THE BROKEN QUEEN

FORSAKEN #2

PENELOPE BARSETTI

HARTWICK PUBLISHING

Hartwick Publishing

The Broken Queen

Copyright © 2022 by Penelope Barsetti

All rights reserved.

CONTENTS

1

RYKER

I was beat.

I searched the Kingdoms high and low, looking for Ivory, questioning everyone I met, bribing strangers for information that never amounted to a damn thing. And the entire time, there was a boulder inside my chest, a guilt that was always present.

She'd warned me about Mastodon.

I didn't listen.

I didn't fucking listen.

We made camp at sunset, a fire in the center of the circle, all the men sweaty from a hard day of riding. My father had given the order, and I led the search party. I was told not to return until I found her.

But days had turned into weeks.

Weeks into months.

I didn't want to let the fear come into my mind, but it was already there.

She was probably dead by now.

Raped. Tortured. And then murdered.

"Ahh!"

My head snapped to the left at the sound, hearing a woman's cries. It sounded just like Ivory. But Ivory wouldn't scream like that. It was just my mind playing tricks on me.

Karl dragged a woman behind him, a blonde in black breeches with boots, her white tunic ripped at the shoulder from where she'd been tugged. She dug her boots into the ground and fought back, her hair whipping around.

"Piece of shit, let me go!" She fought against him then bit down on his forearm. The blood appeared instantly, and Karl screamed.

He threw her hard to the ground. "Bitch."

She scrambled away and tried to break free.

Karl dropped his body on top of hers and pinned her to the ground. "I'll take you right here, then. And then the rest of the men will have their turn." Her hands were pinned above her head, and then her bottoms were yanked off.

Her screams continued to pierce the night.

The sound was too abrasive to ignore, so I stared. I watched her start to cry, all the while trying to buck him off her. She was pretty. Really pretty. Too pretty to be traveling alone in these woods. She must have gotten lost.

Karl would rape her then kill her.

Her family would never know what happened to her—just the way I would never know what happened to Ivory.

That stung. "Karl."

He ignored me, getting her bottoms to her ankles.

"Karl." I left the tree I was leaning up against and walked over. "Knock it off."

He looked up at me, his face flushed with arousal. "Want to go first, m'lord?"

"We slept in a brothel last night."

"But a forced woman is much better than a paid woman." He yanked her shirt up her body, revealing her soft belly and fair skin. He kept going until her breasts emerged, her nipples hard against the cold air.

I admit I stared for a second—because I was a man.

But I forced myself out of it and kicked him in the side. "Off."

Karl groaned as he rolled off. "You goddamn git."

She frantically pulled herself together before she stumbled to her feet, trying to run.

"Miss?"

She tripped to the ground and landed on her palms, but she quickly pushed back to her feet.

I grabbed her by the arm before she could get away. "Calm down."

She twisted out of my grasp and gave me a seething stare. She had bright green eyes and a pretty face, high cheekbones, full lips, an elegant neck perfect for hot kisses in the middle of the night. The tears continued to streak down her cheeks, and that just made my dick hard. "Leave me alone."

I raised both of my hands as I approached. "Whoa. Does it look like I'm going to hurt you?"

She didn't turn her back to me now, her breathing heavy, her eyes still terrified. "If you aren't going to hurt me, let me go."

"Why are those the only two options?"

She took off again.

"Hey!"

She sprinted into the trees.

"Goddammit..." I took off after her, running into the forest, trailing behind her flowing blond hair. She was fast on her feet and agile, jumping over a fallen log like a horse, but I was faster, and I got her by the arm. "Would you just calm the fuck down for a second—"

She twisted out of my grasp and kneed me between the legs.

My knee blocked it, but it still hurt. "You know what? Tried to have a civil conversation with you, but you're being a pain in the ass. So this is how we're going to do this." I locked her hands together, tripped her, and pinned her to the ground. I pressed her hands into the small of her back and kneeled on her so there was no way she could get free—not this time.

She tried to buck me but quickly realized it was no use.

"Fucking asshole, let me go!"

"I will after you chill for a second. Can you do that?"

"Fuck you." She gave another buck.

I kept her still and waited for her to tire out.

After minutes of squirming and bucking, she finally gave up.

"What's your name?"

She kept her mouth shut.

"We're going to be here all night, huh?"

She finally spat out an answer. "Effie."

"Effie. Pretty."

She gave another buck against me.

"You should stop doing that...a bit of a turn-on."

She went absolutely still.

"Why are you out here alone?"

"I needed to get medicine for my mother...and got lost."

"Medicine from where?"

"One of the villages."

"And where are you from?"

"Delacroix."

"I can take you back to Delacroix."

"No."

My eyebrows rose. "You'd rather take your chances out here alone? Lost?"

"Better than being anywhere near *him*."

"He's not going to touch you."

"He just assaulted me."

"Well, he won't do that again."

"Men are pigs, and you have no control over them."

"I do, actually. My father is the Duke of Delacroix."

She went still, her breathing deep and even.

"I'll escort you back there safely. You have my word."

"You're lying."

"Why would I do that? I could have let him have his way with you. Or I could have my way with you right now. Don't see either of those happening. Do you?"

She breathed, her cheek against the dirt.

"I'm going to let you go now. I'd appreciate it if you didn't run. I've been traveling for months, and I'm fucking tired." I released her wrists and got to my feet.

She lay there for a second before she pushed her palms against the earth and rose to her feet. Dirt stained her white tunic, some of it was in her hair, and the wetness of her cheeks made the dirt stick to her face.

She was still a hottie.

She brushed her hands on her trousers.

"Ryker."

"Yes, I know your name. You're out here searching for your sister?"

For just a brief second, I forgot about my mission, and the pain came flooding back. "Yes."

"I'm guessing you haven't found her yet?"

I gave a shake of my head. "Wouldn't happen to know anything, would you?"

"I'm sorry."

It was worth the shot. "Come on. We'll head back to Delacroix in the morning." I took a step back toward the camp and quickly realized she didn't follow. "I gave you my word."

"You can't control other people."

"I can when I can behead anyone I want—without reason."

She still hesitated, as if this was some elaborate trap.

"What's it going to take? Because, clearly, my word isn't good enough for you."

Her eyes dropped down to my belt. "That dagger."

My hand reached for it on my belt, grasping the cool metal of the hilt. "That's not going to do much against a man like Karl."

"It will if you use it right."

If she were anyone else, she would have tried my patience, but those green eyes were so fascinating to me. One moment, they could be fearful and dim, and then another moment later, they could be bright with fury. Back and forth they went, like the balance of an uneven knife. "Alright." I removed the scabbard from my belt and handed it over.

She snatched it from my hand quickly, like I might change my mind.

SHE LAY between me and the tree trunk, the rest of the men spread out around the campfire. They all stared at Effie when we joined them, but they wouldn't dare disobey my orders.

Even though she had my dagger tucked into one of her pockets, I slept easy, knowing she wouldn't try to hurt me when I was the one who saved her. She couldn't sneak up on me anyway.

At sunrise the next morning, we packed our bags and kicked dirt onto the fire to put it out.

"Karl, get up." Bryson gave him a gentle kick with his boot.

The rest of the men were ready to go.

Effie stayed close to my side, always keeping her eye on the rest of the men at all times.

Bryson gave him a harder kick. "Come on."

This time, he rolled over—and he was dead. His eyes were open and empty, and the front of his neck was stained with blood because his throat had been slit. The wound was still gaping open, a couple insects already inside.

Bryson immediately backed up and flashed his eyes on Effie.

I did the same.

She held my stare, her look fierce. "He deserved it."

Speechless, I continued to hold her gaze. Wasn't sure if I admired her or despised her. Now I felt like an idiot for giving her my dagger.

"He was just going to do it to somebody else," she said. "Now, he can't."

The men all looked to me, waiting for my response. She killed one of my own men—in his sleep. I'd never liked Karl, but he was a good scout and a remarkable tracker, an asset we couldn't afford to lose. "I should have you hanged for that."

"But you won't." She held out the dagger to me. "Because you know if you were me, you would have done the same thing."

***

WE RODE BACK TO DELACROIX.

She sat behind me on the horse, her arms hooked around my waist. We rode through the plains, and my eyes continued to search for Ivory in the same dress I'd last seen her in, even though I'd already found it in the abandoned carriage. Her bag was left behind too, the two guards dead on the road.

But I could never make sense of what happened.

Mastodon killed the guards then stopped the wagon. He seemed to take her elsewhere on foot, but I wasn't sure why. Where had he taken her? My first assumption was

that her kidnapping was being used for leverage or ransom
—but no demands were ever made.

It was a fucking mystery.

We reached Delacroix before nightfall. Our horses were
taken to the stables, and we entered the heart of the city.
Peace had reigned in the Kingdoms for eternity, so war was
just a myth.

We made it to the cobblestone streets, the castle on the left
and the village on the right. "Would you like me to escort
you home?"

Effie turned to look at me, a hint of humor in her eyes. "I
killed a man in his sleep last night. Think I can manage."
The sunset was red and orange as it descended over the
horizon of the cliffs. It cast a warm glow on her face, gave
her cheeks a beautiful color. I knew I'd never seen her in
Delacroix before, because I definitely wouldn't have
forgotten her. "But thank you...for what you did."

Her long hair was still shiny and soft after the long day we'd
had, and unlike most girls, she was breathtaking on her
worst day. The women at the Capital donned their best
makeup and clothing, but she still outshined them all. "I
hope your mother feels better."

"Me too." She withdrew the dagger with the scabbard and
handed it to me.

I watched it hang in the air between us before I pushed it back with my palm. "Keep it. And next time you travel alone, bring it with you."

She brought the dagger back to her chest and held it there, as if she'd never wanted to part with it in the first place. "I will." She gave me a final look before she turned around and walked down the path toward the city, her hair moving slightly in the breeze.

My eyes followed her until she turned from the path and disappeared.

2

RYKER

My father sat behind his desk with his hands clutched together against his lips. His eyes were down on the maps laid out before him, but he didn't seem to be looking at them because his eyes were still.

"I've spoken with the emissaries of the Kingdoms, and they have no information." It was hard to accept this news but even harder to deliver it to my father, who hadn't been the same since Ivory disappeared. "No tracks. No leads. Nothing." I felt worthless, searching the lands endlessly and turning up nothing.

He continued to stare at the surface of the desk.

"What do we know about Mastodon?"

He started to rub his knuckles, his eyes still on the map. "He served as a Blade Scion. But where he was prior to that, nobody knows. He can't be traced to a single kingdom. He came from nowhere...and disappeared to nowhere."

None of this made sense. "Why would he steal her and not demand a ransom? Why would he take her and just disappear? He took her for a reason, right? What was the reason?" I waited for that information to be revealed in time, but it never came.

"I do have a theory." He finally lifted his gaze and looked at me.

"What is it?"

"I haven't entertained it up until this point—because it's so unlikely. But our trail has run cold. Mastodon is an unforgettable man, but no one can recall ever seeing him in the Kingdoms."

"The Blade Scions are appointed by King Rutherford himself. He must know something."

"Everything he knows has been fed to him by his servants. That man doesn't do a damn thing himself." He continued to rub his knuckles. "Without Ivory, I don't have access to the Capital, and our entire plan has been foiled."

That was the last thing on my mind. "What's your theory, Father?"

He dropped his hands back to the table. "They've found a way to the top of the cliffs."

My blood suddenly went cold. "Who?"

"The Runes. The Teeth. The Plunderers. One of them."

"And they took Ivory? Why?"

He shook his head. "That, I don't know."

"Then that means Mastodon is one of them."

"Yes. His face was always covered, so he could have been a Teeth and we wouldn't have known it."

My sister was at the bottom of the cliffs—a wasteland. "If that's true, that means there's a way down…"

"Yes."

"Then we find it and go after her."

My father's eyes flicked down again. "I'm not sure that's wise."

My eyes narrowed.

"It's a dangerous place—"

"I don't care. I'll go."

He kept his look down. "Ryker—"

"If my sister is down there—"

"You've heard my stories, but you have no idea what it's like down there. It's hell—frozen over many times. Even if you managed to find her, your odds of getting her back are slim to none."

"I won't abandon her down there, Father."

He lifted his gaze once more. "If my theory is true and she is down there...she'll return."

My eyes narrowed again.

"She's their key into the Kingdoms—and they'll use her when the time is right."

3

EFFIE

I hung the damp clothes with the clothespins, hooking them in place on the line so the breeze would move through the cotton and remove the moisture. A gust of wind came through, billowing my hair back behind my face, and it caught the shirt I'd been holding. "Rude." I chased after it, stomping my boot down before it got another gust of wind and took off down the road for everyone to see. "At least it's not my undergarments..." With the damp shirt in my hands, I turned back to the line where half of the clothes hung.

But now, a man stood there.

Ryker.

He wasn't in his armor or the king's uniform. He looked like anyone else in his breeches and tunic, as if he wanted to be just anyone else. When he caught me off guard, a subtle smile moved on to his lips. "Laundry day?"

I composed myself and attached the shirt to the line.

"Need any help?" He reached inside and pulled out one of my chemises. "Ooh...sexy."

I snatched it out of his hand and quickly checked the windows at the back of the house. Thankfully, the curtains were closed because my parents were both napping. "Do you mind?"

"Not at all." His grin widened.

I continued to hang up the clothes, watching him watch me.

He stood there, thoroughly entertained, even though he'd never had to take care of his own clothes a day in his life.

Not only was he the son of the duke who lived in a beautiful castle, but he was handsome too. He had thick, dark hair that was cut short, bright green eyes that looked as pure as gems, and he had the kind of smile that made women go weak in the knees. Myself included.

"How's that dagger treating you?"

I continued to work. "I keep it tucked under my pillow every night."

"Do you feel unsafe?"

"I'll always feel unsafe after what happened."

His smile disappeared. "You should always be on your guard outside Delacroix. But when you're home, you don't need to worry about that. The laws protect everyone."

I rolled my eyes and kept working.

"You know something I don't?"

"The law doesn't mean shit if you don't get caught. And if you try to report someone after the fact, they'll just kill you. And even if they don't kill you, what does it matter? The deed is done. The law doesn't prevent crime."

His stare was hard now as he listened to every word I said.

"The world is different for you, m'lord."

"Don't call me that." He had a deep voice, and it became even deeper when he was serious.

I grabbed more clothes from the basket and moved farther down the line as I clipped them into place. He moved with me, always watching me.

"No sign of your sister?"

After a long pause, he gave his answer. "No."

I could feel all his pain in just that simple response. It was in the tone of his voice. It was in the tightness of his face as he gave a slight wince.

"I'm afraid I'll never see her again."

"I'm sorry." I stopped my work for just a moment, squeezing the fabric in my fingertips.

"Do you have a sister?"

"I do."

"Hope nothing ever happens to her."

She was a lot younger than me, so we weren't close. But I'd be devastated if anyone ever took her.

"Why are you here?" I hung up the pants then took another step to find room for the shirt.

"Come on, sweetheart." He stared down at me, wearing a sexy, brooding stare. "I didn't come by to help you with the laundry or retrieve my dagger."

"Well, I have a boyfriend."

He didn't even blink. "A boyfriend, huh?"

"Yes." I kept working.

"What's this boyfriend's name?"

"What does it matter?"

"Because you're lying and can't give me one."

I kneeled and grabbed another handful of clothes, unsure how to deflect the conversation. "Henry."

"And what's he do?"

I straightened and kept hanging the clothes. "Blacksmith."

"Really? So, your boyfriend and your father are both black-smiths? What are the odds."

Shit, he'd done his homework.

"Come on, sweetheart. The son of a duke isn't good enough for you?"

I'd officially run out of clothes, so now there was nothing else to do but meet him head on.

He stared as if he could do this all day.

"You aren't my type, alright?"

"Really?" he asked, the playfulness in his eyes. "You like girls? Ooh...that's hot."

I smacked him hard on the arm.

"Hit me in the face next time. That's how I like it."

I almost did. "I'm not naïve. I know how men like you are."

"And that means...?"

"It's just one girl after the next. Mistresses. Brothels. Whores. I'm not going to get involved with someone like that. I want what my parents have—a loving marriage."

"Gotta say...you're making a lot of assumptions." He was a foot taller than me, his musculature visible through the tightness of his sleeves. "All you know about me is that I'm incredibly handsome—and I saved you from a horrible fate."

"You flirt like a playboy."

"Playboy?" he asked, grinning.

"Come on, don't play dumb with me."

He stared at me for a while before he gave a shrug. "Alright, you caught me."

"And that's not something I'm interested in."

"Why not? We could both have a great time. And I promise you, your husband will appreciate having a wife who knows how to please a man."

"Already know how to do that."

"Oh, really?" His smile was back. "You're just making me more intrigued, sweetheart."

I picked up the empty laundry basket, just to have a barrier between us. "You should go, *m'lord*." I crossed my ankles and gave a half-assed curtsy.

He stayed put—as if he had no intention of going anywhere. "I could have looked the other way and allowed Karl to have his way with you. But I didn't. I did the right thing, and I'd like something in return."

"You do the right thing because it's the right thing to do, not because you're going to get something out of it."

He gave a shrug. "Guess I'm not a good guy after all." He continued to wear his smile, like this was all a joke, and the fact that he could pull it off just pissed me off. He was charming, flirtatious, even endearing. "You asked for my dagger—and then turned around and killed one of my men. I could have hanged you for that, but I didn't. Come on, you gotta feel *some* gratitude for me."

"Of course I do." I knew full well that if he hadn't been there, my body would have been left in the forest. "And I thanked you."

"Well, I want you to thank me in a very specific way."

I smacked him on the arm.

He tapped his fingers against his cheek. "Sweetheart, you missed."

I didn't do it—just so I wouldn't give him what he wanted.

"Now, before you jump to conclusions, my request is very innocent."

"Oh yeah?" I asked. "Sure, it is."

He stepped closer to me, his eyes dropping to my lips.

"Forget it."

"Come on, it's just a kiss. And then I'll leave you alone."

"You expect me to believe that?"

"I've proven that I'm a man of my word." He stepped even closer.

"I'm not going to kiss you here when my parents could wake up any moment and look out the window."

"Then come with me." His hand grabbed mine and tugged me away from the clothesline.

My heart raced because this had become real. His hand was warm as it surrounded mine, and when he took the lead, his large shoulders and height blocked out our route. He pulled me with him until we reached the side of the house. Then he guided me against the wall, my back against the surface, his body pinning mine in place so there was nowhere for me to go.

His face was just inches from mine, and that charming smile was long gone. Now it was just his heated stare on my mouth, like he couldn't wait to dive down and reap the rewards of his chivalry.

"Just one."

His eyes flicked to mine again.

I didn't take a breath when I looked into those green eyes, but I could feel my heart pounding like a drum. I'd shared kisses with men in secret. Felt their hands in my hair. Around my waist. But I'd never felt this level of anticipation, this inability to breathe.

He lowered his head to mine, and with the light contact of a bee on a flower, he gave me a gentle kiss. Our lips came together and stayed that way for a long second. My eyes immediately closed, and I finally drew breath.

His lips moved, pulling my bottom lip between his, giving me another kiss that was more intimate than the first. Then he tilted his head slightly, opening my mouth with his so he could give me a small amount of tongue.

My lips moved with his automatically, my actions second nature, and I let him take the lead.

It started off slow and gentle, our lips coming together and breaking apart, but then his pace increased, his mouth devouring mine. "Sweetheart..." One hand fisted my hair, and he brought our bodies closer together, his hard chest pressing against my breasts.

It was a good kiss...no denying that.

His hand reached behind me and gave my ass a firm squeeze.

My palm automatically slapped him across the face.

He barely turned with the hit. There was no anger in his eyes. All he wanted was to continue the kiss—judging by the way he stared at my mouth hungrily.

He had his one kiss. My debt was repaid.

But my back stayed against the wall, and my eyes were locked on his mouth.

His eyes flicked to mine.

I met his.

Then I pulled him back into me and kissed him.

He grinned for a second before he fell back into our rhythm.

My hand yanked on his arm and pulled it back to my ass.

He squeezed it firmly as he pushed me into the wall, his hard dick against my lower stomach. A quiet moan escaped his lips as he started to grind into me, angling his hips down and hoisting my leg over his hip. He pressed his hard outline right against my most sensitive flesh.

My arms hooked around his neck, and my fingers fisted his short hair as he ground against me, hitting me in the perfect spot over and over. An unstoppable moan escaped my lips as I fell into the moment, as I forgot that I was just another pretty girl to conquer. With a mouth like that and a big dick that he knew how to use, he could conquer me all he wanted.

He fisted my hair and tugged my head back so he could kiss my neck, lavish me with his kisses and a few bites. His hips rocked harder at the same time, overloading my sweet spot, and I clawed at him to kiss me again, to muffle the moan I was about to unleash.

But he wouldn't let me.

He kept his grip on my hair and locked me in place, his stare so intense he looked like a different man. His hips continued to rock, to roll his hard shaft right against my wet trousers.

I grabbed on to his arm and felt my body get pulled under. The tears started in the corners of my eyes, and the flush hit my cheeks hard. The moans emerged, unable to be contained, and my nails clawed at his flesh too.

It was like we were fucking—but fully clothed.

He kept me still against the wall as he watched me come, watched the entire show from beginning to end, and he did nothing to keep me quiet. There was no gloating smile on his lips, but there was a different victory in his eyes.

My hands grasped his forearms until the high passed, until the pleasure left my stomach and the area between my thighs. Then reality struck like lightning, and I could feel the wetness of my panties, feel the shame of my choices.

His hand released my hair. "Now, we're even."

WE SAT TOGETHER by the fire, my mother in the armchair in front of the hearth with my sister in her lap. My father had made stew for dinner, and it was a meager meal with no flavor, but it was better than nothing.

I sat on the couch with a blanket over my thighs, my thoughts drifting back to that erotic kiss against the side of my house. I'd gone out there to hang the laundry, and I'd gotten the best kiss of my life. He didn't even need to be naked to achieve what other men could.

Father spoke. "I entered us into the lottery."

My sister turned the page of her book and kept reading.

Mother met his look. "You've entered us into that lottery every time it's been open. We never get picked."

"Maybe this time we will." He scooped his spoon into the stew, which was mostly just bone broth. "We could get a big farm in the Capital. Sell this place and make enough to retire. To pay for your medicine."

Mother wore a bleak look, like she didn't believe that and never would. "We'll see what happens, dear."

Everyone in Delacroix entered their names into the lottery. A family was always selected and ferried off to a better life. The rest of us were left behind. Delacroix was a beautiful city to call home, but we were still poor. Father had destroyed his body through a lifetime of manual labor, and soon I would be taking care of them both because my sister was too young. My parents had taken care of me their entire lives, so I was happy to do the same, but it was hard to earn a living and take care of two aging parents too.

Ryker had no idea what that was like. Didn't have those kinds of worries. Never would. When his father aged, the servants would take care of him, and he would be free to do whatever he wished.

I WENT to the market with the slip of paper in my hand. It was all the produce my mother had requested, squash, lentils, and other vegetables for her stew. And some beef too—if there was enough left over.

The farmers on the outskirts of town brought all their crops for sale, and everyone came first thing in the morning to grab the best pieces of everything. I admired a green squash for a while before I handed over the coins and took it. Then I moved to the next station, looking for the black lentils my mother had requested.

"What's for dinner, sweetheart?"

I recognized that voice, had heard it in my dreams the past two nights, and my heart gave a jolt when my eyes came into contact with his. Deep green, arrogant, beautiful. I'd never expected to see him again, and the relief that washed over me was unmistakable. "Stew." Again.

"Sounds good. You should invite me over." He looked down at me as he flashed his handsome grin.

"I thought we were even." I handed the coins to the farmer and took the pouch of black lentils.

"Sweetheart, come on." He walked with me as we left the booth. "Don't act like you aren't happy to see me." He was in his street clothes, doing his best to blend in and look like one of us. "I saw your reaction before you covered it up."

I moved to the next booth and grabbed the mushrooms and onions.

"How's your mom doing?"

I put all the vegetables into my bag before I moved to the butcher's counter. "A lot better."

"That's good."

I looked into his eyes and saw the sincerity there. "Yeah... thanks for asking."

"My mom got sick and passed away... I know how that goes."

"I'm sorry."

"Yeah." He walked with me to the butcher's counter.

I walked up to the butcher and pulled out the coins I had left. I had less money than I wanted, and I probably wouldn't even get the worst cut of meat.

The butcher quickly counted the coin with just a glance. "I don't have anything for that, girl."

Ryker reached into his pocket and pulled out his coin. He tossed it on the table. "We'll take the biggest cut of meat you have."

"What are you doing?" My head snapped in his direction. "You don't need to do that—"

"It's fine." He closed my fingers around my coins and pushed my hand back to my stomach.

"I have money."

"Keep it, alright? Save it for a rainy day."

The butcher put the meat on the counter, wrapped up and ready to go, and it was big enough that we could have more than stew. With a few potatoes and some greens, we could have a nice dinner tonight.

Ryker picked up the meat and carried it for me.

I returned the coins to my pocket and walked with him. "You really didn't need to do that."

"I understood there was no obligation."

"But I don't need your pity."

"It wasn't out of pity either—"

"Then why?"

That arrogant smile came back. "I did something for you. Now you do something for me."

"Wow...you're a dick."

He chuckled. "Before you jump to conclusions—"

"You think I'm going to sleep with you because you bought me some meat?"

"Hey, I was just hoping for another kiss, but if you want to take it to that level, I'm game."

I smacked him in the arm.

He gave a laugh, his eyes playful. "You know I'm kidding. I would have bought this for you even if you said you never wanted to see me again. But I also knew that was never going to happen."

"Are you always this arrogant?"

"Yes." He spat out his answer like it was instinct. "How about I show you around the castle tonight?"

"I'm not allowed on the grounds."

"Sweetheart, you're allowed anywhere as long as it's with me." He waggled his eyebrows.

I rolled my eyes and gave him a gentle push to the side.

He came right back and gave my ass a quick spank.

My eyes widened, and I stared at him in shock. "You have some nerve..."

"Oh, you have no idea the kind of nerve I have."

"THAT'S the best dinner I've ever had—at least in a while." My dad devoured all his meat and smothered his potato with extra butter. "The butcher just gave this to you?"

"Said it would be bad by tomorrow," I said.

"Really?" Mother said. "It tastes so fresh."

I shrugged and kept eating.

When dinner was finished, we cleaned up and went to bed.

I had my own bedroom, a twin bed against the wall and a desk in the other corner. There was a single window, just big enough for me to crawl through. I left the curtains open so the stars were visible through the glass.

I'd just gotten to the bed when there was a knock on the window.

Already knew who it was.

I unlocked the latch then pushed it open.

He rested his arms on the windowsill and gave me a smile. "Ready to go on an adventure?"

"You have to promise me I won't get in trouble." I spoke in a whisper, and he did the same.

"Your parents will never know you left."

"I meant with the castle. Because I could be killed—along with my whole family."

He rolled his eyes. "That would never happen."

"I don't know...the guards are really strict."

"On those who trespass. But you aren't trespassing. I sneak in girls all the time."

My eyes narrowed.

"Okay...that was a stupid thing to say." He extended his hand over the ledge so I could grab on to it and pull myself over. "But I'll make it up to you—and you know I'm good for it."

I grabbed on and made my way over the ledge, letting him get me to the ground so my feet didn't make a loud thud. I shut the window until there was just a crack to insert my fingers, and we left.

The cobblestone pathway was empty, torches lighting the routes through town. I'd snuck out of my room a couple times, and I was always amazed by the peacefulness of the night, the silence, and the stars.

When we made it close to the castle, he took my hand in his. The guards didn't even look at him as he pulled me through the double doors of the castle, into the grand foyer with the staircase. Torches were everywhere, highlighting the colored tiles, the crown moldings on the ceiling, the armor of the guards who kept watch all night long. Red rugs were everywhere, decorated with the seal of the king.

I'd never been inside a castle before, only admired it from the exterior, and it was a kind of luxury I couldn't fathom. His hand guided me, and I admired the paintings on the walls, the sculptures on the tables in the hallway, the chandeliers that glowed with light.

After a couple turns down the corridors, we entered his bedroom.

Which was bigger than the house I shared with my family.

He had a four-poster bed against the wall, a sizable rug underneath, two nightstands, and a large hearth that could contain a bonfire. His lamps were on, and so was his chandelier, because they had electricity here.

The rest of the city didn't.

He had his own bathroom too, even a separate living room in front of another fireplace. I spotted doors that must have led to a balcony that overlooked the city. It was innately comfortable, and that made me a little bit envious.

If I'd been born into a different family, this could have been mine. My parents could live a life of luxury instead of one of backbreaking work. Ryker had won the lottery, and my family hoped to win a different one.

He uncorked a bottle of wine and poured two glasses. "Would you like to sit on the balcony?"

"I figured the only place you'd want me is in your bed."

He handed the glass to me, playfulness in his eyes. "We've got time for that later. Come on." He opened the double doors to a balcony, with loungers and chairs that overlooked the city below. The torches illuminated the pathways, and the lights from the windows of the homes glowed like stars.

"It's something, huh?" He took a drink before he sat in one of the chairs, setting his glass on the table beside him.

I took a seat too, the glass of wine resting on my thigh. I'd rarely had wine because it was so expensive. Ale and mead were my usual options. Once the taste hit my lips, I really appreciated all the subtle flavors, the sweet grapes, the blossoms, the hint of cedarwood. "This is good."

"From King Rutherford's own vineyards."

Then it was an even greater honor.

He stared at the city for a long time, even though it was a view he got to experience every day of his life. It was a rare moment when he wasn't gloating or making jokes. A seriousness overtook his face, like he was deep in thought about something. He was even more handsome like that—just being himself.

"She'll turn up eventually."

His face gave a subtle wince before he turned his eyes back to me. "You think so?"

I nodded. "No one would take a duchess without a reason."

"That's what my father says."

"Just have to be patient."

"I feel like shit because she tried to tell me."

"Tell you what?"

"That one of the guards in the castle was untrustworthy." He rested his arms on his knees and looked ahead. "He made her uncomfortable. He stared longer than he should. Since he was a Blade Scion, I just assumed she was intimidated. But she was right on the money...as always."

He was still practically a stranger to me, but my heart broke anyway.

"He transported her to the Capital, but along the way, he killed the other guards and took her."

"Do you think someone ordered him to do that?"

He gave a shrug. "Probably. But not sure who."

"If it's someone from one of the villages looking for ransom, that's stupid. The second he hands her over, he'll be killed.

There's no scenario where he gets away with this—and he must know that."

He continued to stare ahead.

"There's no reason to kill her...so I'm sure you'll get her back."

He reached for his glass beside him and took a long drink. "Hope you're right."

"Your father must be distraught."

"He definitely hasn't been the same."

"Are you going to go back out there and look for her?"

"I've looked everywhere. But I'll look again."

"I wish I could help you."

He turned to regard me, his eyes still soft and serious. "Did your family enjoy their dinner?" He brought the glass to his lips and took another drink.

"Yes. My family hasn't eaten like that in a long time."

"Did you tell them that a handsome man came to your rescue?" He gave a slight smile but one that didn't reach his eyes.

"I didn't need to be rescued. And, no. My father would be embarrassed to accept charity."

"Wasn't charity. You're paying for it right now—sitting here with me." He took another drink then set his glass back on the table.

"Even so, he's a proud man."

"I know where you get it from."

I gave a smile. "My father wanted a son—so he raised me as one."

"Reminds me of my sister. He trained her in the sword just as he did with me. But I can tell he still favors me..."

"No surprise there."

"It's ironic because I know she's smarter and a lot more capable than I am." He looked to the city again.

I couldn't take my eyes off him. "That's sweet."

"Not really," he said with a chuckle. "I would never say that to her face. Gods, it would go straight to her head." He turned back to me. "And if you ever tell her I said that, I'll lie until I'm blue in the face."

"Would it be the worst thing to tell her?"

"It would. You think I'm arrogant?" He scoffed. "She's worse."

"I highly doubt that, for some reason."

He gave a light chuckle. "So, what are your plans?"

"What do you mean?"

"In life."

"Well...I hope I don't die here."

He turned to look at me.

"No offense, Delacroix is a great place. But I hear these stories about the Capital. Blue waters that reflect the sunset. Summers that are warm and not humid. Vineyards. Sailboats in the harbor. Unparalleled beauty."

"The stories are true."

"Yeah?"

He nodded. "Makes this place look like a shithole, honestly."

"I hope to make it there someday, maybe after my parents are gone."

His green eyes watched me, set in that handsome face.

"But hopefully I make it there sooner. My father enters our name in the lottery every time it's open."

His eyes immediately dropped to the floor.

"He actually thinks we'll be selected...someday."

He kept his eyes down.

"They'd sell our house and use the money to retire. My father likes working with his hands, but being a blacksmith is just too hard on his body now. Needs something that won't put so much stress on his back."

He looked away, back to the view of the city. "The odds of winning the lottery are very low."

"I know. But it gives my father something to look forward to, so..."

He didn't look at me again. Kept his gaze forward.

"Did I say something?"

"No."

"Because you're different."

He grabbed the glass of wine. "I would never want you to win the lottery."

"Why?"

He gave a shrug. "Because you would leave, right?"

"Well, we both know this isn't going to last for more than a couple of nights."

He continued his stare and took another drink. "You never know."

"I'm sure you're supposed to marry one of the other royals."

"My father wanted my sister to marry one of King Rutherford's sons, but that's gone to shit."

"You could do it."

He cracked a smile, a very small one. "I'm good."

"I hear the women at the Capital are beautiful."

He chuckled into his glass before he took a drink.

"Why is that funny?"

Now his glass was empty, so he set it down. "Just ironic."

"Ironic how?"

"Because when I first met you, I thought you were far more beautiful than all the girls at court. They wear the nicest gowns, have their hair and makeup done, and you still look better than them in breeches and unkempt hair."

———

"I CAN WALK YOU BACK." He shut the doors to the balcony then approached me where I stood at the edge of the bed. "It's getting late." His eyes shifted back and forth as they looked into mine, trying to read the words that I didn't speak.

"It's not that late..."

His eyes dropped down to my lips. "Is this the wine talking or you?"

My fingers grabbed his drawstring and pulled. "Me."

He took a deep breath as his eyes lowered, watching his pants loosen around his hips.

My thumbs hooked into his breeches, and I pushed them down, watching his hard cock slowly emerge from the confines of his trousers. The head popped out, and then the shaft became visible, a ball of hair at the base. His trousers were at his knees, his large dick hanging straight out.

"You said you were hoping for a kiss...but you didn't specify where." My fingers cupped his balls and lightly massaged them, feeling their weight and warmth in my hand.

He took another deep breath, his eyes so hard and hungry.

His excitement made me excited, and I lowered myself to my knees on the rug at the foot of the bed.

His cock gave a twitch.

His throat shifted with a swallow, and his hand immediately slid into my hair as he brushed it from my cheek. He changed his footing and widened his stance, so impatient to slide across my tongue.

I grabbed his muscular thighs and steadied him. "Whoa, boy."

His fingers gripped my neck, and he tilted my head back so he could fill my mouth once my lips opened. "Sweetheart, don't fucking tease me." His voice came out breathless, even shaky, like this was the first time for him.

"I'm going to make you come—and I'm going to watch."

He closed his eyes as his fingers instinctively gripped my throat tighter.

My lips parted, and I flattened my tongue.

He held his stance and watched me inch forward. When contact was imminent, he held his breath then released it as a loud groan when he finally felt the wetness of my tongue. His shaft glided along, moving deeper and deeper, and he rolled his head back when he was fully inside my mouth. "Fuck." He looked down at me again, released a moan that sounded like a growl, and watched me sit there on my knees with a mouth full of dick. "Sweetheart, you look so hot with my dick in your mouth."

I kept my tongue flat and started out slow, timing my breaths when his dick didn't block my airway, and moved forward and back at a steady pace, our wet body parts sliding past each other.

He rocked his hips, meeting my mouth at the perfect time, making saliva spill out from the corners of my lips. He grunted and moaned, burying himself inside me, becoming more aggressive the more he enjoyed it.

I couldn't breathe. I had to resist the urge to gag. My knees were killing me. My wet eyes caused my vision to blur, and tears stung my cheeks. But I loved every second of it. Loved the way my panties started to become weighed down with my arousal. Loved the way his cock thickened even more in my mouth because he was so turned on.

His fingers dug deeper into my hair and supported the back of my head as he continued to thrust, the speed of his hips and his breaths both increasing. "It's coming, sweetheart..."

Tears streaked down my cheeks, and my nails dug into his thighs. Breaths became even more rare, and I just held on as I prepared for his seed to block my throat entirely. I kept my mouth wide open, making sure he had the perfect climax.

"Mouth or face?" he asked, red in the face, barely holding on.

I tugged on his thighs and gave my answer.

He slammed into my mouth hard, and I couldn't breathe at all, tears streaking down my cheeks, constantly overriding my need to choke. His hips suddenly came to a halt, and he came inside me, his entire dick shoved into my body. "Fuck..." He held the back of my head and kept me in place, watching me take his load on my knees.

It coated my tongue right away, warm and heavy, so much of it that it took several attempts to swallow it all.

He finally removed his dick and let me take my first full breath.

I gasped, tears on my cheeks, the taste of him still on my tongue.

"Fuck, that was so good I should pay for it." He grabbed both of my hands and pulled me to my feet. His fingers yanked on the drawstring to my breeches as he guided me back to the bed, his eyes still hungry even though I'd given my best performance. He yanked my bottoms down to my thighs and pinned me against the edge of the bed. My top was pulled over my head, my boots were kicked off, and then he lifted me onto his enormous bed, the bedspread soft and clean.

He got to his knees, scooped my legs into his arms, and then kissed me.

My head immediately rolled back, and I gripped the bedspread with my needy hands. His mouth was as hungry between my legs as it was against my mouth, his tongue so purposeful and strong. I let out a moan to the ceiling, not having to be quiet like we would at my home. The guards stationed in the hallway could probably hear me loud and clear, but all they could do was listen with envy.

The tears. The pain. The choking. He made it all worth it.

My hand fisted his hair, and I ground my hips into his face, wanting more of that expert mouth.

His shoulders supported my legs, and his hand reached up to grab one of my tits. He squeezed me hard as he continued to circle his tongue around my nub, to bring me to the same level of pleasure I'd just given him.

My back arched off the bed, my hips pressed farther into his face, and I came with a tremble, eyes spouting with tears. "Yes..." I could feel my slickness against his face, feel the way my muscles gave out in an avalanche of ecstasy.

When the explosion passed, his kisses turned gentle, bringing me back down from the high. "That's some damn good pussy right there." He raised himself over me, his shiny lips above my face. "Want another go?"

My hand grabbed his shoulder, and I pushed him down.

He gave a chuckle as he returned to his knees on the floor. "Alright, sweetheart."

4

RYKER

I sat at the table with my father, going over the information sent by the emissaries. It was the same thing every day, King Rutherford expressing his desires on paper, and sometimes his servants delivered them in person to oversee our work.

"You will woo Elizabeth, Lady's Quail's only daughter."

My mind had shifted elsewhere, thinking about Effie on her knees in front of me, her small mouth stuffed with my big cock. "Sorry?"

"Elizabeth." He flashed me an annoyed look. "Woo her."

"Why?"

"Because you need to marry her."

"What?" I blurted. "Why do I need to marry anyone?"

"Because your sister can't marry one of the king's sons when she's missing."

"How does marrying Elizabeth get us to the throne?"

"Because she's next in line after the king and his heirs."

"But he has three sons. The only way they would all die is if...they were trapped in a burning building or something."

"Hmm...not a bad idea."

My eyes narrowed. "What?"

"Nothing. Just do as I say."

I knew my father wanted the Capital, but I didn't know he was willing to kill for it. "She's not really my type—"

"That's what whores are for." He threw down the papers he was reading. "We will speak no more of this. Make your preparations for the Capital."

"What about Ivory? We're still searching for her."

"We've searched everywhere, Ryker. We know where she is —in a place we can't follow." My father was heartless. It was as if he presumed Ivory to be dead or useless. "Time to move on."

I could never move on.

Burke entered the room, his cape flowing behind him. "M'lord." He gave a subtle bow before he took a seat. "One of the search parties has returned. Said they discovered a cave at the base of the Mammoth Mountains. There's a ladder inside that descends so deep underground there's no bottom."

My eyes shifted back to my father, knowing exactly what that meant.

Father had no reaction.

"That's where Mastodon took her," I said. "The tunnel must lead to the bottom of the cliffs." All I had to do was follow it, and I would find my sister somewhere in that frozen hell. "I can lead a group of men to find her."

Father was quiet a moment longer before he turned to me. "We've already discussed this."

"But now we have evidence—"

"A cave is not evidence. She's been missing for months. She could be anywhere down there, and trust me, that place is just as big as the Kingdoms—and far more deadly. I will not risk the only child I have left for a slim-to-none chance."

"I can't just abandon her—"

"She will return. I assure you."

Burke shifted his gaze back and forth between us. "Shall I close the passage?"

I answered before my father could. "No."

Burke stared at my father, giving him the final say.

My father kept his stare on me. "No. If that's the only way Ivory can return, we must leave it open."

I FOUND Effie in the market the next day, shopping for tonight's dinner. Her breeches were snug on her ass and thighs, showing the deep curve in her lower back and the strength of her legs. Her long hair trailed behind her, stopping at the middle of her back.

I wasn't the only one who noticed her. The other men in the vicinity eyed her like they wanted to do the same thing to her that I had two nights ago. Hadn't stopped thinking about it. Probably would never stop thinking about it.

I came to her side and gave her ass a squeeze.

She spun the second she felt someone grab her, but she halted when she spotted my arrogant smile. "You almost got knocked out."

"That would have been something." I grabbed her ass again and came close, my lips just inches from hers.

Her eyes immediately softened at my proximity, forgetting all the people who surrounded us for a split second. But she regained her composure and stepped away, a sack of vegetables on her arm.

"What are you making tonight?"

"Stew."

"It seems like you always have stew."

"Well, it's cheap and lasts a long time."

I didn't realize what I'd said until I'd already said it. "Sorry. I didn't mean to sound like an ass."

"It's fine. I've seen how rich you are." She moved to the next stall and bought a couple potatoes.

I trailed behind her slightly, tagging along as she did her shopping. "So...want to come over tonight?"

"Not tired of me yet?" She pocketed some more produce before she moved to the meat stand.

"I don't think I could ever get tired of that pussy."

She turned at my words, her eyes wide because I'd just said that in public.

I gave a shrug. "I don't care."

She bought her piece of meat and placed it in her sack along with everything else. Then she headed back to her family's home down the cobblestone street. "Not tonight. Tomorrow."

The disappointment hit me like a windstorm. "Why not tonight?"

"The lottery is tonight. Every time my dad doesn't win, he takes it pretty hard. He's usually up all night. Not a good time to sneak out."

"Damn."

"You can wait until tomorrow, right?" She shot me a playful look, a soft smile on those full lips, her hair partially covering her face.

"I can barely wait five minutes."

She chuckled and looked ahead again.

I thought about my father's suggestion, that I forge a relationship with Elizabeth, but that sounded so unappealing when I'd already met the most beautiful woman in the world. She was flirty and playful, but she also had the kind of attitude that got me going. And she could suck dick like no other. "So, it's a date, then? I'll come to your window tomorrow night? Couple hours after sunset?"

"Sneaking in to your room to fuck doesn't constitute a date."

So, I was going to get laid? *Yes.* "How about some dinner and wine?"

"I normally wouldn't refuse a meal served at the castle, but I'll have had dinner shortly before that."

"We can have dinner after."

"Yeah?"

"The maid can leave it right at the door."

"You won't get in trouble if your father finds out?"

"He couldn't care less what I do with my dick. He has his whores. I have mine."

She halted in her tracks and looked at me as if she was about to deck me good.

"That's not how I meant it," I said quickly. "Came out wrong."

"It better have come out wrong." She continued forward again.

"I just meant he stays out of my business, and I stay out of his." I stayed at her side, hoping I hadn't just ruined my chances of having her between my sheets tomorrow night.

When we were close to her house, she stopped, probably because she didn't want to be seen with me. "Well, this is where I take my leave."

"I'll miss you." My hand immediately went to her perky ass and tugged her into me.

"Are you sure about that? Or will you be with one of your whores?" Her hand pressed against my chest to keep me back, but her tone was as playful as her eyes.

"I'll be thinking about you all night—*alone*."

"Good." She rose on her tiptoes and gave me a kiss on the mouth. "Because I'll be thinking about you all night —*alone*."

"Ooh, sweetheart." My hand tightened on her ass, and I drew her into me. "You drive me fucking crazy."

———

IT WAS A LONELY NIGHT—JUST me, myself, and I.

I had to get through the next day as well, waiting for the time to pass so I could get that sexy blonde in my bed tonight. Just the two of us, hot and sweaty, going at it in front of the fire while the guards listened to me fuck that wet pussy.

Morning turned into midday. Midday turned into afternoon.

But it took forever.

I sat in my father's study going over field maps when Burke walked inside. "M'lord, the lottery winners have been notified. They expect to be transferred tonight."

Father barely looked up from his paperwork. "Thank you, Burke."

Burke and the other guards handled the lottery. I never interacted with the "winners" and didn't lower them to the bottom of the cliffs either. Since I had no part in it, it was easy to forget about, but listening to Effie talk about how important it was to her family made me a little sick.

I wanted to tell her the truth, but since it gave her family hope, I thought it would do more harm than good. It was always good to look forward to something, to strive for something, because if you didn't, you would lose all purpose.

And sometimes that could be a death sentence.

There were so many applicants every cycle that the chances of her family getting picked were nearly impossi-

THE BROKEN QUEEN 55

ble, so I wasn't concerned that would be their fate. But I did feel guilty that the lottery existed at all—and it was all a lie.

A fucking lie.

My sister never knew the truth. My father said she was too good, too selfless, and if she ever found out, she would do everything she could to expose the truth. It was better for her and everyone else to stay in the dark.

Well, now she knew everything.

And she probably had figured out that *I* knew everything.

I knew she would never understand that it was necessary, that it was the only way to protect the peace of our world. "Father?"

He continued to read. "What is it, son?"

"Do we have to continue the lottery?"

His eyes immediately flicked up, hostile.

"If what you say is true, there're already a lot of people down there."

"And what happens if we stop?" he asked. "We tell the citizens of Delacroix that we've suspended the lottery? How do you think they'll react? It's the one thing that keeps our subjects working hard every single day. It gives them something to work toward, because they can't enter the lottery without money, and they can't get money unless they work. Not only does it keep Necrosis fed, but it keeps order in this kingdom. Keep people busy...and they don't cause problems."

AT NIGHTFALL, I walked along the cobblestone streets and watched the torches get lit one by one. Effie lived farther into Delacroix, so it was a long walk, requiring a couple turns down the alleyways.

I was there early, but I couldn't wait any longer.

When I arrived at the front of her house, I saw the carriage.

I remained hidden around the edge of the next house, recognizing the guards from the castle.

Why would they be there?

Did they see Effie with me the other night? Even if they had, that wouldn't explain this. Lots of girls came and went. It remained a dirty secret that no one ever spoke of, so I couldn't imagine anyone would rat Effie out, especially when they had no idea who she was.

So why was the carriage here?

I snuck down the alleyway and approached her bedroom window. After taking a quick peek inside, it didn't seem like anyone was there, so I pushed on the frame and made the window crack open. "Sweetheart?"

She must have been in bed because she came into view a second later. "Oh, thank the gods." She pushed the window higher so we could come close together and whisper. "I was afraid you wouldn't come in time."

"Come in time for what?" I asked. "Why's the carriage here? Are you in trouble?"

"Trouble?" she asked, bewildered. "No. My family won the lottery."

Oh shit.

Her face lit up in a way it never had before, her green eyes bright with their own luminance. "You should see my dad... I've never seen him so happy."

My face must be pale as milk because her happy reaction slowly faded.

"Ryker?"

What were the fucking odds?

"I was hoping you'd come by...because I wanted to say goodbye. I thought that was why you were here early."

Fuck, fuck, fuck.

"We both knew this was going to end anyway. It sucks it didn't last longer, but..." She gave a shrug. "It was fun while it lasted, right?"

When my mother died, I was heartbroken. When my sister was taken, I was heartbroken then too. That was why I recognized the feeling in my stomach so quickly—because I'd felt it enough times. "Effie, look...the lottery isn't what it seems. Tell them you've forfeited your prize."

It took her a long time to say anything, to overcome her puzzled expression. "What...?"

"Just trust me, okay?"

"What's that supposed to mean? My family has already packed their things."

"Effie, the lottery is a lie—"

"Effie!" A man's voice came from behind the door. "It's time to go."

She kept her eyes on me. "I'll be right there."

He tried the door, but it wouldn't budge. "Why's this locked?"

"I'm sorry," she whispered. "I have to go."

"Effie, don't do this—"

She cupped my cheeks and kissed me goodbye. Quick and sterile. There was no passion, not anymore. Then she shut the window and closed the curtains.

I stared at my own reflection in the glass, seeing the sheer white of my skin and the emptiness in my eyes. "No..."

I RAN down the hallway straight to my father's quarters. "Father!" I tried the knob but it was locked, so I banged my fists against the wood until I got his attention. "Come quickly. It's urgent."

The guards didn't rush me like they would somebody else, but they did grip their swords to prepare for whatever news I was about to deliver.

He finally opened the door, his appearance disheveled, his hair a mess. "Ryker, what is it? Are we under attack?"

"No. We have to stop the lottery."

In the most dire circumstances, my father had a wildness to his eyes, as if he was prepared to carve out the eyes of anyone who was a threat to his kingdom. He was in his breeches and tunic, his sword in his hand rather than the scabbard. "The lottery? What is it? Have they discovered the truth?"

"I know the winner, so I need to stop this."

All the tension in his muscles left his body. "What do you mean, boy?"

"My friend and her family won the lottery...so we can't do that to them. We need to give them land in the Capital like we promised."

"There is no land, Ryker. That's all a lie."

"I know that! But we need to do something because I'm not going to let this happen to her."

"Her?" He stepped closer to me. "This is no friend, then."

"It doesn't matter what she is."

"It does matter. Because I'm not going to spare a whore—"

"She's not a whore. She's important to me."

He gave a loud sigh and looked away. "Ryker, it's too late."

"It's not too late!"

"Even if I had land to give them, I wouldn't. You want to know why? Because they don't deserve it. They've done nothing to earn it."

"Then tell them it was a mistake."

"And let the other subjects see that we don't keep our word? They would never trust us again."

"Then we just tell her family the truth and to keep quiet about it."

He looked at me, his eyebrows high on his face. "Don't be stupid."

"If it's going to save their lives, they'll be quiet."

He held up his forefinger right to my face. "If they tell just a single person...all our power could be dismantled. There would be riots. Uprisings. The lottery wouldn't work anymore, and we wouldn't have anyone to sacrifice. You know what that means? King Rutherford would have my head—or worse, Necrosis would starve and make it up here. I'm sorry that you've developed an affection for this girl, but you know full well you were never going to marry her. She's not your problem."

"Father, I never ask you for anything—"

"Then don't start now." He turned back into his bedroom. "They chose to play the lottery—and they'll accept the consequences."

"But they played it under false pretenses!"

"Doesn't matter. They should have considered themselves lucky to live in Delacroix, to be protected from the monsters down below, to have food on the table and a warm place to sleep in the winter. But they got greedy—and wanted more."

"Wanting a better life isn't greedy."

He stepped into his quarters. "Goodnight, Ryker."

"Come on!"

He shut the door and locked it.

I threw my body against it, pounding my fists into the solid wood to get him to return. "Open the fucking door!" The guards eventually had to yank me away from the door and drag me down the hallway. "Father! Please! I'm begging you!"

"STOP!" I ran down the pathway in the dark, carrying a torch to light my way to the edge of the cliffs. Their structures were visible in the distance, but I couldn't make out anything else. "Stop this now!" After what felt like an eternity, I made it to the area where the guards stood. "Where are they?" Effie and her family were nowhere in sight.

Fuck, was I too late?

The guard held up his torch as he stared at me. "The winners have been lowered to the bottom of the cliffs."

"No..." I ran to the edge and looked down the line of cables but saw nothing but darkness. "Effie!"

The silence echoed back at me.

I leaned over the edge, my toe just over the line, and stared into that dark abyss with agony.

I was too late.

Then I heard it—a faint shout.

It was so faint that my heart heard it louder than my ears.

"M'lord?"

"Raise the cables." I turned back to them where they stood at the cranks.

Neither one of them made a move for it.

"The duke has ordered their return." My torch changed hands, and I came closer. "Now."

The guard glanced past my shoulder.

"Move." I threw the torch down and shoved him out of the way. I grabbed the handle of the crank and started to turn it, immediately wincing because it was a lot harder to raise than lower with their weight at the bottom. I grimaced as I kept turning, my hand burning against the metal.

Then the cable suddenly went slack.

My eyes shifted to the rope—and I watched it disappear over the edge. "No!" There was nothing left to grab. Nothing left to pull. It was over—and there was nothing I could do. I turned back to the crank and saw the blade that had severed the line.

My father's blade.

I turned around and faced him, seeing his face in the glow of the torch. I was slow to anger, didn't hold grudges, and chose to make a joke out of everything, even something serious. But right now, I couldn't remember the last time I'd been so livid.

He was in his uniform now, his appearance no longer wild, and the darkness in his eyes showed his inhuman traits. "Don't look at me like that, son. This isn't my fault. It's yours."

With my teeth clenched tightly together and the dimples in my cheeks caved in, I seethed in silence.

"If you'd told me this sooner, I could have prevented it, and you know I would have. There's nothing I wouldn't do for you. But you waited until the very last possible moment when everything was already set in motion, when there was no going back. If you care about something, do a better job of protecting it."

"How was I supposed to know she'd actually win the damn thing—"

"You didn't. But we could have made sure her name was omitted from the draw, as we do with all the other subjects that we can't afford to lose. If this girl was really that important to you, you would have done that." He stepped closer to me. "So, don't blame me for this. I'm not going to risk everything for a girl you hardly know. We both know you would have had your fun for a short while and gone your separate ways. She could have won the lottery then—and you'd have no idea."

I'd never want this for her, regardless of what happened with us. "She was a good person—"

"They're all good people, son. You think anyone deserves that fate? No. But we must sacrifice the few for the many. We must protect our kingdoms and our people. The gods put us in charge of Delacroix because we're the only ones strong enough to carry this burden, to do what others could not."

I bowed my head, starting to shake.

His hand went to my shoulder. "There was nothing you could do."

His touch used to be savored, but now it made me cold.

"Your destiny is on the throne of the Capital. A worthy wife at your side. Subjects at your feet. Not with somebody like her—a nobody."

————

I SAT on the rug in front of my fireplace, leaning up against the base of my four-poster bed, staring at the fire with eyes that didn't need to blink. My arm was propped on one knee, and I stared at the only source of light in the room.

Didn't bother trying to sleep.

How could I sleep, knowing she was struggling to survive this very moment?

Supplies were dropped with the winners, so they'd have a chance to make it to a settlement, but who knew if anyone ever made it. My father said it was a frozen wasteland, full of yetis and Teeth.

I closed my eyes because the pain was too much.

I could have prevented all this, but I didn't think.

The entire village entered their names into that lottery. What were the odds that she'd be picked?

One in a million.

I turned my head to look out the window, to see the distant signs of sunrise, the way the sky had changed from black to slightly blue.

The decision came to me without any thought, without any inner speech. I just knew what I was about to do—and I got up to do it.

DECKED IN MY ARMOR, my weapons, and my warmest clothes, I went to the stables and took my horse.

The stablemaster watched me, as if he knew I shouldn't be there but didn't dare comment. "Anything else you need for your trip, m'lord?" He placed water canteens in the saddlebags, along with jerky and dried fruit.

"No." I took the horse by the reins to walk to the edge of the city.

"And when the duke asks after your whereabouts?"

I turned back to him. "He'll know exactly where I've gone." I mounted the horse and kicked. In the rising sun, I rode hard, heading to the Mammoth Mountains where the cave was rumored to be.

I would take the tunnel to the bottom of the cliffs and bring Effie home.

If I made it there in time.

5

EFFIE

Dark. Cold. Terrifying.

It was chaos, all of us panicking once we were on the ground, ankle-deep in snow. They gave us clothes to survive the cold, torches that we couldn't light, weapons that we didn't know how to use.

What the fuck?

My father had woken up that morning and bounced around the house like a kid on Christmas morning. He'd had a look in his eyes I'd never seen before, and he talked about the fishing boat he was going to buy after we sold the house, how he would spend all day by the coastline in the sunshine.

But then they forced us onto that wooden platform—and lowered us down.

I didn't have time to feel the cold, to be terrified of the dark, to face the moment.

My adrenaline was so high, loud in my ears, pounding in my heart. I assumed the bottom of the cliffs was the ocean, but now I realized it was a real place, fifty degrees colder than the mild temperatures at the top.

Why had they put us down here?

My sister was the most frightened, and she started to scream.

"Laurie, shh." Mother tried to console her, but that was hard to do in the pitch black.

I reached for the torch they'd left for us and fumbled for the other supplies, hoping they provided a lighter or some matches to get this going.

Laurie wouldn't stop crying.

But my dad was silent—and that was worse.

I finally found the lighter and lit the torch. The ball of heat was hot against my face, so I held it out, seeing the flames reflect on the snow around us. There were two sacks on the ground full of food and weapons, but that was it.

I could see my father's face now.

He was whiter than the snow.

Once Laurie could actually see, her screams stopped. She clutched my mother, with tears that shone like diamonds on her cheeks.

I took one look at all of them and knew they were in shock.

I didn't have the luxury of being in shock. If I didn't get us in motion, we would die out there. "Come on, let's grab our things and get moving."

"Get moving?" Mother asked. "Where? We can't see a damn thing."

"We'll freeze if we don't find shelter." I spoke calmly, but I had no idea how, considering the situation. There was an ache in my chest that they didn't carry, a betrayal marked by a man who'd made me smile more times than I could count. When I reflected on our last conversation through the window, I realized he knew.

He knew.

He didn't stop it. He didn't save me. He just let it happen.

The Duke of Delacroix was evil—and so was his son.

"Come on." I grabbed one of the sacks and threw it over my arm.

Laurie climbed out of Mother's arms and grabbed the other sack.

Dad just sat there, his breath coming out as smoke.

"Dear." Mom took her time getting to her feet, her joints probably stiff from the cold. Her hand reached for his shoulder and gave him a gentle shake. "She's right. We've got to get moving."

He stared straight ahead, eyes devoid of emotion, defeated.

It was too hard to look at him—so I dropped my gaze.

"Dear." She tried again. "Come on, I'm sure there's a place around here."

My dad's face tightened before he covered it with his hand.

Then he started to sob.

WE MOVED THROUGH THE DARK, tripping over piles of snow, and I held out the torch to light our way. Sometimes we took turns carrying it because the warmth of the fire was worth the weight. The sun finally started to rise, and when I looked behind us, I realized we hadn't made it far from where we'd started.

The light grew brighter, and I saw nothing but snow and trees.

Endlessly.

They wouldn't have given us supplies if there wasn't a chance we would survive, so I swallowed the panic and kept going. I kept close to the wall of the cliff, hoping to come across a cave or shelter. It was solid wall the whole way.

If we didn't find something by nightfall, we'd probably freeze. My mother couldn't handle this trek, and my father was still too devastated to participate.

Laurie came to my side. "Why did they do this?"

"I don't know, Laurie."

"Are we supposed to do something down here?"

I repeated my answer. "I don't know, Laurie." I didn't know why a man who made me weak in the knees could approve of this horrendous torture. I didn't know why someone could smile like that but be full of such hate. I didn't have any answers.

———

"LOOK!" Laurie spotted it before I did. "A cave!" She ran ahead, bopping up and down on the uneven snow.

It was a saving grace because we only had an hour of daylight left.

But my high was quickly dampened when I realized the danger. "Laurie, stop!"

She kept running.

"Goddammit, I said stop!"

This time, she froze in place and looked at me over her shoulder.

"Let me check it out first, alright?" I pulled the sword from my hip and crept toward the entrance to the cave.

Dad was in the rear with Mom, her arm over his shoulder as he helped her move forward. "Be careful, Effie."

I glanced into the cavern and didn't see anyone.

But I did see the crates stacked against the wall and the bedrolls in the corner. "It's clear." I stepped inside and saw the cold fire pit with soot and ash along the bottom. The place wasn't in disarray, so it was used regularly.

Laurie opened one of the crates and munched on the food she found. "They have nuts and fruit in here."

Dad helped Mom inside and helped her sit on one of the crates. "We can't stay here."

We all looked to him.

"It's occupied. They'll come back and kill us all."

I looked outside the cave entrance and saw the light fade even further. "We'll die out there."

"We'll die in here," Dad said.

"And we'll die out there," I said. "We won't survive another night. We need to make a fire and have someone stand watch."

"Effie, no," he said. "We'll be fish in a barrel—"

Rooooooooaaaaaarrrrrr.

The sound shook the walls of the cave, made our hearts drop into the pits of our stomachs.

No one spoke. No one addressed the terror we'd just heard.

What the hell was this place?

"I'll take first watch." I grabbed the firewood and set it on top of the cold stones before I lit it with the torch. It came to life in a few minutes, the smoke sucked out of the entrance and to the bare sky. "I'll take the first watch..."

DAYS PASSED, and we stayed put.

There was food storage that would last us a long time and a fire to keep us warm from the chill. We could venture farther out, but what would we find? After that sound we'd heard, we had no idea what we were dealing with in this new place.

"I think we should stay," Mother said. "We have everything we need right here."

"And what about when the residents return?" Father asked.

We had these family meetings every day, trying to figure out how to survive. We had limited options, so we just went around in circles over and over.

"Maybe they'll help us," Mother said. "Clearly, we don't belong down here."

"Or maybe they'll butcher us and eat us," Father said.

Laurie let out a scream and started to cry.

I gave him a glare. "Don't say that in front of her."

He ignored me.

"I think we should try to see what else is out there," I said. "Maybe there's a village or something nearby. If not, we'll just come back here. If there's no way back, we need to integrate with society. There have to be people just like us down here, other people from Delacroix. All the lottery winners. They'd want to help us."

"I agree," Mother said. "They would."

Dad stayed quiet.

"I can go on my own and report back," I said.

"I can go too," Laurie offered, picking up a dagger.

My hand gripped her shoulder. "You need to stay here, kiddo."

"But I want to help!"

"Who's going to protect Mom and Dad while I'm gone?" I rubbed my hand up and down her arm, seeing the same bravery I possessed. Must be genetic. "They need you. I'm just going to go for a short walk and see if I can discover any clues. I'll be back before you know it."

"Are you sure?" she asked, her voice quiet.

"Absolutely." I kneeled and gave her a big hug, squeezing her for the first time in forever.

She hugged me back, her head resting on my shoulder, her arms around my neck.

I gave her a kiss on the cheek and pulled away. "I'll be back in a couple hours. Sit tight." I grabbed one of the bags and filled it with water and food in case I needed it, and then I tied the broadsword to my hip—and hoped I didn't have to use it.

6

RYKER

The ladder never ended. Down, down, down, it went, plunging deeper into darkness. There was no mistake where this path led because there was only one thing this deep underground. The air became damp and stale, and the heat from the surface quickly disappeared as I traveled deeper into the rock.

I stopped to sleep, but sparingly, because I knew time wasn't on my side.

If I took too long, there would be nobody to save.

If I found her dead body in the snow, I wouldn't be able to live with myself. I wouldn't be able to return to my luxurious quarters and go about my life like nothing had happened. How could I be with another woman when I knew the last woman I'd been with was dead?

Because of me.

When the ladder stopped, I took a tunnel that spiraled down, and then I reached a flat pathway, ice crystals in the stones around the ceiling, in the roots from vegetation that grew on the exterior of the cliff.

When I finally saw a dot of daylight on the other side, I ran.

I couldn't bring my horse down here, so I'd had to make the entire trek on foot, which slowed me down, and it would slow me down even more when I emerged from this cave. I didn't have a map. I didn't have experience. I didn't have anything. A lesser man would have turned around a long time ago.

Bravery didn't fuel my path forward. It wasn't courage either. Wasn't even obligation.

Something else entirely.

I stepped directly into the sunlight and got a full view of this new world for the first time. It was covered in snow, the ground white and too bright to stare at. Tall pines extended far into the distance, their green leaves covered with snow. It couldn't be more different from Delacroix, which had mild winters and blistering summers. Now that I was no longer in the shelter of the cave, vapor escaped my breath and my lungs immediately felt dry.

I didn't know where to start.

The cables to the platform had been cut, so it should be lying somewhere in the snow near the edge of the cliff. I'd find that first, and if I didn't see their bodies, I'd keep going south. If they'd survived the fall, they were probably still alive.

Because Effie was tough.

I FOUND THE PLATFORM.

The cables were hidden under the snow, and I saw no signs of blood or injury. The color would be unmistakable against the white backdrop. All their supplies were gone, so that meant they were well enough to carry everything.

A good sign.

I searched the snow for tracks, but the wind had swept them clean a long time ago. Snow must have fallen sometime since then, especially since it'd been three days since she was lowered down there.

I was tempted to call for her, but I had no idea who—or what—was down there. My father had shared stories with me, stories that I never told Ivory, because as brave as she seemed to be, they would have terrified her.

I moved forward through the trees, my boots crunching as they dug into the piles of snow with each step. I'd grabbed extra clothes before I'd left, and it was a good thing I had, but the air was so cold and dry. My eyes already strained to produce moisture to keep them lubricated.

It was quiet down there, really quiet.

Almost peaceful.

I walked that way for a while, my eyes scanning the horizon, searching between the trees for a sign of a campfire. They wouldn't survive out there in the elements, so they must have found shelter. At least, I hoped they did.

Something caught my eye.

Fire.

Just a glimmer of it through a crack in the cliff face.

Hidden behind a pine, I watched, hoping to spot a face.

There was no movement.

I stayed there for a while and realized I wouldn't see anything at this angle. I'd have to approach. It was probably Effie and her family, but I didn't want to get my hopes up, because if someone else was there and they weren't...they were probably dead.

I approached the crevasse in the cliff face, which would have escaped my attention if it weren't for the fire. Too preoccupied with finding Effie, I probably wouldn't have noticed it. Good thing I did.

I approached the entrance as quietly as possible and peered inside.

On a bedroll were a woman and her young daughter.

An older man leaned against the wall, eating a sack of dried nuts.

But there was no sign of Effie.

I stepped inside and lifted my hands from my weapons. "I mean you no harm."

The father's reaction was so slow that he wouldn't have been able to stop me. He wouldn't have even known I was there before I'd killed him. He dropped his handful of nuts onto the stone and looked as pale as the snow. "Who are you?"

The mother and sister jerked up, and the mother immediately put her protective arms around her child.

"A friend of Effie's." He obviously didn't recognize me, and that might be a good thing. "Where is she?"

He looked me over, examining my weapons and armor. "She went to look for others..."

"By herself?" I asked in disbelief.

He held my gaze and didn't speak.

"How long has she been gone?"

"About an hour," the mother said. "How did you get down here? Were you lowered too?"

"I know another way."

Her dad immediately gave a jolt. "You do? Where?"

"Head back in the opposite direction. There's a cave hidden behind some boulders. You wouldn't see it if you didn't know it was there. It's a long climb back up, so it'll take a couple days to make it back."

Her father locked eyes with her mother.

"But don't return to Delacroix," I said. "If the duke sees you, he'll send you back down here." Or, more than likely, just kill them where they stood so they wouldn't be able to talk. "I'll go after Effie if you want to meet at the cave."

They immediately started to deliberate among themselves.

I didn't stop to eat or drink. Effie was out there—alone—and I didn't have a minute to spare.

SHE'D ONLY BEEN GONE an hour, but there was no sign of her.

There was nothing ahead but a snowy landscape, so her dark clothing should mark her like a flag. I eventually came across her tracks, seeing her trail through the tall pines. It took all my strength not to call out her name, but that would put both of us in danger.

Now that I knew I was right behind her, I picked up my pace, running through the snow and kicking up powder everywhere.

Then I heard it.

A woman's scream.

"No." I pulled out my short sword and shield and hustled faster, tripping here and there, completely unfamiliar with snow.

Her voice was unmistakable. "Touch me and see what happens!"

Fuck. I didn't make it this far just to be too late.

I finally saw them through the opening in the trees, Effie holding out her sword with a shaky hand, her inexperience obvious in her footwork and posture.

A group of five men faced her, wearing armor the color of darkness, making the snow look even whiter in comparison. They all had broadswords and bows and arrows. They looked human, no different from the two of us, but there was a paleness to their skin that set them apart.

Their eyes shifted to me once I appeared in the clearing.

"Get behind me." I pushed her back and took my stance, sword and shield steady, showing them that I knew exactly how to use them both. Five against one...not good odds.

Her voice erupted behind me, full of awe. "Ryker..."

I lowered my voice so only she could hear and kept my eyes trained on our enemies. "When I have them distracted, you need to run."

"No—"

"There's a passage back to Delacroix. Hidden by some boulders. I told your family to meet us there." I watched the men exchange looks before they started to move in, to get into formation to take me on.

My father trained me well. Hopefully, he'd trained me well enough.

She came to my side, her sword at the ready, this time steady. "I'm not leaving you."

"Effie—"

"Klaus will be very interested in you both." The man whom I presumed to be their leader stepped forward, distinguished by the heavy coat he wore on top of his armor. "Surrender and remain unharmed. Or let your bloody and broken bodies be dragged there." He didn't withdraw his sword, like this fight would be so short there was no point.

"You think this is the first time I've taken on five guys?" I spun the sword around my wrist. "Let's go."

The leader stared at me for a long time. His eyes were dark, but not dark brown like the average person. They were black, black like his armor, black like the fur coat that kept him warm. His face started to draw back, as if he was about to scream, but instead, long and sharp teeth emerged.

It was like nothing I'd ever seen.

The others followed suit, pushing a throat of teeth outside their mouths.

The leader spoke, his teeth still. "Surrender—or be eaten."

7

IVORY

Thud.

I heard it—and I heard Huntley go silent.

I ran straight to his weapons and picked up his ax before I ran to the top of the stairs.

Queen Rolfe stood over him, her boot against his chest. "Another should do it, Commander Dawson."

Huntley opened his eyes, his face bloody, but he lay still.

Then Commander Dawson walked over and kicked him right in the head.

It was too horrifying for me to react immediately, seeing a mother betray her son as he lay on the floor with a bloody nose. Just minutes ago, we were happy in bed, our bodies and souls tangled up into one. "What the fuck is wrong with you?"

They both snapped their heads in my direction.

My eyes were reserved for hers. "He's your *son*."

Devoid of emotion as always, she gave a nod to Commander Dawson.

I knew what that meant. "Bitch, I'm gonna kill you. I'm gonna kill you for touching my husband."

"*Husband*?" she asked, appalled. "He is no such thing. But you got the bitch part right."

"According to the Priest of Adeodatus, he is."

"I'll make sure that's reversed."

"It's irreversible—"

"We'll see about that." She nodded to Commander Dawson again.

He started to move up the stairs.

I gripped my sword and prepared to take on a commander, a man who outweighed me in every way. "He'll never forgive you." Queen Rolfe looked down at her son's unconscious body then gestured to the men outside the door. They picked him up and moved him to the couch and applied dressings to his wounds.

There was nowhere for me to go. I was trapped. "I'm taking you down with me, so make your best move." I stayed at the top of the stairs, ready to slam the butt of the ax down on his head when he came close enough.

He stopped a few steps down, considering his options.

"That's what I thought, asshole—"

Something hit me in the head—hard. I toppled slightly and saw the book on the floor. "Cheap shot..."

That was enough time for Commander Dawson to find an opening, and he rushed in and circled his arm around my throat and squeezed.

My hands dropped the ax and reached for his arm, trying to pry it free. I gasped for air, twisting and turning to throw him off, but it was useless. I slipped under and went weak in his arms.

Then everything went black.

———

THE FIRST THING I noticed when I woke up was the cold.

It jerked me awake, and when I inhaled my first real breath, I felt it burn the lining of my lungs. My body rocked back and forth continuously, and that was when I realized I was on a horse.

Tied to the man in front of me.

My hands were bound around his waist, and my ankles were secured to the saddle. I was totally immobile, couldn't even see in front of me because his shoulders blocked my view. I looked left and right, trying to make sense of my surroundings.

It was all a blur.

"Shit." My rider addressed the other men in the cavalry. "She's awake."

"Where are we going?" I yanked on his stomach, but he wouldn't budge more than an inch or two. I'd assumed I would never wake up, that Commander Dawson had choked me to death. But here I was—back in the cold.

He didn't answer.

I slammed my head hard into his back and made him jerk forward. "Answer me."

"Fuck." He fell forward over the neck of the horse then slammed his elbow back into my side. "Sit still, bitch."

"Bitch?" I slammed my head again.

He gave an angry groan then brought the horse to a halt. To my surprise, he untied my wrists.

Once my hands were free, I immediately leaned forward to my ankle, trying to get free as quickly as possible.

A man came up from behind and smothered my face with a cloth, a cloth that reeked of death.

I threw arms and elbows, but it was no use. The cloth stayed right in place, and I was pulled into darkness once more.

And I still had no idea where I was going.

I CAME TO AGAIN, but this time, it wasn't cold anymore.

It was mild, just the way it had been in HeartHolme, the breeze pleasant rather than choking. When my eyes opened, all I could see was the ground, dirt instead of snow. My ankles and wrists were still bound.

I was alone.

I rolled onto my stomach and pushed myself to my knees. "Hello?" I looked to the right, and in the far distance, I saw them. Men on horses. They stayed where they were and watched me.

Okay...that was weird.

I looked down at my wrists and started twisting and pulling, doing whatever I could to fray the binds. There was a sharp rock a few feet away, so I fell forward and started to crawl. The sky was blue and purple, with just a tinge of pink, so the sun had already set. In a few minutes, I wouldn't be able to see at all.

I reached the rock and pressed the rope against the sharpest edge. My arms moved up and down as fast as I could, trying to produce both friction and heat to force the threads in the rope to snap apart. "Come on..."

Footsteps. Loud. Distinguishable. Coming from behind me.

"You motherfucker..." I rubbed harder, only a couple threads breaking even though I was producing the speed of someone fighting for their life.

The footsteps stopped.

A black boot was right beside my face. I could feel the piercing stare on my back.

"And if you manage to break your binds, what will you do then?"

I kept going, watching more of the threads become frayed. "Kill your ass."

His boot moved forward and kicked the rock away.

"Hey!" I immediately crawled for it.

His heavy foot pressed into the small of my back and pushed me down. "Get up."

I turned over onto my back and looked up into the face I'd seen before, his teeth withdrawn into his mouth and throat. Eyes black like molten rock, they were empty of a soul. I clenched my jaw tight as I swung my leg as hard as I could, hitting him right in the shin.

He shuffled slightly and gave a slight grimace, but he didn't make a sound. "You don't want me to hurt you. Trust me on that."

"I'm not afraid of pain."

"But you should be afraid of blood." He stepped away, and that was when his men appeared behind him. I recognized one of them from months ago. They both grabbed me and dragged me to my feet.

I looked over my shoulder, seeing the Runes already turn to leave on their horses.

I faced forward again and pictured feathers in dark hair, coldness in her tight lips, evil in eyes that I looked into every single night.

———

IT WAS SO different from HeartHolme and the outpost.

The sweltering heat—that was new.

A river ran to a large lake, the water sparkling and bright, reflecting the sun high in the sky. Pine trees were everywhere, their branches unencumbered by piles of snow. It allowed the leaves to breathe, to let the smell of pine dissipate in the air. It was uphill from where I'd been dropped off, and when I looked behind me, I had a distant view of the snow on the top of the mountains.

I was far away from home.

Both homes.

Their city was built into the side of the mountain, the streets rising higher and higher until it flattened against the wall. It had a view of the forests and the lake. Along the way, I'd noticed all the outposts where the guards stood far down the hill. If an attack was imminent, they would have plenty of time to retreat into the safety of their city.

It'd been a long time since I'd felt sweat on my brow, felt it down the curve of my back. It'd been cold most of my time down here, and I didn't remember life in any other way. Without the fire in the hearth, the heavy furs on top of the bed, my husband's warm body next to mine...I didn't know who I was.

My husband.

I hoped he was okay.

I didn't expect him to come for me. It would be a betrayal of his people, of his queen. Our little plan hadn't worked, and that was a surprise to us both.

The enormous wooden doors that led to the city were wide open for Teeth to come and go. There were cabins throughout the pine forests. I could see them as I passed. But there was no farming, no livestock, no other signs of civilization.

Then I remembered...they didn't need those things.

Even if Huntley came for me, it would take far too long, and by the time he got here, I'd be long dead.

I'd be the feast on the table.

As I was marched forward, I saw other Teeth pass me on the street. Some of them shifted their gazes and glanced at me, like they knew full well that I didn't belong there—and I wasn't one of them.

The only good thing was the shade the mountain provided. It dropped the temperature exponentially, actually left me slightly cold because the sun hadn't hit the city the entire day. We passed dwellings and shops, but if they didn't sell food, I didn't know what they sold. There was no market like at home. The place was nothing like home.

We made it to the very top, to another set of double doors that led to a stone building several stories tall. The second we stepped inside, it was dark, so dark that my eyes needed to take a moment to adjust. Then I noticed the thick rug on the floor, the torches along the walls, the eerie silence.

I knew exactly where they were taking me.

To Klaus.

I was marched deeper inside, down long hallways, and then entered a room with a glass ceiling.

I felt him before I saw him.

On a large throne, he sat, smaller chairs on either side of him vacant. Dressed in all black with one ankle crossed on the opposite knee, he sat there with his arms sprawled down the armrests, his dark eyes on me with subtle interest.

The men positioned me feet from his throne then retreated behind me.

I stared.

He stared.

It was just like it'd been in the snow. But this time, I didn't have a sword. I didn't have my bow and arrow. I didn't have a fighting chance, not when there was nowhere for me to run, not when I didn't even have a butter knife to cut his eyes out.

What I noticed most was the paleness of his features, the way his skin looked like snow while his clothes were the color of night. He was so still he didn't seem to draw breath. His eyes were so serious he didn't need to blink. He bent his arms and brushed his fingers across his bottom lip. "Welcome to the Crags."

"Happy to be here." My sarcasm was all I had. I used it when I was scared to pretend I wasn't. Used it when I didn't have a weapon to do all the talking. I used it when I had nothing left to lose.

"Your sacrifice has prevented a war."

"Not my sacrifice—as I didn't come here willingly."

His stare ensued, piercing flesh and bone. "Then your queen made the right sacrifice—"

"That bitch ain't my queen." I didn't respect a woman who betrayed her own son. Who was so wounded by her own pain that she didn't hesitate to inflict that same pain on others. Someone like that shouldn't be in power.

Klaus made a subtle gesture to the men who'd brought me there. "Take her to my chambers."

Their hands were on me a second later, but I could hardly feel them, because I knew the meaning of his words. "I'm not letting you touch me." I threw my body into the one on the right then bashed my fist into his face. My elbow flew to the other, and then I ran for it, heading to the nearest hallway.

A big guy came from nowhere and struck me hard from the side.

I hit the stone floor and nearly broke my shoulder.

Now all three of them were on me, pulling me to my feet and yanking me down the hallway.

I fought tooth and nail, bit my attackers, kicked, screamed—you name it. But all it did was slow my progression down the hallway rather than prevent it. When I was dragged into the room, I saw the large four-poster bed and the furniture that surrounded it. Everything was high-end and well-made, just like everything at Delacroix.

I was pinned down and stripped naked.

"Fuck. You." I bit into another then felt a hand slap me hard in the face.

Ropes were secured to my wrists and ankles, and I was stuck on my back, like a spread eagle. I wanted to cry, when I never cried. I wanted to give in to the grief for what was about to happen to me. I wanted to escape—and not return to Huntley or Delacroix. I wanted to take on Queen Rolfe —and stab her right through those fucking eyes.

The men vacated and Klaus entered. The door closed, and he shed his cloak and left it on the back of one of the chairs.

I kept pulling and yanking because there was no way in hell I was going to let this happen without a fight.

He stood at the foot of the bed and stared down at my naked body, his hands in the pockets of his pants. His eyes dragged over me slowly, savoring every single inch of my porcelain skin.

I'd never felt so violated in all my life. "Let me go...or I'll kill you."

His eyes met mine, not the least bit wary of those words.

"I swear to the gods..."

"I'm not going to kill you."

"Wish you would. Prefer that over this."

"It'll hurt at first, but you'll get used to it."

"Fuck. You."

His hands pressed into the mattress, and he leaned forward over my hips, his eyes on my left thigh.

I tried to squirm away, but I couldn't move at all. "You fucking bastard!"

He dipped his head and pressed a kiss to my inner thigh.

I bucked against him to hit him in the face.

"You really shouldn't do that." He opened his mouth and slowly pushed all the rows of teeth forward. "One wrong move...and you could die."

I was stunned into silence, seeing all those rows of teeth about to perforate my flesh. My usual sarcasm left me. Everything left me. My fight. My hope.

"I won't kill you. Only take what I need."

It was even more sinister than I realized.

"Now, stay still."

8

HUNTLEY

I jerked upright and gripped my chest.

The pain—it was excruciating.

The darkness was impossible to penetrate with my sight, to check for enemies as they surrounded my camp. I didn't hear a sound. Didn't feel a wound as my hand moved over my heart underneath my shirt.

I felt nothing.

But it was still enough pain to make me keel over.

I ended up on all fours, panting through the agony, weak everywhere. "Fuck..." I fell back to the bedroll and gripped my chest as I gave a groan. It lasted for minutes, the intensity constant, my breath coming out through clenched teeth.

And then it finally stopped.

Just like that.

My body finally relaxed, and my palm fell from my chest. "What the fuck...?"

AT THE FIRST sign of sunrise, I rode my horse through the trees, the temperature dropping deeper the farther I went. It was a three-day journey, but I made it in two because I hauled ass. I approached the gates to the outpost and watched the doors open when they recognized me.

I rode through the gates and immediately dropped down from my horse. "Where's Ian?"

"His cabin, Your Highness." The guard took my horse by the reins and guided him to the stables.

I jogged through the outpost and ignored the questions people tried to ask. My unexpected visit made people uneasy because it could be a sign of impending war. His cabin was close to mine, so I burst inside without knocking.

A naked woman was in the bed covered in the furs, and he was working at his desk with just his breeches on. It was still early morning, so he hadn't even gotten his day started. His mug was full of coffee, and the fire kept the room warm.

The woman was so knocked out, she didn't stir.

He was on his feet instantly with a shirt over his head. "How long do we have?"

"There's no attack on the outpost or HeartHolme, but time is still of the essence."

The woman pushed off the furs then looked at Ian with sleepy eyes. "Keep it down, would you?"

Ian grabbed his coat and his ax and walked out the door.

I joined him, and together we stood a few feet away, the residents watching our conversation.

"What's happened, Huntley?" He was my height and had my same eyes, but his look was even harder to penetrate than mine. A solid wall of indifference, he was a lot like our father, but he may have forgotten that after all these years.

"Mother has given Ivory to Klaus—to prevent a war."

His eyes were lifeless. "The issue?"

I didn't know how to say this, to tell my little brother I wed without his presence. He'd act like it wasn't a big deal, but I knew it would bother him. "I married her."

That cold wall was broken by his authentic reaction. His pupils dilated. His jaw tightened. His breathing changed.

"It was the only way I could protect her...or so I thought."

"I'm not surprised Mother handed her over anyway. You shouldn't be either."

"Well, I am. Because I thought her love for me was greater than anything else. Guess I was wrong."

"You came all the way here to tell me this? But you didn't come all the way here to tell me you were getting married?" There was a bite to his words, a coldness he never showed me—just our enemies and those stupid enough to antagonize him. "What do you want from me?"

"To gather our soldiers and ride to the Crags with me."

He stepped back slightly, giving a small shake of his head. "You want me to go to war. You want me to go to a war that Mother just prevented. For a woman who's not even one of us."

"She is one of us—because she's my wife."

His nostrils flared at his next exhale. "I already helped you once. Mother hates me enough as it is, and now, she'll hate me more."

"She does not hate you—"

"She's never forgiven me for my actions as a child. And she probably never will—especially if I do this."

"You don't need her approval, Ian."

"Easy for you to say...since you're her only son."

My eyes took his in, seeing the pain and the resentment. "That's not true—"

"Don't bullshit me." He stepped back farther. "I went against her wishes once. I won't do it again."

I held his gaze, sickened that I'd wasted two days coming here instead of riding straight to her. "Ian."

He averted his gaze.

"I'm asking as your brother."

"Why?"

My eyebrows furrowed.

He turned his gaze back on me. "Why did you marry her?"

"I told you why—"

"Her protection is more important than the protection of your people? Is that what you're saying?"

"I'm saying that she is our people, Ian. Not just by marriage —but by heart."

His eyes narrowed.

"She's vowed to help me regain our home. Without her, we wouldn't have a chance."

"And you believe her?" he asked incredulously.

There was no hesitation in my voice. "I do."

"She's just using you—"

"I've promised her something in return, yes. But she's not using me. We need to get her back from the Teeth because we have no chance of taking Delacroix and the Kingdoms without her. Mother would see that if she weren't so desperate for revenge. She can't think clearly. You know exactly what I'm talking about."

"But is that worth going to war with the Teeth?"

"It is if our goal is to return to the top of the cliff—and get away from Necrosis."

He averted his gaze again, this time with a sigh.

"Would it make any difference if I told you she meant something to me?"

After a long pause, he looked at me once more.

"Because she does."

When he gave another exhale, his nostrils flared again. "Even after what her family did to ours?"

"It's not her family. Just her father, whom she's nothing like."

He bowed his head and chewed the inside of his cheek.

"Ian."

When he met my gaze, it was with a look of resolve. "You owe me."

The breath left my lungs—along with all the tension. "I know."

"No questions asked."

"Consider it done."

"Alright." He stepped away. "We go to war."

9

IVORY

I was thrown into a room full of single-size beds.

No windows. One bathroom. No fireplace. The ceiling had glass openings, so that gave me some light. But now that the sun was gone, all I had was the moonlight to see my surroundings. I leaned against the headboard of one of the beds, my thigh wrapped in tight gauze to keep the pressure on.

I felt weak. So weak that my dinner wasn't enough to make me feel better.

It could have been worse. All he wanted was my blood—but not my flesh.

Thank the gods.

I sat there for a long time, too weak to even consider an escape plan. They returned my clothes, so I put on my shirt but left my bottoms off to keep an eye on my bloody thigh.

He said he wouldn't kill me, but once his teeth had pierced my flesh, he got excited, so excited that I thought he would devour all of me on the spot.

I suddenly felt this pain in my chest, a pain I'd never felt before.

It was deep inside, not superficial or on the surface, like a knife between the ribs or in the flesh like my current wound. It went so deep that I couldn't identify the location. I just knew it hurt, knew that changing my position or getting up and walking wouldn't make a difference. And it hurt a lot more than the wound in my leg.

It reminded me of the night Huntley and I had bound our souls together for all eternity. When we were together, the euphoria was so potent, so powerful. It cleansed my body of every sorrow I'd ever felt. The joy was unmatched. It was just like that...but in the opposite direction. This pain was stronger than anything I'd ever known. It was beyond medicine, beyond healing. The pain was organic and physical, as if it was a part of who I was.

I JOLTED awake when the door flew open.

A girl my age was shoved forward. Long blond hair. Green eyes. A petite thing. They hit her so hard that she fell forward and caught herself on her palms before she broke her face on the stone.

Just in my top and my underwear, I rushed to her. "You okay?" I took her by the arm and helped her to her feet.

The door remained open, and someone else was shoved inside.

A man with a bloody face. Tall. Muscular. In the armor of Delacroix. He barely caught himself before he hit the floor, and he gave a groan when he did it, like he had three broken ribs and a broken knee.

The guard shut the door, and the lock turned.

The blonde kneeled at the man's side and tried to help him to his feet.

He shoved her off then slowly stood upright, too proud to accept assistance. His left eye was black and swollen, he had a nasty cut on the opposite cheek, and his lips were swollen from the kiss of a fist.

But I recognized him. "Ryker...?"

His entire body went still, and his eyes focused on me. All his aggravation disappeared as he stared me down, his eyes shifting back and forth slightly, his swollen pupil barely visible beneath the inflammation of the tissues.

The blonde looked back and forth between us. "Ivory?"

My eyes remained on his. My heart had never beat like this before. It was like drums at the Harvest Parade. It had taken me all night to feel normal again, and even then, I hadn't felt quite right. But now, I felt stronger than I ever had.

He stepped forward, disbelief on his messed-up features. I hadn't changed since my journey had begun, other than my hair being a little longer, my eyes being a little dimmer. He knew it was me, but it was too good to be true.

Words failed him, and he embraced me instead. His powerful arms wrapped around me and yanked me into his chest, immediately squeezing me tight with his strength. His chest rose with the deep breath he took, and his body gave a little shake when it came back out.

I clung to him just as hard and felt my eyes moisten. He felt the same. He smelled the same. Home was in my arms. "I can't believe you're here..."

"Thank the gods you are." He released me and stepped away.

The blonde watched us before she dismissed herself and moved to the other side of the room to give us privacy.

His eyes stayed on me. "It was the Teeth that took you?"

I shook my head. "It's a long story. Did Father send you?" That meant the cavalry was nearby, that they would attack the Crags and free us both.

His eyes dimmed. "No. Just me."

"You came down here by yourself to find me?" I asked, my voice breaking.

He gave a subtle shake of his head. "I looked for you every-where in the Kingdoms—twice. No one provided any leads. No one had seen you or Mastodon. I'm sorry that I didn't listen to you...by the way."

He was already forgiven. "It's okay, Ryker."

"He's one of the Teeth, then. How did we not notice?"

"Because he's not. He's a Rune."

"Then how did you end up here?"

"Long story...but Queen Rolfe turned me over to stop a war." I didn't have to explain who the Teeth and Runes were, so he obviously knew everything about this place, had known about the cruelty long before I did. "You didn't answer my question."

His eyes immediately shifted to the blonde across the room. His stare lingered for a second before it returned to me. "I came across Effie in my travels across the Kingdoms. She was alone, and some of my men wanted to do what men do best. I returned her to Delacroix, and one thing led to another..."

I had no idea where this tale was headed.

"I discovered that her family had won the lottery. I tried to stop it, but it was too late."

The lottery. It wasn't a saving grace. It was a damnation. And people prayed they would be chosen for that damnation.

"The men discovered the tunnel that leads down here. I took it and found her, but not before the Teeth did. There were too many of them. I couldn't prevail, not on my own anyway. I'm surprised they didn't kill me."

"Because you're no use to them dead."

His eyes narrowed.

"They'll feed off us." I looked down to my bandaged thigh.

Ryker stared at it then quickly looked away, disgusted.

"We'll find a way out of here. It was stupid to bunk us together."

He returned his gaze to my face, his features still pained.

I watched him for a while. "What?"

"Everything is different now."

Unsure of his meaning, I felt my eyebrows strain as I waited for more.

"Between us."

I continued to stare.

"Because now you know that I know...that I've always known."

I was too happy to see him to feel that way. If I'd discovered the truth in the safety of our castle, my reaction would have been different. But not now, not when we had to survive. "Nothing has changed."

"You look at me differently," he said. "You're doing it now."

I averted my gaze because I couldn't meet his. "You said you tried to stop the lottery... How?"

"Went straight to Father."

"And he didn't answer your pleas?"

"Said it was too late for him to intervene."

Too late, or he just didn't want to? "How long have you known?"

He gave a shrug. "I don't know... Always?"

"He asked you not to tell me?"

His eyes filled with guilt as he gave a nod. "He knew how you'd feel about it. Thought it was better to protect you."

"I hope this means you understand how barbaric the practice is now."

His eyes shifted to Effie in the corner. "It's complicated..."

"How is it complicated?" I demanded. "You risked your life for this woman, so you care about her. You care about what happens to her."

"Obviously." His eyes came back to me. "But there's more to the practice than you realize. Father doesn't do it because he wants to. He does it because he has no other choice. King Rutherford commands it, and his Blade Scions make sure his commands are fulfilled. And if he didn't do it, they would come for us."

"And we could fight them all together."

He stared in disbelief.

"If we don't want to live in fear forever, it needs to be done. It should be done. Sacrificing innocent people isn't the answer."

"Ivory." He lowered his voice. "Have you seen Necrosis?"

I didn't answer.

"Because Father has. And I won't repeat what he's told me."

"EFFIE." Ryker sat on the bed beside her, their backs turned to me.

She stared at the wall, her arms crossed over her chest.

"Talk to me—"

"I have nothing to say to you." She got up and moved to another bed.

Ryker stayed put, his eyes still on the wall in front of him.

I pitied my brother, but I also didn't. If it were me, he'd be getting more than just the cold shoulder.

Ryker gave a sigh before he joined me on my bed. He sat at the edge, his arms on his knees, one hand massaging his swollen knuckles.

"Want me to talk to her?"

"You'd just make her hate me more."

"You know I wouldn't."

"There's no point. Can't really blame her, can I? If her father exiled mine to a wasteland of monsters, I wouldn't like her either."

I'd feel the same. "But you came down here to save her—and that's a greater reflection of who you are."

"Save her?" he asked. "No. I just joined her."

"We're going to get out of here, Ryker."

He gave a slight shake of his head. "Always the optimist, huh?"

"No, a realist."

He turned to look at me.

"I remember the path from this room to the exit. The rest of the way...we'll have to haul ass."

"There has to be another way out. If under attack, it doesn't make sense for soldiers to run down all the streets to get to the edge of the city. There's a shortcut somewhere. A ladder or a rope."

His military mind was a big advantage. "I guess you're right."

"But if we don't know where they already are...escape will be futile."

True.

"Can these guys be killed?"

I nodded, remembering Huntley take down a few with his sword. "They're just really hard to kill."

"I couldn't take down a single one. I thought I did, but he popped right back up."

"It's hard to slay an enemy if you don't know what you're dealing with."

"So, you got a plan?"

I looked up at the portion of the ceiling that was made of glass. "That could be our way out."

He lifted his chin and looked up. "We could stack the beds...I could lift you on my shoulders... But how are we going to break it? I can tell that glass is as thick as stone. And if it shatters, it could kill us."

My eyes moved to the corner. "If we could cut a hole big enough for us to climb through right at the edge...it would probably hold. Right at the center is where it'll be the weakest."

"Cut it with what?" His eyes moved back to me.

"That's where we have a problem..."

"A dagger could work."

"Just have to steal one."

His eyes darkened, covered with storm clouds. "You're the one they want, so it'll be up to you. Not sure what they're going to do with me."

"If they were going to kill you, they would have done it already."

He gave a shrug. "I suppose."

"You think Father will come for you?" I asked. "I wasn't enough, but he can't lose his only son."

His eyes moved straight ahead. "I don't know. He vowed never to return."

"I suspect he'll break that vow."

"He's too pragmatic for that. He thinks you've been stolen for leverage and your kidnappers will return you when they're ready to negotiate. With me, he'll know I came down here for Effie. If I don't return, it's because I didn't make it."

The door opened, and we both turned our heads to look at the visitor.

It was the same man who'd escorted me before. He had cheeks that were so hollow he looked malnourished. His eyes possessed a hungry stare, which was reserved for me.

I knew he'd come for me.

The last thing on my mind was the pain I was about to endure. Now I saw it as an opportunity—an opportunity to steal that dagger and get out of here.

Ryker appeared in my view. "Take me."

"Ryker—"

"I'm rested. I'll taste better."

I grabbed him by the shoulder and pulled him back. "Stop—"

"No." He pushed me back again. "I'm stronger. I have more blood than she does."

The guard didn't look the least bit interested. "She belongs to Klaus. And you belong to someone else."

10

RYKER

I was sick to my stomach.

All I could do was sit there and absorb the pain. The bandage on my sister's leg hinted at the damage underneath, and when I pictured those enormously long teeth, I knew how deep they had punctured her flesh. The only thing worse than her suffering was my helplessness.

I couldn't do a damn thing about it.

I leaned against the headboard, immune to the pain in my face because the pain in my heart was so much worse. I didn't protect my sister. I didn't protect Effie. Hopefully, Effie's family didn't wait for us and made it back to Delacroix. At least I'd accomplished that much.

Effie's face came into view as I stared at the opposite wall. The hostility in her gaze was replaced by concern, heartwarming concern. "How's your face?"

My ankles were crossed in front of me, and I was still fully clothed. It was odd to be in full armor but have no weapons. It was a lot lighter, for sure. "I don't even notice it." If I focused, I could feel the throbbing in my face, deep behind my eye and near the bone of my cheek. But the emotional duress was so much more.

"I'm sorry about your sister."

My eyes shifted away.

"She'll be okay."

"I wish they would take me instead."

"I know."

"And I don't know what I'm going to do if they try to take you." That was somehow worse, especially since my father was the reason Effie was down here in the first place. "I can't let that happen."

Silence. Painful silence.

My eyes eventually shifted back to hers.

They were still on me, still dim with sadness. "You think my family made it?"

"I'm sure they did."

She inhaled a slow, deep breath. Held it for a long time. And then exhaled.

"I'm so sorry...for everything."

Her eyes flicked down.

"Effie—"

"All those times I told you about the lottery, you knew what it really was. My father lived for that lottery, and so did countless others. That dream for a better life was all just a sham. You preyed on people's hopes...their dreams. It's like promising a cow golden pastures but taking it to slaughter. How can you do that?" Her eyes flicked up again, filled with venomous anger.

"*I* didn't do anything, Effie. My father is the Duke of Delacroix. Not me."

"But you knew. That's just as bad."

"It's complicated, okay?"

"So complicated that the best solution is to lie to people and send them to their deaths?" she asked.

"It's not like that—"

"It seems like it."

"Look, when I realized what the lottery really was, I questioned him about it. I was just as horrified as you are right now. But he explained there was no other way. And there really is no other way."

She gave a loud scoff then turned away.

"Necrosis needs to feed. And if there's not enough to feed on, they'll go to the top of the cliffs. Once they make it there, it's game over—for everyone. If my father disobeys King Rutherford, he'll be the next one down here. You can sit there and act like you would do something different, but if you were really in the situation, you wouldn't. You know how I know that? Because it's been going on for thousands of years. No one has ever, not once, tried to do something different."

She turned back to me, her eyes still angry.

"So don't act like I'm the asshole. We're *all* the asshole."

Her arms slowly crossed over her chest.

"I tried to stop it, Effie. I begged my father to bring you back, but he said it was too late. I did whatever I could, and when that didn't work, I came down here for you. I risked my life to make this right."

Her eyes dropped once more.

"Sweetheart—"

"Don't call me that...ever again."

It was like a knife right between the ribs.

"You shouldn't have come down here."

Now I did feel the pain in my face, in my abdomen, everywhere they'd beaten me. Everything was suddenly amplified. "Even if I'd known how you'd feel, I still would have come, Effie."

The door opened again, and I straightened in the hope of seeing my sister.

But it was the same guard, and he was empty-handed. "You." His eyes were locked on me.

At least it was my turn instead of Effie's. "Take care of my sister when she gets back." I started to move from the bed.

"Of course..." She got up too, and all that anger she'd felt just a moment ago was gone. She looked on the verge of tears, not for herself but for me. Her hand reached for mine, and she gave it a quick squeeze before she let me go.

I squeezed it back.

I walked past the guard at the doorway and swiped the dagger from his belt with a fluid motion.

The door closed behind me, and I discreetly slipped the dagger underneath my sleeve.

His voice came from behind me. "Go."

"Where, asshole?" I just had to survive this, and then I'd get us out of here. Couldn't be that bad. Couldn't feel worse than I felt right now.

He shoved me in the back. "There."

He marched me down a couple hallways and then inside a bedroom. Torches lit the dark corners, cast shadows along the walls. The bedchamber had a large four-poster bed, chains hooked to each beam of wood. The windows were open, letting the cool breeze waft through the room.

"Take off your clothes."

I turned around and faced him, my eyebrow raised. "You're an attractive dude, but not my type. Not enough tits and ass."

His face remained slack, not even cracking a smile.

"Alright, then..." I started to undress, his eyes on me the entire time. It was hard to hide the dagger and not let it fall with a thud, so I turned at just the right time, caught it, and wrapped it in my tunic before I dropped it on top of my pants without a sound. I turned back around, buck naked.

He moved toward me.

"Whoa, hold on." I raised my palm to stop him from coming any closer. "I'll do the honors, alright?" I climbed onto the bed and hooked the chains to my ankles and then one arm. The other remained free.

That seemed to be enough for him because he walked out.

I lay there staring at the ceiling, waiting for something to happen.

A woman appeared from another room, with long dark hair, bright-red lips, almond-shaped eyes—and she was completely naked. Her skin was fair and unblemished, not a single scar, and she had big tits that were perky and an ass to boot.

Was not expecting that.

She approached the bed and directed my limp hand into the cuffs. "Allow me." She looked down at me, her eyes playful, a strand of hair coming loose from behind her ear and hitting my shoulder. "Aren't you delicious?" Her eyes took me in, and then she placed her fingers right against my chest and dragged down, over my abs, down to the vein right above my dick. "They told me you were handsome, but they still undersold you."

I just wanted to get this over with, so I stayed quiet. The sooner she bit me, the sooner she'd be full, and the sooner I could get back and get the hell out of there.

She crawled onto the bed and straddled my hips—her sex right against mine.

As if this was foreplay, she leaned forward and kissed my stomach and then my chest, her hair dragging behind her, her back arching so her ass was in the air.

This would be hot under different circumstances. Like, if I wasn't about to be eaten and I didn't just get dumped by a girl I actually liked for the first time in my life.

Her kisses continued, and her teeth remained sheathed in her throat. Her hands felt me everywhere, and whenever her sex was against mine, I could feel how wet she was. She straddled my hips once more and sat there. "If he's not your type, then I definitely am." She rubbed her hips, as if that was all she needed to do to get my dick to spring to life. "Is it the bite? It's scary at first, but you'll enjoy it if you relax."

"I might be into this under different circumstances, but you didn't catch me on my best day."

"And why's that?" Her palms continued to stroke my chest.

"I just got dumped."

"Then it sounds like my timing couldn't be better." She had a seductive voice, the kind that was deep but still feminine. She didn't seem like the kind of woman that needed to tie a guy down to get some action.

"But I liked her...*really* liked her."

"If she's forgotten you, you should forget about her." She leaned in close, her lips coming close to mine. "I can help with that."

Too much bad shit had happened for me to feel anything but agony. "Just get it over with, alright?"

Her eyes narrowed and her face tightened—like I'd just said the wrong thing. "This is supposed to be fun, and you just took that away from me."

"Sorry about that."

"Don't appreciate the sarcasm."

"Well, that's all I got."

She sat back, and then her mouth opened, and the teeth slowly emerged.

It was horrifying every time I saw it, like watching a snake unhinge its jaw to swallow prey five sizes too big.

When her teeth were all fixed in place, she brought her face down and bit right into my shoulder.

My instinct was to scream—but I kept my mouth shut tight and waited for it to end.

11

IVORY

Naked and chained to the bed like last time, I waited in the dark bedchamber. My heart raced, pulsing in my neck and my chest. My left thigh still hurt, and I hoped he wouldn't go back to the old wound. But I also didn't want him to make a new scar elsewhere. They were in places most people couldn't see, but Huntley would see it.

If I ever saw him again.

A part of me believed he would come for me, but another part wasn't holding my breath. He would have no aid or soldiers, and by himself, he wouldn't be enough to get me out of here on his own. Would he strike down his mother and commit treason? Or would he just move on and let things be?

But if I didn't get out of here, those dragons would never fly again.

I couldn't let that happen.

The sight of their sorrow still haunted my dreams...among other things.

Klaus stepped into the room, dressed in his black cloak that made his skin appear even more pale. His boots tapped against the floor as he approached me, and a moment later, he appeared in my vision, calm. But his calmness was always sinister. "My Little Rhubarb. Always so sweet."

What an affectionate nickname. "You're just going to feast on me forever?"

"Not forever. But until you're no longer appealing. Then I'll give you to someone else."

"Until I'm not young and hot anymore?" I asked.

He gave a slight smile. "Something like that." His eyes raked over my naked body. "But that won't be for a very long time."

My eyes glanced to his hip, seeing the dagger that hung on his belt.

Now I just had to find a way to get to it.

His eyes were on mine again, as if he could see my thoughts. "A dagger wouldn't be enough to kill me, Rhubarb."

"Don't call me that..."

"That's what you are. Sweet. Juicy. Red..."

The implication was sexual, because he liked me naked, liked my pussy near his face. But all he did was bite me. His clothes stayed on, and he never touched me anywhere besides my legs. Didn't make any sense.

"Delacroix drops unfortunate souls to the bottom of the cliffs to be fed to us and Necrosis. But not you. I can tell." He stared into my eyes, as if he could compel me into telling him the path back to the top. "You know the way."

"I won the lottery, so Delacroix exiled me here—"

"You aren't like the others. You're different. The Runes wouldn't have taken you in, otherwise."

"Then where do the others go?"

"Here." He smiled again.

Now I knew why they had been there that afternoon. They had been hunting for new arrivals. Every lottery winner was brought here—to be food. "They're supposed to be fed to Necrosis—"

"And they are. In every battle, they're sacrificed."

Appalling.

"But don't worry, Rhubarb. I would never sacrifice you."

Think I'd rather take my chances with Necrosis. As long as I had a sword in my hand without chains on my wrists and ankles, that was preferable.

"You're going to tell me the way."

Not gonna happen.

"Not today," he said. "Not for a while, I imagine. But just know that when you are ready to tell me, I'll release you. I'll release all three of you."

For a brief moment, that was an appealing option, because I could get my brother out of here. But I knew what would happen if the Teeth could make it to the top of the cliffs. They would feast on everyone in Delacroix, then the other Kingdoms. They'd all be slaves—and sacrifices.

Not an option. "Just get on with it."

That smile widened, and the rows of teeth emerged. "With pleasure."

THEY CARRIED me to the bed and set me on top.

Now my other thigh looked identical to the first, wrapped in a tight bandage. My entire body was weak, both of my thighs burned from the gashes in the flesh, and I felt so tired. The tray of food was placed beside me, but I was too weak to sit up.

Definitely too weak to steal a weapon.

They left, and the door shut.

"Shit, are you okay?" Effie came to my side, her hand moving to my arm for comfort. "You look really pale..."

"Because I don't have any more blood..." I tried to crack a joke, but it didn't come off that way.

"Come on. Sit up and eat." She gently tugged me up and adjusted me against a pile of pillows at the headboard. She scooted the tray closer to me.

I just stared at it. "Too tired..."

She came closer and put the tray on her lap. Then she fed me by hand.

I cocked an eyebrow and released a laugh. "Girl, I'm not going to let you feed me—"

"Girl, you might die, so open up."

I released a sigh and opened my mouth.

She put the bite of chicken into my mouth, waited for me to chew, and then served me more food. We did that for a while in total silence. Her watching me, feeding me, and making sure I stayed awake.

When the plate was clean, she set the tray aside. "Feel any better?"

"Yeah, a bit. My headache is already going away."

"Good." She glanced at the door like she expected Ryker to walk through it, and when he didn't, she turned back to me. "Were you able to get a dagger?"

"Sorry."

"Don't be. When it's my turn, I'll try."

"I'm sorry this is happening to you. I grew up thinking the lottery was real, that citizens of Delacroix really got big plots of land and enjoyed the harbor at sunset. How naïve I was…"

She turned back to me, her arms crossed over her chest. "It's not your fault."

"I didn't say it was. I'm just saying that it's shitty. Really shitty."

"Yeah."

"I hope your family is okay."

"Me too," she said quietly. "I hope they didn't wait for me."

"I'm sure they're alright. We'll get out of here, and you'll see them again."

"Hopefully."

The silence came, filling the void as we both waited for my brother to return.

I stared at the side of her face, admiring her soft blond hair, her sharp jawline, her pretty features yet humble eyes. "It's none of my business, and I'm not trying to get in the middle of anything, but…my brother is a good guy."

She slowly turned back to me.

"And as much as I hate the lottery and what we're doing to innocent people, I understand how the real world works. People would rather do the easy thing than the hard thing.

Doesn't mean they're terrible people. It just means...there's not a better solution."

"It sounds like you're justifying it."

"Not at all. In fact, my husband and I intend to take the Kingdoms then defeat Necrosis for good. That way, we don't have to live like this anymore."

"Your husband?" she whispered. "I didn't realize you were married."

"Yeah...it was recent. About a week ago, actually. Don't mention it to Ryker."

"Why not?"

"Because he's going to be pretty angry about the whole thing."

"I'm a vault—your secret's safe with me."

"Thanks."

"But everything you said just disproves everything you said before that."

I cocked my head, unsure of her meaning.

"You said people will always do the easy thing, not the hard thing. But you're willing to do the hard thing."

It was never my intention to paint myself as a hero, as someone who was brave. "You should take my words with a grain of salt...because my intentions aren't totally altruistic.

It's the only solution I can find that spares my father's life and gives everyone the lives they deserve."

"How does this spare your father's life?"

"Because my husband wants to kill him."

Her eyes widened.

"It's a long story..."

"How do you plan on taking the Kingdoms?"

"Not sure yet. This brilliant plan is still in the beginning stages, and I have to escape first if I intend to fulfill it."

"You think your husband will come save you?"

"Maybe. But I'm not going to wait around for that."

"Good." She gave a slight smile. "Because I can't wait to get out of here."

"You know, I haven't had a chance to talk to Ryker about all of this, but I'm sure if I did, he would help me. I understand you're upset right now, as you're entitled to be, especially when everything is still a shock, but I know he would do the right thing."

She dropped her gaze.

"And he did come down here all by himself..."

She stayed quiet.

"So, he's nothing like King Rutherford. Nothing like my father. I just hope you give him another chance."

Her eyes flicked up once more. "He had every opportunity to tell me what the lottery really was...and he didn't."

"Probably because he assumed you would never win it."

"But still, he could have warned me."

"And if you told other people, that could have caused a panic and a riot."

"He should have trusted me—"

"Would you honestly have kept that secret?" I asked. "Because you're angry with him for keeping this secret. So if you kept that secret, it would make you a hypocrite. Right?"

Her arms tightened across her chest as her lips pressed tightly together. It was obvious she was searching for a comeback but failed to find one. "Yeah, I guess you're right."

"Then cut him some slack. I know how he feels about you."

"Feels about me?" she asked incredulously. "It was just a fling that barely had a chance to burn."

"Must have been a pretty good fling...since he came all the way down here."

"Guilt. Obligation. Something along those lines. Besides, it's not like this was ever going to be a relationship. He's the son of a duke, and I'm the daughter of a blacksmith. He's supposed to marry one of the girls at court. I'll probably marry a farmer or something along those lines." She looked away, either to hide the pain in her eyes or avoid the pain in mine.

"My husband and I couldn't be worse for each other, but we're bound for all eternity."

She looked at me again.

"Ryker broke all the rules when he came after you. I wouldn't be surprised if he broke more..."

12

HUNTLEY

As if an arrow had struck me in the heart, I gripped my chest and slumped forward over my horse. My world became blurred just for a moment. I saw a man. I saw teeth. And then it was gone—but my body was broken.

Ian noticed my collapse and grabbed the reins of my horse, bringing it to a halt. All the men behind us did the same, stopping the entire army in the middle of the plains. "Huntley."

I slipped off the horse entirely and fell to the ground.

"Huntley!" Ian was at my side instantly, his hands feeling me for injury. "What is it?"

"I'm fine." I shoved him off and writhed on the ground, the explosion in my heart leaving me incapacitated.

"You just fell off your fucking horse. You aren't fine." He grabbed my water canteen and splashed it on my face.

I smacked him away. "Not helping."

"Then tell me what the problem is, so I can help."

I rolled to my stomach and slowly pushed myself up, the pain still white-hot in my veins. "It's Ivory..."

"What?" His hand gripped my shoulder to steady me. "What are you talking about?"

"It's her... I know it is."

"It's her, what?"

I stared at the grass, felt the breeze move through my hair, forced myself to focus. "I feel her pain."

His hand remained on my shoulder.

I breathed through the agony, waited for it to pass—prayed that it would pass.

We stayed that way for a long time, everyone silent, staring at me on the ground.

Minutes later, it began to fade.

My hand left my chest, relieved that her suffering had concluded. My vision cleared, and I could finally distinguish the features of my brother's face. "They're feeding on her." Feeding on my fucking wife. "I could kill her right now..."

Ian seemed to know who I was talking about because he didn't ask.

"How do you know this?"

"I don't know. I feel things...see things."

"That's not something husbands and wives just do..."

"I know. But that's what's happening."

IT WAS TOO dark to see, so we camped for the night. Since we were no longer in yeti territory, it was safe to risk an open fire. If the Teeth saw, it didn't matter, because they would know of our coming eventually anyway.

I still felt a dull pain in my chest. Now it seemed permanent.

Ian sat across from me, full because he'd just finished his roast boar. He sat on the log with his arms on his knees, his eyes on the fire. "Mother must have been livid when you told her."

"Try heartbroken."

His eyes lifted to mine. "What do you see in her?"

I held his gaze, the words not coming to me right away.

"She's pretty. I'll give you that."

"It's not that."

"Then what is it?"

If he expected me to give some grand answer, he would be disappointed. "I don't know."

"You don't know? We're declaring war on the Teeth because...you don't know."

My eyes narrowed. "I don't know because it's complicated. When shit is complicated, it doesn't have an easy answer, alright? Her father destroyed our lives, so it's really fucking complicated. Leave it at that."

"You don't see *him* when you look at her?"

My answer was immediate. "No."

"So, she helps you with the dragons, helps you take Delacroix back, helps you take the Kingdoms. In exchange for what?"

I stared at the fire.

"I asked you a question."

"I'll be king—and she'll be my queen."

He gave a slight shake of his head. "She would betray her own father to have the throne. Guess she's just like him."

I wanted to defend her honor but couldn't, not when I wanted to keep our plan a secret.

"And what about her father?"

My eyes returned to the fire again.

"She's fine with you killing him?"

If I answered his question, he would never forgive me. Never.

"Huntley."

I could tell he already knew, just by the tone of his voice. I lifted my gaze and faced him like a man. "I promised to spare his life."

The seething anger spread into his face, made his eyes burn hotter than the fire.

"It was the only way."

"He *killed* Father."

"I know—"

"He *raped* Mother—"

"Like I'd ever forget, asshole. I was the one who was forced to sit there and watch the goddamn thing. Don't sit here and remind me of the horrors we've endured, because I'll never forget that shit as long as I live. But without her help, we have no chance. It was necessary."

"You better break that promise."

"I'm a man of my word."

"Well, when you see that motherfucker, that'll change. When you see the scratches on his face from Mother's nails, that will change. And if it doesn't, you can't stop me. And you sure as hell can't stop Mother."

I promised Ivory I wouldn't kill him, but I never promised my family wouldn't. She failed to negotiate all the terms, and that was her fault, not mine. But I knew her desires, and that made me feel deceitful. "I know."

IN THE DISTANCE, we saw them.

Hundreds of horses bearing riders. When the black flags drew near, I could see the symbol in the center.

A feather.

Ian slowed his horse. "She's sent out her men to intercept us."

She knew what I would do the moment I left, and she knew what my brother would do too.

Ian turned to me. "I will not raise my sword against our people—not even for you."

"I would never ask you to."

"Then what's your move?"

I watched them come closer, the white horse in the lead more distinguishable. Her brown hair flowed behind her, the white feathers striking against her dark hair. In her armor and weapons, she looked like a queen and an assassin. "She came herself. But that's not going to stop me."

Ian turned to see for himself.

We waited, watching them ride across the plains and come closer, every rider equipped for war.

I knew she'd come to capture me, to secure me in chains and return me to HeartHolme so I wouldn't get myself killed on my crusade. But if anyone tried to touch me, I'd slice their head clean from their shoulders. If my mother cared for her people, she would just let me go.

She tugged on the reins and slowed her white stallion. Eyes reserved for me, she came close, her black uniform tight on her wrists and thick on her shoulders where her cape attached.

She stopped directly before me, authority in her eyes as well as in the rest of her posture. My father had been gone since I was just a boy, so I hadn't had the opportunity to learn everything a boy should learn to become a man. But everything else, I learned from my mother. How to keep your arrow true. How to use your shield as a weapon. How to kill without mercy. I hated her right now, but the soldier in me still admired her.

Her eyes flicked to Ian's, and the look of disappointment she showed was purposeful.

I brought her attention back to me. "You can't stop me."

Her eyes shifted back to me. "I know."

"Then order Ian and the rest of your men to abandon my mission. I will carry on alone." I would infiltrate the Crags and slice their teeth from their throats until I found her.

"You will not be alone—because I am with you."

I continued my piercing stare as if I didn't hear a word she spoke.

"HeartHolme is with you."

I gave a slight shake of my head. "You would go to war for her?"

She tugged on the reins slightly, her horse coming to my side so we were just inches apart. "I would go to war for my son."

13

IVORY

The door opened, and my brother was shoved inside.

He looked just as bad as I did, with droopy eyes, a weak posture, and bloodless cheeks.

Effie rushed to him right away and threw his arm over her shoulder. Before I could even reach him, she helped him to bed, getting him propped up on the pillows.

His arms went limp on the bed.

"Ryker, stay awake." She gave him a gentle slap on the cheek. "Let's eat something." She pulled the tray on her lap then basically force-fed him.

I felt well enough to sit beside him, to watch a strong man too weak to feed himself. I wanted to rub his arm or comfort him in some way, but I didn't want to lure him to sleep by mistake.

Slowly, he conquered his dinner plate. Once his belly was full, the color started to return to his cheeks. He was a little stronger, but still tired the way I was.

"You okay?" I finally asked.

He turned to me, as if he hadn't realized I was there until now. "More than okay."

"Really? Because you look hungover."

He smiled slightly. "I miss being hungover." He reached into his pocket then withdrew a sharp dagger.

"You did it?" Effie clapped her hands to her mouth in surprise.

I took the knife from his hand and examined it like it might be a mirage. "How did you pull this off?"

He gave a shrug. "I'm good. What else do you want me to say?"

I gave him a smack on the arm. "I'm serious."

"Took it from the guard that opened the door."

"I didn't even know he had a dagger."

"Because you're dumb."

I smacked him again.

He chuckled and took the dagger back. "It's almost dark. Are we doing this tonight?"

"You still look pretty weak, Ryker," I said. "And I've seen better days."

He pushed himself up, sitting upright fully. "You okay?" He turned serious, his hand gripping my shoulder.

"Yeah," I said, ignoring the pain in my chest. "Already over it."

"I don't think tonight is ideal either," Ryker said. "I feel like shit. You look like shit. But if they don't take Effie tonight, they'll take her tomorrow, and then they'll take us the following day...it'll just keep going. It's never going to be a good time. One of us is always going to be weak."

I turned to Effie.

She gave a slight nod in agreement.

"We can't even wait a couple hours. That guard is going to realize his dagger is gone once he changes out of his uniform."

"Shit," I said. "You're right..."

"As always."

I looked at the glass ceiling above, trying to select the place where I would begin to carve our escape. "Effie, you think you can help me stack the beds?"

"I'm on it." Effie got to her feet and immediately started working, tugging one of the beds across the floor directly underneath the corner of the roof.

"I'll work on this," I said. "And you rest."

"That works for me." He lay back and got comfortable.

Ryker wasn't the lazy type to excuse himself from hard labor while women did it instead. That meant he still felt terrible, that he needed as much rest as he could get at the moment.

I worked with Effie to stack a bed on top of the first, and then tilt a third one on top of that. It was a linear pile, but it was high enough that someone could climb on top and reach the ceiling.

With the dagger in my hand, I climbed up the wooden frames then stood with my head just a foot beneath the ceiling.

"Careful," Ryker said. "It's swaying slightly."

I went still so it wouldn't tilt and fall over.

Ryker gave me directions from his spot on the bed. "Go for the corner first. That's where it's the most stable."

"Yes, I know." I pressed the dagger right against the corner then tapped the hilt with my other hand, giving a tiny indent so the seam was split. It was thick, really thick, so I had to hit it a couple times before I made a dent.

A chunk of glass fell, shattered against the stack of beds, and then hit the floor.

"Stay back, Effie," Ryker called.

I did the same thing again, sticking to the edges, chiseling away pieces and letting them fall to the floor where they shattered into tiny fragments. The hole became bigger and bigger, big enough for each of us to pass through.

"Shit, you did it." Ryker appeared below, looking up at my work.

I glanced down and cast him a glare. "I do a lot of things, idiot." I slipped the dagger into my pocket then kneeled down. "This thing will topple down if we all get on it at once. So, I'll go first and help you up, Effie."

"Got it," she said.

"Don't cut yourself," Ryker said.

The chiseled glass would be against my back, so I had to make sure I didn't accidentally scrape against it. Otherwise...that would hurt like a bitch. The very top of the ledge was another foot above the glass, so I had to squat down and prepare to jump to catch it.

"Whoa, hold on." Ryker went to one side of the structure. "I've got this side. Effie, you hold onto the other."

"Okay." She moved to the other and secured the base. "Go for it."

I squatted down then jumped as high as I could. My hand gripped the ledge and held on, squeezing it tight so I wouldn't slip. My feet dangled before my boots caught the wall, and I slowly pulled myself up. The cool air hit me right in the face, and it was refreshing like cold water against my cheeks. I pulled myself until I was over the edge and on the roof of the building. It was an overcast night so there were no stars, making it dark. Really dark. I leaned back over the ledge and dropped my arms down so I could catch Effie when she came up.

Effie started at the bottom, climbed up, and then balanced on the very top.

I leaned as far as I could go without tipping back into the room. "Grab my hands and climb up."

Ryker was directly below, stabilizing the base so it wouldn't topple over and wake up all the Teeth...if they even slept.

Effie gave a small jump and clamped down on my hands. She had enough upper-body strength to pull herself up and toward the ledge.

I groaned. "Damn, girl. You're strong."

She reached the ledge and pulled herself the rest of the way. "That's what happens when you help your dad at the forge."

Ryker made his way to the top, the beds swaying slightly underneath him with his additional weight. He went still and waited for it to stop before he looked up at us.

We dropped both of our arms down so he could grab on to us both.

He motioned for us to move. "I can jump to the ledge."

"Don't be annoying, and take our hands." I kept my arms down and anticipated the strain of his weight.

"Ivory, I weigh a lot more than you do—"

"Just shut up and do it." Effie threw down her arms. "Come on."

Ryker released a loud sigh before he gripped each of our hands and started to pull himself up.

We pulled back, lifting him from the ground and to the ledge.

I ground my teeth as my body strained to keep going. "Gods, you're like an ox..."

We made it over the edge and collapsed onto the roof.

Ryker seemed just as tired as the two of us. "Alright, so we have no weapons, no gear, and we're going to sneak out of here and try to make it back to Delacroix in one piece?"

I lay on my back as I looked at the sky, still breathing heavily. "Yep. Pretty much. Maybe we'll eat a yeti on the way."

"Gods," Ryker said with a moan. "If I have to fight a yeti with a dagger, I'm going to be pissed."

"You're going to be dead, more like it." Effie got to her feet and brushed herself off. "Maybe we can steal some weapons along the way. Ryker can sneak up on a guard and take him out with the dagger."

"Not a bad idea." I got to my feet and took a look around. It was dark, only the moonlight breaking through the clouds to give us visibility. "Can the Teeth see in the dark or anything?"

Ryker gave a shrug. "I'd assume they can do anything until further notice."

"Then we have to be careful." I walked to the edge of the building and looked down. "And quiet."

"Well, that's going to be hard to manage with you..." Ryker came to my side and peered over the edge.

I cast him a glare. "If we weren't running for our lives right now, I'd push you over."

Ryker turned to Effie. "You see how she talks to me?"

Effie came to the other side of me. "I'm sure she has her reasons."

"Wow." Ryker looked away. "Now I see how it is..."

I was caught between them, right in the middle of the tension. "Let's focus, guys. I'll go first."

THE GUARD WAS right in front of me, his sword and shield over his back. He paced left and right, looking over the edge to the city beyond. I tiptoed forward with the small dagger in my hand.

But Ryker got there first. Gripped him by the head and snapped his neck. Before the guard's body fell and made a loud thud, Ryker caught him beneath the arms and dragged him behind the building.

I released a growl. "I had him."

"Really? Because it looked as if you were creeping like a scared mouse." He leaned the body right against the wall, so it was less likely to be discovered until morning. "We're racing against the clock. If the Teeth come to feed on Effie tonight, we'll be screwed. Just let me handle it." He took the sword and shield for himself and then handed Effie the extra dagger he found.

I rolled my eyes and bottled my annoyance.

"He's right," Effie said. "He's quick."

Ryker took the lead down to the next level, sticking to the cover of the buildings, his footsteps inaudible. It was a long way down, and we'd have to sneak up on a lot of guards along the way. I was actually relieved I wasn't alone because this would be a lot harder if I were.

When we came up on another guard, Ryker did the same thing, snapping his neck before he could even react. His weapons were harvested off his body, and then his corpse was tucked somewhere off the path. He handed the bow and arrow to me. "I know you're a good shot." The short sword went to Effie.

"I should take the sword too," I said. "I know how to use it."

"Remember what Mom said?" Ryker turned to me. "That you're supposed to share?"

I gave him a glare. "Now isn't the time—"

"You can't shoot and wield a sword at the same time. All Effie needs to do is shove that sword into someone's belly and she's golden. Trust me, she can handle that." Ryker took the lead once again. "Come on."

I turned to Effie when he was out of earshot. "He's just trying to get back in your good graces."

She admired the sword before she tucked it into her scabbard. "I know."

"Is it working?"

She gave a shrug. "Not sure..."

WE MADE it to the bottom, but now we were stuck behind the gate that protected the Crags from invasion. Guards were everywhere, the torches illuminating their dark clothing and weapons. I was out of ideas. I turned to Ryker. "Should we attack them all or...?"

He gave me that look that said, "You're an idiot."

"Well, we can't stand here all night," I said. "We're running out of time."

"Should we climb the walls?" Effie said.

"It's a nasty drop on the other side," Ryker said. "And we don't have rope."

"You don't think there's another way out?" I asked. "Like a hidden door?"

Ryker shook his head. "Not down here. Back in the city perhaps, but..." He remained crouched down, scanning the area as he tried to think of what to do.

Effie did the same. "I see a rope. It's behind that guard."

Ryker didn't pull his gaze away. "I noticed the same thing, sweetheart."

She turned at the sound of the nickname.

Ryker clearly didn't realize he'd said anything he shouldn't have because his eyes were still focused on the rope. "I have an idea."

"Taking them down with my bow?" I asked. "I thought the same thing."

"No." He shook his head. "I'm just going to walk over there and grab it."

"What?" I asked in disbelief.

Effie had an identical reaction. "What?"

"I'm dressed in black, they don't know anyone is missing, and if I walk over there like I know what I'm doing, they'll assume I do know what I'm doing." He turned to me. "Dad always told us that if you don't want predators to think you're prey, don't act like prey. Don't run. Don't cower."

"He was talking about bears, Ryker," I said. "Not Teeth."

"If I get caught, it'll give you a distraction to open the gate." He nodded toward the two levers on either side of the wall. "Pull them at the exact same time. I can tell they're synchronized."

"We all get out of here, or none of us gets out here," Effie said. "We aren't doing that."

He turned to her, and a long stare ensued. One of those stares Huntley and I used to share. Heated. Primal. Aggressive. Looking on felt intrusive, so I turned away and glanced at the guard near the rope.

Then Ryker just stood up—and went for it.

I released a loud sigh because I couldn't shout or beg him to come back.

Effie suppressed her rage too, but beneath her breath, she muttered, "Motherfucker..."

Tall and strong, he walked with a normal pace to the rope, and miraculously, the guards didn't suspect him. He kneeled down, grabbed the rope, threw it over his shoulder and walked off...just like that.

"I can't believe that worked," Effie whispered.

"He's never going to let us forget it either," I said.

He returned—a big-ass grin on his face. "What'd I tell you?"

"You got lucky," I said. "That's all."

"Uh-huh," he said. "Whatever you say." With the rope over his shoulder, he peered out and looked for the best place to make our escape. "We should stay away from the main gate." He pointed to the left, where the wall slightly curved into the mountain. "Over there. But I bet there's a guard or two."

"We can handle one or two." I could fire an arrow into one, and Ryker could take care of the other.

"That should be easy."

"Alright, on my mark." Ryker watched the guards near the gate, watched them change position and move to their previous spots. "And...now." He went first, walking normally with the rope over his shoulder. It was dark with the exception of the fires, so they probably wouldn't even know we were there if they didn't know prisoners were on the loose.

The wall started to slant inward, and we followed it until we found three guards at their posts.

Ryker stopped. "We've got to keep this quiet, alright?" He turned to me. "You fire off that arrow and take him out silently. Headshot, alright? I'll move in for the other two."

"I can take one," Effie said.

"I'm sure you can," Ryker said. "But not when we've got to stay quiet." He set down the rope and unsheathed the broadsword he'd taken off one of the previous guards. "You got this, Ivory?"

The last time I'd shot an arrow was to save Huntley against the Teeth. My aim remained true despite the terror in my heart. I could do the same now. Just place the arrow on the string and hold my breath. "Yes."

"And don't shoot me by mistake."

"Fuck off." I nudged him hard in the side.

He gave a slight groan mixed with a chuckle and moved in.

I got my bow ready and aimed for the guard who had his back turned to us. I held my bow, brought tension to the string, and then released.

Ryker got to his man first and snapped his neck just as my arrow pierced through my guard's neck. Unlike with Huntley, the guy actually went down.

The remaining guard turned at the sound, his short sword immediately out of his scabbard.

But Ryker took care of it before he could scream—by slitting his throat.

The guard collapsed, a pool of blood gleaming in the torchlight.

Ryker gestured for us to come over. "Help me with this..."

Together, we tucked all the bodies near the wall.

"Don't you think people are going to notice the big-ass pool of blood?" I asked, grunting as I rolled a man twice my size against the wall.

Ryker wiped his bloody hands on the guy's tunic. "I think they're going to notice your smartass mouth first."

"Are you guys like this all the time?" Effie asked.

My brother and I both turned to look at her.

She sighed. "I'll take that as a yes."

Ryker retrieved the rope then approached the wall, looking for a way over.

"There's nothing to hook on," I said. "But we can't climb it either because the walls are too smooth."

Ryker tied the end of the rope and made a lasso that farmers used to capture cattle. "I can hook it on one of the spires at the top."

"But that's..." Effie craned her head farther back to look. "Really high."

"I can do it." Ryker started to flick his wrist and whip the rope in a circle.

"It's dark," I said. "You can barely see."

"I'm not blind." He continued to whip the rope around and around, gathering momentum, his eyes gauging the distance high above. He threw his entire body into it, whipping the rope high into the sky—and missed.

"Wow, that was really close..." Effie came to my side, her arms over her chest because the cold was deepening as the night progressed.

Ryker righted the rope again and started the process over. "I'm going to get it this time."

He was so close last time that I actually believed him.

He threw his body into it again, and it soared up high and landed right around the spire.

Ryker tugged hard, making the rope cinch into place. "What'd I tell you?"

I was astonished that he'd accomplished it, and I quickly realized that Ryker wasn't just my younger brother. At some point over the years, he'd grown into a man, a man who could take a life, a man brave enough to willingly venture to the bottom of the cliffs to save someone, a man who could survive what shouldn't be survivable.

"The rope should bear all our weight." He gave it another tug to check it. "Effie, you go first. Ivory and I can handle company if it comes."

Effie looked at me, as if she felt guilty for taking the rope first.

"Girl, go." I gave her a gentle pat. "We've got to hustle."

Effie took the rope from Ryker and began the climb. She had no experience, and it showed based on the way she slid down a couple times, the way she struggled not to swing left and right. But she didn't give up and continued to move as fast as she could.

Ryker watched her go. "She's got one hell of an ass, huh?"

I smacked him on the arm. "We could get caught any second, and that's all you care about?"

He gave a shrug. "Would you rather me stand here and panic—"

A loud horn blew. Really loud.

We both looked up to the top of the city where the sound came from and looked at each other once more.

Ryker gave another shrug. "Shit, guess it's time to panic." He grabbed the rope and brought it to me. "Go."

"Effie isn't at the top yet."

"Doesn't matter. We just gotta hope the rope holds."

"I should stay with you—"

"I'll be right behind you. Now, go." The joking taunts were cast aside, and he looked just like Father, giving out orders with his same ruthlessness. His expression tightened in just the same way, becoming heartless.

I took the rope and started the climb.

Shouts rang throughout the city, everyone searching for the prisoners who'd escaped. I could hear them grow louder like they were headed down to the gate to see if we'd made it that far.

When I was halfway up, Effie reached the top and perched on the edge. I looked down to check on my brother.

With his short sword in hand, he kept watch, waiting for the men to realize where he was.

I kept going, hustling as fast as I could as I felt the rope burn my hands. When I reached the top, Effie gave me her hand and helped me off the rope and onto the edge. I wanted to keep my voice quiet, but Ryker wasn't paying attention, so I had to give a loud call. "Ryker, come on."

He sheathed his short sword and grabbed on to the rope. He was much quicker than the two of us, as if he'd done this before.

"Ivory." Effie pointed to the guards below. One was close, carrying a bow and arrow.

"Shit." I grabbed my bow and prepared it, but we had so little room that I would probably topple over after firing. "I need your help. Hold me."

Effie grabbed on to me and secured me in place.

I placed the arrow to the string, aimed, and fired.

I hit him right in the neck, and he fell to his knees.

"Damn, that was a good shot."

My focus was extraordinary, probably because my brother's life was on the line. I grabbed another arrow and took down the next guard who ran to the wall.

"You're going to have to teach me."

"Be happy to."

Ryker made it to the top of the wall, out of breath, but that didn't stop him from tossing the rope to the other side and sliding down, probably burning his hands along the way. "Quick, we've got to get moving." He made it to the bottom and prepared to catch us if we fell.

We both made it to the bottom, and the second my boots hit the earth, the gates started to open.

"Shit, we gotta go." Ryker took the lead, sprinting straight into the forest outside the city.

I'd never run so fast in my life, but I knew if I were recaptured, I would never escape again. They'd make sure to keep me chained day and night, and they would separate us this time around.

It was even darker in the forest without the moonlight through the canopy, but hopefully that worked in our favor. Ryker kept up the lead, glancing behind him from time to time to make sure we were still with him.

I don't know how long we ran for, but it felt like a lifetime. All the muscles in my legs screamed from the fatigue, and I had to stop because I couldn't go on any farther. Effie stopped with me, keeling over like she was just as exhausted as I was.

Ryker came back to us. "We've got to keep moving. They'll have horses."

I couldn't even talk I was so out of breath. "I...can't."

Ryker peered behind us, checking the trees for company. "You have thirty seconds. But we have to keep moving after that. If you don't want to be sucked off by a leech again, you won't stop this time."

THROUGH THE NIGHT and the early morning, we ran.

I wasn't even sure where we were going, and I hoped Ryker did. Without a compass or the sun, there was no way to determine our direction. We had no water or food, so we might have escaped their clutches, but we would probably die out there anyway.

That was fine by me.

We finally stopped under the shade of thick trees, the air colder than it was near the Crags. That must have meant we were going in the right direction. "We just have to follow the cold..." I dropped to the ground and leaned against the tree, sweaty and exhausted, not to mention starving.

Effie lay straight on the grass and curled into a ball like she might sleep right on the spot. "What do we do now? I'd like to keep going, but I don't think I can."

"Me neither." The cold didn't even bother me because I was that tired.

"I'll let you guys get some sleep," Ryker said. "I'll hunt." He took my bow and quiver of arrows from the ground. "By the time I'm done cooking, you'll have had enough rest to keep moving."

"What about you?" I asked through heavy-lidded eyes.

"I'll be fine," he said. "I slept less while I searched the Kingdoms for you."

My heart tightened into a fist and squeezed.

"I won't be far, so call if you need help." Ryker marched into the forest, and his footsteps disappeared.

Effie lay on her side and looked at me. "If we really get out of this, it'll be because of him."

"I know."

14

HUNTLEY

The Teeth knew we were coming.

They already had a cavalry waiting for us, their soldiers on their horses as they barred the way to the Crags. We were evenly matched, only because we couldn't drain all our forces for this single fight.

Klaus stepped out from his line of men and rode his black horse toward us. It was well-groomed, the dark hair of its tail in a braid. It was also geared with armor to protect its chest as well as its flank. Klaus was dressed similarly, in his armor and weapons, his cape blowing behind him.

Queen Rolfe stepped out from the ranks, riding her pristine white horse.

I did the same because this was my fault.

She glanced at me but didn't bother to command me to stay back.

We both knew I wouldn't have listened.

Klaus stopped and made us come the rest of the way.

In the center, we met, our horses facing one another, each of us armed to the teeth.

Klaus reserved his stare for me, cutting into my flesh with his eyes. The last time we'd seen each other, it had been under the same pretenses. He wanted to kill me and take Ivory, but that blew up in his face.

I should have killed him when I'd had the chance. Should have chased him down like my mother said. My hands squeezed the reins through my gloves because I couldn't express my anger in any other way. He had my wife trapped, and I knew exactly what he was doing to her. "We didn't come here for a war. Neither one of us can afford the causalities, not when Necrosis hasn't struck in months. So, let's negotiate. Give me what I want, and I'll give you what you want."

Klaus didn't acknowledge my mother, as if she wasn't even there. This was between him and me. "She's what I want, Huntley."

My hands squeezed the reins tighter. The possessiveness was sickening. He couldn't possess something that didn't belong to him. She was my wife, and she belonged to me. "Give me back my wife—or I'll kill you this very moment."

His eyes narrowed. "Your wife?"

"By keeping her, you're declaring war against the Runes. If you want to avoid that, then you better oblige, because I'm not bluffing." I kicked my horse slightly and brought myself closer to him, in case I wanted to pull out my dagger and nick the artery in his neck.

"War is pointless because I don't have her."

"Don't fucking lie to me—"

"They escaped last night. We've been searching for them ever since, but their tracks have gone cold."

"They?"

"She and two others. My cavalry isn't here to intercept you. It's for her."

The pride in my chest was indescribable. I'd amassed an army to free her from this freak show, but she was long gone before I could even assemble my forces. She didn't need me. "Abandon this mission. It's over."

His eyes shifted to Queen Rolfe. "Her Highness gave her to me as a peace offering—"

"That was before I knew my son had wed her," Mother said. "Now that I'm aware of their connection, she's one of us, a Rune. Don't waste your resources searching for her— not when she belongs to us. Is that understood?"

Klaus stared, like he was tempted to open his mouth and show his razor-sharp teeth.

"You attacked the outpost, a declaration of war, but I'm willing to pardon your actions if you withdraw your search party."

Klaus shifted his gaze back to me. "She knows the way."

I kept a straight face.

"And you know she knows it."

"She was lowered from Delacroix—"

"Lies." He snarled. "I've tasted her blood. It's royal."

Tremors ensued down my arms, and my hands latched on to the reins tighter so I wouldn't undo all this diplomacy we'd just established.

"There's a path to the top of the cliffs, and she knows it." His eyes remained steady on my face, and he hadn't blinked once since this interaction had begun. His body didn't have the same needs as ours did, not with his eternal life. "A Rune would never marry one of them without reason. She's priceless—and don't pretend otherwise."

"Queen Rolfe has commanded you to withdraw your forces. Do that now, or there will be bloodshed."

His stare continued, reserved just for me. "From this moment on, we're even."

My eyebrow cocked.

"The attack on the outpost is absolved, in exchange for my withdrawal."

That put us back to where we were—and that wasn't exactly reassuring.

Klaus pulled on the reins of his horse and retreated to the line of his men.

Queen Rolfe watched him for a long time before she shifted her gaze to me.

I felt it burn my cheek, felt her anger melt my flesh.

"I hope she is worth it, Huntley."

"We both got what we wanted. You got peace—or whatever the fuck you want to call it—with Klaus. And my wife is free. Yes, she is worth it."

She pulled on the reins of her horse to turn the other way. "We will scour the land until we find her. She'll be heading to the tunnel that leads back to Delacroix. We can intercept her on the way."

"That's not where she's going."

With a perfectly straight posture that exuded her power, she regarded me.

"She's going to HeartHolme—to find me."

"For the first time, she's free to go where she wants. And you're the last place she'll go."

"You're wrong."

The corner of her lips kicked up in a sarcastic smile. "She'll return to Delacroix and warn her father what has transpired. The path to the top of the cliffs will be destroyed—and you'll never see your wife again. She'll leave you here to sacrifice your soul to Necrosis so she'll never have to sacrifice hers."

I didn't believe that, not one bit.

"And then you'll realize that I was right—as always."

15

IVORY

The dinner Ryker caught filled our stomachs, and the berries Effie found in the wild were enough to wet our mouths and give us some hydration. But nothing could replenish the sleep that we'd lost, and we were all exhausted.

We stuck to the tree line as we ventured toward the cold. I could feel the temperature plunge a little deeper with every passing day, and then I realized a problem I hadn't foreseen earlier. "Once we get to the snow, I'm not going to survive." Ryker and Effie had warmer clothes than I did because that was how they were dressed when they came down here. Ryker lost his armor, but his warm pants, tunic, and jacket were still on him.

"We'll share our clothes with you," Ryker said up ahead. "And if I see a bear, I'll take his fur."

"We can't eat that much, so I don't want to waste it."

"You want to survive or not?" He looked at me over his shoulder.

I could hunt if I needed to, but to be wasteful left a sickness in my stomach. "You think they're still searching for us?"

"Always assume the worst until told otherwise," Ryker said. "But if they knew where we were, they would have found us by now."

"What about our tracks?" Effie said.

"I've made false tracks in other directions to throw them off the scent," Ryker said.

Effie walked beside me, so she looked at me. "I didn't know your brother knew all this."

"I didn't either. Before all this happened...I still saw him as a boy."

"Well, this *boy* is the reason we're going to make it out of here."

After walking all day, we camped for the night.

"Can we make a fire?" I asked. "It's a little cold."

"Too dangerous." Ryker shed his coat and dropped it over my shoulders. "Not just for the Teeth...but whatever else is out here." We had nothing to sleep in, so we tried to find the grassiest places to cushion our backs. The spot we selected was between a group of trees, providing a bit of cover from the rest of the forest. It was a clear night, so the bright stars in the sky provided some illumination.

I didn't hear a sound. No hooves against the earth. No calls into the night. Nothing.

We were alone.

Effie lay on the ground near the base of the tree and curled into a ball to stay warm.

I leaned against the tree because I assumed I would take the first watch. Ryker had done all the hard work since we'd escaped, and he deserved to rest more than anyone else. "You should get some sleep."

He leaned against the tree beside me and rested his forearms on his knees. His eyes were on Effie across the clearing. "A part of me thought Father would send forces after me... Guess not."

"You can't take horses down the path."

"I'm sure he could get an army down here if he really needed to."

"You don't know that he didn't." Ryker was used to being the favorite, being the child my father valued and respected. To think that he was expendable was a fresh wound he'd never received before, not like all the scars I carried.

"Not sure what to do with Effie when we return to Delacroix."

"Help her locate her family."

He gave a slight shake of his head. "If her family is smart, they will keep a low profile. Because Father will kill them if he knows they're alive."

Because they'd tell everyone the truth.

"So, they're either already dead or in hiding."

"Then where will Effie go?"

"I don't know."

"You could take her to the Capital."

"I guess."

"Or you could marry her."

His head snapped in my direction. "*What?*"

"He's not going to execute your wife, right?"

"Sure...but marriage? I haven't even slept with her yet."

"You haven't?" I asked in surprise.

"I didn't get the opportunity...because she won the lottery."

"Wow, talk about a cockblock."

He gave a chuckle. "That's exactly what it was."

Now was the time to tell him the truth, that I was married to a Rune, and after I got what I needed from the library at the castle, I would be back down here...in HeartHolme. But I knew how he would react. He wouldn't just be angry, but completely incredulous. "Does this change anything for you?"

"What do you mean?"

"You've always known about the lottery, but now that you've seen what's down here...does that change anything?"

"It's cruel, no doubt."

"Does that make you want to stop it?"

"Sure. But what's the alternative?"

I tightened his coat around my body. "Not sacrificing people to the Teeth and Necrosis..."

He glanced at Effie to make sure she was asleep before he looked at me again. "Look, I hate it as much as you do, but there is no other way. If we don't feed Necrosis, they'll grow so hungry they'll come for us. It's the few for the many."

"Not if we defeat Necrosis."

He rested his head against the trunk and sighed.

"You've seen what's down here. There are Teeth. Runes. Yetis. If we combine our forces—"

"In what universe would that ever happen?" he asked. "You're talking about an alliance between the top of the cliffs and the bottom. That just won't work, Ivory. And if Necrosis could be defeated, someone would have done it by now."

"Or maybe no one's tried."

He gave another sigh. "You've always been an optimist, and I love that about you...but what you're suggesting is impossible."

"I disagree."

He looked away.

"There's something you don't know about Father..."

He turned back to me.

"We aren't from Delacroix. Or the Kingdoms. Or the top of the cliffs."

Even in the dark, I could see the focus in his eyes.

"He used to be a Plunderer, a barbaric group of men. They made it to the top of the cliffs and murdered the King of Kingdoms. Took his place. He did other horrible things... but I'm not sure if I should tell you."

"Who told you this?"

"My—" I'd been married to him for less than a day when I was taken away, but I was already used to calling him that. This time apart caused a pain in my heart, not just because I was scared, not just because I feared I would never see him again, but because I missed him. "The Runes told me."

"And how would they know?"

"Because their queen and her two sons survived the attack...and were forced to start new lives down here."

He didn't speak.

"She said...Father raped her...and made her eldest watch."

His eyes were empty. "She lies."

"I didn't believe it either—"

"He would never do that, and you dishonor our family by even entertaining the accusation. They're just trying to get inside your head—and you let them."

———

RYKER WAS in a sour mood for days. His carefree attitude and his quick wit had evaporated with our conversation. He didn't even talk to Effie. It made our cold journey to the tunnel more unbearable because we didn't have each other's company to pass the time.

Effie walked beside me in the rear. "What happened with you guys?"

"I told him something about our father that he didn't like."

"Oh."

"In his defense, I didn't believe it either. It wasn't until I saw solid proof that I could even begin to process it."

"What kind of proof are you talking about?"

"A person."

She wore a look of confusion but didn't press her curiosity. "I'd thought you told him about your husband."

"I was going to but...chickened out."

"He'd be that upset?"

"Oh, you have no idea." I was eternally bound to the enemy. The enemy in his eyes, at least. "I'll tell him when we get back to Delacroix because I'll be leaving shortly afterward."

"And going where?"

"Back down here."

Her eyebrows were high up her face. "You're coming back here...alone?"

"I need to get back to Huntley."

"But you're going to do that alone? Ryker will never let you go."

"He's not the boss of me, so that doesn't matter."

"No offense, girl. But you'll die out here."

"I know the way."

She gave a shake of her head. "But still..."

"What are your plans when we get back to Delacroix?"

She breathed a drawn-out sigh. "Find my family, I guess."

"And you and Ryker?"

She looked up ahead to see him leading the way in the distance. "I don't know..."

"He's a good guy."

"I know. It's just complicated."

My life had been simple until Huntley kidnapped me and brought me down here. Then my perfect world became complicated. Really complicated.

"You miss him?"

Our arrangement was purely political, but now that he wasn't at my side, it was like a piece of me was missing. We used to be together nearly every waking moment, and now I struggled to tolerate his absence. "Yes."

Her eyes softened. "I bet he's looking for you."

"I don't think he is. Not by choice, but by force." His mother knocked him out cold without further thought, so she'd probably locked him up somewhere so he couldn't come after me. The only way we would be reunited was if I went to him with everything I promised to deliver. I was a prisoner with the Teeth, but he was also a prisoner at HeartHolme.

THE MILD TEMPERATURES dropped to an icy cold, and the lush landscape turned into snow. The wind picked up, like daggers in the eyes, and the freezing cold made our bodies numb. "I think I recognize where we are..."

Ryker turned around, ankle-deep in snow. "I think I do too. I remember that mountain over there. Looks like an eagle." He pointed to the snow-covered mountains, an eagle's head carved out of the rock.

I recognized it because of the cluster of trees to the right. "Once we get past this ridge, we're going to want to turn right. There's a cave with supplies on the way. We should stop there and recuperate."

"How far is it?" Ryker asked.

"I know the cave you're talking about," Effie said. "Two days at this speed. One if we hustle."

Ryker stopped and turned around. "We aren't going to survive another night out here."

We found a decent place under a stand of trees, the branches catching most of the snowfall. We cleared it with branches and lit a fire so we wouldn't fall asleep and never wake up again. It was a risk, but if we didn't take it, we would die anyway. "I agree."

"So, we hustle?" Effie asked. "We'll sweat—and we don't have many berries left."

"There's water in the cave," I said. "I say we haul ass and get there before dark."

Ryker nodded. "Then you guys need to keep my pace." He took off and headed straight. "Come on, I know you can do it."

———

WE MADE it to the cave at dark and ended up spending a few days holed up inside. We replenished our fluids, caught up on rest, filled our stomachs with as much food we could handle. Too tired to have conversations, we spent those days in silence.

On the third day, we departed and headed for the secret tunnel. We took the canteens we'd found in the crates and grabbed a sack and stuffed it with dried fruits and nuts. We were much better prepared for travel now, so the three-day trek through the tunnel should be a slice of cake.

Ooh...cake.

When Effie stepped through the entrance to the cavern, she let out a shaky breath. "We're going to climb all the way to the top?"

"It's not that bad," Ryker said. "It's mostly a lot of walking. But there's a long ladder at the end..."

That ladder had been a bitch to climb when gravity was on my side. Going in the opposite direction...it was totally going to suck. "It'll be over before you know it."

16

HUNTLEY

When the gates opened to allow the riders entry, I moved forward to get a better look.

She wasn't with them.

Weeks had passed and there'd been no sign of her—not here at the outpost or HeartHolme. The disappointment was too much, made me taste acid in my mouth.

The riders hopped down and handed their reins to the stablemaster.

"What did you see?" I immediately asked.

The man removed his gloves. "No signs of anyone anywhere."

Fuck.

Ian walked up to me, coming from the stone keep. In his hand was a scroll that he had already read. "She hasn't returned to HeartHolme."

If my wife could escape the Teeth, she could navigate her way to the outpost or HeartHolme. I'd seen her in action and knew she was too smart to get captured by the Plunderers or cross paths with a yeti. She was out there somewhere. "Let's send a search party."

"Huntley." Ian released a frustrated sigh. "It's like searching for a needle in a haystack. She could literally be anywhere. It's a waste of manpower."

I gazed through the open gates, as if she would pop out of the snow.

Ian stared at the side of my face. "She must have gone to the tunnel—"

"She would come to me first." She would want me to know that she was alright. She would want to know that I was alright too. "She would never betray me." I regarded my brother, warning him to tread carefully.

Ian didn't speak, but his stony expression said it all.

Weeks had come and gone, so she had either returned to Delacroix...or she was dead.

17

IVORY

After what felt like a lifetime, we finally made it.

The castle shone brightly in the sun at the top of the hill, the flags at the keep flying in the wind. It was a clear day, warm, peaceful. My heart gave a squeeze when I saw it because I still had affection for this place despite its gory history.

We were just outside the city, on foot because we didn't cross paths with other travelers with horses. I had to be at least ten pounds lighter since I'd started my journey, with all the goddamn walking and no eating.

"I hope my family made it..." The wetness in Effie's eyes reflected the sun as well as her emotion.

Ryker looked at her. "I'm sure they did. We'll find them."

I lagged behind because this sunny moment I had to confess everything to Ryker. A part of me wanted to walk into that castle with him at my side, to see Commander Burke, the maids, my father. I wanted to smell the jasmine outside my window. I wanted to see Quinn, just to assure him I was alright since he was probably worried sick. But I couldn't do any of that. "Ryker?"

He looked at me over his shoulder.

"Hold on a sec..."

We were close to the city, so close that I could hear the hammer in the forge, hear a horse neigh from the stables, hear one citizen shout to another. I was right on the doorstep—but I couldn't cross the threshold.

Effie lingered behind because she knew what was coming.

Ryker walked up to me, his irritated eyes focused on my face. "What is it, Ivory?"

"I...I need your help with something."

His eyebrows furrowed. "What is it?"

"I need to get into the library...unseen."

He'd never looked so confused in his life. "Unseen? You've been away from home for months, and all you care about is going to the library?" The lightness in his eyes was suddenly heavy, and he looked angry like my father. "Walk through the front door and grab whatever you want."

"It's not that simple, okay? There's something I need to tell you."

"I'm not going to like this, am I?"

Nope. "I need you to promise this stays between us."

He gave a shake of his head. "Depends on what it is."

"Promise me first."

His nostrils flared when he pushed the air out of his lungs. "You're going back down there, aren't you?"

"I made a promise to someone, and I have to keep it."

"To whom?" he demanded. "The Runes? Fuck the Runes—"

"Just listen to me, okay?"

He looked livid.

"Fine, don't promise me. I know you'll keep my secret."

"Not if it puts my people at risk."

"It doesn't," I said calmly. "What I told you about Father is true—"

"Not this shit again—"

"I didn't believe it either. Trust me, I was livid. But when I met her...I knew it was the truth."

"Her?" he asked.

"Our half sister."

His eyes shifted back and forth quickly, stunned.

"She looks just like me."

He was still speechless.

"I didn't want to believe it. I refused to. But when I saw her, I couldn't deny it. And it broke my heart. I can't picture Father doing that...but he did."

Ryker dropped his chin. "It was a long time ago—"

"Don't make excuses for him. It doesn't matter how long ago it was."

"I just mean, he was a young man, probably my age—"

"And how many women have you raped?"

He looked away.

"All of this that we see...it's not ours. It belongs to the Rolfe family."

He stepped away for a second, rubbing the back of his neck as he gathered himself. "Ivory, regimes rise and fall throughout history. They're conquered, and a new era ensues. I know it's not a fairy tale, but it is reality." He came back to me, his eyes harsh. "Even if everything you say is true, what does it matter? You think we can confront Father and he'll just step down like it's no big deal? In case you've forgotten, this world is about survival, not doing what's right."

"But life should be about *more* than survival. It should be about living. And only a select few of us are. Now that you've seen what's down there, how can you abandon all those innocent people?"

"*Innocent?*" he asked incredulously. "Are you talking about the people who feasted on our blood?"

"There are others."

"Ivory, you need to let this go—"

"And you need to be better than this. You can't just look the other way while innocent people are dropped below so they can either be eaten by the Teeth or Necrosis. That's not you. I know it's not."

"Look, there's nothing I can do to change it—"

"Yes, there is. We can unite against Necrosis."

"Father would never agree to that."

"Then we replace him."

He took a slight step back, his eyes wider than before. "You want to overthrow him?"

"You just said regimes rise and fall every day. Perhaps his is almost over."

All he did was blink. "I can't believe what I'm hearing."

"I can't believe you don't realize what kind of person Father is."

"Blood is blood. And I'm not going to kill mine."

"I would never…" Just the thought made me sick. "But this world isn't going to be more tolerable until we do something about it."

"You said we were Plunderers before Father took the throne? That means the former rulers abandoned us all down there first. Sounds like they wouldn't do anything differently if they had the opportunity. It sounds like Father got fed up with the bullshit and gave them what they deserved."

My heart slipped into my stomach. "Nothing warrants what he did."

"I'm just saying, he's not some heartless murderer. They had every opportunity to bring everyone up here, but they didn't. So he took matters into his own hands. That sounds a lot more kingly than what the Runes did."

I loved my brother with my whole heart, and it was so painful to be at odds with him. "The Runes want what I want. They want to unite all of us—and defeat Necrosis once and for all. That's why I'm helping them."

He shook his head. "That's why you're betraying us."

"I'm not betraying anyone. I'm just trying to do the right thing here."

"Family comes first, Ivory. Everything else can be damned."

A long stare ensued, each of us looking at the other with our guard high. We'd always been close, especially after Mother passed, but right now, we felt like enemies across the battlefield. When I spoke, my voice was calm, trying to neutralize all this hostility. "Talk to him about everything I told you...and see what he says."

"Why?"

"That way, you'll know what kind of man he is. And I promise you, you aren't the same."

"I don't agree with that."

"Ryker, you went all the way down to the Bottom of the Cliff to save Effie. You're nothing like him."

He did his best to keep his eyes hard, to show no kindness.

"Effie told me how you met, that you protected her."

His eyes remained hard like a shield.

"I know this is a compromising situation. But I also know in my heart that you and I are different than he is. That we're like Mother...may the gods protect her soul." My eyes shifted back and forth between his. "How many times have I tried to talk to him and he rejected me because he'd rather be with his concubines? I tried to warn him about Mastodon, and he dismissed me because I'm just a woman. None of this would have happened if he'd just listened to his daughter's pleas for help. I wouldn't have been taken down there, and I wouldn't have learned these horrible truths. I've come to realize who he really is...and he's someone I don't know."

Ryker still had nothing to say.

"Please help me."

His hands went to his hips, and his head dropped. "Fuck, man."

"Get me into the castle without being seen. I just need to find something in the library, and then I'll be on my way again."

"Ivory, you can't go back down there by yourself."

"I'll be fine, Ryker."

"You expect me to just lie to Father?" he asked. "Lie through my teeth and say I haven't seen or heard from you?"

"I think that would be best, yes."

He released an angry sigh.

"Please."

"You know that castle as well as I do. You know how to come and go."

"But I need you to keep my secret. Can you do that?"

He stared me down, breathing heavily. "How are you helping them?"

"They need me to heal one of their creatures, but it's the type of wound I've never treated before."

"You're doing all of this for *that*?"

"I would do it for a person. What's the difference?"

"Why is this important to them?"

I held my silence.

"You do realize you're asking me to help you, which is the same thing as helping the enemy."

"I'm not the enemy, Ryker. Father isn't the enemy either. You know who is? Necrosis."

He gave a sigh.

"Convince Father to form an alliance against Necrosis. I've already secured safety for both of you, so neither of you is in danger."

"You know that would never happen."

"Then you know why I'm doing this. I want to live in a world where people aren't sacrificed. Children aren't sacrificed. Where there aren't people at the top of the cliffs and those at the bottom. We're all one people, Ryker. No one is willing to do the work to change that, but I am."

My brother seemed defeated because no more arguments came from him. "I can talk to Father. But I don't think it'll go anywhere. He also intends to get me as close to the throne as possible, in the hopes that we'll be the ruling family one day. If I really can take over the Capital, then you would have the Kingdoms."

"The king has sons."

Ryker gave a shrug. "He said he would take care of it."

"Take care of it how?"

He gave another shrug.

"And you still don't believe me?"

This time, Ryker looked away. "I'll get you into the castle as a concubine. Work in the library during the night and sleep in your bedchamber at night. They only clean your room once a week now, on Mondays."

"What is today?"

"I don't fucking know. I must have lost track sometime between when I was captured by the Teeth and then bitten by one." He turned back to the castle. "Come on, you guys can stay in one of the houses. At nightfall, I'll come for you."

18

RYKER

With my hood, no one seemed to recognize me.

I wasn't sure if the people of Delacroix even knew I was missing. The guards should be searching for me, but they seemed to think I was long dead, judging by their carelessness.

There were homes in Delacroix that belonged to my father, homes used to house King Rutherford's men when they came to inspect. I assumed none of them were there now, so the accommodations were unoccupied. I didn't have a key, so I had to pick the lock to get the girls inside.

We stepped into the home and shut the door behind us, the curtains drawn so no one could see inside. It was a well-furnished residence with a kitchen, living room, and several bedrooms down the hall. It was nicer than most of the homes in town, except for some of the shopkeepers who did very well for themselves and paid handsome taxes from their earnings.

Effie took a quick look around before she turned back to me. "It's been so long since I've been inside a house..."

"Not too shabby," Ivory said. "Especially for the royal guard."

"I'll find out when they're coming next," I said. "In the meantime, you should be safe here. There's money in the drawer to purchase whatever you need." I wasn't sure how long I'd been gone, but it must have been a significant amount of time because this place didn't feel quite the same. "I'll return this evening."

"You know what I'm going to do first?" Ivory headed down the hallway. "Take a damn bath."

That left Effie and me alone, the first time we'd really been alone together since our adventure started. Her arms were tight around her chest, and the light in her eyes was long gone. The emptiness was there, the loneliness, the fear.

"I'll find your family, Effie."

She lifted her eyes to me.

"I'll get you a nice place at the Capital, and you can start over."

"And what about everyone else?" she whispered. "The next lottery winners?"

I was too ashamed to look at her, so I dropped my gaze. "I'm working on it..."

Once I made it to the castle doors, the guards immediately rushed to relay the news to my father.

Would he be relieved?

Or just pissed off?

I knew he would be in his study, so that was where I went, and when I walked through the open door, I saw him conversing with Commander Burke. Their conversation immediately died at the sight of me.

My father was rigid behind the desk, looking at me with eyes that gave nothing away.

Commander Burke silently excused himself and shut the doors behind him.

I couldn't read my father at all right now.

He finally rose from the desk, walked around it, and headed right toward me.

On instinct, I held my breath.

His arms opened, and he brought me into his chest, holding me like I was still a boy who had wandered too far off. His palm cupped the back of my head, and he held me there, held me for the first time since I'd become a man.

He let me go.

"Father—"

He slapped me across the face. It was practically a punch against my cheek, full of momentum, full of anger.

I jolted at the hit because I hadn't seen it coming. My guard was dropped, and my heart was vulnerable.

"What the fuck, Ryker?" His angry eyes pierced my flesh like hot daggers that sliced the skin and cauterized it at the same time. "I sent my men after you, and they never came back. All of them have died—for you."

So he did send help.

"Their blood is on your hands—not mine."

I didn't apologize because that would sound insincere to both of us.

"You brought them back?"

I lifted my chin and looked him in the eye, my cheek on fire. "They didn't make it."

"Not even the girl?"

"Yeti..." I knew what would happen if I told him the truth. He would execute her, execute her family too. They knew too much. Were far too much of a liability. My pleas wouldn't make a difference.

His eyes shifted back and forth as he looked into mine—like he knew. "You put yourself at risk...all for nothing. I sent my men down there...all for nothing. Your behavior is shameful. You're the future Duke of Delacroix, the future King of the Kingdoms, and this is how you behave."

"I cared about her."

"First lesson of being a man." He stepped a little closer. "Never care for your whores."

I kept my anger between my clenched teeth.

"Pay them—and kick them out the door." He moved away and returned to his chair behind the desk. "I'm sure your trip down there has given you a hard lesson in reality. I'm sure it's taught you why the lottery is necessary. It's taught you that I have to make hard decisions every day—to protect our people."

At nightfall, I left the castle and walked down the same cobblestone road I'd taken countless times. Torches illuminated the homes and shops, reflecting on the pavers underneath my boots. A breeze brushed through my hair, blowing a scent of jasmine with it. It felt exactly the same— like nothing had changed.

I was the one who had changed.

I made my way to the home and saw the gentle glow through the curtains. After a light knock on the door, I let myself inside and found the girls on the couch in the living room, empty plates on the coffee table.

The counter was covered with fruits and vegetables, and a piece of steak was sitting on the cutting board. They'd taken the money left behind and made themselves a satisfying dinner. "Smells good."

Effie rubbed her stomach. "I ate so much. But I have no regrets."

"I never have regrets when it comes to eating." Ivory finished off her glass of wine before she got to her feet. "So, how's Father? I imagine he was happy to see you." With her arms crossed over her chest, she walked up to me.

I gave a shrug. "You know how he is."

Her eyes moved to my cheek, like it was still noticeably swollen. "Let me find something to wear, and we'll go." Ivory disappeared down the hallway, probably to find a jacket or shawl to cover her face.

My eyes went back to Effie, and I could feel that vibration in the air, the tension that stretched between us. Her hostility was still present, but so was everything else we shared.

She got to her feet then faced me, looking brand-new after a bath. Her soft hair was shiny again, and her fair skin was no longer hidden underneath spots of dirt. With eyes that were green like the trees in the forest, she stared at me. "Now what?"

"Well, I have good news."

"Yeah?"

"My father sent men down to retrieve me, and they never came across from your family. I don't think your family was with the Teeth either. Otherwise, we would have been captured with them. So, I'm pretty sure they got away."

She took a deep breath and let it shake her body on the way out. "You think they're here in Delacroix?"

"Not sure. They know if they're recognized, they'll be captured again. Might have gathered supplies and headed for somewhere new...like the Capital or another town along the way."

"Gods, I hope you're right."

"I'm sure that I am. And I'll help you find them."

She had to tilt her chin back to look at me because of our height difference. It reminded me of the night when she was on her knees in my bedroom, and I had to drop my chin to my chest to watch her.

"Until then?"

"You'll stay here until I can get away from Delacroix."

"And if King Rutherford's men come?"

"I'll sneak you into the castle, and you can stay with me."

"You don't have to help me, Ryker. You already got us out of there. You don't owe me anything else."

"I'm not doing it out of obligation." I was doing it for a much stronger reason than that. A reason I didn't even understand.

Ivory returned to the room, bundled up with her face concealed. "I'm ready."

I turned back to Effie. "I'll come back when I can. Just sit tight."

"Alright." She turned to Ivory. "I hope you find what you need."

"Me too." Ivory moved in and embraced her with a big hug.

Effie did the same and placed her head on her shoulder as she gripped her tightly. "Good luck."

"You too." Ivory pulled away, and the two of us walked out the front door and back into the night. The walk was spent in silence, the flames of the torches loud every time we passed one. The temperature was mild, just borderline cold. Now when I glanced toward the cliff, I saw something else entirely. A whole new world.

"I think she'll forgive you."

I gave my sister a side look.

"Don't throw in the towel just yet."

"I don't know... can't exactly blame her."

"The institution is at fault, not you."

"She's never looked at me the same since."

"In her defense, she's been struggling to survive every minute since she learned the truth. Reunite her with her family. I'm sure she'll feel differently then."

"Maybe." When we were close to the castle, I put my arm around her waist and drew her close like she was a lover I'd bought for the night. The guards didn't cast a second glance as I took her inside and to the stairs.

Guards were on watch throughout the castle all night long, but most of the hallways were cleared, especially the ones near her bedchamber since she was no longer in there. When we were alone, I whispered. "Are you going to the library now? Or in the morning?"

"Let me get everything I need now so I can work in my bedroom."

We approached the doors to the library then snuck inside. It was dusty and abandoned—exactly as I remembered it. The lights were flicked on, and the frosted windows near the front filled with a glow.

Ivory got right to work. She went down the shelves with her lantern held high, reading the spines as she searched for what she needed.

I stood there and waited, feeling as if I were torn in half right down the middle. I wasn't sure how she was helping the Runes, but I was certain it was something to help my father lose his place on the throne. I was a simple man with simple ideologies, but my world was no longer simple.

Ivory started to stack the books on the table. "I think these could be helpful..." She grabbed a couple more, making a stack of five textbooks. "Now I know why these are in here and no one knows about them."

"Why?"

"Because our family didn't create this library. The ancestors of the Rolfes did." Once she had all her books, she scooped them up and leaned them against her chest as she moved toward the door. "All the paintings on the walls...not our family."

I had to confront my father about everything she'd told me, but now I didn't want to. I didn't want to hear it from his mouth, that we weren't an ancient family that founded this land and made it our own, that we didn't have the blood of kings. We had the blood of thieves. The blood of conquerors. Of rapists.

"Ryker?"

My eyes shifted back to hers.

"You okay?"

"Yeah...was just thinking about something."

"Well, can you stop thinking and get the door?" She nodded to the mahogany wood because her hands were occupied holding the stack of books.

I poked my head outside, made sure the coast was clear, and then we snuck down the hallway toward her room. The guards weren't posted in this quadrant of the castle during the night, not when there was nothing to protect. We made it to her bedchamber, a door I'd looked at countless times with dread. I hadn't stepped inside it after she'd left. It would just hurt too much.

The door was unlocked, so we stepped inside.

Ivory gave a grunt when she set the heavy books on the table. "Gods, those are heavy." She dusted off her hands on her trousers before she flicked on the lamp at her bedside. The room was set aglow, revealing her crisp white bedspread, the white nightstands and dressers trimmed in gold, the place she used to call home. "Wow...it looks exactly the same."

"But it smells a lot better."

She grabbed one of her pillows and chucked it at me.

"Ouch," I said sarcastically.

She parted the curtains and opened the window, letting the breeze air out the staleness. The scent of jasmine was noticeable a moment later. With her arms crossed over her chest, she looked at the city below, the torches flickering in the breeze.

"Nice to be home?"

She was so quiet for so long it was as if she hadn't heard me. But then she spoke, her voice practically a whisper. "Doesn't really feel like home anymore..."

19

IVORY

I spent all my time in my room, working at my desk, reading in bed, sometimes sitting on the floor. Books were open everywhere, and even though I felt guilty for marking them, I made notes in the corners. I made notes in my notebook too, but the highlights made it easier for me to go back and find the important stuff.

Ryker snuck me food and water. Whenever he had meals, he got extras and delivered them. He never stuck around because he had stuff to do, and I basically spent all my time in solitude, surrounded by books. He hid me in his room on Monday when they came to clean.

I kept the window open all the time, just as I did when I lived here. It was nice to have the fresh air, which was warm and soft on my lungs. I could smell all the scents of home, feel the breeze move through my hair just like old times. Sometimes I would sit at the foot of my bed and look out the window, seeing the hawks pass in the sky, the cloud-less day.

Everyone below...they didn't enjoy days like this.

I wasn't even sure how they had reliable harvests with their kind of weather.

I lay on my side across the bedspread, an open book in front of me, but all the reading lulled me to sleep. With my head in the crook of my arm, I slipped under, the breeze hitting me right in the face from the window.

But then the breeze stopped.

The curtains rustled.

The floorboards creaked.

After months of traveling in the harshest conditions, of having to sleep with one eye open, my mind was trained to pick up any sound it deemed unusual. My eyes flew open, and I saw the man standing there.

In black armor with two short swords at his hips, he stood with broad shoulders and powerful arms. His back was to the window, as if he had climbed all the way up the rocks, past the guards, and straight into my open window.

I recognized the blue eyes from my dreams, but now they were different.

Livid.

His stern face was harder than usual, his jaw clenched with the same tightness as his closed fist. When he stepped forward, his boot was heavy against the floor, heavy with the weight of his muscles and armor.

I sat up, still unable to believe he was right before me, that this wasn't a dream. "Huntley—"

With the speed of a hawk catching a mouse from the grass, he gripped me by the throat and squeezed. "You betrayed me."

My hands immediately reached for his wrists, and when I tried to speak, I just lost air I couldn't afford to lose.

He lowered me back to the bed, using his weight to pin me down. "You humiliated me."

I tried to shake my head, but his grip was too tight. My head was submerged in a lake, and every time I drew breath, I just inhaled more water.

"I led an army to the Crags to get you back. But you were already gone." His face came close to mine, his eyes angrier than I'd ever seen them. "I assumed you would come to me at HeartHolme. At the outpost. But you never did."

I tried to kick him off, but it was like slamming your toe into a wall. I tried to peel his hands off me, but his lock was as strong as a viper's jaws.

"My mother told me you returned to Delacroix, but I told her she was wrong."

"She—" Now I really started to suffocate.

He gave me a hard shake. "You ran the first chance you had —and broke your promise to me."

I couldn't fight. I couldn't breathe. My mind was about to slip away, and judging by the insanity in his eyes, I wouldn't wake up again. The maids would find my corpse eventually, and no one would ever know what happened.

My hand reached for his chest, and I planted my palm over his heart. That was where I could feel it, feel the pain in my chest during our separation. I stared at it as I felt my vision tint black, as my world faded away.

Just when I closed my eyes, I drew breath.

Gasped it deep inside me.

My eyes popped back open, and I gasped again, inflating my lungs over and over.

He stayed above me, his hostility burning white-hot.

"I...didn't...betray...you." I should wait until the oxygen was fully restored to my body, but I couldn't. He needed to know that my promise had been kept, that my loyalty hadn't faded. "It's not what you think."

His blue eyes were as cold as ice.

"I came here for the books." I reached for one beside me.

Like he thought I would smash it into his skull, he knocked it onto the floor.

"I'm telling you the truth."

"You should have come to me first."

"I was with Ryker, and it was safer to travel with him and Effie."

His eyebrows furrowed as his eyes narrowed.

"It's a long story, but the Teeth had Ryker too. They captured him when he went after Effie. The three of us escaped, and it just made more sense to travel with them here, get the books, and then go back."

He didn't believe me. It was in his eyes. "It looks like you went back to your old life pretty quickly."

I moved to sit up.

He slammed me back down.

The way he looked at me, the way he distrusted me...hurt. "My father doesn't know I'm here. Ryker snuck me in. The books are too heavy for me to sneak out, so it was easier to read them and make notes. Look at the books if you don't believe me."

"Who's Effie?"

"She won the lottery."

His eyes narrowed.

"She and Ryker are a thing...were a thing, so he went down to save her."

His eyes shifted back and forth.

"I was going to come back. I promise."

"I don't believe you."

"I was worried about you—"

"Don't believe that either."

Now my patience waned, because I was telling the truth, but he was too stubborn to see it. "If I came back, your mother would have captured me and probably killed me, and you wouldn't have even known I'd returned. At least by having this information, I had some leverage if that happened."

"Then you know how to save the dragons?"

"Not yet, but I'm working on it."

He gave an aggravated sigh.

"Why would I lie to you—"

"Because I'm so fucking close to killing you." The last time we were together, it was morning, the sunshine coming through the window. Naked and wrapped up in each other, we were happy, the bond between us unbreakable. Now he was a different man, a man I hadn't seen since he hijacked my carriage.

My hand returned to his chest, right over his heart, right where it hurt the most. "Did you feel this?"

His hard stare burned into my face.

"Because I did..." My hands slid up his chest to his shoulders, to his neck.

His features remained the same, unresponsive to my touch.

"I would never betray what we have."

An eternity passed as he held my gaze, as he peered all the way down to my soul. One hand moved to his waist, and with expert fingers, he popped the buttons of his trousers and got his bottoms down.

My heart raced in a way it hadn't in a long time. Not in the way it did when I was chained to the bed about to be devoured. Not in the way it did when I ran for my life. It was a different excitement, one that I only experienced with him.

I was already just in a loose shirt and my underwear, so he pulled those down with his big fingers and got me naked from the waist down. He yanked me down to the foot of the bed and squeezed his narrow hips between my thighs. With eyes locked on mine, he guided himself inside me, pushed past my tightness...and sank.

I gasped when I felt him, gasped as if I'd forgotten how this felt.

How good he felt.

Even when his fingers were around my throat, I was wet. When he looked at me like he might kill me, I wanted him. It was my body's natural reaction to him, regardless of the context.

He sank until he was balls deep then gave a quiet groan that sounded almost like a growl. He rolled his hips slightly, his body getting reacquainted with mine. His eyes dropped to my lips as he remained still, absorbing my wetness through his skin.

That was when I felt it, that throb in my chest. It was beautiful like music from a harp, soft like a fresh pillow on the bed. It felt warm, like sunshine on a winter day. Like nothing had transpired in the last few weeks, we were back in his bed, waking up after a passionate night together.

He felt it too—it was in his eyes.

My hands reached for his chest, but instead of the hard muscle of his pec, I felt the cold armor. I wanted flesh. I wanted blood. I wanted warmth. My hands clicked the locks until they came loose, and then he removed it and tossed it on the bed above my head. His eyes watched my hands as I removed his tunic so I could feel him—palm to chest.

My hands glided up, feeling the divots between different sections of muscle, feeling the inferno his body produced. It used to keep my bed warm during a blizzard, used to be my own personal fire.

He yanked my shirt up so my tits were exposed and started to rock into me.

I moaned at the first thrust because it was so good.

One of his big arms hooked behind my knee as he deepened the angle, his body directly above mine. His sweltering anger was long gone, now replaced by that dark possessiveness. He looked at me like I was his and his alone. In the bedroom that had once belonged to him, he reclaimed me, made me his wife all over again.

I breathed deep and hard, like I was the one doing all the work, when my only job was to lie there and take it. My fingers curled, and my nails started to dig into his skin. My breaths turned into moans. My lips turned hungry.

His head dipped so our mouths were close together, our breaths hitting each other in the face.

My hands glided up the back of his neck then fisted his short hair. It felt like a dream, being able to touch him like this, to feel our bodies and souls connect on a level I couldn't describe.

He seemed to be teasing me, dangling his lips close to mine but never giving me what I wanted.

I pulled him into me and got the kiss I craved, got his sexy lips and the scruff that surrounded them.

He withdrew right away, his eyes on my mouth. "I'm still angry, baby."

Not that angry if he was calling me baby again. "I know."

His head dipped again, and his lips pressed against mine. It was euphoric—the heat, the softness, the passion. It started off slow, our mouths coming together in a delicate dance.

But then his kiss turned intense, his mouth parting my lips harder, giving me his tongue, devouring me.

I let him take me, all of me, my nails slicing into his skin, nearly drawing blood.

My kiss faltered once I felt it approach, that sweltering pleasure only he could deliver. It started everywhere at once, but it intensified as it came to the center. My entire body tightened in preparation, like the string of a bow, inching farther and farther back before release.

Then it released—and the arrow went flying.

I kept my mouth buried in his to stifle my pleasure so it wouldn't echo through the castle and shake the windows. My moans would normally be unbridled, but now they were suppressed winces and heavy tears.

His cock thickened noticeably inside me, swelling just a little more before release. His face and neck were blotchy and red, all the blood reaching the surface as his body worked for this moment. His eyes fixated on me, watching the tears flow like streams, and he gave a quiet moan as he released.

As he gave me all of him.

I was a dry riverbed now engorged with a stream. It filled me completely, spilled out over the shores. It'd been so long since I'd felt this full, since my husband had made me his wife like this.

My husband.

I'd said it more times in our separation than in his presence.

The rocking slowed to a halt, our breaths changed from ragged to soft, and we remained connected on the bed. I felt him soften slightly, but he was still so thick inside me, making his presence known.

His lips dipped back to mine, and he kissed me, soft once more.

He thickened all over again, plumped back to full mast, and the rocking motion started again.

I moaned against his mouth as I felt him take me a second time. "God, I missed you..."

———

A QUIET KNOCK sounded on the door.

Huntley was naked in my bed, the sheets at his waist, his thick arms folded under his head. His eyes flicked to the doorway then to me, silently interrogating me.

I threw on some pants then cracked the door open, seeing the tray of food on the floor. I opened it wider and whispered. "Ryker?"

He was just down the hall, so he turned around and came back. "What?"

"Can I have another one?" I picked up the tray off the floor, seeing steak, potatoes, greens, and a bowl filled with pieces of freshly baked bread.

He flashed me an irritated look. "Why?"

"Because I'm hungry."

"You're going to eat *all* that—"

"Shut up and just do it." I walked inside and shut the door in his face.

His voice was audible on the other side. "Pain in my ass…"

Huntley hadn't moved from his relaxed position, not the least bit afraid of whoever was on the other side.

"You must be hungry." I carried the tray to the nightstand beside him and set it down.

He seemed more interested in me than the food.

"Ryker is bringing me another one."

He pushed himself up and propped his body against my wooden headboard. "He'll suspect you have company."

"I don't care if he does."

"Then you told him about us."

I sat at the edge of the bed, feeling the puncture of his hard stare. It'd been so long since I'd been the target of his eye, since we'd had these quiet conversations in the middle of the night. We fit together so well, it seemed as if we'd spent no time apart. "No."

There was a subtle shift in his eyes, a delicate tightening.

"It's not the time."

"When is the time?"

"I don't know..."

"What does he know?"

I inhaled a deep breath because I'd rather go back to fucking than discussing politics in this fucked-up world. "I told him what happened to your family, that we're Plunderers by blood. I told him what Father did to your mother, but he didn't believe me." I dropped my chin and looked at my hands on my lap. "I don't blame him. It took me a while to accept too."

With no expression on his handsome face, he stared.

"He's conflicted."

"He rescued a woman from the bottom of the cliffs, a woman put there because she was unlucky enough to win the lottery, a lottery that his father and the king instated. There's nothing to be conflicted about."

"He detests the practice, but he believes there's no other way. Sacrifice the few for the many..."

His gaze hardened, and I knew him well enough to read his thoughts.

"Ryker has a good heart."

"Does he?"

"Yes." I held his gaze with my confidence because I would vouch for my brother always.

"Did you tell him our plan?"

"Yes."

"And?"

"Said it was impossible."

"So, he won't be much help to us."

"He will."

"I can't depend on someone I don't trust."

"You can trust him."

He gave me a cold look.

"He snuck me into the castle, got me the books to help you, sneaks me food every night, and hasn't told my father or anyone else that I'm here. That's pretty trustworthy to me." My brother and I fought like cats and dogs, but our loyalty to each other was unquestioned.

He absorbed those words a long time, his stare hard.

"He just needs some time to come around. That's all."

The same stare. The same powerful eyes. "When you tell him you're a Rolfe, I'll trust him. Because that will mean you trust him too."

OUR DINNER WAS FINISHED, the trays on the table near the door. With the window open and the breeze gently flapping the curtains, I worked on the couch, the light from the lamp brightening the pages.

When I felt his stare, I flicked my eyes up. "You aren't tired?"

He was up against the headboard, his massive body taking up most of my king-sized bed. "Why would I be?"

"Because you climbed all the way up here."

"I've completed harder challenges—like riding day and night to get an army to take on the Teeth." His eyes hardened a bit, the anger still in his visage. "Like taking the tunnel back to Delacroix without rest and then trekking across the Kingdoms to see the light in your bedroom window. Climbing up some goddamn rocks is inconsequential."

I shut the textbook in my lap. "I thought we were past this."

"Never said I was."

"I told you—"

"I heard you the first time. Doesn't mean I'm not angry."

"Then what should I have done—"

"Get your fucking ass back to me as fast as possible." His voice was raised, loud enough that someone would hear outside the door if they were standing close enough. "So I know that you're okay. So I can sleep. So I don't have this goddamn pain in my chest that won't go away."

"Lower your voice—"

"Let me save you some time, baby. Don't tell me what to do. This marriage will go a lot smoother the sooner you learn that."

"Why do you keep calling me that if you're so pissed at me?"

"Because you're still my baby regardless of how pissed I am." He looked away, tightening his jaw as he ground his teeth together. The undercut of his jaw was sharper now, the cords in his neck thicker in appearance.

"I guess that means you didn't fuck anyone else while I was gone…"

The look of anger he gave me was indescribable. The rest of his face matched his eyes—livid. "Fucking you twice in one go didn't make that clear enough for you?"

His stare was too much, so I looked away. My books were thick with boundless knowledge, but it was like searching for a needle in a haystack. What I needed was really specific, and there was nothing listed in the appendices.

We turned quiet, but the animosity was still palpable.

"I said I was sorry, alright?" I said, still not looking at him.

"No, you didn't."

I opened the book again and dismissed the conversation.

"Tell me you're sorry."

"I already did—"

"No, you didn't."

I slammed my book shut and glared at him. "Sorry."

"I'll take it." He looked at me again.

"Are we good now?"

He turned away again.

"So, you're just going to be mad forever?"

"Probably."

I rolled my eyes and went back to the book. It took me a moment to focus on the pages, to actually absorb the words I read, and when I was finally back at work, he interrupted me.

"Come here."

I lifted my chin and stared at him. "This is a two-way street. Don't tell me what to do either."

"That's not going to work."

"You bet your ass it is."

"It's not going to work because you like it when I tell you what to do."

"No, I don't!"

He patted his lap. "Get your ass over here. Now."

Defiant, I just sat there.

"Don't make me ask again."

"That was asking?" I asked incredulously.

He threw off the sheets like he would drag me by the hair.

"Fine." I set the books aside and came over, back in the long shirt I'd worn when he arrived. At the edge of the bed, I stood, still wearing that look of defiance even though I'd caved.

His big arm scooped around my waist and dragged me on top of him. His hungry lips went straight for my neck, kissing me everywhere, his other hand in my hair. The sheets were kicked away, and my underwear was pulled to the side so he could shove himself inside me. He gave a groan against my throat. "I missed you, baby."

THE LAMP WAS STILL on even though it was sometime in the middle of the night. We lay together in my bed, the sheets soft and crisp at the same time, my thigh hiked over his hip as we shared a single pillow.

It'd been a long time since we'd done this.

His jawline had a heavy shadow from his long travels. His eyes were as sharp as ever, but now, they showed signs of fatigue. His fingers lightly kneaded my ass under the sheet.

I knew he could feel the gauze wrapped around my thighs, feel it rub right against his skin, but he never asked about it. "When I was at the Crags—"

"We aren't going to talk about that."

"I just wanted to explain—"

"I know what they are, and I don't want to talk about it."

"Huntley, I'm fine."

"Doesn't matter."

"And Klaus didn't...you know."

His gaze remained steady.

"So, I'm fine..."

"You'll have those scars for the rest of your life."

"Whatever. I'm sure I'll get more along the way."

"I should have killed him that day." His eyes dropped again. "But I promise, if I get that chance again, I won't waste it."

"None of this would have happened if I hadn't run away. So, really...it's my fault."

He raised his eyes again.

"Don't feel bad."

"I would have done the same thing, baby. And I don't think we'd be here now if you hadn't."

WHEN I WOKE up the next morning, I had to make sure he was beside me.

Make sure it wasn't all a dream.

My hand reached out for his hard chest, and I felt it. Felt the slab of muscle. Felt his beating heart. My eyes were too tired to open, so I kept them closed, lulled by his warmth and smell. But then I felt my body move, felt my thighs separate, felt a mountain shift over me. Then I felt him.

That woke me right up.

It was sloppy and lazy, his face in the crook of my neck, his hips rolling against mine.

My fingers latched on to his back with my eyes closed, and I took it. I took his slow thrusts, felt his hips rub against my inner thighs, listened to us make subtle groans as we moved together.

We were both half asleep, so it took almost no effort to reach our high. My knees squeezed his torso as my toes curled so hard they began to cramp. My lips released a quiet whimper, and I expressed most of my euphoria against his chest.

It was over as quickly as it'd begun, and he rolled off me to start his day. His footsteps receded into the bathroom, and the door shut a moment later.

I was about to go right back to sleep, but there was a knock on the door.

Must be breakfast.

I was far more tired than hungry, but I managed to get dressed and grabbed the door.

Ryker was there with a single tray.

I didn't complain. I was too tired to be hungry, so Huntley could have my food. "Thanks."

His eyes scanned over me before he glanced into the bedroom.

"You mind?"

His eyes came back to me. "Is someone in here with you?"

"Is that any of your business?"

He curled his bottom lip into his mouth and chewed slightly, swallowing his retort as he tried to subdue his anger at the same time. "Based on our circumstances, I'd say it is my business. Nobody is supposed to see you, so if you're fucking one of the guards—"

"Ryker, don't worry about it."

"How can I not worry about it? This guy tells another guard, and then Father finds out I'm lying to him—"

"He's not a guard, alright?"

His eyes narrowed. "You're supposed to be a virgin—"

"Say that shit to me again and I'm going to slam this tray into your head, alright?"

"You know I don't give a shit, but if you were to marry—"

"Not getting married." Because I was already married, and he didn't give a damn how many guys had come before him. "Are we done here?"

"Ivory—"

I shut the door in his face and set the tray on the coffee table.

Huntley stepped out of the bathroom as he scrubbed the towel over his head. "Tell him that your husband doesn't give a shit." He dropped the towel, fully naked, his hair a little uneven. "But I appreciate his concern."

I rolled my eyes, and now that I was too awake to go back to sleep, I hit the books.

He started to get dressed, as if he was leaving.

"What are you doing?"

"Going out."

"Why?"

"Don't expect me to stay cooped up in here all day."

"But what are you going to do? You're the most wanted man in Delacroix."

He gave a shrug as he headed to the window. "Get a drink."

"A *drink*?" I asked, flabbergasted. "You're willing to risk getting caught for a beer?"

"More like scotch or rum. And I won't get caught." He parted the curtains then sat on the windowsill. "You need to focus, and if I have to sit here and watch you bite your lip all day, you aren't going to get anything done."

"I still don't think this is a good idea. You're going to crawl up the walls in broad daylight?"

"No offense, baby. But I've worked security here before, and it's pretty lax." He threw both legs over the edge then hopped down.

20

RYKER

Even after days had passed, it wasn't the same.

He was still pissed.

Hardly said a few words to me. Burke ignored me. My usual duties were revoked. I felt like shit even when I hadn't really done anything wrong. I went to the bottom of the cliffs to save an innocent person...and I was the bad guy.

At lunchtime, I brought two trays to Ivory's door. I was pretty annoyed that she was shacking up with some guy the second she got back, but it wasn't my place to say anything. The last thing I wanted to do was think about my sister's private life, so I chose to block it out.

When she opened the door, she let it open fully, giving me a full view of her bedroom.

That meant nobody was there.

"Thanks." She took the trays and set them down on the table near the door.

I glanced left and right and saw no sign of life. "You still need two if you're alone?"

"Probably not. Want to eat with me?"

I was lonely as fuck, so why not? I shut the door and came inside.

She tucked the towel under the crack in the door to keep out the light.

Her bedroom was messy, her sheets rumpled in disarray, books stacked everywhere.

We took a seat together on the couch and ate.

I stared at the cover of one of the texts as I put the piece of chicken in my mouth. "Any luck?"

"I think I'm making some headway."

"And what are you trying to accomplish?"

"I told you I'm trying to heal a creature."

"But what creature? And why is it so hard for you to do?"

She took a few bites of her food and never gave an answer. "How are things with Effie?"

I gave a shrug.

"You haven't talked to her?"

"And say what, exactly?"

"Ryker, I told you she would forgive you."

"Well, maybe she shouldn't."

She stopped eating altogether. "You aren't the bad guy here."

I didn't know what I was anymore.

She read my mood and dropped the conversation. "How are things with Father?"

"He's not talking to me."

"He's not?"

"No."

"I think that's harsh."

"He was happy that I returned unharmed, but he gave me the cold shoulder afterward. I questioned the lottery...he didn't like that."

Now she was quiet.

"I'm pretty lonely, honestly."

Her hand went to my forearm.

"He's not assigning me tasks right now. As punishment."

"You know how he is. He's just...passive-aggressive."

I knew that all too well.

"I really think you should go see Effie. I'm sure she'd be happy to see you."

I kept my eyes on the floor.

"If you think you're lonely...imagine how she must feel."

I SAW his life through a different lens.

Because he didn't censor it, not like he did with Ivory.

So, I saw the whores. I saw the drinks. I saw the drunken stupors she knew nothing about.

The doors to his study opened and he stepped out, but the women were visible in the background, naked on the bed behind his desk. Long hair. Tits. Rumpled sheets. He was in his breeches and a loose tunic, his brow marked with a shine from old sweat. In his hand was a glass, and he knocked it back as he approached the table where Burke and I sat.

He didn't even give me a glance.

"There's been no sight of her, m'lord." Commander Burke sat beside me, ready for battle even though it was a quiet night. "She's either dead or has been taken from the Kingdoms."

Father dropped into a chair. "I know exactly where she is."

I studied his face, noticing the tint from the booze.

He set down the glass. "She's been taken to the bottom of the cliffs, and when the time is right, our enemies will use her as leverage."

I felt my anger tighten my jaw—because he sent men after me but not her.

"Then we'll know exactly who we're dealing with." He pushed his empty glass aside, and even though he was right across from me, he never looked at me. Not once. It was the coldest shoulder I'd ever been given.

"The Blade Scions will be here tomorrow," Commander Burke said.

My eyes shifted to him.

"We'll select the next winner of the lottery tomorrow," he continued. "That's what they're here to see."

Good thing they weren't here last time.

Father gave a nod in agreement then slouched in the chair. Arrogance was evident in his body language, his stare, the way he seemed indifferent to everything.

I used to interpret it as confidence. "I'm your son, and you can't look me in the eye."

He stilled. Burke stilled. The entire room held its breath.

My eyes pounded his face, waiting for acknowledgment, some sign of respect. "I'm home and your daughter is still missing, but you don't seem to care about either of those things."

His head slowly turned so his eyes could regard me.

I kept up my stare.

"Anger is like grief. Everyone manages it differently."

"Well, you should manage it better." The chair slid back over the floor as I stood up. I made my exit, turning my back on my father and walking out of the room with the same indifference he showed me.

21

EFFIE

I stayed cooped up in the house, day and night.

At first, it was a welcome reprieve. I slept in a soft bed every night, had a fire to keep me warm, had food in the kitchen that kept me full. There was money in the drawer if I had any other needs. It was a blessing after the arduous journey I'd gone through. But once my basic needs were met, my reality hit me like a pail of cold water.

I worried about my family.

If the duke hadn't reported their deaths, then they must still be alive.

But where?

How would I ever find them?

My thoughts were shattered when the lock clicked.

"Shit." I jumped out of the armchair and ducked out of sight before it opened.

"Effie?" It was Ryker. He shut the door and locked it behind him. "You here?"

I emerged from behind the wall. "Wasn't sure if it would be you."

He came closer to me, taking his time with his steps, his muscular arms stiff by his sides. Instead of donning his armor and weapons, he wore breeches and a dark tunic, looking like a regular citizen rather than royalty. The playfulness in his eyes had been snuffed out like a low-burning candle. Now they were dim and dark. "You doing alright?"

I bottled my complaints because he seemed to be having a worse day than I was. "It has everything I need. Haven't felt this pampered in a long time."

He gave a slight nod. "Good." He took a look around, but it just felt like a reason not to look at me.

"You seem down."

While still avoiding my gaze, he said, "I'm fine."

"No, you aren't."

He stilled at my words, and after what seemed like a long internal debate, he turned back to me. His green eyes now looked tired—really tired.

"What happened?"

He gave a slight shake of his head. "You don't want to hear about it."

"Then why would I ask?"

"It's about my father."

The man who ruined my life. The man who lowered my family down to a frozen hell.

"Like I said...you don't want to hear about it." He stepped around me and headed for the couch. He took a seat on the edge, his forearms on his knees. There were shelves against the wall around the fireplace, holding dusty books that no one ever touched.

I knew because I was bored enough to look. I took a seat beside him. "I do."

He rubbed his palms together before he gave me a side glance. "He was so relieved that I returned. But in the same breath, he slapped me across the face." His eyes shifted straight ahead. "Haven't talked since. I just told him off and walked out."

"He's mad you went after me?"

"He's mad I could have gotten myself killed."

"Well...then, it sounds like he just cares."

"Has a funny way of showing it." He dropped his gaze to his hands as he rubbed his palms again. The calluses were there on his fingertips, in the center of his palm where he gripped the hilt of his sword. I remembered those hands on my body, remembered their roughness against my soft skin.

"He'll come around."

He kept his focus on his hands. "I'm not sure what to do."

I studied his face, unsure of his meaning.

"After everything Ivory told me, everything that happened with you...I'm just so confused."

"I don't think there's much to be confused about."

His motions halted for a moment, probably because the bitterness in my voice had a bite to it. "It's not a matter of what I think is right or wrong. It's a matter of changing it. I'm not sure how to do that."

"Ivory said align all the Kingdoms then defeat Necrosis."

He finally turned and looked at me head on. "And you think that's going to be easy?" His eyes shifted back and forth in incredulity. "That is literally the most complicated plan ever. That requires cooperation from not only my father but King Rutherford, and I can tell you right now, neither man will be on board with that."

"Have you tried?"

"You don't know my father..."

"But I have a pretty damn good idea what he's like. You know, since he sacrifices innocents without losing sleep."

Ryker looked away. "I can try—but I don't think it'll go anywhere."

"And if it doesn't? What will you do?"

He gave a shrug. "No idea."

I knew I was being too harsh. He was the one who had confided in me, and it would be wrong to judge his every thought and emotion. "How's Ivory?"

He gave a slight chuckle. "She's good."

"What was that about?"

"What?"

"The laugh."

"She's getting laid, so I'd say she's doing really good."

"What?" I blurted. "By whom?"

He shook his head. "No idea. Don't really care. But I don't want us to get caught."

She'd told me she was married, that she missed him, so jumping into bed with some other guy just didn't sound right. That must mean...he was in the castle. Right under Ryker's nose. Under the duke's nose. "I wouldn't worry. She's smart."

His hands broke apart, and he looked at me head on. "So...I have some bad news."

Oh no. My parents were dead.

"The Blade Scions are coming. That means you'll need to come with me to the castle."

"There's no other place you can put me?"

He shook his head. "Not on such short notice."

"It's okay. I can wait it out in the city."

His eyes shifted back and forth, the disappointment settling in like the setting sun. "You don't want me. Made that loud and clear. I'm not the kind of guy that doesn't take no for an answer."

I doubted any woman had ever said no to him.

"You can have the bed. I'll take the couch. When the Blade Scions are gone, I'll bring you back here."

"And we're just going to do this forever?" I asked incredulously.

"Just until we figure out our next step." His green eyes watched me, both authoritative and sad. "We're going to have to play this by ear for a while."

I'd lost everything in the lottery, and now I had nothing left. I was completely dependent on him—because I had no other option.

He rose from the couch and stepped away. "Come on, we should get going."

———

HE SNUCK me into the castle, and like last time, the guards didn't even glance at me. My face was covered with a shawl so my face was hidden, but I doubted anyone here would remember me from last time, would know that I was the one who'd won the lottery.

The castle was a special place, with the crystal chandeliers, the thick rugs that spanned the full-length hallways, stone statues, and oil paintings on the wall. It also had electricity, something the rest of Delacroix lacked. It gave all the rooms a gentle glow, like the heat of a fire that spread to every corner of a room. When the nighttime chill settled on the land, the castle stayed warm. The only sign of the cold was the frost that pressed up against the glass.

Ryker escorted me the same way as last time, turning left and right, and then approaching his door in a quiet hallway. We stepped inside, and once we were in his large bedroom, I looked at the rug at the foot of the bed.

I remembered exactly what happened there. Could taste him on my tongue. Could feel the tightness in my throat and the blockage of my airway. The heat settled in next, warming my skin from head to toe.

If he had the same thought, he didn't show it. He stepped into the room first and bent down to start the fire in the enormous hearth. He got it going quickly, the flames licking the wood quietly. "Hungry?"

"Already ate."

He got to his feet then headed to his private bar. The bottle of wine was uncorked, and he filled two glasses. He didn't offer one to me, as if he were afraid I would misinterpret the offering. He set his glass down on the coffee table in the sitting room then disappeared down the hall.

I stood there, unsure what to do. It was nice to have company, to dispel my solitude, but the tension prickled my skin so hard. The heat from the fire was hot on my skin. My throat was dry even though I was far from parched.

He returned moments later, in pants that seemed to be made of wool, and his tunic was replaced by a shirt with no sleeves. Everything looked soft and comfortable, like it was meant to be worn in the house and nowhere else. The pants were low on his hips, and the shirt hugged his muscular torso. He took a seat and brought the glass to his lips for a deep drink. "You want something to sleep in?"

"I'm okay."

He took another drink and kept his eyes on the table.

I finally grabbed the other glass and took a seat across from him. Once I had a drop on my tongue, I was taken back to that night, a night that felt pure and magical. Sneaking around with the son of a duke was wrong, but it felt so right at the time. "Where did he bite you?"

His eyes lifted. "She."

"Oh..."

He gripped the neckline of his shirt and tugged it down, revealing the deep scar on his chest. It was almost a perfect circle, the outline of the mouth distinct, the teeth marks still visible. After he gave me a good look, he released his grip, and the shirt bounced back to how it'd been before.

I was so disturbed I felt my face go pale. Felt my fingers go numb. Felt everything hurt. "I'm so sorry."

He took another drink of his wine. "Don't be. I'm fine."

"You'll have that scar the rest of your life."

He gave a shrug. "If you aren't covered in scars by the end of your life, did you really live?" He swirled his glass, made the dark liquid spin in a circle, and then took another drink.

"Still...I'm sorry."

"Don't worry about me, sweetheart." He seemed to realize his slip because he quickly looked away and took another drink. His stare was focused elsewhere, like if he pretended it didn't happen hard enough, I would think it didn't happen at all.

But I couldn't pretend it didn't happen—not when I loved the way it sounded. "Will anything happen to you?"

His eyes shifted back to me.

"Now that you've been bitten?"

"The bite is nearly a week old, and I don't feel different. So, I don't think so."

"I hope so. I just wonder...how does someone become a Teeth? Are they born that way? Born with all those teeth...?"

"Good question. I have no idea."

"There's a whole world down there, and we don't know anything about it."

"Yeah." His glass was empty, so he set it down and relaxed farther into the couch. His knees were far apart, and his arms were crossed over his hard stomach. He spent most of his time staring at anything else but me.

"Look...it's not that I don't like you."

His eyes shifted back to me.

"Because I do. I still do..."

His eyes watched me without blinking.

"I just..." I'd put myself in this situation, and now I didn't know how to get out of it. Any time I was with him, these feelings were there, still there despite what his father had done. He was part of the ruling class that believed their inferiors deserved to be sacrificed so they could continue to live. We were worthless. Expendable. But my heart still pounded like the hooves of a racing horse. "It's hard."

He sat up, his forearms moving to his knees. He had such a cut jawline that it cast a shadow under his neck. Handsome, strong, brave...he was unlike most men I knew. When the jokes were cast aside and he looked at me like that, I felt weak in my knees, felt weak everywhere. "What can I do to make this right?"

"You already made it right when you saved us."

"I mean between us." His palms came together, a single one bigger than both of mine together. "Because I want there to be an us."

My knees grew weaker. If I had to stand, I'd probably just crumple to the floor. "I don't see how there ever can be."

"I told you I don't agree with my father's policies. No, I'm not drawing my sword and threatening to kill him unless he stops, but—"

"That's not why. I need to start over somewhere, far away from here, and you're here. Not to mention, you're going to have to marry soon, and I'm not having an affair with a married man."

"Marriage isn't high on my list of priorities right now."

"But it will be soon."

His eyes darted away for just a moment. "None of that stuff matters right now. Do you want to be with me or not?" He looked at me with that authoritative gaze, his green eyes exuding power, not from his birthright, but what he earned on his own. "Because I will make it work. I will be loyal to you. I will be faithful to you. I travel to the Capital regularly, and we can be together during those travels."

"Have you ever done this before?"

"Done what, exactly?"

"Commitment to one woman."

He gave a subtle shake of his head.

"Then why do you want to do it now?"

His eyes remained the same, hard and focused. "I just do."

"But why me—"

"I don't have a reason. If you think I'm going to sit here and recite a poem about my feelings, that's not going to happen. I can't explain the way I feel. I can't justify it. But I just know that's what I want. I don't want to lose you, and right now, I'm willing to do anything just to be with you."

I'd known if I came with him, this would happen. I'd end up in his bed, his hips between my thighs, my sweat dampening his sheets. But I hadn't expected it to happen like this. I expected him to initiate it, but I was the one who put the conversation on the table. I was the one who I said I still wanted him.

I was the reason all of this had happened.

He remained still, his eyes piercing into me like daggers.

I was too tense to move. Nearly too tense to breathe.

"Be with me."

I'd never met anyone like him. The other guys felt like boys. Ryker felt like a man. That was why it was too hard to think logically about this, because my entire body wanted him even though my mind knew it would only end in heartbreak. But I decided to worry about that later, to pick up the broken pieces of my shattered heart at another time. "Okay."

———

HE PULLED his shirt over his head and tossed it aside before his hand dug into my hair. He pulled it from around my face, pinned it against the back of my head, and kissed me with passionate restraint. His arm hooked around the small of my back, and he drew me close, squeezing me against his rock-hard body.

Like a fresh piece of chocolate, I melted against his heat. His lips took mine with authority but also gentleness. Every kiss was purposeful, full of passion and dominance. He kissed me good and hard then slowed it back down as he guided me toward the bed.

His lips went to my neck, and he kissed me as he tugged on my breeches and got them over my hips. He descended my throat, his hot breaths melting my skin, his tongue tasting the salt from my sweat.

I held on to him and let him devour me, felt my breaths come out uneven, felt my heart race like it might explode.

When my pants were pushed down all the way, his thumbs hooked into my panties and scooped those away too, letting them hit the floor and join the pile. He released a quiet growl as he looked down at my naked body, from my small tits to the hair between my legs.

My hands went for his breeches, and I tugged them down, getting his underwear too, and the big dick I remembered popped free. It could barely fit into my mouth, and I knew it was about to barely fit somewhere else too.

He lifted me onto the bed and moved over me, his thick arms and legs holding up his massive weight without effort. His mouth moved to my neck once again, and he kissed me as he hooked my thigh over his hip. He started to grind, bringing his throbbing cock right against my clit.

I'd never felt a man do that before, so I clawed his back and moaned. He pushed with the right pressure, mimicking the hold created by my fingers, and soon his length became smeared with my arousal.

I was already going to release, so I steadied his hips. Wanted to save it for the right time.

He must have read it in my eyes because he kept going, kept pushing me in the perfect spot. "We've got all night, sweetheart." With his face close to mine, he drove me into the finish that I tried to stall.

I was glad he continued—because it was so good.

So good that my nails sank deeper than they should. So good that my eyes moistened into forming tears. So good that I let out a moan as if there was nobody but us in the castle.

He barely let me finish before he sank inside me, giving a loud moan when he was sheathed, from the aftershocks of my climax. The tightness. The wetness. It gave him pause, made him stop to breathe. "Fuck." He breathed the word into my face, let it come out as a whisper for only me to hear.

My satisfaction was already complete, and desire kindled into a brand-new inferno. My thighs squeezed his hips as we rocked together, as his massive size took up every inch like it had in my throat. My fingers were in his short hair, down his back, over his biceps...everywhere I could touch.

His thrusts were slow and steady, like anything more would set him off. He wanted to hold off, but based on the tint of his skin and the clench of his jaw, he was enjoying it far too much. His breaths were uneven and more like pants, and every time he rolled his hips, he gave an involuntary moan.

It was so sexy.

I grabbed on to his hips and guided him harder, faster. "We have all night..."

He gave another groan, this one low and masculine, from the back of his throat.

I tugged him far inside me, taking his entire length, even wincing a bit because I wasn't deep enough for a man like him. "Come inside me."

This time, he closed his eyes and reared his head. "Fuck." He thrust against me hard as he finished, his green eyes dark with intensity, his cock thickening just a little more with release.

I could feel it, feel how thick it was, feel the weight of this man.

He grunted the whole way through, as if this was the best orgasm of his life. "Sweetheart..."

His dick already made me sore, but I wanted to keep going. Wanted to keep going until neither one of us could go on any longer.

With sweat on his chest and satisfaction in his eyes, he looked down at me. The intensity was still there, as if that climax hadn't made a dent in his desire. His dick stayed hard, so I assumed that was just the beginning. He started to rock again, sliding through the wetness of our come. "Fuck, that feels good."

"So good you should pay for it?"

The corner of his lip didn't kick up with a smile, and the playfulness didn't enter his eyes. His look remained intense as he started to rock into me. "I don't have to pay for it—not when you're mine."

22

IVORY

When it grew late, I started to worry.

Huntley had been gone a long time, far longer than required to have a couple drinks at a pub. Every time I looked out the window, I didn't see the guards dispatched to the streets in a manhunt. The horns didn't blare. Everything seemed quiet.

But he still hadn't returned.

I couldn't focus on the books any longer, so I started to pace. My stomach growled because Ryker hadn't delivered my dinner, but I was too concerned about my husband to really care about food right now.

I heard the floorboard creak and pivoted to the window.

There he was, looking exactly the same as he had when he left. His hood was pulled back, and he showed his handsome face, the chiseled jawline, the authority in his gaze.

He was completely relaxed, oblivious to the worry he'd put me through.

My closed fists moved to my hips. "I was worried."

He loosened his cape then started to unbuckle his armor, all the while looking uninterested.

"Did you hear me? You were gone all day and all night. You couldn't have been drinking that entire time."

"Then you don't know me very well." The armor came undone, and he stacked it on one of the chairs. "I drink like I fuck—nonstop."

I crossed my arms over my chest. "I'm still pissed that you had me worried—"

"Good. Then you know exactly how I feel."

"Wow...so, this was all just to make a point?" I threw my arms down. "That's not petty at all."

He walked up to me, each step of his boots loud and heavy. He came right up to me, his chin tilted down so he could look me straight in the eye. "You make me petty. That's your fault."

"Don't you dare blame me. It's not my fault you can't let anything go. Like, *ever*."

His eyes shifted back and forth between mine, the fires of anger visible on the surface.

"Look, I don't want to fight—"

"Yes, you do. Because that's all we ever do. Fight and fuck."

"Well, can we skip to the fucking part, then—"

He threw me down on the bed then pinned my face to the mattress. My cheek was against the sheets, half of my eyesight obscured because half of my head was buried in the sheets. My ass was in the air, and my panties were already at my knees.

Then he thrust himself inside me, his big dick making its entrance with a savage push.

Thank the gods my moans were stifled by the sheets.

He locked my wrists together at the small of my back and kept one hand on the back of my neck even though I wasn't going anywhere, and he fucked me so hard I felt like a whore he'd paid for the night.

I was locked in place, his massive dick ramming into me and making me wince every time it hit me with its full force.

"This is what you wanted."

I panted and moaned against the bed.

"Say yes."

I could barely talk, my face was pressed so deep, my body was shaking so hard from his thrusts.

"Come on, baby. Say it."

"Yes..."

His grip tightened on my throat. "Again."

"Yes."

He gave a moan at my defeat, his dick thickening a little more. "That's my baby..."

HE SAT on the couch in just his underwear, one foot propped on the coffee table, his elbow on the armrest. As if he hadn't just fucked me senseless, he looked at the door, his mind somewhere else.

I pulled my shirt back over my head and got my underwear back on. "Ryker hasn't come with dinner yet."

"He's not going to."

"What do you mean by that?"

He turned slightly my way, his eyes as hard as the stone of this castle. "I saw him."

My heart leaped into my throat like a frog. "Did he see you?"

"No."

"What was he doing?"

"He took a blond girl from one of the king's homes and escorted her toward the castle. So, you aren't getting your dinner tonight."

"That's Effie."

"I surmised."

They must have worked out their differences...and he forgot about me.

Huntley shifted his gaze back to the door. "How long is this going to take?"

I joined him on the couch, the books in front of me. "It's not like the answer is listed in the table of contents."

"Not what I asked."

I grabbed the last book I'd been reading and opened it in my lap. "It's hard to say. Regrowing limbs isn't exactly part of healing..." I flipped the pages and found the place where I'd left off.

"I can get you something to eat."

"How?"

"I'm sure a pub is still open somewhere."

"No, it's okay. I don't want you going out there again."

"But I know how my baby gets when she's hungry."

I rolled my eyes as I kept my eyes down on the book. "I'll be fine."

His arm moved over the back of the couch, right against the back of my neck. It was instantly warm, instantly inviting.

I automatically shifted over and rested against his body. My head used his shoulder as a pillow, and I tucked my knees close to my body. Comfortable silence ensued, the breeze ruffling the curtains, the pages of the book turning.

After several pages with little to no information, I tilted my head back so I could look at his face. "I have a question. Why are these books in your library?"

He met my gaze with silence.

"You have so many about the magic of healing... Where did they come from?"

"The library was around long before I was born. Long before my father was born. So I can't answer that."

"There's so much literature about healing, about healing different creatures, and I think my father has no idea the information is right at his grasp. I don't think anyone knows about it since I'm the only one who goes in there. Ryker wouldn't read a book if his life depended on it."

"Neither would I."

"Yes, I know you're more of a slash-and-stab kind of guy." I turned back to the book, and while the information was interesting, it wasn't helpful toward my goal. Those dragons would never escape that island without my help. They would wither and die there, and the thought broke my heart. I had to figure this out.

"When I was a child, my mother told me there had been a healer in the family. My great-great-great-grandfather. Something like that."

I lifted my head and looked at him again. "Then...maybe these were his."

"Possibly."

I looked down at the book again, feeling connected to someone who had passed on long ago. "I wonder where he learned everything. If he took these books from somewhere else...or if he authored them himself."

"We'll never know."

"Is this...why you heal so quickly?"

His eyebrows quirked at the question.

"Because you possess the blood of a healer."

His stare continued, his reaction as hard as ever. "Possibly."

"Do your mother and brother have this ability too?"

He shook his head. "Just me."

I studied him for a moment longer, feeling a new connection to him. All my knowledge came from his ancestors, the ancestors who gave him healing blood. "Does that mean our children will have this ability?"

"Probably. Along with your stubbornness."

"*My* stubbornness? Honey, my stubbornness doesn't compare to yours."

"Then they'll be very magical and stubborn children." The corner of his mouth rose in a slight smile, and for once, that playfulness reached his eyes.

It was infectious, and all my offense evaporated. "Maybe you could be a better healer than I ever could."

"Maybe. But that's not the life I've chosen."

"Slash and stab, right?"

His playfulness remained. "Lead and defend."

Now my eyes softened, thinking about the way he took the rear to protect his men at the front. "You'll be a great king."

"And you'll be a great queen. I will protect my subjects, and you'll heal the ones I fail."

"I don't think you'll fail any of them, Huntley."

His arm scooped around my shoulders, and he pulled me closer. The book was forgotten now, closed on my lap. His chin rested on the top of my head, and we sat there together, my cheek against his warm flesh.

Then a knock sounded on the door.

"Guess he's not too busy after all."

I pulled on my pants, Huntley stepped out of view of the doorway, and I opened it.

Ryker practically shoved the tray into my arms. "Here. Gotta go." He immediately took off.

"Whoa, hold on."

"What?" He turned back around, but most of his body pointed toward the hallway, like he couldn't get away from me quick enough.

"What's going on?"

"I delivered you food. Now I gotta go."

"Are you and Effie back together?"

He stilled at the question. "Why would you ask that?"

"Why else are you in such a hurry?"

His clothes were wrinkly like he'd put them on in a rush, and his hair was ruffled all over the place. His skin was shiny too, like he'd been sweating a lot this evening. "The Blade Scions are coming in the morning. I needed Effie to relocate to my quarters."

"And that clearly worked out well for you."

His eyes narrowed in annoyance. "I don't pry into your business." He glanced past me, into the open doorway where my guest was hidden. "Don't pry into mine."

"But you did pry into mine. Said I should have stayed a virgin."

"Well, you're supposed to. I'm not saying I agree with that, but that's just the rules—"

"Fuck the rules. You can fuck whoever you want without question, but when I take a lover, I'm some kind of a whore? That's ridiculous."

"Trust me, I think it's ridiculous too. Imagine how much more sex I'd be getting if girls weren't committed to remaining pure until marriage and all that bullshit. It sucks for me as much as it sucks for you. But I'm in no mood to debate the social expectations of women right now. I've got somewhere to be." With that, he walked off and veered right.

I closed the door and set the tray on the table. "We can split this."

"I ate while I was out." He returned to the couch, his hard body bulging with muscles from his strong physique.

I pulled the tray into my lap and cut into my meat.

He sat forward and looked through the pile of books sitting there.

"I'm glad Effie forgave him."

"Just because she's fucking him doesn't mean she's forgiven him—as I've proven the last few days."

I cast him a glare. "I don't think anyone else on the planet holds a grudge the way you do."

"I have a good memory. Others don't."

I continued to eat and let the conversation die.

"You need to figure out how to heal the dragons soon. Because I can't stay here much longer."

I chewed my bite as I stared.

He answered my unspoken question. "The man who took everything from me sleeps in this castle. All I have to do is walk into his quarters and slit his throat. It's not wise to keep me here longer than necessary."

"You promised me you wouldn't kill him."

"And that promise is getting harder to keep the longer you keep me here."

"So, that's our next move? We heal the dragons first."

"If we want to take over the Kingdoms, we're going to need the upper hand. Three fire-breathing dragons is that leverage."

"The Capital alone is a big place. I don't think a couple dragons are going to cut it. Besides, getting them to fight for us is another obstacle we'll have to tackle. Not even sure how to communicate with them. Not to mention, there are innocent people all over the Kingdoms. Burning everything is the same as mass executions."

"Then what is your idea?"

"Diplomacy."

He actually rolled his eyes.

"I'm serious."

"Women love to talk, but trust me, men do not. We like action. We like threats. We like getting shit done. We conquer Delacroix first, then move on to the other Kingdoms until we reach the Capital. King Rutherford can surrender if he wants to protect his people."

"You know, a lot of things have to go right for that plan to work. How are we going to do this without horses? We can't get them up the tunnel."

"We take the horses here in Delacroix."

"There's not enough for the soldiers and all the Runes."

He looked away.

"The purpose of this is to unite everyone against Necrosis—not kill a bunch of innocent people."

"You're a woman. You don't get it—"

"Use my sex as a justification again, and I won't be your wife anymore."

He slowly turned to regard me, and the ferocity on my face must have been enough to make him back down. "You couldn't stop being my wife even if you wanted to be. We're eternally bound—in case you forgot."

"Not if I kill you."

He met my look, anger licking at the corners. "I'd like to see you try, baby."

We were like fire and ice. We came together and formed an inferno of blue flames. Sometimes those flames were stoked by passion. Other times, they were stoked by our anger, egos, and stubbornness.

"Are you going to shoot me in the neck again? How'd that work last time?"

I set my tray down and met his look. "Maybe I'd shoot you in the eye this time. Or better yet, the dick."

He gave a slight chuckle. "That's the last place you'd shoot me. You love my dick, baby."

"Not when you're being an asshole."

"Yeah?" He grabbed me by the ankle and tugged me down, getting me flat on my back on the couch. He was on top of me a second later, ripping off my underwear and yanking my shirt up.

I slapped him across the face then shoved my hands into his massive shoulders. "Get off me."

The hits just turned him on more, and he got me into position and shoved his big dick inside me.

My entire body went limp, just as it always did when he was inside me.

He gripped the back of my hair and rocked into me. "Tell me to stop."

It felt so damn good every single time. A man had never made me feel this way. Ever. Every time we came together,

I was paralyzed by it. I could tell he felt it too, in the way his eyes softened so subtly.

"Tell me to stop." His fingers were tangled in my hair, and he maintained his grip like the strands were reins to a horse.

"No..." My hands hooked under his arms, and my nails anchored into the muscles of his back.

"Don't threaten me again." His head dropped close to mine, his eyes on my lips.

I rocked with him, breathing hard, clawing savagely.

He didn't blink, not remotely uncomfortable by the daggers in his back. "Understand me?"

"Yes." I hated my obedience. I hated the way I crumbled so easily. But I lost all my strength when it came to this man.

"Yes, husband."

"Yes...husband."

WHEN I WOKE up the next morning, I was in his arms. It was a king-size bed, but we only used half of it. Only used a single pillow. We were on my side of the bed, our naked bodies wrapped around each other.

I loved waking up like this. My nights had felt so lonely during our separation, and now that he was here with me, it was as if those horrible nights had never happened. The pain on my inner thighs was gone as if I'd never been bitten.

His eyes opened a moment later, locking right on mine.

I kissed his shoulder, and when his hand moved for my neck to tuck my hair away, I kissed the inside of his wrist. "I'm sorry that I threatened to kill you last night." My temper got the best of me, and words I didn't mean just flew out.

"It's fine. I like it."

"You like it when I threaten to kill you?"

"I like it when you tell me off for being an asshole. It's sexy."

"You were being an asshole..."

His eyes turned playful.

"This is the part where you apologize to me."

He grinned. "It won't happen again."

"Still not an apology..."

"How about I fuck you instead?" He rolled on top of me and opened my legs with his.

"Nope." I planted my palms against his chest. "I want that apology."

He pressed against my entrance then slid inside, filling me with his length and thickness. We both took a couple breaths as we became acquainted with each other, as if this was the first time when it must have been our hundredth. Then we started to move together, nice and slow.

My palms slid up his chest, and I cupped his face and the back of his neck.

He bowed his head and gave me a kiss as he continued to move. "I'm sorry, baby."

"WAIT..." I flipped back through the pages, going over the words I'd already highlighted.

Huntley sat beside me, his eyes on the fire in the hearth.

I flipped back and forth then checked my notes. "Wait, wait, wait..."

Huntley turned to me.

"I think I got it..." I showed him my notebook. "According to the healing elements, it's possible to restore what once was. So if they once had wings, I should be able to restore them." I grabbed the book. "This one talks about the process of regrowth from the soul, finding the seed of destiny and watering it with the mind...so I think that could apply to this." I looked up at Huntley, expecting a good reaction.

His expression was as hard as ever. "None of that means anything to me. You think you can do it or not?"

"I won't know until I try, but this is the answer. It's just a matter of pulling it off."

"You can pull it off, baby."

"I've had no practice."

"The dragons are practice. Keep practicing until you get it right."

"Well...they're dragons. I doubt they're going to give me many opportunities to get close."

"We'll have to make sure they're fed first."

"Yeah, that doesn't make me feel better either."

He stared at me. "I promise I won't let anything happen to you."

The strength in his eyes, the depth of his voice, it did make me feel better. "We'll leave when the sun goes down. But first, I've got to talk to Ryker."

"You told him about the dragons?"

"No. I told him I needed to heal something, but that was all."

"So, you don't trust him."

"It's not that."

"It sounds like it."

"I just know he's still...processing all this. But if he and Effie have reunited, then I imagine he's our ally."

"What are you going to tell him?"

"That I'm leaving...but I'll return. In the meantime, he needs to make my father come around."

"That's not going to happen."

I sighed. "Won't know until we try."

"Are you going to tell him about us?"

I looked away because I didn't have an answer. "I'm not sure how to handle that."

"When we return, it'll be to conquer, so this may be the only chance you get."

"We aren't conquering anything. We're removing my father from power if he refuses to comply."

"I'm removing him from power whether he complies or not —because this castle belongs to me. This bedroom belongs to me. Delacroix has been in my family for generations— and it's mine." His soft-spoken words turned maniacal, and the man of bloodshed emerged. His look was so enraged I couldn't challenge it. "I will grant him the option to surrender with dignity for you. But if he refuses, I will remove him in a very undignified way. Personally, I hope he chooses the latter."

I looked away because his anger was too much to bear.

He seethed in silence for a while, needing the time to recover from his rage.

"I'll tell Ryker to work on my father. I'll also tell him to work on a plan for the Capital. If we take the Capital, we take the Kingdoms. It'll be a lot more efficient."

"Ryker won't be able to make a dent in that place."

"He's a lot more capable than you realize. Let's not forget he was the one who saved me."

"You would have saved yourself whether he came or not."

I turned to look at him.

"I know my baby." He had been pissed off just a second ago, but now he looked at me with confidence and affection. It was the same look my father wore when he was proud of me...which had only happened once or twice. "Not everyone at the Capital is loyal to King Rutherford. There are some who know the truth."

"The truth?"

"That the lottery is a sacrifice. That King Rutherford gets a kickback from our neighbors to the north for keeping Necrosis at bay."

My eyes narrowed because I had no idea what he spoke of. "Our neighbors to the north...?"

"A short distance across the sea, there's another country. Another kingdom. Another ruler. He trades with the Capital in exchange for keeping the Runes, Teeth, Plunderers, and everyone else at the bottom of the cliffs. The Blade Scions are responsible for not only trading with them, but protecting the Kingdoms from potential attack. They have a strong army, and the only reason they haven't conquered us is because they know we're keeping Necrosis out of their lives."

All of this was brand-new information. I stayed quiet because I didn't know what to say.

"The Blade Scions know the truth—and some of them aren't happy about it. If Ryker is looking for allies, that's where he should start."

"Is that why you became a Blade Scion?"

He nodded. "The corruption goes deep. And I'm sure there's more we know nothing about."

"I wonder if Ryker knows this."

"I doubt it."

"So, even if we beat Necrosis...we might have another war on our hands."

"Potentially. Or they might be smart and realize it would be a really stupid idea to attack a country that defeated a foe such as Necrosis."

"Do you think that's where the outcasts are from? The dragons?"

"Could be."

I felt like this problem only grew bigger and bigger as time wore on. "I'll talk to Ryker and have him sneak me out. I'll meet you in the city."

"I'm going to miss this bed."

"Yeah, me too."

"But I guess a tree will have to do."

"A tree?" I asked. "We're going to sleep in a tree?"

"No." He turned to me, his eyes hard. "We're going to fuck against a tree."

———————

RYKER APPEARED that evening with my dinner.

"Come in."

He clearly just wanted to leave the tray and run off, judging by the conflicted look on his face.

"I need to talk to you."

He gave a sigh of irritation before he joined me in my quarters. "What?"

"I need you to sneak me out tonight."

He glanced at the books behind me. "Got what you need?"

"Yeah."

"And now what? You're going to go back down there?"

"Yes."

Now all his irritation was gone, replaced by a look of concern. "Ivory, you shouldn't go alone. I know you're tough and all that, but even I wouldn't make that trip alone —only if I had to. I would take you myself, but I can't leave Delacroix again, especially not when I have Effie here."

"I won't be alone, Ryker."

"Then who will you be with?" he blurted.

The time had come. The truth was inevitable. "His name is Huntley...and he was the one staying with me."

His eyes narrowed. "We don't have a guard by that name."

"Because he's not a guard. He's a Rune..."

When the understanding descended, his eyes looked cold.

"He's one of the sons I told you about—Mastodon."

"Wow..." With a clenched jaw, he gave a slight shake of his head. "That's who you're fucking? He kidnapped you."

"I know—"

"He wants to destroy our family."

"No, he doesn't. His anger is reserved for Father—and rightfully so. He has no ill will toward either of us."

He backed up, his eyes glowing with fury. "I can't believe this."

"I already told you I was helping them. What does it matter if I'm sleeping with him?"

THE BROKEN QUEEN   279

"It just does."

"How is it any different from Effie sleeping with you? Her family would be appalled if they knew about you two. Would you want her to stop?"

That shut him up really quick.

"Huntley is the strongest man I know. He'd never let anything happen to me."

"Except being given to the Teeth in the first place."

"That wasn't him—"

"But he couldn't protect you from it either."

"He amassed an entire army to free me, but by the time they got there, we were already gone."

His green eyes turned still.

"After I help him, we're going to return and begin our plan against Necrosis. I need you to get Father on board before I return."

"Or what?"

"Just...get him on board."

"Otherwise, Mastodon will kill him?"

"His name is Huntley. And he promised me he wouldn't kill him."

"And you believe that?" he asked incredulously. "He wants nothing more than to defeat Delacroix with an army and slaughter Father. If it were me, I would do the exact same thing. He may have made you a promise, but there's no way he's going to keep it."

"He will."

"He won't—"

"Yes, he will. He will because he's my husband."

Totally shocked, he didn't have a reaction. Not for a couple seconds. Not for nearly a minute. He just stared at me, speechless. Then the hurt moved into his eyes. The pain of betrayal. "What the fuck, Ivory..."

"He married me to protect me from the Teeth. It didn't work, but...we still forged an alliance. We agreed to take the Kingdoms and defeat Necrosis together—as husband and wife. I know this is hard to digest—"

"Hard to digest?" he exclaimed. "You married the enemy."

"He's not the enemy, and neither are we. We're doing this for the good of everyone, so no one is sacrificed at the bottom of the cliffs, so there aren't soul-sucking monsters ready to kill us all at a moment's notice."

He stepped back and dug his fingers into his hair. "Fuck. Do you realize that marriage is permanently binding? You can't just divorce this guy and marry someone else once this is all over."

"I don't want to divorce him."

He turned silent once again.

"It's not just a political arrangement..."

He turned away altogether, releasing a heavy sigh.

His disappointment was like a hot knife between the ribs.

"Ryker—"

"I'm done with this conversation." He turned back to me, his hands on his hips. "Let's go."

"There's something else I need to say—"

"Then fucking say it." Now he didn't care if anyone overheard us. He spoke as loudly as he wanted.

"While I'm gone, you need to work not only on Father, but you need to work on the Capital."

He gave me a blank stare, as if he couldn't believe what I'd just asked him to do.

"Huntley used to be a Blade Scion, and he told me what they do for King Rutherford. Apparently, there's another kingdom to the north of us. They give us supplies in exchange for keeping Necrosis confined to the south. Not all of them are loyal to the king. A lot of them don't agree with his practices at all. Connect with them, and you have allies."

"Ivory, I never agreed to do any of this. I said I would think about it—"

"You know it's the right thing to do."

He looked away.

"You know this world needs to change. You're just saying this because you know Father won't cooperate."

"Well, he won't."

"Then we need to find another way. I'm sorry."

With his hands on his hips, he bowed his head.

"I know this is hard."

"Really? Doesn't seem hard for you at all—since you married a traitor."

"He's not a traitor. *We* are the traitors, Ryker."

He raised his chin and looked at me.

"I know you don't want to believe it. I didn't either. But it's the truth. Try to talk Father into it, and if he says no...which he probably will...we need to execute this plan instead. He can have a nice house when this is all over. He can have a normal life. We can still be a family. It just won't be in a castle anymore."

"Well, you would still be in the castle."

"That's not why I'm doing it."

"It's not? You aren't as power-hungry as Father is?"

"I just told you that's not why."

He looked away. "Whatever you want to tell yourself..."

His insult was like a bite from a snake. "You know me, Ryker. You know that's not how I am."

"But I also know the kind of blood that runs in our veins. We're conquerors. Thieves. Rapists. Liars. Maybe you aren't as good as you think."

The insinuation hurt. "That's our past but not our future. My only desire is to make this world a better place. For me to do that, I need your help. I need your loyalty. I need to know that you're doing this while I'm away."

He directed his look toward the window, which was now closed. The curtains no longer flapped in the breeze. The room was already stale. "I want this world to be a better place too...so I'm in."

I knew he would be.

"But I already lost Mom, and I'm not going to lose him too."

"I already negotiated his safety, Ryker."

"I don't want Effie to be found and killed. I don't want her family to be killed. I don't want anyone else to win the lottery."

"I know you don't—because you have a big heart."

He dropped his hands from his hips and regarded me. That look of anger slowly faded, slowly turned into the softness of a sunset. "Let's get you out of here."

23

HUNTLEY

I waited in town at the designated spot. A torch burned above me, illuminating my silhouette so she'd be able to find me. I saw their dots at the top of the hill, and they became bigger the closer they came. Ivory was covered in a cloak and a shawl so none of the guards would suspect she was anything more than a lay Ryker had paid for.

I was uneasy throughout the separation, afraid something would go wrong and one of the guards would see through her disguise. Or worse, Ryker would change his mind and drag her to his father. Then I'd have a tough time seeing her again.

Now any time she wasn't in my grasp, I was plagued with the kind of anxiety I'd never known.

I was afraid I would lose her again.

They drew close, their visages visible in the torchlight.

She removed her shawl and showed her face, her bright green eyes, her fair cheeks.

One look at Ryker told me he knew exactly who I was.

Not Mastodon—but Ivory's husband.

It was all in his eyes, which were sharp like daggers. He sized me up as an opponent, marked me as an enemy without giving a great speech before a battle. His stance on our marriage was perfectly clear in his silence.

It was the exact reaction I expected.

Ryker finally spoke. "I'll fetch you a fresh horse."

"Thank you." Ivory placed her hand on his shoulder.

He quickly twisted away and disappeared.

My eyes took her in, watched every little reaction as it moved over her beautiful face. Her eyes crinkled in the corners, her lips pursed together to swallow a painful retort. She watched him depart before she turned back to me. "I told him."

"I can see that."

"I tried to make him understand...but he couldn't."

"Don't blame him."

Her eyes narrowed.

"How can he understand what he hasn't experienced? He doesn't know our journey."

"He feels betrayed."

"Because he was betrayed. You married the man who intends to take all of this away."

Her eyes slashed at me with anger. "You aren't making me feel better."

"Wasn't trying to."

She looked where Ryker had gone, trying to see him in the dark. "Asshole."

"I'm giving it to you straight. That's my job."

"Well, that's not what I need right now." She continued to look away, all the anxiety riddling her expression.

"Once he gets to know me, gets to know our world, he'll feel differently."

She turned back to me, her expression cautious. "Are you just saying that?"

"My job is to give it to you straight, isn't it?"

She held my gaze for a while before she turned back to Ryker.

He returned with a saddled horse, guiding it by the reins. "I know a way you can slip out of the city."

We followed him, moving down the cobblestone alleyways until we reached the edge of the city. It was dark up ahead, so dark we wouldn't be able to see much. But if we didn't leave now, we'd be spotted during daylight.

Ryker handed the reins to Ivory. "Be careful, alright?"

She nodded. "Tell Effie I said goodbye."

"I will."

"What's your plan with her?"

He gave a loud sigh. "No idea. But we'll figure it out."

"I told you she would forgive you."

His eyes dropped.

"I hope you can forgive me someday."

His eyes stayed down for a while, like it was too hard to look at her.

She moved into his chest and hugged him.

His response was immediate, and he gripped her hard. "Please be careful."

"I will." She was the first to pull away. "See you soon."

He gave a nod before he turned his gaze on me. There was cold indifference there, no longer the hatred he'd possessed earlier. "Take care of my sister." He could have said a lot of other things, but there was only one thing he really cared about.

And that made me respect him. "With my life."

WE TRAVELED BACK the way we'd come, heading across the wide-open spaces, through the forest, and to the secret path that led to the bottom of the cliffs. The horse cut our travel time down to half of what it had taken me to get here.

Ivory was in a solemn mood the whole way, like that final conversation with her brother left a lasting effect on her. When we made camp at night, she wasn't in the mood for conversation or anything else.

I let her be.

In the morning, I took the reins, and she held on to me. Hours of silence could pass, and we didn't speak a word. It was the sort of comfortable silence I shared with Ian and my mother, a kind of familiarity that was born over a lifetime. But with Ivory, it was natural.

We arrived at the tunnel at nightfall. "I'm afraid your father is going to destroy it."

"He won't."

I stared at her face in the light of the moon.

"Ryker told me he's leaving it open so I can return...or the people who captured me can return me."

He was less heartless than I realized.

She got comfortable in the bedroll, sticking as far to the edge as possible so there would be room for me. She was on her side, facing the other way, still forlorn—unlike the woman I'd married.

I joined her in the bedroll, kept my weapons on the grass beside me within a hand's reach. She turned toward me and got comfortable, her arms hooking around me for warmth, but it still wasn't the same affection she usually showed me. "Tell me, baby."

"Tell you what?"

My eyes were on the glimpses of sky between the tops of the trees, the white spots that marked the stars. "What's bothering you."

With her face on my shoulder and her arm over my stomach, she released a drawn-out sigh. "My choice of a husband isn't the only reason Ryker's upset. He didn't say it, but I could feel it."

My fingers moved into her hair, and I gently ran them through it.

"It's because he wasn't there. Wasn't part of the moment. Part of the day. My brother isn't an emotional or sentimental guy, but we've always been close."

"I'm sorry."

"I am too. And I know my dad...he'd be really hurt."

That was hard for me to imagine, but I kept the doubt to myself. "Listening to my mother cry...that was hard. I knew it wasn't the woman I had married that brought her to tears, but the fact that she couldn't bear witness to the moment I'd dedicated my life to another, to the woman who would bear her grandchildren."

"Yeah..."

"When the time is right, we'll do the ceremony again."

"Can we?"

"Yes. We can do it in front of the entire kingdom. It won't just be our wedding. It'll be your coronation as well. Both of our families will be there. I'll gladly slice my palm for you again. And I'll bed you like it's our first time, too."

———

WE DESCENDED INTO THE TUNNEL, taking the ladder for hours until we reached the bottom. We both wanted to get the trek over with, so we hardly spoke but a few words so we could complete the journey quicker.

As we descended the path farther underground, it grew cold like last time, and Ivory's jacket wasn't enough to keep her warm. Her breath escaped as vapor, and her teeth chattered so loudly I could hear it echo off the walls.

Nighttime was the only time she felt warm. We both slept in the bedroll naked so the heat would fill the enclosure and bounce back at us. Her face was against mine, her leg hooked over my hip, her arm around my neck.

Her hair was across the pillow, and her eyes were heavy with fatigue. "How much longer?"

"Another day, probably."

She watched me for a while, her eyes dull from the endless journey. "I don't know what I would do if you weren't so warm."

"Die."

She gave a slight chuckle. "Obviously..."

"I remember the first time we did this—when you stared at my dick."

"Oh my gods..." She closed her eyes in shame then turned away, looking at the ceiling instead. "I did not."

I grinned because she was so full of shit. "I watched you."

"I was making sure you didn't have a dagger under the blanket."

"You know I could kill you with just my fist, so I wouldn't need it."

Still too embarrassed to look at me, she kept her eyes on the ceiling.

"Didn't realize you possessed enough humility to feel embarrassed."

"I'm not embarrassed."

"Then why won't you look at me?"

"Because I'm comfortable on my back."

"Sure."

She rolled her eyes.

"So, what did you think?"

"About?"

"Come on, baby." I continued my grin because this was a good time. "You know exactly what I'm talking about."

She stayed quiet.

"Is that the reason you came back to save me from the Teeth?"

"Oh, get over yourself." She gave me a smack.

I chuckled and pulled her back into me. "Alright, I'll go first." My arm hooked around her waist, and I anchored her to me so she couldn't roll away. "The first time I kissed you, I stopped. Do you remember that?"

"Yes."

"I stopped because I didn't expect to like it. I don't kiss women. They kiss me—on their knees. But when our mouths came together...I felt fire." I remembered that night so vividly, and now it had new meaning after everything we'd been through. When I'd slept with her, I hadn't realized she was the last woman I'd ever sleep with, that it was the first time I was bedding my future wife. "Your shirt came down...and I liked those tits. Small but firm, with nipples perfect against my tongue. Soft against my lips. Warm to the touch. They pebbled every time I came close, every time I exhaled a breath. I love staring at them when you're at the foot of the bed, your nipples so fucking hard they're sharper than my ax."

Her breathing had quickened a bit, and the paleness to her cold cheeks had tinted to a beautiful rouge. The embarrassment was long gone, replaced by a look I'd seen more times than I could count. "I thought you had a really nice dick..."

That's my baby.

"A big dick."

I already knew all this, but it was still fun to make her say it.

"Now that dick is all mine, and I'm not going to share."

When she thought she'd caught me with another woman, she'd stabbed me with a dagger and twisted it to make it hurt. But I loved it. I loved the way it drove her crazy. I loved the way it forced her hand. And I loved that nothing had changed since. "Quinn was never good enough for you."

"Quinn?" Her eyebrows furrowed in genuine confusion.

"The guard you snuck out of your room."

It took her a couple seconds to catch up. "He was a nice guy."

"Scrawny."

"He had nice eyes."

"Not as nice as mine."

A slow smile came on to her lips, the kind that reached her eyes. "Look who's jealous..."

"Not jealous. Just judgmental."

"You can't get mad about a guy who was before your time."

Before my time. It was hard to remember when that time existed. It was hard to remember the whores who slept in my furs at the outpost because Ivory had erased their memory. Her presence was so large she filled my past as well as my present, became a memory that I never actually had. "It's hard to believe there was a time when you weren't mine."

Her hand moved to my face, her fingertips brushing along the coarseness of my beard. "It's weird, isn't it?" Her soft eyes were locked on mine, and with a lover's touch, she caressed me.

My arm tightened around her back, and I tugged her into me, bringing us together as a single person under the blanket. My face rested against hers, my eyes down on her lips. We lay that way, cocooned by the rock in eternal silence. I missed our nights in a bed, but I forgot how hard the rock was when she was with me. I forgot about the frost on the walls. The yetis in the snow. The Teeth who wanted blood.

I forgot it all.

———

THE SNOW SHONE so bright in the sun that I couldn't look directly at it. Heat bounced off the surface and hit me right in the face. The air was cold, the snow was two feet high, but I was burning up inside my coat.

"Ugh."

I glanced over my shoulder.

"I hate it down here."

"You're a Rune." I moved ahead, scanning the horizon for tracks in the snow, for weathered branches, for any signs of the Teeth waiting for the next lottery winner. "You better get used to it."

"I'm a Rolfe, not a Rune."

"They're the same thing."

"Technically, you're a Delacroix, so you aren't a Rune either."

I turned back around. "Water is thicker than blood. The Runes are just as much my people as the ones at the top of the cliffs."

She lagged behind me because the snow was a bigger obstacle for her small stature. She tried to step in the places

I'd already trod so she could keep my pace, but that didn't make much of a difference.

I kept going.

"How did you guys survive the fall?"

The fall. The boot to my back. The wind in my face. Clouds in my vision. Moisture so cold it made my eyelashes freeze. And then the snow spiraling up at me. "We landed in a lake."

"A lake? I haven't seen a lake over here."

"It's still there. Just can't see it."

She caught up to me, winded as she tried to keep my stride, but she had too much pride to ask me to slow down for her.

My kind of woman.

"It's underneath the snow?" she asked between breaths.

"Yes. It's frozen over with a thick sheet of ice."

"Are we standing on it right now?"

"No."

"Even then...that water must have been freezing. If you weren't knocked out, you must have been in shock."

"Ian was. We got him out of the water. We thought he was gone, but miraculously, he came back."

"My gods..." She didn't give me that look often, tenderness wrapped up in sympathy, but she gave it to me now. Like she could feel exactly what I went through.

"My mother kept us alive. It was my father's responsibility to raise us from boys to men, but the task fell to my mother. She changed us from victims to survivors. She made us strong, vengeful, and ruthless. We weren't allowed to complain about our broken bones, to voice our hunger, to do anything besides press on. I know I'm a heartless man, but I wasn't raised to be anything but fierce."

Her soft eyes continued to regard me. Without judgment and without pity, she stared. There was something deeper in her expression, the same emotion my mother showed me when I was in her good graces.

Respect.

"Now I feel stupid complaining about anything..."

WE MADE it to the cave at nightfall, and I noticed the supplies were beginning to run low.

Ian would need to make a delivery soon.

"I'm not in the mood for seeds and nuts. Not a goddamn rabbit..." She grabbed her bow and quiver of arrows. "I'm going to hunt before it gets too dark." She stared down at me, as if she expected me to tell her otherwise.

I gave her a slight nod. "Don't go too far."

She left the cave, her sword on her hip, her bow over her back, her ass nice and tight in her trousers.

I watched her go before I readied the fire. The wood was piled on and then kindled. Soon, the orange flames heated the space, melted the snow at the entrance to the cave. Shadows sprawled across the walls and the ceiling. I stared at it, thinking of old memories as I listened for signs of trouble.

Just when the night turned pitch black, she returned, two squirrels in her hand. "It's not much—"

"I don't like rabbit food either."

I prepared the meat for the fire then roasted it on a spit. The juices started to bubble and make the fire hiss below. I watched her across from me, her eyes tired, her hair messy after the long journey. She leaned against the other wall with her knees pulled close. Her eyes were on the fire most of the time, but sometimes it was on me. "I didn't realize princesses ate squirrels."

Her eyes narrowed right on cue.

I grinned because I loved pissing her off. It inevitably led to sex. Good sex.

"I was never a princess, but even if I were, I'm definitely not anymore." She took the spit away from the fire and divided the food between us. We ate in silence, just the way Ian and I would after a hunt. I'd hunted with women.

I'd fought with women. But I'd never done these things with a lover.

"Did you guys travel to HeartHolme, and the Runes welcomed you with open arms?"

"We went to the outpost first. They took us in for a while."

"And then your mother became queen?" she asked. "That's one hell of a story."

"It didn't happen that quickly. Her reign didn't begin until a decade later."

"How?" she asked. "How did she pull that off?"

"By being the fiercest warrior. By being selfless for her people. By giving everything to everyone else and leaving nothing for herself. When the king passed away, his son wanted to take the throne. But the Runes wanted my mother instead."

"That must have pissed him off."

"It did. But he was too young for the role anyway. Too spoiled by luxury that was given and not earned. My mother has led them ever since, and her wish is for me to take her place when her time comes."

"But the people will have to vote?"

"Yes."

"And what if they vote no?"

I took another bite and didn't answer until I was done. "I will always embrace the will of my people. But ruling HeartHolme has never been my destiny. My destiny, as we both know, is to take back my father's throne and rule Delacroix and the Kingdoms."

"Then who will rule the Runes?"

"Ian—if they'll have him."

"If Necrosis is defeated and there's no barrier between the top and the bottom, would there still be different kingdoms? Wouldn't they all be united under one banner?"

I gave a slight chuckle because she was so naïve.

"What?"

"There's no such thing as happily ever after. Peace isn't eternal. It's temporary, a pause between wars. Without Necrosis as their primary adversary, I imagine the Runes, the Plunderers, and the Teeth will wage war until there's one sovereign."

"Can't they just chill out instead?"

"No."

"There's more to life than power."

"No, there's not."

She finished her last bite then studied me across the cave.

"Power is everything."

"Maybe to an egomaniac like yourself..."

"It would be easy to be indifferent, to step away and live in your own world. Have a farm somewhere. A quiet life providing for your family with the gifts of the earth. But every time you step away, someone else will step forward. There will always be a power-hungry egomaniac wanting to rule. Their interests will be vile and selfish. They will send innocents to war and conquer the weak. What's the only way to prevent that from happening? By already having someone occupy that throne—someone worthy of the throne. Someone who can prevent those things from happening."

She gave me a deep stare, her eyes unblinking, her chest not rising.

"My mother will have to conquer the other factions if she wants to survive. I'll provide her aid, obviously."

"They can't have a truce?"

"Do the Teeth seem like people who make truces?"

Her eyes dropped. "In the battle with Necrosis...would the Teeth be their allies?"

"Probably."

"So, shouldn't we conquer them first? It would make it easier to take on Necrosis."

She had no military experience, but she was innately strategic. "If they find out we've taken back Delacroix, they may retreat from the Crags and join the Necrosis in their lands. In war, you have to play everything by ear. If you make a plan and refuse to change it despite your circumstances, you'll perish."

She gave a slight nod, as if I'd just assigned her orders.

The fire continued to burn between us, and the darkness outside the crack in the wall felt like a looming shadow. The smoke drifted toward the opening and disappeared, fading into the black. It was quiet out there, no sign of the heavy footfalls that belonged to a behemoth in white fur. The Teeth rarely emerged in the darkness, so I didn't suspect their prying eyes. It was just the two of us in this cold wilderness.

"What's the plan? Do we return to HeartHolme or go to the dragons?"

If I had the option, straight to the dragons. But that wasn't possible. "The outpost. HeartHolme. Then the island."

"Oh goody…I'd love to see your mother."

My lips lifted into a slight smile at her sarcasm.

"Seriously, what if she orders her men to kill me?"

"She won't."

"Uh, she knocked you out cold and handed me over to the Teeth like I was a box of berries. I wouldn't be surprised if she shoves a broadsword right through my gut the second she sees me."

My feelings toward my mother were complicated. That hadn't always been the case. I used to revere her and nothing else. But now...it was complicated. "I grabbed what men I could from the outpost and marched on the Crags. She intercepted me with the army of HeartHolme."

"She's quite vindictive, isn't she?"

"Actually, she came to help."

Her eyes narrowed.

"Her fear of losing me was stronger than her hatred for you. So, she arrived with her sword at her hip and her army at her back to return you. When we return to HeartHolme, she won't touch you. I imagine her angry crusade is over."

Ivory gave a pause, like she couldn't believe anything I'd said.

"You don't need to be afraid anymore."

"Psh," she said with a laugh. "I was never afraid. Just thought she was a psycho bitch."

I let the insult pass because my mother deserved it.

"I imagine she'll always hate me, but now she won't be trying to kill me and have me raped all the time."

"Yes."

"Hallelujah." She raised both fists in the air. "That'll be a nice change."

THE SKY WAS clear and the air was cold when we arrived at the outpost. The sunshine had melted the snow, making it far easier to manage as we progressed toward the high gates. Ivory kept up with me, eager for a hot bath and a soft bed.

The guards along the wall recognized me, and the gates swung inward to allow us to enter.

"Home sweet home."

We entered the outpost and were instantly warmed by our surroundings. All the homes and shops provided a cocoon of heat that couldn't be found in the open countryside. Torches were lit, bonfires were in the middle of the dirt roads. The men informed Ian of my arrival, and I took Ivory to my cabin.

Our cabin.

I grabbed the hidden key and unlocked the door.

She stepped inside and immediately shed her coat, looking more at home than in her bedroom at Delacroix. "I'm going to bathe."

"I'll return shortly." I shut the door and walked across the outpost until I entered the stone keep. Ian was there in his heavy fur cape and his black clothing, a beard along his jawline. He spoke to one of the men near the big bonfire before his eyes shifted and locked on mine. Once he spotted me, he tuned out his guard and headed straight toward me.

When I reached him, I greeted him by gripping his shoulder.

He did the same to me. The relief was in his eyes, as if he'd feared I wouldn't return from Delacroix. "Did you find her?"

"Yes."

"So, she fled?"

"She was with other travelers headed to Delacroix, so she decided it was best to join them since she needed something from the castle anyway."

His eyes shifted back and forth between mine—stoic.

"It took her a few days to uncover what she needed to heal the dragons. That was when we departed."

"And you believe her?"

"Yes."

His eyes continued to shift.

"I have no doubt."

"But you also have no sense when it comes to this woman."

"She's not a woman. She's my wife."

"Doesn't matter what she is. She should have come straight here."

"She had good reason to return to Delacroix. She saved us a lot of time—and now we're ready to recruit the dragons into our army. It won't be long before we take the castle with fire, teeth, and claws."

Ian retained his cold composure.

"We can trust her."

"She could have told her father everything."

"He had no idea she was there."

"You don't know that—"

"I stayed with her for about a week. Her brother snuck her all her meals, and no one ever came to the door."

"Her brother was in on it?"

"Yes. He was a prisoner with her at the Crags."

His eyebrow cocked. "How'd he end up down here?"

"His girl won the lottery, and he came down to save her."

Ian paused as he digested the tale.

"That's the reason why he helped her, because he doesn't agree with the policies they enforce."

"And you believe him?"

I considered the question for a long time. "I'm not saying I trust him fully, but if he were going to snitch to his father, he would have done it by now. Will he openly oppose his father? Probably not. But in the dark, he's loyal to his sister."

"I don't understand why she's helping you. I don't understand why she's turning her back on her family for you. Love isn't the reason because love isn't strong enough for that kind of betrayal."

I wanted to tell him the truth. He was more than just my brother. He was my best friend. But I knew exactly what his reaction would be. "Because she knows I'm the one true king. She knows her father's claim to the throne is false. She wants to make it right."

"Even so..."

"You know I promised her I wouldn't kill her father."

His eyes narrowed. "That's a promise you never should have made."

"It was the only way to get her cooperation."

"Then you keep your promise, but that promise doesn't apply to the rest of us."

It was a loophole she hadn't foreseen, and now that I was buried deeper in this plan, I felt like shit about it. "If she gets us the dragons and hands us the keys to the Kingdoms, I think it's the least we can do."

Ian held his silence, his jaw clenched hard. "The second Mother steps foot in that castle, she'll stab her sword straight through his throat—just the way he did to Father. No amount of gratitude will change that."

No, it wouldn't. It would be up to me to convince her.

"What's the next step?"

"Ivory and I will ride to HeartHolme, rest, and then venture to the island."

"After she heals them, how do you plan to earn their allegiance?"

"If I fix their wings, they'll be indebted to me."

"Do dragons understand such a thing?"

No idea. "I'll figure it out. We'll leave in the morning."

He gave a slight nod. "Ride hard."

I STEPPED into the cabin with two trays of hot food.

Ivory was asleep in bed, the sheets below her arms so her tits popped out slightly. Her hair was all over my pillow, and the furs were pulled up toward the headboard to keep her warm.

I set the food on the table before I undressed and had a bath. It'd been five days of solid travel, and the second dirt and oil were off my skin and hair, I felt like a new man. I dried off with a towel and returned to the main room, the fireplace greeting me with its warmth.

Ivory was awake now, eating in the armchair near the fire, wearing one of my shirts she must have found in a drawer. Her eyes were still heavy like she was dead tired, but she couldn't turn down a hot meal.

I put on my underwear and sat at my desk. We ate in silence, hardly looking at each other.

She scarfed down her food, but I still finished before she did because I ate like a bear. When I was done, I watched her, watched her eat every single crumb before she sucked off her fingers and wiped them with a napkin. Then she left the tray behind on the table and climbed right back into bed. She turned and faced the opposite wall, as if she would fall asleep the second her head hit the pillow.

"Baby."

"Hmm?"

I got under the covers and pressed my body to her back. My hand moved down her stomach to the area between her legs, and I rubbed the little nub that I could taste on my tongue without even kissing her. She gave a slight moan and rocked her hips just a little bit, but she didn't turn over. "I'm so tired..."

My head dipped to her shoulder, and I pressed a few kisses to her soft skin. My lips made their way up, moving to her neck and her jawline. My fingers continued to rub her in a circular way, slowly increasing the pressure and pace. "You think I give a damn, baby?" My arm slid under her neck, and I cradled her head toward me, my lips catching hers.

The landing was soft, the combination of our lips like a flame from a candle. Slow and purposeful, our mouths moved together, and within seconds, her hips were thrusting to meet my fingers and her hand was in my hair.

My dick was between her ass cheeks and against her lower back, drooling at the tip out of eagerness. It'd been five days since we'd left Delacroix, and fucking against the cavern wall wasn't the same as against a soft mattress with clean sheets.

I rolled her onto her back and moved between her open thighs. Without our lips breaking apart, I sank inside her, and when I was balls deep, I let out a drawn-out sigh of pleasure. My eyes opened and I looked into hers, seeing the same fire in her eyes that burned in mine.

I felt it, that weight in my chest, that connection between our souls that was both painful and exhilarating. It hurt, but it hurt in the most addictive way. Sex had always felt good, but it had never felt like this. I'd been with a lot of women in my lifetime, but the pleasure had never moved beyond the physical. With Ivory, I could feel it everywhere, in my blood, in my heart, in my soul.

She tugged on my ass and panted against my mouth. "Huntley..."

I could feel every inch of her, feel her in such intimate detail that I could anticipate every change before it came. So many nights spent this way had taught me everything about her body. What she liked. What she really liked.

What made her say my name. What made her toes curl. Right now, I could feel her ironclad grasp on my length, and I knew she was just inches from the edge. "Come on, baby."

Her nails scratched my back.

"I want to give it to you." My thrusts remained steady. I couldn't go any faster, not without releasing my load too soon. I always let her go first, always let my wife writhe in pleasure before I followed.

She gave a moan as her nails started to cut me deep. "Yes..." Her eyes turned glossy with unspent tears. "Huntley..."

I was lost at the sound of my name. My thrusts quickened as I exploded, grunting like an animal, releasing all the tension I'd carried on our long trek here. Balls deep, I gave it to her, filled my wife for the hundredth time.

Her face moved into my neck as she finished. She grasped on to me hard, moaning and dissolving her tears into my skin.

We both breathed as we came down from the high, our bodies loosening around each other. I gripped her by the back of the head and pulled her back to the pillow. "Don't you ever tell me you're too tired again."

A tear escaped and rolled down her cheek.

"Say yes."

Her answer was immediate. "Yes."

I pulled out and rolled over, lying on my back with the sheets at my waist.

She was on me right away, curling up into my body, holding on to me like I was her favorite pillow. It was the same position we took every night, whether it was in a bedroll under the stars or in the comfort of my cabin. When she was gone, I forgot how to sleep, how to get comfortable. And now it felt like she'd never left.

24

IVORY

First thing in the morning, we had breakfast then departed the outpost.

It was strange to be there again, especially when my last memories of this place were when Huntley and I were enemies. Never in a million years did I imagine we would be married shortly after we left. And I never imagined how complete our nuptials would make me feel.

Ian met us by the gate, the reins of the horse in his hand. "You have supplies for three days. Ride hard—because a storm is coming."

"Why does it seem like there's always a storm coming?" I blurted.

Ian shifted his eyes to me. "Because there always is."

Huntley took the reins. "Anything you need me to bring to HeartHolme?"

He withdrew a tied scroll from his pocket. "May as well save an emissary."

"For Mother?" He tucked it into his pocket.

"Yes." At Huntley's height, Ian looked just as much a king with that fur cape over broad shoulders. His eyes were the same color, but they had a greater sharpness to them than Huntley's did. They possessed more pain too, like he carried the world on his shoulders. Or perhaps he carried his mother's resentment instead. "Our scouts say the Plunderers are passing to the west. Be careful not to cross their path."

"I will." Huntley brought him in for a one-armed hug.

Ian reciprocated then quickly withdrew.

They reminded me of my relationship with Ryker—just with less talking. "Thank you for the horse."

Ian shifted his gaze back to me and stared.

"And for riding with your brother to rescue me."

He turned his back to me and walked off.

"So, my mother-in-law is a bitch...and my brother-in-law is an asshole...and my half sister-in-law is also my half sister, and she hates me." I gave a slight nod. "That's fine...totally fine."

"He's not an asshole." Huntley turned back to me. "He just trusts less easily than I do."

"So, that means you trust me?" I asked. "Because when you climbed into my bedroom, it didn't seem like you trusted me then. In fact, you were about to kill me."

He stared down at me, his gaze hard. "Are you trying to piss me off?"

"Just making a point."

"I'm not in the mood for your points, Ivory."

"Ivory?" I asked because I never heard him say that name. "Don't call me that again."

The anger faded from his eyes. It was a subtle movement, hardly noticeable.

"For this to work, we need to trust each other. And I trust you—implicitly. I need the same from you."

He pivoted his body closer to me, his height nearly rivaling the horse's.

"You should have trusted me when I went to Delacroix. I would never betray you, and you would never betray me."

He continued to stare. "I trust you, baby."

I released a drawn-out breath, feeling the relief. "I just don't want us to get separated again, and you wonder if it was intentional or I have a trick up my sleeve or something..."

"We won't get separated again. Not letting you out of my sight."

Good. Because my world didn't feel the same without him in it. I felt lost, like a piece of myself had been left behind.

He continued his stare, as if he could hear my thoughts as I spoke them in my mind. "You will earn my family's trust as you've earned mine—and they will treat you like family."

"I can't see that ever happening with your mother..."

"I didn't see it happening with me either, but look at us now."

I CONSIDERED myself an outdoors kind of girl. I could work in the heat, get so sweaty that my shirt clung to my back, and it didn't bother me one bit. But these long travels by horseback got old...quick.

When we got to HeartHolme, we would leave again, and I was already dreading that.

Maybe I was a princess after all.

Huntley kneeled by the stream and refilled his canteen before he took another drink. Our horse did the same, his hooves submerged in the cold water as he drank his fill. We stopped for a short break, the sun high in the sky, the earth now dark with dirt because the snow didn't fall this far south.

"How much farther?" I asked, enjoying the shade under the tree.

"A day."

My back was sore from sleeping on the ground, and my thighs were bruised from straddling a horse for two days in a row. I couldn't wait to be home, to be upstairs in our bedroom with the fire roaring. The sun rose and filled the bedroom with warm light, and that was my favorite part of waking up in the morning.

"I can tell this isn't your thing." He filled his canteen again and took another drink.

"Do you hear me complaining?"

"I know exactly what you're thinking without you sharing a single word."

I rolled my eyes. "Alright...it's not my thing."

"You'll get used to it."

"Yeah, I don't think I will."

"You're strong, baby. Don't underestimate yourself."

"I know I'm strong. I know I can do anything. But actually enjoy it? That'll never happen."

He rose to his feet as he capped his canteen then wiped his mouth with the back of his forearm.

"Do you enjoy it?"

"I enjoy being in the wild. I enjoy the solitude."

That didn't surprise me. "Is that your dream?"

He turned to look at me, a behemoth of a man, his weapons across his back, his shoulders broad like a mighty oak.

"To have a quiet farm somewhere...raise a family?"

He joined me under the tree then squatted down so we were eye level. With his forearms on his knees, he considered the question. "Yes."

"That's hard to do if you're king."

"But one day, our son will take my place."

"Or daughter."

His gaze held mine.

"Your mother is Queen of the Runes."

"It's different in Delacroix."

"Then change it. You'd have the power to do that."

After a long consideration, he gave a nod. "You're right."

"Damn right I'm right."

He gave a slight grin. "I can't imagine you giving up the castle for the wildlands."

"If you build me a nice house with a fireplace and a bath, I'm happy."

"So, you'd move with me?"

"Of course. What else would I do?"

His stare continued, piercing into my eyes with his intensity.

"You said you'd never let me out of your sight again, right?"

He nodded then rose to his full height once again. His head turned to the left, and he suddenly became very still.

"What?"

He raised his hand to silence me.

That wasn't good.

When I strained my ears, I heard it. People were approaching.

He turned to the horse and tugged it away from the stream even though it was mid-drink. "Hurry."

"Who is it?"

He mounted the horse then directed the beast toward me. "I said come on." He leaned down and extended his hand.

Just when I grabbed his hand and he pulled me into the saddle in front of him, an arrow whizzed by, hitting the exact place I'd been just a moment ago.

He kicked the horse hard and tugged on the reins. "Move."

The horse took off at a sprint, and I tried to find something to grab on to. I was always behind him, but now I was in front, shifting forward over the saddle as the horse flew across the dirt. I grasped the pommel with both hands.

Huntley hooked one arm around my waist and anchored me to him so I wouldn't fly off the horse. With a single hand, he grasped both reins and directed us through the trees, forcing us both to duck under branches that would knock us clean off the saddle.

"Who's chasing us?"

"Plunderers."

"Why?"

"Why not?"

The chase ensued, but we were running so fast that I couldn't even see who was chasing us. Even if I wanted to look, Huntley's massive size blocked them from view.

"How do you know they're still behind us?"

"Because I do." He made a sharp turn around some rocks then halted behind the boulders.

The galloping grew louder, and then a moment later, they rode by, their heads covered with animal skulls. They didn't even notice us because they were riding so hard. I released a heavy breath, relieved it was over.

"We can't outrun them to HeartHolme. You're going to have to help me."

"What do you need me to do?"

"Get out your bow and shoot them down as I ride."

"What?" I asked incredulously.

"You're a good shot, baby."

"But I've never done it on a horse."

"You can do it."

"I'll miss—"

"Then don't miss." He kicked the horse and took off again. "I won't let you fall, alright? Trust me."

Fuck.

The Plunderers doubled back quickly, realizing what Huntley had done. They were on our tail once again.

"It's either this, or I hide you and keep riding."

"I'm not leaving you."

"Then shoot down these fuckers."

It took me a second to find the strength to release the pommel, my only lifeline. His grip tightened over my stomach, locking me in place so I wouldn't tip over and fall. I fumbled for my bow and arrow then tightened it to the string. There was so much bouncing, so much veering left and right that I couldn't hold my arrow steady.

"I know you can do it, baby."

"Get me a shot."

"We've got a guy on our left."

I turned the other way and aimed. There were two riders, and one was equipped with a bow and arrow too. I pulled the string and released, and my arrow completely missed the mark.

"Hold your breath," he said. "Focus."

The other rider fit his string with an arrow and released.

It hit Huntley right in the side.

Huntley gave no reaction—like he didn't even feel it.

But it pissed me the fuck off. "You're going to die, mother-fucker!" I put that arrow on the string so fast and fired.

It hit the rider right in the head, and he went down, knocking off the archer behind him. The horse rode off elsewhere now that he was free.

The smile was in his voice. "That's my girl."

Another rider came up on our right, and I did the same, hitting him in the chest on the first try. "Bye, bitch!"

More riders came, all firing arrows at us.

I nocked several arrows to the string and fired at once, taking down more than one guy at a time.

Huntley kept me steady and kept the horse on track, letting me do the rest.

I must have killed off enough of them because they stopped coming.

"Where'd they go?" I peered around Huntley to get a look and saw them pull back. "That's right! Go fuck yourselves! All of you!"

"Alright." Huntley pulled me back in front of him. "Enough."

"Cunts..."

"Take the reins."

"What?"

He forced them into my hand. "Just take them." His hand moved to the pommel, and he slouched over me slightly.

"Huntley?"

He was quiet.

"Oh my gods, you're hurt."

"Keep riding."

"We need to stop—"

"They can't see us stop. Otherwise, they'll come for us again."

AFTER AN HOUR of riding and no pursuit, I stopped in the middle of the trees and dismounted.

Huntley practically fell off. He had to grip the horse as a crutch the entire way down, and he nearly lost his footing when he reached the ground. He lowered himself to his knees on the grass, and that was when I saw the damage.

Several dozen arrows were lodged in his back.

"No..."

He lowered himself to the ground and lay on his side. His face was ghostly white, and for the first time, he actually looked weak.

"I...oh my gods...Huntley." I was in shock. The whole time we were riding, he was taking those arrows to his back, and he didn't give any indication that it was happening. He was calm the entire time. His body didn't jerk every time they sank into his flesh.

Now I knew why he'd put me in front.

I sawed the arrows down to the tips so I could remove his cloak. His armor was underneath, but it hadn't been enough to stop all the arrows. There were dents where other arrows had struck and bounced off. Others had only impaled the material and not his flesh. But the rest...made it through.

There were at least six of them.

"Get the arrows out."

"You'll bleed out."

"I heal quickly...remember? I can't heal...can't heal...if they stay inside."

I could barely see right now. The tears were too much.

"Baby...I'll be fine."

I fisted the first one and tugged.

He gave a grunt when it pulled free, some of his flesh on the tip.

The tears got worse.

With a steady hand, I did each one, tugging it out and letting the pool of blood drip to the ground. I rushed to the horse and grabbed the emergency supplies Ian had packed for us. I found cotton gauze and returned to wrap him up, to put pressure on the wounds to stop the bleeding. "I've never fixed a person before...but I can try."

"It's fine." He closed his eyes. "I just need a minute."

I remained squatted down beside him, my tears dripping onto his arm.

"Stand guard."

I did my best to swallow my tears and get to my feet because he was right. We were in the middle of nowhere, stopping without taking a look around, and I had no idea what new dangers awaited us.

I stepped away from him and scanned the area.

We were alone.

My gaze passed over the brush and trees. It was all green, but then there was a spot of black, and I halted. My head slowly turned back to see what had caught my eye. It was probably a rock. A boulder that was dark like the nighttime.

My eyes settled in place...and my heart leaped into my throat.

We weren't alone.

He stood just on the outskirts of the tree line, almost blending in with the surroundings because he was so still. His eyes were so dark they looked like graphite, and his pronounced cheekbones made his expression seem feral. He looked young, not more than a few years older than me, and his dark-blue garb was a color I hadn't seen anyone wear before. But the most telling aspect of him at all was his skin.

It was fair in most places...but black in others.

My breaths came out shaky, and for the first time in my life, I felt fear in its purest form. As a prisoner in the Crags, I was scared, but that felt like a vacation compared to this moment. He wasn't Teeth. He wasn't a Plunderer. He wasn't a Rune. Wasn't an outcast.

Necrosis.

Without taking my eyes off him, I withdrew my blade from the scabbard and gripped the hilt with both hands. A level of focus I'd never known descended on me, a second vision, a surge of energy. My life was on the line—and so was my husband's.

He held my stare without blinking. Without breathing. He was the stone in the mountain, an inanimate object, not a living person. His thoughts weren't written on the surface of his face, like he was empty inside.

It made me more afraid. It made me afraid because I didn't understand my opponent whatsoever. Couldn't gauge his thoughts. Couldn't gauge his emotions. His intentions. I continued to grip my sword and wait for him to step into the clearing to fight me. Huntley was too unwell to take up his sword, so it would just be me.

Then he disappeared.

It happened so fast, I didn't actually see him leave. He was there. And then he was gone. The blackness faded from the greenery, and the only indication I had that he had been there was the rustle of the bushes nearby—like he just passed through.

WITH MY SWORD IN HAND, I made sure my eyes never left the greenery where he'd been.

Like he'd come back at any moment.

Nearly an hour passed, and I still couldn't drop my guard. My fingers never loosened on the hilt of my blade. I was ready for a battle that would probably claim my life.

Huntley got to his feet. "Let's get going."

I didn't turn around to regard him, to check if his wounds had healed.

He untied the horse from the branch and brought him close. "Baby?"

It took all my strength to finally pull my gaze away from the last spot where I'd seen him. It. Whatever it was. Once my eyes were locked on his blue ones, the relief swept through. "You sure you're alright?"

He nodded before he mounted the horse. "I wouldn't have been if you couldn't get those arrows out. I would have bled out on the inside."

"I can't believe you were taking those arrows the entire time and never said anything."

He extended his hand to me. "I've been through worse."

"I sincerely hope that's an exaggeration." I took his hand and let him help me up. This time, I sat behind him, and my eyes immediately darted back to the tree line where I'd seen the thing watching me.

Huntley kicked his boots into the horse and took off. "Let's get home."

———

THE LARGE GATES opened up ahead, and we passed through into the protective walls of HeartHolme. The second we were cocooned in safety, I finally let my muscles relax, finally took my first real breath.

Huntley handed the horse over at the stables, and we walked into the city that had become home. "My mother will want to see me straightaway."

"I think you should rest first."

"I'm already healed, baby."

"Doesn't mean you don't need rest, Huntley."

He stopped to look at me. "I know she's been worried about me every moment since I left—and now I know exactly how that feels."

The guilt washed over me.

"I'll take you home first."

We walked through the city until we approached the two-story home behind the gate. He got it unlocked then we stepped on to the property, the rosebushes in full bloom. He got me through the front door, and the second we walked inside, it felt the same...but also different.

I looked down to where I last saw Huntley collapsed on the floor.

"I'll be back in an hour." He turned back to the door right away.

"Huntley?"

He stopped at the door, his hand on the knob.

"There's something I need to tell you."

"Can it wait?"

"No." I shook my head. "It definitely can't wait."

After his eyes narrowed, he shut the door behind him and drew close. "What is it, baby?"

"While you were resting and I was standing guard...I saw Necrosis."

There was no reaction on his handsome face, as if he'd only gotten one part of the story and was waiting for the rest.

"He had these big eyes...hollow cheeks...and black coloring to parts of his skin."

Now there was a reaction. A deep breath. A tightness to his face and neck. "What happened?"

"Nothing. We stared at each other for a long time...and then he left."

"Why didn't you tell me?"

"You were incapacitated...and I didn't want to speak a word."

His heavy stare continued, his eyebrows shifting slightly as he processed all that. "Are you certain of what you saw?"

"No doubt. I could make a perfect sketch if you want."

"Why didn't he attack you?"

"Beats me."

He was quiet for a long time, thinking all this through. "I think you should come with me."

"Where?"

"To see Queen Rolfe."

25

HUNTLEY

It was dark now, the city aglow with torches. Lights from the castle were visible through the windows. There was only one direct way into the castle, over a stone bridge that crossed a gaping hole in the rocky outcropping, and we passed over that to the guards standing watch at the entrance to the castle.

Their eyes were on Ivory, someone they couldn't identify.

"This is Ivory Rolfe—my wife."

Her head turned slightly my way, probably because she'd never heard someone say her full name before.

The guards let us pass without opposition, and then we were inside. Guards were everywhere, but they held their silence as we passed through the grand foyer and up the stairs. Lit torches were abundant, highlighting the heavy rugs on the floor, the oil from the paintings on the wall.

We made it to the top floor where my mother's quarters were located, and Asher was there, like a cold sore that never went away. He rose from the table at the sight of us, his eyes always a little hostile, and he directed his stare on Ivory. He didn't speak a word, but his look said everything. "I'll inform Her Highness that you're here. She's been worried." He disappeared down the hallway.

Ivory looked around, admiring the large table in the center of the room. "You think it's a good idea to have me here?"

"She needs to get used to it."

A moment later, my mother walked down the hallway, regal in her queen's uniform. It was gray and tight around her waist and arms. The feathers in her hair were the same color, bringing out the fierceness in her blue eyes. She had a sword on her hip. She was one of the few rulers I'd known to carry her own blades, to fight in her own wars.

As if Ivory wasn't in the room, her eyes were reserved for me. "I'm so relieved you've returned." Her hands cupped my cheeks, and she pressed a kiss to my forehead. She used to do it every night before she tucked me in when I was a boy. Now, she only did it after great stretches of separation. Her hands dropped to my shoulders, and she brought me in for an embrace. "My boy." She was a foot shorter than me, but she could still get a hold of me, surround me in a blanket of her affection. "Are you okay?" She pulled away and searched my gaze, unaware of all the arrows that had pierced my back on the way here.

"No misfortune befell me, Mother."

She squeezed my arms before she let me go. Then the woman I'd known since birth disappeared and the ruthless queen returned. The warmth in her eyes faded as a winter storm covered the sun. Her shoulders shifted back, her neck elongated, and her face was stoic once more.

Her eyes shifted to Ivory—and stayed there.

Ivory held her gaze. She was still. Quiet. She showed no sign of intimidation.

After an eternity of tense silence, my mother looked at me once more. "She's not permitted on the castle grounds. If she returns, I'll consider that trespassing. And you know what I do to trespassers."

When she'd met me on the battlefield, I'd hoped that meant everything had changed. That she'd let go of her anger and resentment. But all that had changed was her murderous desire. She wouldn't rape or kill Ivory. And she wouldn't hand her over to an enemy either. But that was it. "She's a Rolfe—whether you like it or not."

"Not for long."

"You can't break that kind of magic."

"I can do anything, Huntley." That warm greeting we'd just exchanged...it was like it never happened.

"Then I'll marry her again—and again."

That pissed her off. It was written all over her face.

"Our bond is unbreakable. Don't waste your time."

Ivory turned her head to regard me.

I kept my eyes on my mother. "Let go of the past, Mother. Because she's a Rolfe now. She will always be a Rolfe. She will birth my children, and she will be buried beside me in death. And our souls will walk together in the afterlife."

The pain was in her eyes. The betrayal. "Leave us."

Ivory walked out and shut the door behind herself.

Once she was gone, Mother spoke. "Why are you doing this to me, Huntley?"

"I'm not doing anything to you."

"You married her so I wouldn't throw her to the wolves. That threat is over, and now we can dissolve this union."

"I still want to be married to her."

"Why?"

"Because I do." Because I couldn't imagine my life in any other way now.

Her eyes shifted back and forth frantically, unsure what to make of my testimony.

"Ivory got the information she was looking for from her books in Delacroix. She believes she has everything she needs to heal the dragons now. So when I return, we'll have a weapon none of our enemies can fathom. She's the reason this is happening, so you need to drop your prejudice."

"I don't care what she does. I don't trust her."

"Well, I do. I trust her with my life, which she's saved several times now."

She continued her hard stare.

"You need to let this go."

That comment made her turn away, turn her back on me entirely.

"Mother—"

"You'll never understand."

"I was there."

"Still not the same thing."

"Doesn't the fact that she's helping us make you see that she's not like him? She wants to do the right thing. She knows the throne doesn't belong to her family—and she's trying to give it back. What more proof do you need?"

"My eldest son deserves someone better." With her arms crossed over her chest, she looked out the window.

"Your eldest son deserves to be with the woman he wants—and she's the woman that I want."

She slowly turned around and gave me a look I'd never seen before.

"I know that's not what you want to hear, but that's the truth. And it would mean a lot to me if you just tried. Tried to put the past behind you and see her as a different person. I know if you gave it a chance, you'd like her."

She gave a slight shake of her head and looked away.

"She's a lot like you."

"Don't insult me."

"It's not an insult. It's a compliment. Because that woman always has my back."

"She fled to Delacroix just like I said she would."

"To get the information we needed. She never told her father she was there. The whole thing was clandestine."

She kept her gaze out the window.

"It's not going to change, so you may as well accept it."

"And when she betrays you and your entire family, I'm just supposed to accept it?" She turned back to face me, her eyes hard like the butt of my ax.

"She would never do that."

"You really think when we take Delacroix she'll be able to look her father in the eye and not falter?"

"I won't lie, it'll be hard for her, but she would never betray us. She wouldn't have gotten this far if that was her intention. She wouldn't have married me if that were the case. She fought for the Runes at the outpost and saved lives when she sprayed that yeti. She came back for me when the Teeth cornered me. When I followed her to Delacroix, I found her nose stuck in a book, trying to figure out how to heal the dragons. Then on the way here, we were attacked by Plunderers, and she took them all down so we could escape. What more does she have to do?"

For the first time ever, my mother was speechless.

"I know what kind of woman you want for me, what kind of daughter you want to raise your grandkids. You don't want a damsel in distress who sits on her ass while I'm fighting wars. You don't want a woman who doesn't know how to grip a sword, doesn't know how to look death in the eye without blinking. You want me to have a partner—and that's exactly what she is."

The silence seemed to overwhelm her because she didn't speak.

"You need to accept her—for me."

Silence.

"Please." It was a word I'd never spoken before, except perhaps when I was a child and my mother tried to teach me some manners. But those manners were abandoned long ago, and now I never asked for anything—just took it without remorse.

Her arms tightened over her chest, and she dropped her gaze. An eternity of silence passed before she gave a slight nod.

An actual nod. "Thank you." I turned away and returned to the door. Ivory was on the other side of it, near the banister so she could look down the staircase to the floor below. "Baby, come on."

She turned to me but hesitated, like she didn't want to be in my mother's presence longer than she had to. I didn't expect the two to ever be friendly, that this hostility would ever fully wane, but I hoped they could be in the same room together without dread. She joined me, and we returned to my mother.

Mother addressed me. "What else?"

"After we evaded the Plunderers, we stopped to rest. That was when Ivory saw Necrosis."

My mother shifted her gaze, her entire focus, back to Ivory. "It can't be."

"I saw him through the hedges," Ivory said. "He stared at me...and I stared at him."

"Did you kill him?"

"No." Ivory shook her head. "He never attacked me."

Mother's eyebrows furrowed in confusion. "He just left?"

"Yes."

"That's not like Necrosis." Mother turned back to me, expecting more evidence.

"He had black marks across his skin."

"So, you saw him?" she pressed.

"No," I said. "But Ivory's description is more than enough to convince me."

"If Necrosis found you two alone, a strong man and a young girl, he wouldn't have spared you. He would have eaten your souls." Her gaze switched back and forth between us. "To just walk away without provocation is impossible."

"Well, that's what happened," Ivory said. "He disappeared in the trees and never returned."

Mother looked at me once more. "If what she says is true... then Necrosis is ready to feed."

"Yes."

"We must be prepared for war. I will send an emissary to your brother. Now the question remains, should you stay until Necrosis arrives, or should you continue your mission?" Instead of barking orders, she made me feel like a part of the decision, something I respected about her as a ruler. "You're one of our greatest fighters. But I understand how important these dragons are to our success."

She left the decision up to me. "Just because we've spotted Necrosis doesn't necessarily mean they're ready for an attack. It could have just been one that left their lands to feed. He didn't attack us...so his intentions are even less clear. The dragons are our priority, and I'm not sure how long this mission will take. Even if Ivory can heal the dragons, we still have to figure out how to gain their allegiance."

"Giving them the ability to fly isn't enough?" she snapped. "Make it very clear that without the promise of their servitude, they will never leave that island, unless it's by death."

I knew Ivory wouldn't like that attitude, but at least she kept her opinions in check. "I'm not sure how we'll communicate with the dragons. There's a lot we don't know. So I imagine I'll be gone for some time."

"I understand." She gave me a slight nod, as if I was dismissed. "When will you leave?"

"Two days," I said. "We need time to recuperate from our travels."

"I want to see you before you leave," she said. "You're dismissed." The conversation concluded, and she walked away from me like I was a soldier whose only purpose was to follow her orders.

"Yes, Your Highness."

I FISTED a handful of hair and locked her in place against the bed. Her ass hung over the edge, and one of my arms was pinned behind a knee to keep her where I wanted. The fire crackled in the hearth, and the sheets already smelled like us, as if we never left. I stood at the foot of the bed and thrust into her as if it'd been weeks since I'd last had her rather than a few days. The pain in my back was forgotten because the pleasure between her legs was so damn good.

Her hands gripped my hips, and she tugged herself back into me every time I thrust, the two of us sweating and panting as we devoured each other. Her eyes were wet and reflective, old tears from her last climax.

I could fuck her forever.

When her body tightened around my dick again, she raised her head as she began to writhe, but I yanked her back down to the mattress and kept her in place. My fingers tightened on her hair like a leash, and I fucked her that much harder.

"Huntley..."

Fuck yeah, baby.

Her eyes closed as she came, and her little screams filled our bedroom.

"Look at me." I tugged on her hair.

Her eyes snapped open as she gripped my arm.

My cock moved through her wet tightness, slathered in her cream and mine. My dick gave a twitch because it felt so good, and I shifted my body a little closer for the finale. I wanted her to take every drop of my load, to watch it drip down her thighs on her way to the bathroom.

I gave it to her deep and hard, made her wince slightly with every thrust, and that just made it feel better—because she was too proud to complain about my big dick. Too proud to look weak. Too proud to ever admit she was wrong.

My kind of woman.

I released inside her with a loud groan and felt the hot spasms of pleasure all throughout my body. Every time felt like the first time, and it also felt like the best time of my life. With her little body folded underneath me as I dominated her mind, body, and soul, it was so fucking satisfying.

That was why I never got tired of her.

And I got tired of all the rest.

I let my dick soften inside her before I pulled out and let everything spill to the hardwood floor at the foot of the bed. I wiped off my dick with a cloth then pulled my clothes back on.

She lay on her side in the middle of the bed, her eyes already closed like she was ready for bed.

I secured my sword to my hip then walked out.

"Excuse me?"

I turned back, seeing her propped on one elbow with tired eyes.

"You just fuck me and leave without saying a word?"

I continued my hard stare. "Yes."

"Where the hell are you going?"

I stepped back to the bed, her naked body on full display, and her neediness almost made me stay. "Elora."

"Well...a heads-up would have been nice."

"Really want to pull at that thread, baby?"

Her eyes narrowed at the jab.

"I would have been pretty ticked if I'd woken up and you were gone."

"Why?"

"Because of what I just said."

"You know I'll come back."

Frustration entered her eyes because she wasn't getting what she wanted out of me.

"Do me a favor. When I come back, don't stab me again."

"Wow...another grudge. Just don't sit at a bar with a woman I don't know, and we won't have a problem."

"Trust me and don't follow me around. How about that?"

I knew I'd won the argument when she didn't have anything to say.

"I'll be back in a couple hours." I turned back to the door.

"That's all you had to say..."

I turned around again once I was in the open doorway. "I'll bring you some dinner on the way back."

As if our bickering had never happened, her eyes softened. The tightness in her shoulders disappeared, and she got comfortable on the bed once more. "Thanks."

WITH AN ANNOYED EXPRESSION on her face, Elora opened the door. But that quickly changed once she saw me on the other side. "Well, well, well...look who it is." She opened the door wider, and her eyes lit up like the torches that made the city glow throughout the night. "My asshole brother."

The corners of my lips tugged into a smile at the affectionate nickname. "Want to get a drink?"

"Only if you're buying." She moved into my chest and hugged me hard. "And you know I drink a lot..."

My arms locked around her as my chin rested on her head. I returned her affection with a bear hug, squeezing her tightly before I let go. "Then it's a good thing I brought all my savings because I drink more than you do."

We left her house and walked to our favorite pub, a place we'd been going to since I could remember. Ian was usually with us, but now that he was stationed elsewhere, it was rare for the three of us to be in a room together.

We took our seats at the bar and ordered our rounds.

Elora immediately took her glass, tipped her head back, and downed it in a single swallow. "Keep 'em coming."

I hadn't even touched my glass yet, so I cocked my eyebrow as I stared at her.

"Just a warm-up." She grabbed the next full glass from the bartender then pivoted on the wooden stool to look at me head on. "So...how's the wife?"

My eyes immediately dropped down to my open palm on the table, where the scar was still visible in the skin. It would always be there, a token of my marital commitment, the only physical sign of my connection to Ivory. "Angry that I left."

"Left the house?"

"Yes."

"Hmm..." She took a drink. "Sounds a little high-maintenance."

"My baby just doesn't like to share me—with anyone."

"My baby?" she asked incredulously. "Really?"

I called her that so often that I forgot she had a real name. "That's what she is."

"What happened to her being a pain in the ass?"

"Oh, she still is." I gave a slight smile. "But I can handle it."

She took another drink. "I thought this was just a marriage of convenience. I didn't realize you actually liked the girl."

The feelings were slow to develop, like the ice that began to thaw at the arrival of spring, but it still took until summer for the snow to become a stream. "She's hard not to like."

"Really?" She swirled her glass. "Her family took everything from you. I'd say it'd take a lot for you to tolerate her."

"Elora, she wasn't even born when everything went down. You're treating her like a criminal when she hasn't committed a crime."

"I'm treating her like a threat—because that's what she is."

"She would never betray me."

"Oh, did her magic pussy tell you that?" She threw her head back and downed the contents again. Then she motioned for the barmaid to refill her glass. "Thanks, girl. I really need this tonight."

"She wouldn't."

She rolled her eyes. "You're smarter than this, Huntley."

"She has the most magical pussy in the fucking world, but it hasn't clouded my judgment. In every moment of uncertainty, she's proven her loyalty. You've respected my judgment up until this point, and there's no reason you should stop respecting it now."

She gave me a hard stare before she rolled her eyes—real slow.

"Elora."

"What?" She slammed her glass down. "You really expect me to believe that someone would turn their back on their family like that? Isn't that the least bit concerning to you? Even if he is a rapist and a murderer, he's her father. And she would just cut ties?" She snapped her fingers. "Like that?"

"If Mother were just as evil, I'd turn my back on her too. In a heartbeat."

She dropped her gaze down to her glass and began to swirl it.

"She asked me to spare her father—and I agreed. So she hasn't completely turned her back on him. She's not as heartless as you think. In fact, she has more heart than anyone else I know."

Elora was quiet for a while, more interested in her glass than me. "I'll kill her if she hurts you, you know?"

"I know."

She lifted her gaze and looked at me. "I'm not joking."

"Trust me, I know." I took a drink and let it burn all the way down to my stomach.

"How's your mother handling it?"

"*Our* mother."

"That bitch ain't my mother, and you know it."

"She is. She just...struggles with it."

"I haven't spoken to her in three months, Huntley. I don't think that's a normal mother-daughter relationship."

"Well, I don't have a good mother-son relationship with her either. She gave my wife to the Teeth, and I had to march there with an army to get her back. She's threatened to break our marriage with magic, and I've threatened to marry her over and over again so she won't bother. Grass is always greener on the other side…"

"But Mother loves you. Me… She couldn't care less what happens to me."

"That's not true."

"Come on." She slammed her glass down again. "She couldn't care less about me, and that's perfectly fine. I'm not up in the middle of the night crying that my mother doesn't love me, that my father was a jackass." She took another drink to wash down her bitterness.

I didn't support my mother's behavior, but I did understand her thought process better than anyone else. I was the one who was there. I was the one who had to watch her watch me, had to watch all her pride and dignity be stripped away in the vilest way possible. She wanted that part of her to die in the past, but it couldn't, not when new life resulted from it. "I'm not saying I agree with her behavior, but give her some sympathy."

"Sympathy?" She rounded on me. "You just told me this woman gave your wife to the Teeth."

"And I got her back." Well, she got herself back, technically.

"Why do you always make excuses for her?"

"I'm not making excuses."

"That's exactly what you're doing. Right now."

I took a breath and steadied my anger, but that was nearly impossible to do. "You don't understand. And be grateful that you don't understand."

She shook her head, her visage angry.

"I understand because I was there."

She didn't absorb my words fully. It was obvious because she didn't understand. She didn't have a reaction.

"Elora."

She turned to me, the rim of the glass at her lips.

"I understand because I was forced to watch the entire thing."

WE SAT THERE for a long time, neither one of us really saying anything. Elora was quick to fire like a cannon, but now she simmered like a warm pan on the stove. Her eyes were on her drink most of the time because she didn't know where else to look.

It wasn't hard for me to get the barmaid's attention, and I ordered something hot to eat to go with all the booze I'd drunk. There were other people in the bar, regulars I recognized, others I didn't. I gave her plenty of time to speak, and when she didn't, I decided to move on. "Seeing anyone?"

She stirred slightly at the question. "I'm sorry, Huntley... I just don't know what to say."

"You don't need to say anything."

"I can't even imagine...but I guess now I understand. I understand why she's so deranged...and why you always put up with it."

"Trust me, I don't always put up with it."

"You know what I mean."

The barmaid put the roast beef sandwich in front of me, so hot with steam I couldn't touch it for a couple of minutes. "You never answered my question."

"Like I'd walk into that trap..."

"What? I talk to you about Ivory."

"And that's it. Ivory is the only woman you've ever mentioned."

"Because she's the only one worth mentioning. Is there someone worth mentioning in your life?"

She turned on the stool and faced me. "You don't need to do the dad thing with me. I'm perfectly capable of taking care of myself."

"The dad thing?" I asked.

"You know exactly what I'm talking about, Huntley." With her fingers wrapped around her glass, she stared at me. "You did it the whole time I was growing up, but now I'm an adult, and you don't need to do it anymore. Just be my brother."

"I am asking as your brother."

"I see the way you scare off the guys who stare at me."

"Doing that as your brother, Elora."

She chuckled before she took a drink. "Alright. His name is Victor."

"Victor...stupid name."

"Wow, couldn't even get past the name." She laughed before she took another drink.

She was right. I already didn't like him. "Tell me why he's good enough for you."

"He's not good enough for me. But that's not what I'm looking for right now."

I didn't like that one bit. "Don't waste your time, Elora."

"So, you can waste your time with whores, but I can't? Why can't there be a brothel for women? With a bunch of sexy men ready to service our needs?"

I suddenly lost my appetite. "I'm going to be sick."

"Hey, you went there."

"No. You're the one who talked about going to a brothel for women."

"And isn't that a genius idea? Women like sex too, you know."

"Trust me, I know." Ivory had woken me up in the middle of the night throughout our entire stay in Delacroix. I'd be dead asleep, and then she'd be on top of me, her thighs straddling my hips.

She scrunched up her nose in disgust. "Anyway...we're just having a good time."

"Where did you meet him?"

"He delivered my materials to the forge. He flirted. I flirted back. You know how it goes..."

"Elora, you can have any guy you want. Don't waste your time on a deliveryman."

"And you could have any woman you want, but you waste your time on the daughter of the man who raped your mother and murdered your father." She raised her glass in the air. "Touché."

She was a lot more than that, but I was tired of repeating it. "If you gave her a chance, you'd see that you're wrong."

She finished her final drink and left the empty glass on the bar. "When do you leave?"

"Day after tomorrow."

"Already?"

My food had finally cooled off, so I started to scarf it down. "Ivory and I are returning to the dragons."

"That's going to go really bad...or really well."

"I hope it's the latter."

"Yeah, me too. It'd be pretty badass to see you return home on the back of a dragon."

I had a feeling it wasn't going to happen like that. "On our journey here, Ivory saw Necrosis in the wildlands."

"What? You're asking me if I'm seeing anyone while sitting on this the entire time? What's wrong with you?"

"I don't know what this means, but Queen Rolfe is preparing for war."

"You mean, another war."

"I'm sure Ian and the others will return to HeartHolme. They're too vulnerable at the outpost."

"Hope you're right. Wait... So that means you're still going to leave?"

"We don't even know if Necrosis will actually attack, so I can't wait around. Getting the dragons is our top priority. Not having Ivory and me in the fight won't change the outcome."

"I know not having her around won't change a damn thing."

"She's actually great with a bow and pretty decent with a sword."

"Not as decent as I am," she said coldly.

"I need you to be careful, Elora. Always have your armor ready to go. Make sure you've got your best weapon ready."

"Psh, this isn't my first time…"

"But treat it like it is. Confidence is the key to success. But arrogance is the path to failure. Don't become complacent and lose your head. I'm not ashamed to admit that Necrosis is an enemy that I dread to face—even after all this time."

With the serious tone as the backdrop, she ceased her sarcastic quips. "Come on, you know I'm always careful. I doubt I'll be in this fight. I'm usually tasked with weapons duty…"

"And it's a pretty important duty, Elora. Our lives depend on it."

She gave a nod in appreciation.

I waved down the barmaid. "I'll take another one of these to go."

"You're that hungry?" Elora asked, her eyebrow raised.

"Oh, it's not for me."

"That little girl can eat something like that?"

I gave a slight grin. "Like I said, I think you'd really like her if you gave her a chance."

26

IVORY

I woke up to a scratchy beard against my face and soft lips against mine. My mouth parted, and a breath filled my lungs. Then my lips felt the pressure again, the caress of a lover.

My mouth reciprocated as my eyes opened to see intense blue eyes.

"Wasn't sure if I should wake you or not."

"If that's how you're going to do it, you should always wake me up."

He walked away as he pulled his shirt over his head. "Dinner is on the table. I'll get the fire going again." He dropped his breeches too, getting down to just his underwear. Sculpted muscles on top of sculpted muscles comprised his strong physique. Even without armor, he was protected.

I noticed the little scars on his back with a twinge of anger. "What'd you get me?"

"Roast beef sandwich and mashed potatoes."

"Oh my god...that sounds amazing." I hurried out of bed and sat in the armchair near the fire. In his baggy shirt, I ate everything he brought me, licking the juice off my fingertips as I went. The squirrel in the cave never tasted this good. "How's your sister?"

He sank into the other armchair, his massive shoulders like two boulders. "The same."

"Which is?"

"A brat."

I chuckled. "I know you don't mean that. I have a brother too, remember?"

He kept his eyes on the fire.

"Really. How is she?"

"Still not happy about you."

"Well, she's gotta come around sometime, right?"

"I don't know...she's pretty stubborn."

I scraped the potatoes out of the box with my fork, enjoying their buttery fluffiness. "What did you say to your mom at the castle?"

His eyes shifted to me. "I told her she needs to accept you."

"Ha." I took another bite. "Nice try."

"She listened."

"Doesn't mean she'll actually do it."

"Said she'd try."

"Well...I'll believe it when I see it." I would always be dirt underneath that woman's shoe. She would be totally indifferent to me if she didn't hate me so much.

"She doesn't trust you, but I vouched for you."

"She'll never trust me—and that's perfectly fine."

"Ivory."

The way he said my name silenced me. The fact that he said it at all silenced me.

"I got my mother to come to the table. Now I need you to meet her halfway."

"And how do I do that?"

"Be yourself."

"I've been myself this entire time...and she didn't care for it."

"Well, now she's ready."

I wasn't exactly thrilled about having any kind of relationship with that woman, not after she'd tossed me to the Teeth and caused me these scars on my thighs for the rest of my life. But holding the grudge wouldn't get me far, and this seemed important to Huntley. "Alright."

He turned back to the fire.

"I'm actually more interested in a relationship with Elora."

He gave me a side glance.

"You know, because we're related."

"You think I'm stubborn? You think I hold a grudge? I've got nothing on her."

"Yes, I know... She was lovely last time we spoke."

"Then let it go."

"That's hard to do, knowing she's my sister."

"She's not your sister, baby. You're related, but that doesn't make you family."

I could hear the protectiveness in his voice, the way he guarded her like she was the treasure that everyone wanted. It reminded me of the way he protected me against those who wanted my head on a pike. "Are you going to be gone all day tomorrow?"

"No."

"Then can we have sex all day?"

He turned and gave me his full look, a slight smirk on his lips. "Sure, baby."

"Can't wait." I wiped my hands on the linen cloth before I kissed him on the shoulder. "I'm going back to bed." When I stepped away, he grabbed me by the arm and pulled me back. After a tug, I ended up on my ass across his lap. His arms cradled me to him, placing me right against his chest.

My arm hooked around his neck, and I dropped my head to his shoulder, the hardest but most comfortable pillow I'd ever had. The fire crackled in the background, and he rested his chin on my head, his powerful arms keeping me close to him. We stayed like that for a long time, until I fell asleep.

"I DON'T WANT TO LEAVE." The day had passed in the blink of an eye, morning becoming afternoon, and afternoon becoming night. The fireplace was lit once more, filling our bedroom with heat and light. "Can we stay another day?"

He lay beside me with my leg hiked over his hip, his eyes across from mine. "No."

I gave a sigh of disappointment.

"It's too important."

"You do realize we'll be there for a long time, right?" We wouldn't just arrive, I'd heal their wings, and then we'd take off back to HeartHolme. There would be hiccups along the way, and then communicating with the dragons...not even sure how to go about that.

"Yes."

That meant uncomfortable nights in a bedroll, terrain filled with murderous outcasts, insects flying around all the time. "Maybe we should take some men with us."

"The fewer people who know about this, the better."

"If we return with the dragons, where will they go?"

"We have a large cavern in the rock."

"I don't think dragons are going to want to live underground."

"That's the only place we have that's big enough for them to sleep. They can spend the rest of their time flying around and doing whatever dragons do."

Burning and eating everything? "I hope I can heal them..."

"I know you can."

"Reading about it in a book isn't the same thing as doing it."

"It might take some time, but you'll figure it out." His blue eyes shone with confidence, like he truly believed I was capable of this. It wasn't smoke up my ass. It wasn't a manipulation.

I wouldn't be able to leave that island until I fixed them. I wouldn't be able to forgive myself if I left them in the same state as when I arrived. I would do everything I could to give them back their wings, whether they helped us or not.

He must have read the unease in my eyes because he said, "You've got this, baby."

"How do you know? How do you know I'll pull this off?"

"Because I know how much you care."

———

BRIGHT AND EARLY, we gathered our things and left the house that had become my new home. When I returned to Delacroix, the bed I'd slept in for years didn't feel right. It didn't feel like the bed I shared with Huntley. It was hard to say goodbye, like I was leaving behind a piece of myself.

When we left through the gate, Elora was there.

It was just after sunrise, and the tired look in her eyes indicated she wasn't a morning person.

Same here, girl.

Her eyes were reserved for Huntley.

"I thought it was unnatural to see a sunrise?" Huntley had a teasing tone when he spoke to her, the kind of affection I'd never witnessed him share with anyone else, not even his brother.

"Be careful, okay?" She lowered her voice a little bit further. "Watch your back."

"I've always had eyes in the back of my head. But now I've got another pair."

Me.

Elora rose on her tiptoes to embrace him. "I'll keep my eyes on the skies—and when I see a glorious dragon, I'll know that you've returned." She gave him a squeeze before she let go.

He gave her a pat on her shoulder before he let go. "Take care of yourself, alright?"

"Always do."

"And ditch the loser."

"He's not a loser."

"Well, he's not a winner either." He stepped away and grabbed his bag from the ground. "Goodbye, Elora."

She didn't say it back, and she flicked her gaze to me instead. The affection faded, and her look filled with a powerful stare of spite. "Remember what we talked about?" She grabbed her dagger out of her belt and held it up, as if she was going to start carving my face like a roasted turkey.

Huntley stared her down. "Elora—"

"It's fine," I said. "She can make all the threats she wants. They're empty anyway."

She gripped the dagger a little harder and went for me. "I'll show you empty, bitch."

Huntley stuck out his arm and caught her.

I didn't flinch. "They're empty because I would die before I let anything happen to your brother."

She lowered the knife and stopped her charge, and Huntley dropped his arm too. He turned to look at me, to give me a hard expression he'd never shown before.

It was almost too much to look at. "Come on, we've got a lot of ground to cover."

AFTER WE STOPPED by the castle for Huntley to say goodbye to his mother, we grabbed a fresh horse from the stables and rode out into the open. The area before Heart-Holme was an open field of weeds and resilient flowers. It was enormous, making it impossible for an enemy to approach the city without being visible from leagues away.

My arms were wrapped around his hard stomach as I held on, and I couldn't see anything ahead because Huntley's enormous body blocked everything from view. All I had were the sights to my immediate left and right. "Why don't we take two horses?"

"Because I'm the better rider."

"I can ride a horse pretty damn well."

"Not well enough to evade enemies if we're attacked."

It was a long day of riding, bouncing up and down, the cold air freezing my hands in front of his stomach. But it finally came to an end at nightfall, and we settled in the shelter of the forest near the stream.

Huntley took care of the horse first, leading it to the stream and then feeding it oats.

I immediately pulled out my bedroll and lay down on the grass, exhausted even though I wasn't the one controlling the reins.

Huntley tied up the horse then built a fire before he started to grill a fish.

I opened my eyes and watched him by the fire. "Where'd you get that?"

He gave me a cold look.

"I know, the stream," I snapped. "But how did you catch it?"

"With my hands."

"What are you? A bear?"

He ignored the question and kept cooking.

He was definitely the size of a bear. And he was mean like a bear too.

When dinner was ready, he served me a dish, and we ate in silence. The firelight was a welcome reprieve from the never-ending darkness of the forest. It also masked the sounds of the wildlife, of the hooting owls and snapping twigs from nighttime predators. But I knew it would be snuffed out the instant we were finished.

He finished first then sat with his forearms on his knees.

"What did your mother say?"

He was looking into the distance when he shifted his look back to me. "To be careful."

"I can see how much she loves you." It was the only time she didn't look like a heartless bitch. She embraced her grown son like a boy, wore her heart on her sleeve, blinked through the moisture that built in her eyes.

His eyes shifted to the fire. "She's a compassionate and fair ruler. You've never witnessed it because she can't see straight when it comes to you. She loves her people the way she loves me. She'd sacrifice herself in a heartbeat to keep them safe."

If Delacroix were attacked, my father wouldn't be on the battlefield. He would send his soldiers to fight for him instead. Queen Rolfe didn't take that approach. She was in the thick of it all, her sword and shield in hand, kicking ass. "If things had been different...perhaps she and I would get along."

His gaze flicked back to me. "Things will never be different, but you're going to get along anyway."

That seemed like a hopeless endeavor to me.

"You're going to do it—for me."

"She handed me over to the Teeth to be eaten, and she tried to have one of her guys rape me. And you really think—"

"It's in the past now."

"Oh? It's in the past? Because I don't think my scars are going to be in the past."

His stoic expression remained, his eyes devoid of emotion. "She agreed to try. I need you to do the same—"

"She was going to have me *raped*."

"And I don't regret that one bit."

"Excuse me?"

"I don't regret it because it led to this."

My body sucked the air deep into my lungs. It was so quick, it actually burned a bit. My heart rate became irregular and unpredictable, painful. "That we're married...?"

He didn't shift. He didn't blink. He didn't anything. "Couldn't imagine being married to anyone else." His look remained unapologetic. He spoke words I was too afraid to say myself. "So, you're going to try for me. And that's final."

WE FINALLY MADE it to the harbor outpost, and after a night of sleep in a real bed, we took off in the sloop. The fogbank was as thick as smoke, and it burned our lungs with every breath we took. I could barely see a few feet in front of me, but Huntley seemed to know exactly where we were going.

He controlled the wheel and barked orders at me, telling me to turn the sails so he could catch the right amount of wind when he needed it. Leaving the coast was the hardest part—because we were going right against the waves.

Several hours later, we broke through the waves and the fog, out into the open sea.

It was beautiful, in a sort of lonely, terrifying kind of way.

I stood at the bow and stared at the never-ending blue horizon, imagining the small dot of the island at the edge of my vision. I had no idea where it was, but I pretended I did.

Huntley came up behind me, pressing his chest to my back. "What do you see?"

"Nothing...and it's terrifying."

"Come on, baby. You know you don't have to be scared with me."

"I didn't say I was scared. I just... It's unnatural being so far from land. I don't even know how to swim."

He stepped forward and came into my view. "You're on a ship, and you don't know how to swim? You told me you could."

"Well, I lied. It's not like I lived near a lake or anything."

"I'll teach you. You know the sword and the bow...but you don't know how to swim. You don't know how to fight either."

My eyes narrowed on his face.

"I'll teach you that too."

"Are you sure that's a good idea? Wouldn't want your girl to be able to beat you up."

That handsome smirk came onto his face. "I'd love that, actually."

———

WE HIT a rough patch in the sea, and the constant rocking of the boat against the big waves made my stomach squirm uncomfortably. I clung to the edge and spilled my guts overboard three or four times.

Huntley took care of the wheel and the sails without a hiccup. The man didn't get sick. He didn't get injured. The guy was invulnerable. "You alright?" He turned the wheel, hitting the wave head on so we wouldn't capsize.

I clung to the edge. "Do I look alright?"

"I can't take care of you right now."

"Asshole, I don't need you to take care of me—"

A wave splashed over the side—and soaked me to the bone.

He kept his eyes ahead, but there was a smirk on his face. "There's a bucket down below. Use that."

My boots slipped on the slick floorboards, and I had to grip the edge so I wouldn't go flying. "It's so stuffy down there..."

"Well, you're going to freeze if you stay soaking wet, so just do as I say."

"Do as you say—"

"Yes." This time, he turned and looked at me. "Now."

I was freezing and sick, so I darted back into the hatch and returned beneath the deck. The ship swayed dramatically left and right, and I lost my footing more than once. I grabbed the bucket and got into bed, just waiting for the nightmare to be over.

At some point, I fell asleep, and when I woke up again, the ship was steady. It bobbed in the water naturally instead of teetering and nearly throwing me overboard. The bucket was at the bedside, but all my vomit was gone from the bottom.

Huntley must have thrown it out.

He wasn't in bed beside me, and my soaked clothes were gone from the floor too.

I rummaged through my pack until I found an alternate outfit then headed back up through the hatch. He was at the bow of the ship, eating an apple as he looked across the smooth water into the horizon. It was early morning, and fluffy clouds made it overcast.

The nausea had passed, but I still didn't have an appetite. He could keep that whole apple to himself. "How much farther?" I came to his side and sat beside him on the bench.

He didn't flinch, as if he'd heard me before he saw me. "Less than a day."

"Good."

He finished his bite before he regarded me. "You look a lot better."

"I can't believe you dumped my bucket. I could have done that myself."

"Didn't want our room to stink."

"But still..."

He sank his teeth into the skin of the apple and ripped off a chunk. "You don't have to be embarrassed."

I looked forward over the horizon, searching for a little dot that indicated the location of the island. "I felt so sick, I thought I was pregnant or something." My hand moved over my stomach, right over the most tender parts.

He chewed his bite, his eyes on the side of my face.

My eyes turned back to meet his. "Why aren't you freaking out?"

"Why would I?"

"Because of all the nausea and vomiting...and what I just said."

He took another bite—as if we were discussing the weather. "Pregnancy is a result of sex. And we have a lot of that, don't we?"

"Still, you're really calm about it."

"I'm not a coward. I don't hide away from my responsibilities."

"I'm confused... Do you want that responsibility?"

He took another bite. "Whenever it happens, it happens."

"Well, I'm not ready to be a mother, so I hope it doesn't happen right this second."

"Then I'll keep taking my herbs."

"What herbs?"

"Herbs that make you temporarily infertile. I've been taking them since I became a man."

"Oh...good to know. Not sure why you didn't mention this before."

"I assumed you would tell me when you were ready to get pregnant, and I would stop taking them."

Again, he spoke about us having a family together so nonchalantly. "And I have full authority over this?"

"Always."

It was just a couple months ago when we were strangers, when he kidnapped me from my home and threatened to kill me. Now we talked about having a family like it was no big deal, like we'd been together for years. "Then that means it really is just seasickness."

He tossed the apple core overboard and finished his bite. "You seem sad about that."

"Just surprised. You seem like the kind of man not interested in children unless his hand is forced."

"You'd be a good mother. Raise my sons to be men. Raise my daughters to fight like men."

That old pain returned to my chest, the throb that intensified in our separation. This time, it hurt, but it also felt good too. It was too much to contain, like too many coins in a treasure chest. "You'd be a good father."

27

HUNTLEY

"We really can't just sail to the other side?"

I dropped anchor and brought the ship to a halt near shore. "No."

"It took days to cross last time."

"And it'll take days again."

She gave a loud sigh when she didn't get her way.

"I can take down any motherfucker who comes our way. But these guys...they're different. The best way to keep me alive and you safe is to sneak through, not parade our boat along the shore and announce our presence."

"What if we sail in the dark—"

"I said no."

Her eyes turned furious. "I'm just throwing out another idea—"

"And I don't give a shit about your idea. This is what we're doing. *Period.*"

Her look only became angrier.

"Let's go." I prepared the rowboat and extended my hand to help her aboard.

She ignored the help and got in herself.

I rowed us to shore and let our bow anchor into the sand. Most of our clothes were left behind on the sloop, so we were just in short-sleeve shirts and pants. Ivory threw her hair up, and while I liked it down and around her shoulders, I loved seeing all of her face, her slender neck, and sharp cheekbones.

She was fucking beautiful.

I moved to the tree line and pulled out my ax. "Ready?"

"Sure."

I continued to stare at her. "Drop the attitude. We're here to survive."

"You want me to drop the attitude? You just treated me like a child—"

"Because you acted like one. You're lazy and would rather take a shortcut."

"Lazy?" She looked like she might slap me. "Every time we move through this jungle, we risk getting caught. Just thought sailing under darkness would be a better choice.

Let's get something straight. This is never going to be a marriage where you just make all the decisions. I'm going to have opinions too—a lot of opinions."

"I've noticed."

A flash of anger moved across her gaze, and for a split second, I thought she was going to slap me.

"Are we done with this? Because we have shit to do."

"Yeah," she said coldly. "We're done."

IT WAS the kind of heat that never left your skin. You sweated everything out, but then absorbed it back in right away. It was a never-ending cycle. Moisture glistened on the fat leaves on the trees, and fruit encased in thick husks was along the ground. I could still make out the last path we'd taken, judging by the slash marks in the foliage, so we followed that without issue.

At nightfall, the torches lit up the island, and that was when mayhem ensued.

One tribe had captured the leader of another, and as he hung from a rope made of vines, they chopped off his arms. They only partially removed one of his legs before he bled out and died, and once it wasn't fun anymore, they just let him hang there. I watched the whole thing, just to understand my enemy, to understand where we were.

Ivory faced the other way, and every time she heard a scream, she closed her eyes, as if that would make it go away.

Now I realized she hadn't made the other suggestion because she was lazy.

It was because she was scared.

Yeti. Teeth. Necrosis. They didn't faze her. But this island full of the worst of the worst...that's what made her lose sleep at night. Having me beside her wasn't enough to chase away all the fear that she would end up just like the guy hanging on the vine. "You should get some sleep."

"Not a chance," she whispered. "Not until we get to the dragons."

"You know I would never let anything happen to you."

"But I'm afraid something will happen to us both." Her knees were close to her chest, and her arms hugged them tightly. "I know it's different for you. They'd kill you. But with me...we both know what they'd do to me."

I didn't let myself consider it when she was with the Teeth, and I wouldn't let myself consider it now. "Not going to happen."

"You're the one who should get some sleep, Huntley. You're the one who's going to keep us alive."

DAYS PASSED, and we traveled in silence.

She stood guard most of the time so I could sleep, and as the days wore on, her eyes became redder. Her face lost its color. She was just going through the motions, waiting until we reached our destination.

Thankfully, we didn't draw unwanted attention, and we made it across the island and deeper into the jungle. Once it became dragon territory, I dropped my guard a bit, knowing the outcasts wouldn't venture this far toward the beasts.

They couldn't fly, but they could still rip a man into two separate halves.

Ivory walked ahead so I could keep an eye on her, and she was too tired to pay attention to her movements, because she tripped on a pebble and nearly smacked her face into the earth.

I caught her by the arm just in time. "We'll stop for the night so you can get some sleep."

She let me pull her back up and didn't give an argument.

That was when I knew how tired she was. I scooped her into my arms and cradled her against my chest.

Her arms locked around my neck, and she rested her head against my chest. Her eyes dropped like heavy curtains, and she was immediately out.

She was lighter than the feathers in my mother's hair, so I carried her deep into the jungle without any exertion. It was easier than letting her walk on her own, at least when she was this tired and might snap her ankle on a branch.

Hours later, I made camp in the thickness of the trees, and she immediately went to sleep in the bedroll. Didn't eat dinner. Just went straight to sleep. I made a fire to cook the meat I'd caught, knowing we were far enough away from the outcasts to get away with it. With only the fire and my wife's deep breaths for company, I looked at the stars between the branches and pretended we were somewhere else.

28

IVORY

When I woke up, the first thing I noticed was how hungry I was.

Correction. How starving I was.

My stomach gave a loud growl as I sat up and blinked through the sunshine. It was definitely past morning. I could tell by the heat level. I sat up and saw Huntley come into my view.

He handed me a plate of meat, potatoes, and some exotic fruit.

I was so hungry, I took it without question.

He gave a quiet chuckle before he stomped out the fire. "You slept for over twelve hours."

"No surprise there..." Traveling across the island felt like a terrible dream that I'd imagined in my head. The dragons should be far more dangerous than the outcasts, but I'd take a dragon over those psychopaths any day.

He took a seat on a nearby boulder, one knee up with his forearm against it.

In silence, I ate, and the stiffness in my back made me miss our bed at home. When I finished everything, I felt like a new person, a person who got a full night of rest and a full breakfast and dinner combined into one. "How far are we?"

"Maybe fifteen minutes."

"Oh, I didn't know we were that close."

"Ready for this?"

I'd read all the books and made all the notes, but there was no way for me to prepare for this part. "Uh...I guess."

"That doesn't sound promising."

"I'm sure I can heal them. The question is, will they allow me to heal them? Because I have to touch them."

"Last time we were here, the dragon didn't seem hostile."

"Maybe because we'd just fed him."

"Well, I have a boar to bring with us." He nodded to the carcass on the ground. "As a peace offering."

"Hope that's enough..."

We left the camp and approached the edge of the forest toward the mountainside. The trees began to thin, and more of the searing sunshine made it through the disappearing canopy. Farther we went until we saw the caverns.

In the exact spot where we were last time, we peered into the shadows and saw nothing.

"You think they're in there?"

"If they weren't, you'd know."

I stood behind the last tree before the open clearing, peering into the darkness, wondering if they were staring back at me this very moment.

Huntley dragged the boar away from the trees then tossed it in front of the open cave. He cut the animal right down the middle, opening the body and revealing the entrails so the smell would be fragrant.

Huntley returned to my side, and we both waited.

Nothing happened.

For a very long time.

I turned to him. "I'm not walking in there."

"Didn't tell you to."

"What if they don't come out?"

"They will."

Then I felt it. A tremor underneath my feet. My eyes darted back to the cave, and the vibration of the earth became more powerful, more distinct. "They're coming..."

The footfalls became audible, and then the shiny scales of the first dragon came into the light. Dark green scales and dark eyes, he looked like the lizards on the ground...but infinitely bigger, with teeth the size of my whole body.

He stared at the carcass on the ground before he lifted his gaze and looked at the trees.

As if he knew.

Dragons weren't like horses or other animals. They had intellect. I could see it in his eyes that very moment.

He inched closer and dipped his head to smell the offering. His nostrils flared, and for just a moment, I could see the swirling flames all the way in his lungs. They closed, and he took a bite, breaking through the bones like they were twigs.

He chewed as he lifted his head again, looking at the tree line where we were hidden.

"I'm going to go for it."

Huntley turned to me. "And by go for it, you mean..."

"Walk up to him."

He released a loud sigh of disappointment but didn't issue an argument. "I don't have a better idea. I'll have my arrow trained on him. That'll give you enough time to run for it."

"I don't think it'll come to that. He knows we're here."

Huntley withdrew his bow and nocked an arrow to the string.

I left my weapons behind and inched past the final tree, letting the sunlight hit me right in the face.

The dragon stilled when he saw me, and his nostrils immediately flared as he sucked in the air around him, as if trying to smell me.

I raised my hands gently. "Uh...hi?"

Still as stone, he stared. The look reminded me of Huntley's, actually.

"The boar is from me... I'm not sure if you remember me from last time."

Dragons must not blink because he hadn't blinked once.

"You have no idea what I'm saying, do you?" I should just be grateful that he wasn't trying to burn me alive right now, but I was disappointed there wasn't a more obvious way to communicate with him. The people who'd exiled him there, could they communicate with him? Those people may not even speak English, for all I knew. "My name is Ivory. I think I can fix your wings."

The same stare continued.

I made the motion with my arms, flapping them up and down like a bird. "Wings." Then I pointed at him. "I want to fix your wings."

He turned his head to look at his own flank as if he understood.

"Yes!" I threw my arms up in the air. "Exactly!"

He gave a quick flinch and ducked his head lower, getting in a defensive stance.

"Shit. Sorry." I lowered my hands again. "Sorry, sorry. Just got excited. I didn't mean to startle you. I just... I think I can fix your wings, if you'll let me try." I made the gesture with my arms again, like an awkward bird trying to fly.

His dark eyes started to shift back and forth, examining me with his shrewd intelligence.

Then I felt it, a cloud of emotion. It pushed against me like a wall, so thick and potent, it felt like ash was in the air and I couldn't breathe. It was overwhelming, the intensity.

My knees went weak, and I found myself lowering to the ground.

"Ivory."

The dragon turned and looked at Huntley behind me.

"I'm okay." My palms flattened against the earth, and I steadied myself. "I think he's...trying to tell me something."

The dragon turned back to me, and once his focus had returned, the sensation grew heavier. It pushed against me from all sides. It was emotion in a physical form, telepathy without need of words. Like swords against my skin, the feelings pierced me everywhere, trying to get deep inside me.

Grief.

Despair.

Hopelessness.

Death.

I felt it all, like he put everything in my hands.

Then I felt the weight lessen, as if he took things from me. Pain. Anguish. Tears. He took them from me like he picked my pocket.

Then the wall vanished.

"What was that?" I looked to him for explanation but knew I wouldn't receive one.

"Ivory, what happened?"

I held up my hand to silence Huntley. "I think he's trying to communicate with me." I got back to my feet and brushed off the dirt from my breeches. "I want to help you. Please let me help you."

He stared at me with that shrewd gaze, those dark eyes ageless in their depth. Then he looked at his flank once more and moved the limb on his back, the limb where his wing should be attached. A quiet whine escaped his ferocious jaws, like a dog in pain.

Within a single breath, I became choked up. Tears burned my eyes because I could feel all his despair with just the single sound. "I'm so sorry they did this to you..." I raised my palms slightly, showing my empty hands. "But I think I can fix you...if you let me try."

He stared at me again, as if deliberating my words, like he somehow understood every word I said.

"You can trust me. I'm not one of those assholes. I would never hurt you."

He took another step closer to me and dropped his head. His eyes were level with mine, his toothy jaw so close to my face I could feel his warm breaths fall across my face.

I closed my eyes—my display of trust.

His nostrils flared as he drew breath, as he pulled my smell deep into his lungs.

Then I felt the thud on the ground.

I opened my eyes and saw him right in front of me, on his stomach.

A smile moved on to my face, but the tears continued to come. "Thank you..."

I CLIMBED up the dragon's body, latching on to the hard scales and spikes as I pulled myself up. The ground had to be at least ten feet below, and I was taller than most of the trees in the jungle.

I examined what was left of his wing, just a nub that had been sawed down to the bone. I examined it for a while, seeing exactly where the blade had hacked and sawed. Just touching it riddled me with physical pain, like I knew exactly how it felt. My fingers made contact with it, and a vision hit me.

A man in armor, hacking and sawing. His face was covered with a metal helmet. Chains were wrapped all around the dragon, so he couldn't escape. He was subjected to the torture then shipped out here to suffer.

I yanked my hand away as if I'd just touched a flame. "You're going to burn this motherfucker alive when I'm done with you."

A quiet growl escaped his lips.

"What is it?"

"Ivory." Huntley emerged, his weapons on his hips, his bow on his back.

"He's with me," I said quickly. "He's not going to hurt you."

He held up the little bag I'd brought with me, which was stuffed with medicinal herbs that I had gathered on our journey. "Here." He tossed it up to me.

I caught it with one hand and set it beside me. "Thanks."

The dragon continued to growl, his head following Huntley's movements.

"Next time you come out here, drop the weapons," I said.

Huntley kept his eyes on the dragon as he walked back to the trees.

"That's my husband," I said. "You don't have to worry about him. I promise." My hands touched the nub everywhere, trying to focus my mind to feel what was left of the nerves, tissue, and bone. It would be hard to recreate the wing, especially when I had no idea what a dragon wing looked like, what the anatomy was comprised of. In this instance, I would have to rely on the memory left in the tissues, in the hope that they would direct my ministrations. "This is going to take a long time, so be patient with me. And it's probably going to hurt a little bit."

He gave a grunt—like he understood.

HOURS PASSED AND NOTHING HAPPENED.

I focused my mind, tapped into the nerves of his body, but no matter how hard I concentrated, I couldn't get anything to happen. I pulled out my notebook, checked my notes a couple times, and tried again.

The dragon looked at me over his shoulder and gave a grunt.

"I told you it would take a long time. So, get comfortable."

He lowered his head to the ground.

"Baby, how's it going?" Huntley kept a far distance away, steering clear of the dragon's jaw.

"Uh, it's not going—as you can see."

"I can also see it's starting to get dark, so we should call it a night soon."

"No. I almost got it."

"Ivory, there's no rush—"

"I said I almost got it. Give me some space."

Huntley stood there, arms across his chest, his weapons still all over him.

Every time I tapped into the electric current of his body, I followed it to the injury, but I couldn't get it to push out. I knew that made no sense. It wouldn't even make sense to another healer because I wasn't healing anything. I was tapping into the body's natural directory to regrow cells and teeth...and trying to apply that to his wing.

I pushed and pushed, my hands feeling the scales burn hot from the energy underneath. Then I felt my hands shift underneath me as something jerked upright.

Roooooaaaaarrrrr.

I jerked back when I heard the dragon cry out. I fell on my back and quickly pushed myself up again.

There it was.

More of his wing.

It wasn't much, just some regrowth of his bone, but it was something. "Oh my gods..."

The dragon looked behind him to examine the wing.

"I did it... I fucking did it!"

He moved the limb and winced at the same time, but he was so happy that he couldn't stop. The whine he gave earlier was replaced by a quiet growl, a growl of satisfaction. His dark eyes shifted to me and held my stare.

"You're going to fly in no time."

HUNTLEY SAT across from me on the other side of the fire. The dinner he'd caught roasted on the spit, and every few minutes, he turned it to char a different side of the meat. Drops of juice dripped to the rocks below and sizzled on impact.

I'd worked all day, but I wasn't the least bit hungry.

I was too overwhelmed.

"You did good, baby." He seemed to understand I was in a mood, so he gave me plenty of silence to process what had happened that afternoon.

"I can't believe I did it..."

"I can." He reached forward and rotated the stick.

"It's going to take so long to finish..."

"We're in no hurry."

"If Necrosis is about to attack, I'm not sure I agree with that."

"We don't know that for sure, and if we don't return with dragons, we won't be able to make a difference. Queen Rolfe has defended her people from every attack on Heart-Holme. She'll continue to do so."

"Do you view her as different people?"

His eyes shifted to me.

"As a queen...and then as your mother?"

"I have to. The relationships are different. As her royal subject, I'm her servant. As her son, I'm her priority. If we don't separate them, no one will respect either one of us. We can't have nepotism in our politics."

In rare glimpses, I saw her as a mother. The rest of the time, it was just a ruthless queen with an iron fist.

The food was finished, so he removed it from the fire and separated it onto two plates he'd packed for the trip. We ate in silence, letting the fire die out on its own. Shadows were cast across the glade, everything farther away obscured in darkness. "I can tell he's in pain."

"He'll be fine."

"The only way I can stop the pain is by healing him...but I can't heal him if I want the wing to regrow."

"All he cares about is having his wings back. The pain is inconsequential."

"I still don't want him to suffer."

"I know you pity him because his wings were massacred, but don't forget he's a ferocious dragon, not a weak dog. When those wings are restored and he's back to his former glory, he won't need your pity."

FIRST THING IN THE MORNING, I found him outside the cave, waiting for me.

"How are you feeling?" I continued to speak to him like he could understand every word I said. Maybe he didn't know the words, but I was sure he could detect the inflection in my voice, my tone.

He lowered his chin to the ground so I could climb aboard.

Thud. Thud. Thud.

"Ivory."

I looked at Huntley, who was looking past me.

I turned to the large cave entrance and saw another dragon emerge. His scales were cobalt blue, the color of semiprecious stone. He was about the same size as the first, and his stare was just as sinister.

He examined me with a predator's gaze, as if sizing me up.

"I'm here to help."

He came closer then looked at the wing of his friend. He gave a growl then nudged him with his snout, as if trying to push him out of the way.

"He wants you to heal him first." Huntley came close to me and was careful not to draw any of his weapons.

"I'm going to heal both of you, okay? But let me finish with him."

The cobalt dragon continued to nudge him.

The green dragon gave a growl and snapped his jaws.

"Hey." I whistled loudly and waved my arms. "I can heal you both. No need to fight, alright?"

"I wonder if they're brothers."

"Why do you say that?"

"Because it reminds me of Ian and me."

"Does not," I said. "You would let him go first. You always let everyone go first."

He turned his head to regard me, giving me that hard stare. "I'd let you go first. No one else."

The cobalt dragon flared his nostrils with an angry breath before he turned back to the cave.

The green dragon dropped his snout back to the earth so I could finish my work.

"Do you have a name?" I asked.

He released a breath, steam coming from his nose.

"How about Pyre? Because you burn your enemies to a crisp."

Another puff of steam came out.

"Alright. Pyre, it is. I'll have to find a name for your friend." I started the climb, grabbing on to the scales as I hoisted myself toward the sky. As I did, I could hardly believe my actions. Could hardly believe I was climbing up a goddamn dragon. I reached his flank and positioned myself at his wing. It was exactly as I left it yesterday, the stump several feet bigger than before. "Alright...let's go to work."

A WEEK CAME AND WENT.

Every day, I worked on Pyre, getting his limb to regrow. At first, it was just the bones at the base that enlarged, but soon, the scales began to thin and the skin branched out into a web. I could see the nerves and blood vessels in direct sunlight, see them break off like rivers. The work was exhausting, and by the end of every night, I felt like I'd run all the way from the Teeth back to HeartHolme.

It was growing dark, so dark that I could barely see my ministrations, and that was when Huntley ordered me down.

"Ivory."

"I'm almost there."

"You can finish tomorrow—"

"Just shut up." I bent the wing slightly, trying to gauge the force it could handle at this point. Regrowing the wing was easier in the beginning because there was only one direction for the growth to take place. But now that the bones had branched off and the wing had become wider, it was a lot more challenging. It was like painting an image from memory—but a memory I didn't have.

I wiped the sweat from my forehead with the back of my wrist before I focused my thoughts once again. I closed my eyes, tapped into the energy at the very edge of the wing, and pushed.

Crack.

Grooooooowl.

"Sorry, sorry." I opened my eyes and looked at the difference.

The wing was complete. "Pyre...look."

He turned his head over his shoulder and examined it.

I let go and backed up so he could move it around.

At first, he just raised it up slightly then back down again. But then he opened the wing wider and gave a hard flap down.

He nearly tipped me off.

"Does that feel right?"

He flapped it harder again then gave a loud cry.

"I can't tell if that's a good sound or not...."

He gave a loud growl before he moved his face to mine, putting his teeth right in my face. A wall of hot breath hit me, blew my hair out of my face. Then he curled his lips over his teeth and rubbed his snout against me.

I realized what it was—a hug. "Aww...you're welcome." I reached my hand out and felt the scales of his face, seeing that they were even harder around his large teeth. "But let's not get too excited. We've got to do the other side now."

He got back on the ground so I could climb safely down.

It was really dark now, and without the sun, all we had was the starlight. It glinted off his scales, giving a faint glow. I felt him before I saw him. Huntley. He grabbed my hand and pulled me away.

In the darkness, I could hear the flapping sound, Pyre testing his wing, too excited to wait until tomorrow.

Huntley took me to our camp in the jungle where we left our supplies during the day. Without our usual fire, it was dark, so dark I could barely see in front of my face. He guided me to the bedroll.

"We should make a fire. I can barely see."

"No fire tonight."

There was something in the sound of his voice that caught my attention. "Why?"

"We don't need one." He dropped his equipment to the ground beside him and got into the bedroll.

"Huntley."

He pulled the covers back and guided me in beside him.

"Why do I feel like there's something you aren't telling me."

"I didn't anticipate us staying here so long."

"And what does that matter?"

"Because having a fire in the same spot for an extended period of time implies there's a camp. And if someone thinks there's a camp, it's only a matter of time before they come to investigate."

All the excitement of today evaporated into thin air.

"It's just a precaution, baby. No one is coming to get us."

"For now..." I lay in the bedroll beside him, afraid of what lay further in the jungle, what could creep up on us while we slept.

His hand cupped my face, his fingers brushing the hair from in front of my eye. "I'd never let anything happen to you."

"It's not just me that I'm worried about..."

"I wouldn't let anything happen to me either." The backs of his fingers lightly grazed over my skin. "We've got too much shit to do—together."

"YOU WOULD THINK I'd be faster this time around, but...nope." I'd been working on Pyre's other wing for a full week, manipulating the bone and tissue to grow back to their usual size, but it took a lot out of me every single day. I was losing weight, not because I was moving around a lot, but because I used so much energy with my mind and hands.

Pyre was getting anxious. His head was permanently turned over his shoulder to face me, to watch me manipulate his wing a little more each day. Sometimes, he flapped the wing involuntarily, and I almost rolled to the ground headfirst. "Pyre, you need to chill. It's going to take me longer if you keep moving."

Huntley was nowhere to be seen, somewhere in the jungle. He might be refilling our canteens or hunting. Or he might be cooking our dinner over the fire, since a fire was far less risky during the day as opposed to at night.

Pyre gave a quiet whine.

"I think I can finish this today...so just stay still."

The blue dragon emerged from the cave and watched Pyre be worked on. He sat there and watched, as if he were standing in line, waiting his turn. I pushed my mind over and over, regrowing veins and nerves, getting the structural stability back.

"Ivory."

"What is it, babe?" I didn't take my eyes off my work, knowing I was racing against daylight.

His voice grew louder because he came closer. "Babe?"

I didn't even realize what I'd called him. It just came out. I'd never even used the endearment before, not with anyone who came before him. "You've got a problem with that?" I lifted my gaze from my hands and met his stare down below.

He wore that rock-hard expression, his usual intensity spreading into his powerful shoulders and the rest of his body. Then he gave a subtle smirk, just the corner of his lip rising a bit. "Pyre can't take off when you're done."

Pyre turned to face him, like he understood every single word.

"Why not?" I asked.

"Because the outcasts will know we're here if they see a dragon flying around."

"Oh..." That thought hadn't crossed my mind.

"He has to wait until dark at least."

I rubbed his hard scales, not sure if he could even feel my touch through his rough exterior. "Pyre, is that okay?"

He issued a low growl.

"There're some bad people on this island. They would hurt us if they knew we were here."

He slowly bowed his head, and that was enough to express his disappointment.

Huntley watched the whole thing. "He understands what you're saying."

"Yeah, I think so too."

"When the sun goes down, you can take to the skies," Huntley said. "Just a couple more hours, man."

"Man?" I asked.

Huntley shot me a glare.

I got back to work on his wing. It took a few hours, but I grew the last bit that he needed. An audible crack filled the night, and that was when I knew I was finished.

Pyre wiggled his wing and opened it to its full length.

"Beautiful, huh?"

He flapped it a couple times, a quiet whine escaping his lips.

"I know, honey..." I rubbed his back, knowing how much this meant to him.

"Baby." Huntley nodded toward me. "Come down here."

I climbed down halfway then dropped to the bottom. Huntley had a lit torch in his hand where he stood in front of Pyre's face. I walked over, getting closer to the glow, closer to Pyre's features.

The second we made eye contact, I saw them.

The tears.

They dripped down his face, reflective in the light like diamonds.

That made me cry too. "Pyre..." My palms flattened against his snout without thinking twice about those incredible teeth, and I pressed my forehead right against his jaws. "I'm so happy for you."

He rubbed his snout against me, one of his tears dripping right onto my head. It felt like a bucket of water had been dumped on top of me, soaking my hair and all my clothes. The moisture traveled to the skin instantly, but I didn't mind the inconvenience.

He lifted his snout and turned away, raising his head up high to look at the stars up above. He stared at them for a long time, his wings folded against his body like he'd forgotten he had them.

"You can do it, honey."

He let out a heavy breath before he opened his wings wide. Enormous, with claws at the very tips for extra damage, they were straight at his sides, ready to flap down to lift him off the ground. He took a few steps before he started to pound his wings, to get the air underneath the webs. His feet didn't leave the ground, and he kept running, like he didn't trust his own body.

But then it happened.

His feet left the ground.

And he soared into the sky.

The only indication he was there was the way he blocked out the light from the stars. A shadow moved across the sky, enormous and powerful.

I didn't notice my own tears until they landed on my lips and layered my tongue with salt.

Huntley's thick arm moved around my waist, and he pulled me a little closer. "I'm damn proud of you, baby."

29

IVORY

The cobalt dragon nearly charged me down when I stepped out of the tree line the following morning. Murderous eyes bored into mine, and instead of steam erupting from his nostrils, it was a black smoke.

"Whoa, calm down. Why do you think I'm here?"

He continued to huff and puff.

Huntley was beside me. "Check the attitude, man. Otherwise, she won't do shit for you."

My eyes popped wide open, and I turned to give him an incredulous gaze. "Did you just say that to a dragon?"

"I don't care. No one talks to my wife like that."

"He didn't say anything—"

"He didn't need to."

Pyre came out of the cavern next, a new spring in his step. He flapped his wings, as if to show them off.

I smiled. "Lookin' good."

The cobalt dragon looked at him with a sneer.

Pyre walked up to me and dropped his head so he could rub his cheek against my body. Not understanding his strength, he knocked me flat on my ass. Huntley was there to pick me up and lift me back to my feet.

"Huntley, didn't you say there were three dragons?" Ever since I'd been there, I'd only seen two. The third never revealed himself.

"Yes."

"Have you seen him?"

Huntley peered to the caverns, as if the third dragon would appear.

Pyre raised his snout and exchanged a look with the blue dragon, a silent conversation passing between them.

"Something happened to him..." Maybe I could speak dragon because I felt as if I understood the exchange between them.

Pyre turned to stare at the cavern for a long time, and he slowly turned back to me, the sadness in his eyes.

Huntley seemed to understand too. "He didn't make it."

I bowed my head and shut my eyes because the guilt that overcame me was too intense to keep up appearances. If I'd been able to heal them when I'd arrived here the first time, the outcome could have been different. "I took too long."

"Don't do that."

"If I'd been here sooner—"

"If I'd trusted you like I should have, we could have gone to Delacroix first and saved time. If you want someone to blame this on, blame me. Not that I feel responsible, because the person responsible is the asshole who put him here in the first place."

The blue dragon lowered himself to his belly against the dirt just the way Pyre had and wiggled one of the stumps of his former wing. He issued a whine as Pyre had, eager for me to get to work.

Huntley stared at me. "You couldn't save him, but you can still save these two. That's what matters."

I felt the moisture in my eyes, felt the hot tears that were only growing in size. "Yeah...I guess."

Pyre bowed his head again and gave me a gentle nudge.

I suddenly felt a layer of affection move on top of me. Warm air. White shores. A cloudless sunset. I felt the wind in my hair, felt like a bird in the clouds. It was peaceful. Easy. "Thank you."

I turned back to the other dragon. "I should give you a name. How about...Storm? Your scales remind me of the ocean at its deepest."

That seemed to be agreeable to him because he lowered his snout onto the ground so I could climb up.

"Well, I've got work to do." I turned to Huntley. "I guess I'll see you later."

"I'll bring you some lunch." His hand moved to my ass and gave it a squeeze.

I smacked his hand away. "Did you just squeeze my ass?"

Both dragons moved in, their snouts pressing close.

He wasn't the least bit apologetic. "And I'll do it again." He gave my ass a hard smack before he walked away.

———

HUNTLEY HAD COOKED dinner in the daylight, so it was cold when we ate. But it was filling and good, along with the potatoes he sautéed. He'd harvested more fruit from the jungle, and there was an assortment on my plate, acting as a small dessert.

He sat beside me, his back against the tree, his arms on his knees. "How'd it go with Storm?"

"He's a lot more impatient than Pyre. Kept snapping his jaws at me."

He gave a quiet chuckle. "He seems bossy."

"Bossy is the perfect word. Pyre is a sweetheart."

"I have a feeling I'll be more compatible with Storm than Pyre."

"Or less compatible—since you're similar."

He looked at me. "We're the same, and we get along just fine."

"We are so not the same. You're stubborn and angry..."

"And you aren't, baby?" He wore a slight grin, like this was all amusing.

"No."

He looked forward again. "Sure. Whatever you say."

"I'm not."

"Okay."

I smacked his arm. "I said I'm not."

"You just smacked me, but yeah, you aren't angry."

I released a loud growl similar to Pyre's and told myself to let it go.

The silence passed for a while, neither one of us saying anything.

"I still can't believe Pyre has wings."

"When he can fly in the daylight, it'll feel real."

"How are we going to get them back to HeartHolme?"

"That's your job."

"Mine?" I asked.

"Pyre likes you, so that should be easy."

"Well, Storm is still pissy with me because I didn't fix him first."

"He better change his attitude. If it weren't for you, he'd never fly again. They may be dragons, but never forget they're forever in your debt."

"I didn't do it so they would owe me. I did it because it was the right thing to do."

"Doesn't matter."

"I'll try to talk to them about it. But now that they have their wings again, I imagine they won't want to fight for strangers."

"Where else are they going to go?" he asked. "They can't go back to where they came from. Remember how they got here in the first place."

How could I forget?

"So, they need a new home anyway."

"I guess that's true."

My back was sore from sitting upright on the dragon all day long, and the rest of my body was exhausted from focusing so hard throughout the day. I wanted to get into the bedroll and pass out, but Huntley and I hardly spent any time together. If we were back at home, we'd at least be doing it all night long, but it wasn't as enjoyable on the hard ground. Most of the time, we did it up against a tree or on my knees, but it wasn't the same as having a nice mattress beneath our bodies. "I'm excited to go home soon."

Huntley stared straight ahead.

"I thought I was an outdoors kind of girl...nope."

Nothing.

"I need a bedroom and a fireplace—"

"Ivory." The tone of his voice silenced me like a slap in the face. His stare remained forward, peering into the darkness, as if he could see something. Or hear something.

It was hard to hear anything over my loudly beating heart. I strained to hear the sounds around us, to search for the snap of a twig under a heavy boot. It became even harder to hear when my breaths grew deep and labored, when the fear started to take off.

Huntley got to his feet and withdrew his ax.

Shit.

I got up too and immediately returned my sword to my hip and threw my bow over my shoulder.

Then I saw it, the glint of torches.

They were so close.

And there were so many. At least twelve.

Huntley continued to face the enemy. "Run."

"What?"

"You heard me." He gripped his ax with both hands.

"I'm not leaving you—"

"Do as I fucking say."

"No—"

He grabbed me by the shoulder and shoved me hard. "These men aren't Teeth. They aren't Plunderers. You know exactly what they'll do to you—and they'll make me watch. I'd rather fucking die."

"Huntley—"

He shoved me hard again. "If I mean anything to you, you will do this." With that, he turned back around and approached the tree line, and the fire got brighter, the torches only a few feet away.

I took one look at his back before I sprinted away.

Sprinted for my fucking life.

I could hear a man's voice, fading the farther I ran. "That's a nice ax there. Fancy sword. Why do I get the feeling you aren't from around here?"

Fuck.

"Tie him up. We'll have a nice conversation back at camp... where we can really get to know one another."

I sprinted in the dark, getting scratches on my face from sharp leaves, and stumbled over invisible rocks and made my knees crack. When I was far enough away, the voices disappeared, but I knew exactly what was happening.

Huntley was right. I would be useless to him.

But he couldn't take on twelve psychopaths by himself.

But I knew someone who could.

I broke the tree line and entered the open clearing before the large cavern. A blanket of stars was overhead, glistening like diamonds in the vast emptiness. I reached the cave and let out a scream. "Pyre!"

Silence.

I didn't have a torch to light my way, and since it was even darker inside that cavern than out here, I stayed put. "Pyre!"

Thud. Thud. Thud.

I backed up, knowing he was coming.

A minute later, he emerged, his wings folded to his body. He looked down at me and seemed to read my unease, because he dropped his head and brought it close to my face. His snout even gave me a gentle rub.

"I need your help."

He raised his head so our eyes could meet.

"The bad men on the island took Huntley...and I can't save him."

Pyre stared at me with his big eyes.

"Please."

He looked up past me, as if he could see the action in the forest. *No.*

I heard the word in my head, heard it echo like it was spoken in a vast chamber. "Did you just...talk in my head?"

His eyes dropped back to mine. *Yes.*

"What...how...wait..." I had so many fucking questions, but now wasn't the time. "Why haven't you spoken to me before?"

I needed to trust you first.

"Okay...if you trust me, then you need to help me."

No.

"Pyre..." The tears fell from my eyes, because if I didn't have his help, I would never get Huntley back.

I'm finally whole again. I can't risk my wings.

"You wouldn't have those wings if it weren't for me, and now I'm begging you to help me."

He shifted his gaze away.

"Pyre, I know you're scared, but don't forget who you are."

He looked at me once again.

"You're a fucking dragon. You can burn this whole island to the ground. You can snap a man cleanly in two with your ferocious bite. You've got scales thicker than any armor. I know you're traumatized by what happened, and that's understandable...but don't forget who you are. *What* you are."

No more words were forthcoming. He remained in front of me, wasting precious time.

My tears came on thicker. "Please...I love him."

HIS HEAD GAVE a slight drop in defeat before he lowered himself to his belly. *I will try.*

"Thank you, Pyre." I ran to his flank and climbed up the mountain of scales until I was at the top. I'd never ridden a dragon before, but I immediately clamped down on the last spike protruding from the back of his neck. It was similar to a pommel on a saddle, and I leaned far forward just like I did on a galloping horse.

Pyre opened his wings wide apart and looked up to the sky.

"You can do it, Pyre."

He squatted down on his powerful legs then jumped, his wings flapping instantly.

My body was pushed down against his flank at the momentum, and I nearly flattened against his scales.

He beat his wings harder and left the ground, gaining height into the sky toward the stars.

The wind was in my hair. It was colder than it was on the ground, fresh instead of soaked with humidity. I could barely see anything except the torches from the camps down below.

Where is he?

"They took him from our camp, so they're somewhere in the jungle heading back."

Then I will burn it down. He glided down to the trees then opened his jaws to spray his red-hot fire.

"Wait, wait. Huntley is down there with them. You'll burn him too."

I'm not going to land on the ground.

"We'll look for their torches. They'll leave the jungle soon, and we'll see them."

Pyre glided away, flapping his wings to get to a higher elevation.

I kept my eyes on the ground below, searching for signs of the outcasts who had taken my husband hostage. Flying became second nature, and I held on to the horn without a tight grip.

Pyre didn't seem to mind soaring the skies as we waited.

"I can't wait to see you fly in daylight."

I can't wait to hunt like a dragon should.

We circled the island, still searching.

I finally saw it, the flicker of torches out in the open. "Pyre, I see them."

Where?

"To the left."

He flattened his wings and soared to the left, getting them in our line of sight.

My heart leaped into my throat as we drew closer, afraid of what they'd already done to my husband. "Kill them all."

Pyre dipped down nearer to the trees and inched forward, their torches more distinct now that we were so close.

They came into sharper view, the twelve men with torches.

"I don't see him..." My eyes searched for Huntley, and I feared it was too late. They'd slayed him right there at the camp and just left him there. Then I saw him. Two men pulled a rope across the ground, the end secured around Huntley's ankles. His hands were bound behind his back, and they dragged him like dead boar. "Burn them! Burn them all!"

Pyre opened his jaws and released a jet stream of pure fire. It lit up the sky, so bright that every other person on the island couldn't miss it. He sprayed it down over them, engulfing every single one of them in a ball of fire.

"Yes!"

The men shrieked as they burned alive, their arms flailing about as they tried to put it out. Some dropped and rolled on the ground, but that was no use either. Others ran for the ocean, but barely made it a few yards before they collapsed.

"That's right, motherfuckers!"

Ivory. The rope.

I looked down at the rope that bound Huntley. It was on fire—and headed straight toward him. "Put me down."

I won't land.

"Put. Me. Down."

Pyre released a roar before he glided to the earth and landed. *Hurry.*

"They're too busy being burned alive to do anything, Pyre." I slid down his smooth scales until I hit the ground and buckled underneath the gravity of the fall. I pushed myself up and sprinted to where Huntley tried to wiggle free.

Others will come. Hurry.

I slid to my knees at Huntley's feet and hacked the rope with my blade, sawing it in half so it came apart.

"Hands." Huntley sat up and displayed his wrists to me.

I slashed the rope with my blade then moved to his ankles.

Huntley didn't say a word to me. He was on his feet, and he snatched the sword out of my hand.

"What are you—"

One of them had managed to escape the fire, and he came down on Huntley with his ax. I hadn't even noticed him because all I cared about was getting to Huntley as quickly as possible.

Huntley parried his attack and stabbed my sword clean through his gut.

"Oh shit."

Huntley grabbed my hand and yanked me to my feet. "Stay behind me."

Ivory!

I looked back at Pyre, who had a crazed man swinging a machete at him.

I snatched Huntley's ax off the ground and sprinted to the dragon. "Coming!" I made it to the outcast and slammed my ax into his back. The blade went deep, and he went down right away. "Why didn't you bite him? Pyre, you could step on him, and he'd flatten like a leaf."

I want to leave.

"Hold on."

I turned back to Huntley, who'd just executed the last man standing. Now he had blood all over him, and I wasn't sure if it was his or his enemies. He searched through the charred bodies and gathered everything they'd taken from him. "You okay?"

With his weapons returned to his body, he marched back to me, a streak of blood on his neck. His intense eyes were focused on me, and he looked livid, maniacal. It seemed like he was going to shove me again, but he grabbed me by the arm and yanked me into his chest, smashing his mouth against mine. It was a hard kiss, crushing our lips together as he tightened his grip on my arm. His other hand moved down my back to my ass and gave it a hard squeeze before he let me go. Then, as if nothing had happened, he walked up to Pyre. "Let's go." He climbed up the scales like he'd done it before and left some room in front of him for me to sit. He leaned out slightly, his hand dropped down for me to take.

It took me a second to get over that kiss before I could move a muscle. I eventually snapped out of it and climbed up to grab his hand. He yanked me up, putting me right in front of him.

That was when I felt it. All of it. Right up against my back.

"Pyre, let's head back to the caverns." He grabbed on to the horn with one hand and circled his arm around my waist.

Pyre obeyed—and leaped into the sky.

WE LANDED OUTSIDE THE CAVERN.

"You need to get to work on Storm's wings." Huntley didn't address what just happened, that the outcasts would have claimed his life if Pyre and I hadn't interceded. He was all business.

"I will in the morning—"

"We don't have the time. The whole island saw that spectacle, and it's only a matter of time before they come to investigate. If they know there's a dragon that can fly, they're going to do everything they can to use him to get off this land."

"I can't see—"

"I'll make a fire for you." With that, he marched off into the jungle to retrieve firewood.

I turned to Pyre. "He's grateful—even if he doesn't say it."

You're the one he should be grateful for. I never would have come if you didn't ask.

"And I really appreciate that you did." I circled my arms around his foreleg and gave it a squeeze. "Thank you."

He rubbed his closed mouth against my head. *You're welcome.*

Storm stepped out of the cave a moment later, his eyes cold like Huntley's.

"Looks like I'm going to work on your wings tonight."

Don't tell him that we speak.

I wanted to ask Pyre why, but I realized I couldn't without revealing the secret he'd asked me to keep. "Once your wings are repaired, we'll need to leave the island. Those outcasts will come for all of us."

Huntley returned with a bundle of firewood he'd just chopped down, and he made a pile before he stepped back and made a gesture to Pyre.

Pyre inhaled a deep breath and then exhaled the fire.

The wood caught instantly, the flames leaping high into the air.

"No reason to hide anymore." Huntley dusted off his hands. "Baby, get to work."

AFTER A COUPLE HOURS, I couldn't go on any longer. "I'm too tired. I need to sleep."

Storm examined his one working wing and flapped it a couple times.

"I'll try to finish it tomorrow."

Storm positioned his body to show it to Pyre.

Pyre didn't change his expression, but there seemed to be a smile in his eyes. There must be a whole conversation going on between them, words that Huntley and I couldn't hear. Both dragons walked deep into the cave until they were swallowed up in the darkness.

Huntley already had our gear inside the cave. "We'll sleep here from now on."

"That's a good idea." I'd feel a lot safer with two ferocious dragons just a few feet away.

"Come on." He stepped away from the entrance and moved around the perimeter. The fire he created burned low now, nearly snuffed out completely.

"Where are we going?"

He continued to walk, moving farther around the edge of the rock so the cavern was no longer in view.

"Huntley?"

He suddenly grabbed me and pinned me against the rock. His hands were instantly under my shirt, his palms on my tits, and he gave me that same crushing embrace that bruised my lips.

The air was sucked from my lungs, and my fingertips and toes turned numb. It was like kissing fire, white-hot fire. My mouth opened further to him, and I moaned when I felt his thumbs flick over my hard nipples. I moved farther back into the wall as he smothered me, devoured me like an animal.

I felt like a feast for the taking.

He squeezed my tits the way he squeezed my ass—hard.

It made me moan and wince at the same time. He never handled me gently or like I was the princess he teased me about being. He always treated me like a woman who could handle his manliness.

All the fatigue evaporated when he took me like this, when he revitalized my entire body with those kisses and touches.

His hands dropped down to my breeches and yanked the drawstring until it came loose. He lifted one leg then the other, yanking off my boots until he started to tug the snug material over my hips and ass. He did all this as he kissed me, getting me naked from the waist down.

My hands did the same to his bottoms, getting them loose and tugging them down so his cock could come free.

With his breeches at his knees, he lifted me up into the air then lowered me right onto his length. It was a slow entrance, his hands gripping my cheeks as I sank onto his length. He was bigger than he'd ever been, so it was a good stretch.

He got me right to his base and squeezed my ass cheeks as he held me there. He didn't pin me up against the rock to support my weight. He carried me with his large arms, not the least bit tired.

My arms hooked around his neck, and I looked into his dark gaze, seeing the blue eyes that had struck me the first moment I saw them. They had been meaningless to me at the time, but they'd slowly become everything to me. They were the eyes I saw first thing in the morning. The eyes I saw before I went to sleep. They were the eyes in my dreams too. Beautiful. Powerful. Intense.

He began to raise and lower me over his dick, my wet body smearing his length with dripping lubrication. The only reason we fit together so well was because he could make me wetter than I'd ever been.

With just the power of his strong physique, he guided me up and down, his arms thick like tree trunks. But a labored breath never escaped his lips. A look of fatigue never entered his hard expression. "I told you to run."

I breathed louder every time his dick moved inside me, his big size stretching me to the limit. He was back in my arms, safe and sound, hardly a scratch on him, and my life felt complete once more. "You should know by now that I never listen."

He increased the pace, his core perfectly still as his arms did all the work.

"I'd never leave you."

His arms moved faster, and he fucked me savagely, his face tinting, his expression hardening.

"Never."

He released a heavy breath that came out as a moan. "Fuck, baby."

My arms tightened on his neck, and I felt the pull start in my belly. It was warm and deep, an ache that felt almost painful. The feeling stretched out everywhere, migrating to my limbs, hitting my toes. My breaths turned deep and ragged, and soon I was moaning into the darkness. "Babe…"

He moved hard, his hips getting into it too. "Yes, baby."

My moans turned into loud screams, and I clawed at his back as I felt it all at once. It felt so good, made my vision blur with tears, made my nipples harden so much they ached. My face dropped into his neck because I couldn't do anything else except writhe.

Both of his hands squeezed my ass hard as he gave a loud groan.

I could feel it. Feel the way his cock thickened. Feel the weight he'd just deposited inside me.

It felt so good that I clawed him even deeper. "Yes…"

He approached the finish, his arms slowing their pace. Soon, he came to a stop altogether and held me against him, his forehead pressed to mine, his cock still deep inside me. It didn't go soft like it did most nights. It stayed rock hard, as if that was only the beginning. "Watching you come for me on a dragon…fuck me."

30

ELORA

The sun had barely peeked over the horizon when I was out of bed and on my way to the forge. Without the sun, the wind stung with cold, and sometimes I closed my eyes just to avoid it.

I turned the corner and headed down the alleyway toward my shop. My finger dug into the corner of my eye and rubbed the balls of sleep out of the crevice when I noticed my front shop door open and close. "What the...?"

A man with his back turned to me inserted a pick into the keyhole and locked it back into place...like he had a fucking key. He wore a cloak with the hood up, hiding his face from view. But I could see his broad shoulders, discern his formidable height, see the muscles in his legs. So, I was no match for this guy, not without my sword.

But that didn't stop me. "Hey, asshole."

He froze for a split second, his back still turned to me.

"That's called breaking and entering—and you could be hanged for that."

I expected him to turn and run, but instead, he pivoted his body and faced me head on.

I stopped when I saw his face.

He was my age or somewhere close. Youth was prominent in his smooth skin, in the brightness of his eyes. They were blue, almost the color of my brothers'. His jawline was so cut it seemed to have been carved with a sharp knife. There was a beard there as well, like the scruff had been growing one too many days. He had tanned skin, like he spent a lot of time outdoors working with his hands based on the musculature of his body. He didn't carry a weapon—at least, not one I could see.

He sized me up at the same time.

"What were you doing in my forge?"

His fixed stare remained, as if he was deaf.

"Asshole, I asked you a question."

"You're the blacksmith."

It wasn't really a question, but it felt like one. "You got a problem with that?"

He stared.

"That was a question—in case you couldn't tell."

He turned away and walked off.

"Whoa, hold up. What the hell were you doing in my shop?"

He kept going.

I went after him. "I'm going to kick your fucking ass—"

He spun around and pinned my wrist down quicker than I could evade the attack. "I didn't take anything." He had a deep voice and wore hostility in his eyes like two beacons. His fingertips squeezed me, as if to make a point. "Now go about your day." He released me and continued on his way.

"Not until you tell me what the hell you were doing on my property."

He kept walking.

"I wasn't joking about the ass-kicking."

He ignored me, not seeing me as a threat whatsoever.

I sprinted, ready to jump onto his back and throw him down.

He sidestepped the attack as if he had eyes in the back of his head.

I hit the cobblestones with a groan. "Asshole..." I breathed through the pain in my knees and didn't rise, my whole body taking a hit when I struck the hard surface. Then a hand appeared in my line of sight.

I stared at it before I looked up at him. "Are you kidding me with this?"

He kept his hand there as an offering.

I released a loud groan before I took it and let him help me up. "You're still an asshole."

He didn't crack a smile. "Necrosis will be here in two days."

I had to blink a couple times before I could process what he'd said. "I'm sorry...what did you just say?"

"They're coming for HeartHolme. You're going to need better weapons if you're going to stop them this time."

More blinks. More confusion. "How do you know this?"

"Does it matter?"

"Uh, yes. It does fucking matter."

"I left Ice on your workbench. It'll only make a couple swords, but that's better than nothing."

"Ice?"

"Infuse your blades with it. Kills them much quicker."

Now I had no idea who this guy really was. "I don't know what Ice is."

"Because it's rare. So rare, no one has even heard of it."

My eyes narrowed. "Who are you?"

He was a foot taller than me, so his chin was tilted down slightly to watch me. "Necrosis isn't here to feed. Not this time. They're here to destroy. So their entire army is going to appear at your gates in the deepest part of the night. Asking me questions will only waste time, time that you don't have right now."

I wanted to ask my questions, but he hadn't answered a single one, so I didn't bother. "If you're right about the Ice, how do I find more?"

"I've given you everything I have."

"Where did you find it?"

No answer.

"Your plan was just to leave it out and hope I used it to make a sword?"

"The moment you saw it, you wouldn't have been able to resist." He stepped away.

"Can you at least tell me your name?"

"I'll tell you next time."

"Next time?" I asked. "If what you say is true, there may not be a next time."

He turned back to face me, his eyes sharp like broken glass. "And if there is a next time, you'll owe me."

I gave a slow nod. "So that's what this is about. You want something from us."

"Not *us*," he said. "You."

IT LOOKED like a pile of broken glass. The shards had sharp corners, so sharp they could slash a wrist quicker than you could feel the cut. All the chunks were uneven, like pieces that belonged to other puzzles. There was also a vapor that rose from the pile, thin and faint, like sweltering heat on the horizon. I placed my hand close, and that was when I felt it.

The cold.

It was cold like ice.

The closer I came, the colder it felt, like ice directly against the skin.

It was pretty too, like freshly fallen snow with little flecks of gold in the powder. I studied it for a long time, and just like he said, my interest was too great. I was already considering how I would use it, in what quantities, and in what weapons.

I decided to divide it into two halves and create two swords. I mixed it with our lightweight steel since the Ice would do most of the damage anyway and created two swords that were featherlight. It took me the entire morning to create the two, to handle the Ice gently so I wouldn't cut myself or accidentally destroy it. By the time I was done, the light was high from all the windows.

I took the first sword in my hand and tested out the balance as I rolled it around my wrist. It was like a knife in hot butter, gliding through without friction. Couldn't even hear the wind whistle in my ear.

It was light and easy to use, but I couldn't attest to its deadliness. I didn't have Necrosis to practice on, so I wouldn't know its effectiveness until they marched on HeartHolme. But if that really happened, then I could only assume everything he'd shared was the truth.

I had to tell Queen Rolfe.

AKA...my loving mother.

IT WAS mid-afternoon when I left my forge and headed to the castle. The streets were inhabited by people now, instead of quiet like they were bright and early that morning. Most of them had brown sacks of produce, dinner they'd purchased from one of the markets throughout the city.

I turned to the main road and nearly bumped into my brother. "You're home."

His blue eyes sagged with exhaustion, and the coldness in his gaze suggested he wasn't interested in a chat right now. "Just arrived."

"Good. Necrosis is coming."

"Just a rumor—but better to be safe than sorry."

"I don't think it's a rumor, Ian. They'll be here in two days. Well, less than two days."

He had the same look Huntley had when he was thinking, a narrowing of his shrewd eyes. "How do you know this?"

"It's a long story. I'm not going to repeat it twice, so if you want to hear the tale, come with me to the castle."

He turned back the way he'd come and joined me. "Huntley's gone?"

"He took What's-Her-Face to get the dragons."

"What's-Her-Face?" he asked, a slight tone of humor in his voice. "You mean his wife?"

"Don't tell me you actually like her."

"I don't love the situation, but that doesn't mean I hate her."

"Really?" I turned on him. "She's my half sister. You don't think that's weird?"

Ian shrugged. "She's good with a bow. Pretty good with a sword."

"And that's enough reason to like someone?"

"It's enough reason to respect someone."

I rolled my eyes and looked ahead.

"Elora, they're married, eternally bonded for this life and the afterlife. I suggest you just get over it."

I released a booming laugh. "Just get over it...got it. You're really telling me you weren't upset when you found out?"

He looked ahead as we approached the castle. "I was."

"You better have been."

"But I was more upset that I missed it."

I turned back to him, surprised by the confession.

"I know Mother was upset for the same reason. In addition to all her other reasons..."

"Well, I don't trust her. I think once she's reunited with her family, she'll stab Huntley in the back."

"Maybe. But I doubt she would have come back down here with him if that were the case."

"Are you an idiot?" I stopped.

He stopped too.

"She wants those dragons, and she can't get there by herself. That's why."

His eyes stared into mine.

"Once she has what she wants, she might kill Huntley and leave him on that island and take the dragons back to Delacroix. Then we'll be trapped down here forever, and your mother will hate us even more because we'll never compare to her favorite son."

Those words stung, judging by the shift of his eyes.

"I told him to watch his back. I hope he took that seriously."

"I trust Huntley's judgment. He knows her better than we do—"

"He knows her wet pussy and that's all, Ian. I could make a fool out of any guy in HeartHolme by rocking his socks off. He'd leave his wife, abandon his kids, turn his back on everything he knows just because he's been hypnotized by magical pussy. All men are the same. They give in to temptation just as fast as a kid in a candy store."

Ian didn't know what to say to that, given the way he stood there and stared.

I rolled my eyes and continued forward. "Hope I'm wrong...but whatever."

He matched my pace. "You may be right. But I also think you're equally hypnotized by your anger."

I looked at him.

"You know what she is—and you can't see straight because of it."

WE MADE it to the castle and checked in with Asher. "We need to speak to Queen Rolfe. It's urgent."

The servant trailed down the hallway, and his voice carried back to us as he announced us. "Elora and your son are here to see you."

Wow...okay.

"Which son?" Her voice came back to us. "Has Huntley returned?"

Ian gave no reaction, probably because he was used to the favoritism.

"Ian."

After a pause, she said. "I'll be there in a moment."

Asher returned and gestured for us to enter the study. He poured two glasses of water then excused himself so we could speak privately.

Queen Rolfe made her entrance in her regal attire, a long-sleeved black dress with a chain hooked across the front. The dress flared out, and around her waist was the black belt that would hold her weapons if she were leaving the castle. She looked at me first, but the stare didn't last for more than a second or two before she focused her attention on Ian. "You've returned."

That was how the hierarchy worked in my family.

Huntley.

Ian.

Me—in dead last.

Whenever Huntley and Ian were in the same room, it was as if Ian didn't exist, but once it was Ian and me, I took third place.

Felt good.

With a straight posture and his hands behind his back, he gave a nod. "The road was quiet. We made good time. The outpost has been abandoned, but hopefully no one realizes that it's unprotected. We made an enormous bonfire that should last for days."

"We can always rebuild a lost outpost," she said. "But we can never rebuild the people we lose to Necrosis—or their souls. I'm glad that you and our people have returned. You must be tired, so you should get some rest."

Ian gave a nod.

She turned to me, her stare noticeably different, with just a tint of resentment. It was the same look she wore any time she looked at me. Huntley was the only one who basked in the glory of her affection and respect. "What is it, Elora?"

She pissed me off so much that I'd nearly forgotten why I was there. "When I went to my forge at sunrise, someone had broken in to my shop. I'd never seen him before. When I cornered him, he informed me that Necrosis would be here at nightfall tomorrow."

Her resentment vanished—and her authoritarian look ensued.

"He didn't take anything from my forge. In fact, he left behind an element called Ice." I pulled the blade from the scabbard and displayed it to her on my open palms. "It's thin and sharp like glass, but it's forever cold. It doesn't melt like snow. It retains its coolness eternally. Even now, with it embedded in the blade, it's cold to the touch."

Ian stepped forward, getting a closer look at the sword.

"He said Ice can kill Necrosis much quicker than any other blade. Maybe it's the truth. Maybe it's a lie. We won't know for sure until tomorrow night."

Queen Rolfe took it from my hands and pressed the blade to her palm. The second it made contact, she yanked her fingertips away, like she felt the cold sting her fingers.

"I thought you should have it."

She kept her attention on the blade for a long moment before she looked at me. "How many blades can you forge?"

"That's all the Ice he gave me."

"Where can we get more?"

"He said it's so rare I'll never find it again."

She lowered the blade to her side, her fingertips gripping the handle. "Did this man have a name?"

"He wouldn't share it with me."

"How do we know this man isn't just spinning lies?" Ian asked.

She turned to him. "How do we know he's not? If Necrosis marches on HeartHolme tomorrow night, then I can only assume this Ice is real." She lifted her blade to him. "Touch it, son."

He dropped his hand on the hilt and gave a slight flinch at the chill.

Never once did she call me daughter. I was always Elora and nothing else. I felt more like a niece who became the queen's burden after my parents were killed in war.

"We'll prepare for battle." She turned back to me. "Supply the wall with everything they need for the siege."

"Yes, Your Highness."

"Did this stranger say anything else?" she asked.

He did say one more thing—one very terrifying thing. "Necrosis isn't here to feed. They're here to destroy Heart-Holme. Their forces will not be scattered to the Teeth or the Plunderers. They're coming for us—and us alone."

She processed that statement with a stony face.

Ian spoke. "Should we call for aid?"

She kept her eyes on me, the anger entering her gaze as if I was the one who had made the threat rather than just delivered the message. "No. Nothing would make them happier than if Necrosis wiped us out for good."

31

ELORA

HeartHolme was always supplied with enough weapons for the army, in case there was ever an attack on our city. But arrows constantly needed to be replenished—and there could never be enough of those.

It was also rare to know of an attack before it came, so that gave me the opportunity to fortify the wall even more. I took the basket of arrows out of the rear of the carriage and carried it to the first cannon.

"What have you got there?" Ian appeared, in his full armor with his short sword at his hip. His broadsword and shield were hooked to his back. He never carried a bow and quiver of arrows because he was more lethal with a blade than an arrow on a tight string.

"We use the cannons to wipe out our enemies, but the radius of impact is so small. So, what if we fill the cannons with arrows instead?"

"Do we have enough arrows for that?"

"I've spent every waking hour making them in the forge, so yes, I think we do." I piled them tightly inside, making sure they would continue to point straight once the cannon exploded. They would fan out on their own once they were in the sky and hopefully hit their marks accurately. "Want to give it a try?"

Huntley aimed the cannon over the wall before he lit the string. "Cover your ears."

"You think I don't know that?" I'd fought down with our soldiers on the ground before, just like Huntley and Ian, but I never received any credit for it. I covered my ears and stepped back.

The cannon exploded, and the arrows instantly shot over the wall.

"Open the gates," Ian ordered.

The guys activated the gears and slowly began to pull them apart, leaving a crack just big enough for us to slip through. We crossed the field and approached the line of arrows that had punctured the soft earth with their ends in the air.

I crossed my arms and grinned at my handiwork. "Not bad, huh?"

Ian walked around, counting the ones that were flat on their sides. "Ten didn't hit their mark."

"But a hundred did." I moved down the line of arrows. "And look at this radius. If these were Plunderers, we would have taken out a hundred already."

"Potentially."

"Oh, come on. Don't be jealous."

"I'm not jealous. I want this to work more than you. I fucking hate Necrosis."

"Ian, you've got nothing to worry about. You're a great fighter."

"Doesn't mean it's not fucking exhausting. Exhausting watching your men die around you while you continue to lead. Exhausting watching the ones who are too weak to get away lose their souls to those monsters." With his hands on his hips, he raised his chin to look over the horizon, a breeze moving through his short hair. "Any time we've ever faced Necrosis, it's always been to feed. Nothing personal. But if your intelligence is right...then this will be a very different fight."

"That's why we're going to take down as many as we can from behind the wall. Protect our people as much as possible."

"We may not have a choice—depending on how many are in their army. Because if there're tens of thousands...the wall won't hold them for long. We'll have to send our soldiers, and they'll know full well they're going to die."

When I prepared for battle, it was always in an idealistic way, imagining how I would claim the lives of our enemies by providing the best weapons, the best arrows, the best strategy to maximize our lethalness and minimize our losses. But I forgot all that other shit nobody wanted to think about. "At the end of the day, we're going to win. And that's all that matters."

He gave me a side glance. "You should never assume an outcome like that. It makes you lazy. Complacent."

"HeartHolme has my full confidence. I believe in her."

He looked forward again.

"I believe in our soldiers. I believe in our queen. I believe in you."

He gave a sigh before he crouched down and pulled the dirty arrows out of the ground. "I think you should sit this one out, Elora." He pulled a few more and bundled them into his hand.

I squatted down beside him and did the same. "Why?"

"I think this is going to be the great battle of our lives."

"Then I should be on the front lines with everyone else."

"Or you should be running that forge constantly."

"I've already prepared HeartHolme for the attack. I would just be making surplus at that point."

"And depending on how long this battles wages, we may need surplus."

"Ian, you don't need to protect me—"

"I can't focus out there if I'm worried about my little sister, okay?"

"You aren't worried about your mother."

"She's the queen. It's different."

"I'm just as strong of a fighter as she is."

"I don't know about that..." He shook his head slightly. "You haven't seen her in action—not close-up. She's got eyes in the back of her head. She fights better than most men I've faced on the battlefield. But that's not the point. You should stay behind. Your talents would be better spent elsewhere. What if the army falls and Necrosis makes it into HeartHolme? You'll need to arm the citizens in a final stand—which means you need more weapons."

"They have no idea how to fight—"

"But they deserve a fighting chance—and you'll lead them."

32

IAN

I slept a long time.

Instead of being anxious all night long, I was indifferent to the terrors that lay ahead. Nothing I did could stop it, and nothing I did could increase our chances of success. So, I did the one thing that could prepare me for the long night—and slept.

Plush lips pressed to the back of my shoulder then migrated down my arm. Silky strands of hair brushed over my skin, soft like rose petals. Her warm hands gripped my chest, and she pulled herself closer to me, her lips landing on the shell of my ear.

I was pulled from sleep by a woman's eagerness, and my eyes opened to the dead fireplace that had been snuffed out sometime in the middle of the night.

Her hand moved down my stomach underneath the sheets, ready to stroke my morning wood and get back to business.

My dick was hard, but I wasn't in the mood. Not when today was the day Necrosis would march on HeartHolme and potentially annihilate us. I pulled her hand away and rolled to my back. "What time is it?"

"The sun is almost at the highest point in the sky." Her hand caressed my chest as she rested her head on my shoulder. "We weren't even up that late..."

"Got a lot on my mind." I sat up and threw my legs over the edge.

"Something wrong?"

The army was aware of the potential assault and prepared for battle, but most of the citizens had no idea what might befall us that evening. Didn't want anyone to panic, not when there was nothing they could do to affect the outcome of the battle. I'd had Hadlee over last night to get my mind off everything—and it worked.

But now I was in a different headspace.

I walked to the drawer and pulled out a pouch of coins. Without counting it, I tossed it on the bed. "You should go. I have a long day."

She didn't stir from the bed. "You know I don't want that."

I pulled on my underwear then walked to the window. I peeked through the curtains, seeing the sunshine reflecting off the cobblestones. People came and went, enjoying their final afternoon before everything changed. "If you're good at something, never do it for free." I dropped the curtain and moved back to the bed, diving my fingers into my hair to push it from my face.

She propped herself on one elbow, her tits poking out from the sheet. "You're the only one I do it for for free."

My heart tightened into a fist at her words because I could read the meaning between the lines. Frozen to the spot, I held her stare, unsure what to do.

She got tired of waiting for words that would never come and left the bed. With her back turned to me, she pulled on her underwear and everything else. Layers of clothing hid her beautiful skin from view. The last thing she pulled on was her shoes, and she walked right past the coin pouch on the bed on her way out.

"Hadlee." I heard her stop at the door.

I turned around to face her, arms by my sides, my heart still clenched. "It would never work between us."

"I know. I'm a whore, and a whore doesn't deserve a man like you."

"That's not what I meant—"

"But it's the truth. I get it." She opened the door and prepared to leave my home. "You know where to find me." With that, she left, her payment still on the bed.

It was money I didn't even need, and I wished she would take it, especially since I might die tonight. I tossed it back into my drawer then moved for my breeches.

A knock sounded on the door.

I assumed it was Hadlee, returning to say something she hadn't before. In just my breeches, I opened the door to Elora. There was still sleep in my eyes and my hair was a mess from Hadlee fingering it all night, and it would only take my sister a moment to realize what I'd spent my night doing. "Give me a second to get dressed."

"Save the vanity." She let herself into my bedroom and took a quick sweep of the messy bed. "I see you enjoyed your last night alive."

I grabbed a shirt and pulled it over my head.

"Don't be embarrassed. I did the same."

"Does it look like I want to hear about it?"

"I'm a grown-ass woman. You have your whores, and I have my—"

"I don't want to hear about your conquests, and I don't want to share mine. Now, what do you want? I just woke up, and I haven't eaten anything, let alone taken a piss."

"Ooh...then you had a really good night."

My stony face only became stonier.

"Alright...not in the mood. Got it." She untied the scabbard from her belt and presented it to me. "I want you to have this."

I stared at the blade she held out to me but didn't take it. "I have a sword. Several, actually."

"None like this." She grabbed it by the hilt and removed it from the scabbard, showing the little flecks of Ice throughout the blade.

"You gave it to Mother."

"I gave *one* to her. But I made two. Intended to keep one for myself, but...looks like I'm sitting this one out." She continued to hold it out to me.

I stared at the frozen specks in the blade before I took it with my hands. I brought it close, and instantly my palm burned from the coldness. I grabbed the hilt instead and tested out the weight, the way it glided through the air like a feather, the way it reverberated with power I didn't understand.

"And, just to clarify, this is a *borrow*. You're giving it back to me once this is over."

I was relying on the promise of a stranger that this could do serious damage to Necrosis, but it was a risk I couldn't afford not to take. I was more comfortable with the broadsword I'd been using forever, but this sword was just as good as what I already had, so I didn't have much to lose. "I'll make sure to give it back to you."

"You better." She gave me a small smile. "Well, I've got a lot of work to do today. Thought it would be smart to light up the bonfires in the field. You know, since they're coming at night. Won't be able to see them otherwise."

"That's a good idea."

"If I had more Ice, I could make a ton of arrows and that would be so helpful, but I don't."

"If this Ice is as powerful as we hope, then we'll find more."

"The guy made it sound like that was impossible."

"If he already found this, then it's not impossible. We'll comb this world until we find it." I returned the blade to the scabbard and set it on my bed. "If our army were equipped with it, then Necrosis wouldn't have as much power over us. I'm sick of them invading our lands and feeding on us like we're fucking livestock."

"Yeah, me too."

A knock sounded on the door again.

Elora turned at the sound. "Looks like your lover is back for more..."

I rolled my eyes and opened the door, coming face-to-face with Commander Dawson.

He glanced at Elora before turning his focus on me. He was in his full uniform, the black plate armor on his shoulders and chest, his cape behind him. "Her Highness requests your presence."

"I'll be right there."

He stayed in my doorway, as if my agreement wasn't enough.

"Look, I just woke up. I need to eat and take a piss, alright?"

Commander Dawson stepped away, his cape flowing in the breeze behind him.

I turned back to Elora. "I guess I'll see you later."

"In case we don't speak again..." She moved into my chest and hugged me tight.

My arms automatically dropped down, and I returned her embrace, my chin on her head.

"I know we'll make it through this. We always do."

I didn't share the same confidence.

"Take care of yourself out there."

"I always do."

She pulled away without looking at me, like one more look would just be too much.

———

MY BROADSWORD HAD BEEN REPLACED by the sword of Ice that Elora had forged for me, and I was in my full armor and cape. The black metal completely covered my body, the chainmail underneath it protecting the open areas at my joints. My vambraces were jagged and sharp, and the backs of my boots had the same sharp edge if I ever needed to kick my way free of a hold. The weight was noticeable, unlike my other armor I wore at the outpost. It was hard to move around in, but when it came to Necrosis, one hit could be the difference between life and death.

Queen Rolfe was in her study, standing above a map covered in chess pieces. She was in the same armor, her long hair in delicate curls and interwoven with feathers. Her Ice sword was at her hip. She didn't raise her chin to look at me. "I've sent an emissary to the coast. They'll inform Huntley of our situation the second he arrives."

I'd never fought a battle without my brother. I always had his back, but he also always had mine. No one else would look after me the way he did, not even my own mother. Her only concern would be slaughtering as many Necrosis as possible. Since she was my queen, I had to share her heart with the rest of her people. I wasn't necessarily more important than they were, but I knew those same rules didn't apply to Huntley. She would betray her own people for him in a heartbeat. But for me...she wouldn't do the same.

I tried not to take it personally.

"I won't lie." She raised her chin and looked at me. "Morale won't be as strong without your brother here to rally them. He's a symbol of strength and hope to our people, the future king."

With a stony expression, I blinked.

"I can't be everywhere at once, Ian. I need you to lead our people when I'm unable to."

"As I do at the outpost every day." I couldn't keep back the retort, not this time. I'd proven myself a million times over, but she never fucking noticed. It was impossible to be seen when there was this enormous shadow always cast over my face.

"Battle is different."

"Whether at war or peace, I lead just the same."

She turned back to the map. "Commander Dawson will lead the first charge."

Commander Dawson appeared from the other room, his helmet tucked under his arm, his other hand at his back.

"I will lead the second. Your job is to keep our men working on the wall. Take out as many Necrosis as you can before we reach them."

"I think my talents are better suited on the battlefield."

"And I think someone needs to rule in the event of my death." She raised her eyes with anger, provoked by my disagreement.

I would never stop disagreeing, especially when Huntley disagreed with her all the time and it never deflated his standing. "We've never had a battle like this. They've never wanted to defeat us before, just feed on us. I imagine they'll bring numbers we can't even fathom."

"Or they'll underestimate us and bring far fewer."

"Either way, our wall is impossible to breach. We can take out a lot of Necrosis while they're on the ground, saving lives in the process."

"And how will we open the doors to release our soldiers when they're right on top of us?" she asked. "You think you know better than me?"

"We won't need to open the doors when we can defeat them from the wall. Elora has created additional apparatuses that will help us take them down. Or perhaps we can plant our first wave elsewhere, so we can attack them from the rear. They'll have a war on two fronts, and they won't know which way to go."

Mother stared at me, angry. "You sound like a coward to me."

It was a knife right in the stomach.

"You'd rather hide behind your wall than protect your people."

It was so offensive I almost marched out of there. But the anger made me stay. "There's a difference between fighting hard and fighting smart. I choose the latter. Because I fucking care. Not just about the lives of my people—but their afterlives too. You've already proven to everyone that you're just as fearless a leader as you are a warrior. Is this about what's right? Or about proving your worth?"

She was silent, staring me down with eyes that could cut me clean through.

"Commander Dawson should hide his first wave out of sight outside the gates. When we sound the horn, he'll come from the rear and attack their forces from behind. It'll cause confusion, and if it causes enough, then we can send another wave through the gates. We have no idea what we're up against, so it makes more sense to make those decisions as the battle rages on. Making a plan and sticking to it at all costs is how you lose."

Her hands left the edge of the table, and she straightened, her shrewd stare seeing right through me.

Commander Dawson shifted his gaze back and forth between us. "Your Highness, I will follow whatever orders you give, but I agree with Ian."

Now she really looked like she hated me.

You'd think I wouldn't care anymore, but it still hurt—every single time.

She addressed her commander. "Then that will be the plan. Let's prepare for war."

THE SUN WAS BEGINNING to set, and judging by the panic in the streets, everyone knew what was to come. I headed back toward my home to get my final meal for the night. Potentially my last meal ever.

My eyes were on the ground, and my helmet was tucked under my arm—just in case. Huntley and I spent our free time in our favorite pub, drinking beer and eating roast beef sandwiches with extra gravy. A couple women might come up and flirt with us, but most of the time, we weren't interested because we were only interested in each other.

A pain filled my heart at the thought of him.

I hoped Elora was just paranoid—and Ivory wouldn't turn on him.

Because I couldn't live without him.

I was almost to the pub when Hadlee ran up to me. She was in slim-fitting breeches with boots that reached high on her shin. Her white tunic was loose at the top, showing her pushed-up tits where the tunic opened. "I just heard. I went to your house, and you weren't there."

"Going to get something to eat before I have to report to the wall." I should be less calm about this, but I was so defeated by my mother's treatment. When she gave me the outpost, I was relieved to be away from her, to find my own way in life. And a little part of me hoped I'd also win some favor with her...which was stupid.

Hadlee's hands went to my forearms, but then she quickly pulled away when she saw the spikiness of my vambraces. There was no good place to touch me, not when my armor was strong enough to deflect a razor-sharp sword. "They say it's Necrosis..."

"Yes."

She inhaled a deep breath.

"They won't breach the wall, Hadlee. We'll keep you safe—as we always do."

"That's not what I'm worried about, Ian." Her eyes turned watery, reflecting the sunset. "It's you that I'm worried about..."

"Don't. I've fought them before. And I'll probably fight them again after this."

Her eyes were still scared, as if that gave her no reassurance.

"I'm not afraid, so you shouldn't be either."

"It's a lot easier to die than lose someone you...you care about."

I'd rejected her affections more than once, and I didn't have the heart to do it again now. "We're well prepared. We had the upper hand, knowing they were coming before they started marching. I hope this battle ends by morning, and once the fires die out and the smoke disappears from the air, it'll be as if nothing ever happened."

"You're unbelievable, you know that?" She gave a sniff. "Consoling me when you're the one who has to face them."

"Like I said, I'm not afraid. It's an honor to defend my people. There's no other way I'd wish to die than in the service of HeartHolme."

Her eyes dropped, the tears catching in her thick eyelashes. "You look so handsome in that..."

"Maybe you can help me take it off when this is over."

Her eyes flicked back up again, a smile coming on to her lips. "I'd love to."

THE BONFIRES WERE LIT at the edges of the field, giving us illumination in the darkness. We would be able to see them, and they wouldn't be able to see us, not past the wall at least. It would make our arrows more accurate. Make our cannons more deadly.

Two riders came from the distance, their horses riding as hard as they could, like they were being chased.

I gave the order. "Open the gates."

The gates cracked just wide enough to allow them passage. They rode through and yanked on the reins to halt the horses.

Queen Rolfe went to them straightaway. "What news do you bring?"

"They march from the south," the rider said. "And they're headed this way."

A cloud of disappointment formed over all of us, even though that was the news we all expected to hear.

"How many?" Queen Rolfe asked.

He took his time answering, as if he didn't want to say. "Twenty thousand...if not more."

I couldn't hold my breath in at the number. It fled in a rush, leaving my lungs deflated. Everyone broke out in whispers to one another, sharing the same unease that just punched me in the stomach.

Even Queen Rolfe couldn't respond. It took her a solid ten seconds to react to that news, and for the first time ever, I saw her look scared.

Fuck.

Elora exchanged a worried look with me. "That's too many. We don't stand a chance."

"You aren't the only one thinking it," I whispered back.

Queen Rolfe didn't have words of encouragement. She needed time to process the deathblow that had just struck us down.

I'd had no idea their army was so massive. Any time we'd fought them, it'd only been a few thousand at a time. But now I realized what we were truly dealing with. It was a force bigger than the Runes, Teeth, and Plunderers combined.

We stood no chance.

I was worried that Huntley hadn't returned—but now I was relieved he hadn't.

He would live. And the rest of us would die.

Queen Rolfe finally recovered from the shock. "We may be outnumbered, but our gates have never been breached. They can't pass through the mountain. They can't get to HeartHolme through any other entry. We hold the gate—and we hold HeartHolme."

"Even if we survive, this battle will span several nights," I said. "At least."

"Shit...I need to make more arrows. More everything." Elora took off at a run and headed straight to the forge.

I left the wall and climbed to the bottom, where Queen Rolfe and Commander Dawson spoke in private. "Commander Dawson shouldn't take an army outside these walls. With numbers that big, he'll be massacred."

"But can we take down an army of twenty thousand from behind the gate?" Commander Dawson said. "We would have to be killing them by the thousands every few minutes to keep them back, and I don't think a volley of arrows and cannonballs will be enough for that."

"It won't," Queen Rolfe said. "It'll buy us time. But not enough."

I took a look around, examining the rocky crevasse that expanded into the city beyond. "I have an idea. But it's not a good one."

"What is it, Ian?" Queen Rolfe asked.

I nodded to the rocky crevasse of the mountain. "Once they breach the wall, we can fire at the walls with the cannons.

The mountain will come down on top of them. If we time it right, we can take out half their army. They'll be trapped, and the rest of the ones that aren't will be forced to retreat."

"We'll also be trapped," Commander Dawson said. "Inside HeartHolme."

"It'll take months to rebuild the path and the gate," Queen Rolfe said.

"Months of hard labor is preferable to death. We have enough food and water to keep everyone fed for months. If it saves HeartHolme, then none of that matters." It was the only option we had from where I stood. "It's the worst-case scenario...if they breach the walls."

Queen Rolfe exchanged a look with Commander Dawson. "If we don't have a choice, that's what we'll do."

33

IAN

I could see their army—even in the darkness.

They were just shadows inside of another shadow, but sometimes a light would catch their armor, and that small reflection was enough to see them—for just a second. Their footsteps became audible next, like the sound of a thousand horses pounding their hooves against the earth. They weren't in unison, so it was a cacophony of noise.

On top of the wall, I stared, watching their army step into the light of the bonfires.

Their features were difficult to distinguish from this distance, but I could see their blue armor, see how close their bodies were packed against one another because there were so many. A few Necrosis rode steeds, Clydesdales, and I could distinguish the leader based on his armor.

He was the only one in black.

Everyone behind the wall was silent, their hearts no doubt racing just as mine did, watching the biggest army in existence march on our gates.

Elora made it to the top of the steps, her quiver full of arrows, and she stopped to look over the edge—to see the horrific sight. She went still, seeing the armor marching in silence, seeing the murderers that wanted to kill us then harvest our souls.

I didn't have any words of encouragement. Not when they wouldn't be believed anyway.

She pulled out the quiver and added the next stock of arrows to one of the crates along the way. "I guess he was right."

"Without his warning, we wouldn't have stood a chance... not that we really do anyway." I kept my voice low so only she would hear, so the rest of the men wouldn't lose what little hope they had left, if any at all.

Elora didn't argue with me—which was a first. She would normally say some bullshit about beating the odds...not giving up...the stronger fighter doesn't necessarily win... But she had nothing to say now. "I think it's time to pray to Adeodatus."

"I thought you didn't believe in the gods."

"Shit, I'd believe in a raccoon if I thought it could help." She left the wall and disappeared.

I hoped Adeodatus could send us a miracle...because that was what we needed right now.

THEY WERE in closer view now, their faces distinguishable. They looked no different from humans, no different from us, no different from the Plunderers. Their features were just more pronounced, like the height of their cheekbones, the hollowness of their faces. And their eyes—they were full of malevolence. Heartless. Vile. Hungry. That was the biggest tell that set them apart from us. It was like looking into the eyes of a dead person—but who somehow wasn't dead.

Their leader held the reins of his horse as he looked up at us, dark hair on the top of his head, eyes brown like a dark piece of chocolate. The glow from our torches lit up his face, showing the sharp contours that made up his visage. He looked up at us with that same expression the rest of his army had—full of loathing. "You stand no chance." His eyes dragged across the wall, stopping on me. "Surrender."

I could feel the frost transfer from his eyes to mine. I could feel the wrath, as if we'd done something that deserved his ire. I felt my throat in his hands. But I didn't blink an eye over any of it.

Queen Rolfe rose up the steps, her boots loud against the stone because everyone was dead silent. I didn't turn to look, but I knew it was her, ready to face off with the monster that was about to try to take everything from us—including our souls. She snatched a bow from one of the archers, fit the arrow to the string, and aimed it right at the leader of Necrosis. She drew her elbow high—her aim right on his face.

His look remained the same. "Surrender—and half of you will be spared."

She fired her arrow.

All he did was lean slightly to the side, and the arrow flew right past his head.

"Your request has been denied. Prepared to feel the wrath of HeartHolme."

The drums started, loud and echoing against the mountain, the music to intimidate our enemies and grant us courage.

Necrosis smiled. Actually smiled.

The power of the drums wasn't enough to stop the shiver that moved down my spine.

He pulled on the reins of his horse and rode straight through a divide in his army, retreating to the rear.

"Coward." She handed back the bow and marched across the wall. "A coward hides behind his army." She raised her voice so all could hear. "A king rides into battle first—and shows his men how it's done. Light 'em up, boys."

Their first line of soldiers sprinted toward the wall.

I stopped thinking about the odds. I stopped thinking about my brother. I stopped thinking about everything. "Archers, light your arrows." I leaned down over the wall. "Cannons, fire on my command." I looked to the field below, seeing the markers Elora and I had put down to know exactly where the arrows would land.

Necrosis ran forward straight to the wall, as if they were about to climb it.

I waited until the right moment. "Now." I threw my arm down.

The cannons exploded, and the arrows sprayed the sky. They followed their arc and rained down again, a hailstorm of sharp missiles on Necrosis. Their army halted momentarily as the momentum made their bodies jerk, made some of them drop dead, but only those that took five arrows or more. The rest continued forward as if nothing had happened. "Archers, fire!"

They lit their arrows from the torches and aimed their fire down at the enemy. Arrows impaled necks and limbs, taking down most, but not all.

And t another wave of Necrosis was coming behind them.

We'd have to move fast if we were going to keep this up. "Cannons, fire!"

Nobody did.

I looked over the wall. They were frantically putting the arrows inside the cannon, lining them up as Elora instructed. "Fuck. Come on, hurry!"

They moved as quickly as possible, but by the time they launched, they missed the second wave and hit the third. The second wave sprinted to the wall, our archers doing their best to take them out.

Elora ran down the path, carrying more arrows.

"Elora!"

She looked up at me, out of breath with the quiver to her chest.

"It's taking the cannons too long to reload. Create something so it saves them time."

"I...right now? I have to make arrows—"

"Figure it out. Now!"

She dropped her quiver on the ground and got to work.

I turned back to the wall and grabbed my own bow and fit an arrow to the string. Necrosis was starting to pile up at the base of the wall, standing on top of one another to build a human ladder. I fired down at them, hitting a single Necrosis three times in the head before he finally went down.

Fuck, that wasn't good.

The next cannon of arrows finally fired.

They landed on the next group of Necrosis, taking out at least half.

I lowered my bow and looked back to Elora. She was tying the bundles of arrows together with a string and then dropping them into the cannon. Then she would cut the ribbon before the cannon fired.

I knew she'd figure it out.

"Keep firing," I ordered. "Don't stop." I turned back to the edge of the wall and lit my next arrow. "It's going to be a long night..."

THERE WERE TOO MANY.

We didn't have enough arrows, and even if we had, it still wouldn't have made a difference.

Necrosis brought ladders from the rear and pushed them up against the gates.

We pushed them back down again, but their archers would shoot us.

My men would topple over the edge and land right on top of them—and I had to watch them be trampled or eaten.

Queen Rolfe was beside me, hacking up the Necrosis that managed to scale the wall. She sliced down every single one, toppling them back over so they landed on top of their own. "Ian, push the ladder off." She sliced and hacked as I grabbed the ladder and gave it a hard shove.

But then there was another ladder to replace it. And another...and another.

At this point, we weren't getting anything done, just expending our energy and stalling for time.

Archers rained down with fire, and while that took out Necrosis, it didn't take down enough. There were just too many.

We'd lost.

I looked to the rocky passageway, my worst-case scenario now my only scenario. "Mother, we have to retreat."

She stabbed one through the gut then sliced his head clean from his shoulders. "No."

"We lost. It's time to save people—"

"I said no." She slashed at the next one, and he went down right away.

More ladders hit the wall, and that was when a horde of them came.

She was so focused on what was right in front of her that it was up to me to guard her back. I pulled out my blade of Ice and sliced clean through the first one. What would normally take four or five power hits took only one.

It made all the difference in the world.

"Mother, it's time to go." I kept them back, seeing a pile of my own men on the ground, their skin already desiccated because Necrosis couldn't resist taking their souls in the middle of battle. The black blotches on their skin were now fair and white, their energy fully restored. Now they were more powerful than before.

She pulled back and finally came to her senses.

"I'll hold them back."

"No." She pushed me aside and held up her own blade, taking down two at once. "Go, Ian."

"No—"

"I said go!"

I took down a few men as I went, then headed down the stairs to the cannons. "Load the cannons."

"We have no more arrows—"

"With boulders." I pointed at the wall of the mountain. "And aim for the mountain."

The guard hesitated.

"Just do it."

All the men turned the cannons then prepared to drop the boulders into place.

Commander Dawson and a few of his soldiers joined my mother on the wall, chopping down all the Necrosis that breached the top. But more washed up over the edges like a high tide, and soon they were running down the steps toward us below.

I met them at the bottom, taking them out before they could reach everybody below. My sword sliced through flesh like it was warm butter, and I took the life out of the eyes that wanted to take the life out of mine. The fatigue screamed in my muscles, but I didn't stop.

"When do we fire?" one of the men asked.

Other soldiers helped me at the bottom, hitting every Necrosis five times for one of my hits. I looked back at the wall, saw my mother and Commander Dawson on the wall, and realized there was no chance to retreat. The second they turned their backs, they would be hacked to pieces. I could run, but at the sacrifice of the men who took my place. "Fire!"

Nobody heard me.

Their eyes were on the sky.

ROOOOOOAAAAR.

I followed their gaze, seeing nothing but darkness overhead.

Then I saw it...a stream of pure fire.

34

IVORY

I worked on Storm all day, but after midday came and went, I needed a break. I took a seat in the shade of a tree, eating the roasted boar Huntley had caught and prepared for me.

Pyre took a seat across from me, lying flat on his belly, his wings folded against his body.

Storm had returned to the shadow of the cavern to take a nap.

Huntley was gone, purposely giving us alone time to talk.

"Thank you for everything you did."

He shifted his tail back and forth slightly, his head raised above mine.

"I would have lost my husband without you."

I couldn't say no to you. Not after what you've done for me and Storm.

"I appreciate your loyalty."

He lowered his chin, resting it on his claws.

"Why can't Huntley know you speak to me?"

He had the most magnificent eyes. They were dark like coal, with specks of gray throughout the color. But they were also illuminated from within, making them visible even in the dark. They were expressive too, showing his mood. *Because our ability to communicate is supposed to remain a secret.*

"Why?"

If we can communicate, that means we can be controlled.

"No one can control you unless you allow them, Pyre."

His eyes fixated on me.

I felt like I'd said the wrong thing. "I'm sorry…I didn't mean to sound insensitive."

When will Storm have his wings?

"Probably tomorrow. Are you two brothers?"

Yes.

"And the third dragon?"

He never answered.

"I'm sorry..."

Without our wings, we're no longer dragons. We're just big lizards. That knowledge was too much for him. He stopped eating. Stopped drinking. The grief swallowed him whole... and he just stopped breathing.

"I wished I'd gotten here sooner..."

Me too.

"So...who did this to you?"

King Dunbar.

"Who is that? I've never heard of him."

He lives far away from here.

"Why did he do this to you? Why on earth would anyone do this to a dragon?"

As punishment.

"For what crime?"

Not to punish us—but to punish our mother.

"Why?"

Dunbar wanted more eggs. She refused. He didn't like that answer, so he punished the three of us and threatened to do the same to our sisters if she didn't comply. Since they haven't come to this island, I assume that means she agreed to mate with Regar. His dragon. He's a vile creature.

"Why doesn't he have another dragon mate with Regar?"

Because she's the last remaining female dragon at the age to reproduce.

"Oh...what happened to your father?"

Dunbar killed him.

"Geez...I'm so sorry." In my world, we had corruption and Necrosis. But we didn't have anything as horrific as that.

He sawed off our wings right in front of her... His eyes closed. *I'll never forget the sound.*

I abandoned my lunch, my appetite completely forgotten. "You have your wings back now. You can show them to your mother when you see her again."

I hope so.

"Is that where you guys will go? Once Storm can fly again?"

If we return, he'll just do the same thing to us. Storm and I aren't enough to defeat him.

"How long have you been on this island?"

I don't know...a year.

Then his home could be a much different place by now. "I have an idea."

He opened his eyes again.

"I could really use your help back at home. It's a really long story... Do you want to hear it?"

Yes.

I told him exactly what I needed him for, to regain the Kingdoms, and unite everyone to defeat Necrosis.

He listened to every word but didn't display a reaction.

"Is that something you'd be willing to do?"

You want to use me...

"I wouldn't put it like that."

Is that why you came all the way here? Why you helped me?

I wouldn't lie—not to him. "Yes."

His nostrils flared with the big exhale he released.

"But I would have helped you even if you refused to help me."

Why should I believe that?

"Because I care about you, and you know that."

He studied me in silence, his mood simmering. *I'm not a ferocious dragon—not anymore. I can't fight in wars. I can't destroy armies. After everything I've been through...I just want to live in peace.*

"Well, you could fly off and find another island somewhere. You and Storm could start over. But...would you ever be able to really find peace, knowing your mother is captive and everyone we know will be taken by Necrosis? It'll just be mental torture, and you'll never truly be happy. You can't run from it."

His eyes dropped down.

"I think you should help us."

I told you. I'm useless.

"You are *not* useless," I snapped. "You just need to get your confidence back. You need to remember who you really are. What you're capable of. Remember that you can bite off the head of anyone who says a single damn thing you don't like. You have fire in your lungs and teeth longer than a sword. I know you've forgotten what you are...but you'll remember."

He kept his eyes on the ground.

"You're the single most terrifying thing in the world. Terrifying—and beautiful."

He looked at me again. *I want to save my mother. I want to save my sisters too.*

"Good. I know you can."

But I can't do that alone. So, I do this for you...and you do something for me.

"Do what, exactly?"

Help me kill Dunbar. Help me release the dragons in his captivity.

"I...I don't know how to help with that. I'm just one person."

But if I help you take the Kingdoms and defeat Necrosis, you have an entire land under your rule. Sail your army to my lands—and help me defeat the king who has slain and imprisoned my family.

I held his gaze, not expecting the ultimatum.

Agree—or I won't help you.

I could unify the entire continent under one rule, but then I'd have to send everyone off to a war that had nothing to do with us. It would be a terrible first decision as queen, but without dragons to help us now, we'd have no chance to succeed.

And Storm will never agree to help you—not unless he gets his vengeance in return.

Then I really didn't have a choice, and Huntley would understand. "Alright. I agree."

I FINISHED Storm's wings that night, and before he even let me climb back to the ground, he took off, flapping his wings hard to leave the island behind. I rolled off his scales and dropped down, but instead of feeling hard dirt, I felt strong arms.

Huntley pulled me back to my feet. "I knew he was going to do that."

I looked to the sky and couldn't even see him anymore. He blended in with the night, part of the stars.

"Now that they're both ready, we need to leave." Huntley kept his eyes on the sky, as if he could see the dragon even though he was practically invisible. "The outcasts will be on top of us any minute."

Pyre emerged from his cavern and lifted his head to the sky. He seemed to know exactly where his brother was, because his head would turn slightly, as if following something.

"I figured out a plan, but I'm not sure how you're going to feel about it."

Huntley's face immediately hardened at my announcement.

"Pyre agreed to help us take back the Kingdoms and defeat Necrosis."

"There's got to be more...because I don't have a problem with that."

"He wants something in return."

"You mean getting his wings back?" he snapped. "Because we already did that."

"I traded that in when he helped me save you."

He gave a slight shake of his head. "Those debts aren't equal."

"Well, now he knows the only reason I healed him was to use him..."

"You would have helped him, regardless."

"I told him that, but he's right. The only reason I ended up here was because your intentions toward him were selfish, not altruistic. Anyway...he wants revenge against the man who did this to him and Storm."

"I anticipated that."

"His name is King Dunbar. I'm not sure where he's from."

Huntley didn't have a reaction, and that made it seem as if he was unsurprised.

"You know him?"

"No. But I suspect he's our neighbor to the north. The one I told you about."

The one who would conquer us if we weren't keeping Necrosis at bay. "He's taken their mother captive. Forcing her to mate with his dragon. When she refused, he butchered Pyre and Storm. He threatened to do the same to her daughters if she didn't comply."

He looked away slightly. "And I thought your father was the definition of evil..."

The insult didn't sting anymore, not like it used to. "We don't have another choice, so I agreed."

"He's a very submissive dragon." He turned back to me.

"Can you blame him?"

"It's not about blaming him. But if I want to take back the Kingdoms, I need a dragon that's not afraid to spill blood."

"He'll get back into it—in time."

"What about Storm?"

"Pyre is supposed to talk to him."

"I'm assuming I would ride Storm and you would ride Pyre, so Storm needs to communicate with me."

"I'll let Pyre take care of that." I followed Pyre's gaze into the sky, looking in the same area he did, but I didn't see a thing.

"Tell him to get down—because I want to get the fuck off this island."

"Then that means you agree?"

He turned back to me. "My first act as king will be to send my people to war. Not a great way to start my reign."

"Like I said, we don't have a choice. We have no chance of succeeding without the dragons."

His eyes were full of fury, but there was no argument from his lips. "That's the only reason I'm agreeing."

35

HUNTLEY

The sun was barely over the horizon, and we were ready to depart. The only reason the outcasts hadn't attacked was because they were organizing, probably forging alliances with other tribes in preparation for the onslaught. Capturing a dragon was enough reason to put aside their blood lust and work together. Only one person could use a dragon to their advantage, so even if they were successful, a bloody war would take place afterward.

I wouldn't allow either one of us to be here to witness it.

Pyre spoke with Storm all night, doing his best to convince him to speak with me, to help us in the war that was about to come. It wasn't until the morning that I learned the outcome of that debate.

Storm stared at me with his angry eyes. They were yellow, like the full moon on a haunted night, and he had a lot more bite than Pyre did. Even his subtle movements were aggressive, the way he turned his head, the way he put one foot in front of the other. He was definitely far more compatible with me than Pyre was.

I waited for him to speak first, but he was just as stubborn as I was.

"Are we doing this or not?"

Ivory turned to me, her eyes pissed off. "Do you know how to talk to people?"

Storm's eyes contracted, his pupils dilating.

I ignored my wife and kept my gaze fixated on the dragon. "I need you for something. You need me for something. It's that simple. For as long as you're my ally, I will protect your scales. I will not enslave you as my own or allow my people to do so either. This is an alliance, and once that alliance is fulfilled, you're free to go. Unlike most men, I don't need a dragon to be powerful. I have my ax and my shield. Your fire and strength do not tempt me."

His snout gave an exhale, a little bit of steam coming out. *Why should I trust you?*

I heard the words loud in my head, heard them echo in my mind. "I never asked you to trust me. You should never trust anyone—that's my best advice to you. But I can tell you that my ambitions are far bigger than enslaving a dragon. My ambition is to return to my family home and reclaim the throne that was taken from me, to rule a world in peace and not war, to defeat corruption. Nothing else matters to me."

That seemed to be enough for him because he turned to regard Pyre.

Ivory looked at me. "We really need to work on your people skills."

"I'm not a people person."

"You're going to need to be if you want to be king."

Storm turned back to me. *I accept.*

"If we're all in agreement, we need to depart the island immediately." I looked over the hill that led to the inhabited part of the island, where the outcasts were preparing for war. "Because they're coming for us."

Both dragons looked in the same direction before they turned back to us.

"It's a week-long trip by boat," I said. "So, if we fly, I imagine we can make it in less than two days. Are you capable of that?"

Yes.

"You're sure?"

Dragons are meant for the sky—not the earth.

I turned to Ivory. "Then it's time to leave. Are you ready?"

She released a breath like she was nervous, a gesture I'd only seen her make a handful of times. "I guess."

"What is it?"

"It's a far trip... What if they don't make it?"

"Then we'll swim."

"I told you I can't swim."

"Then I'll swim for you."

I MOUNTED STORM, climbing up his scales the way I'd seen Ivory do every single day. I straddled his back just like a horse, my legs split over his spine, and I secured my essentials to his scales with a tight rope. I sat just behind his head, a sharp spike at the back of his neck that I could grasp like a pommel.

Ivory was already ready to go on Pyre, in her element. "It's wild, right?"

"Just like riding a horse."

Storm snapped his neck toward me, issuing a loud growl, one of his yellow eyes on me.

That was the wrong thing to say. "Bad joke."

He issued another growl and stared ahead.

Ivory looked as if she wanted to smack me across the face.

Pyre took off first, opening his wings wide and leaving the ground in a powerful jump. His wings flapped in the morning light, and he soared. Ivory leaned forward and gripped the spike, her back arched and her ass sticking out.

Fuck, she'd never looked hotter.

I clicked my tongue in my mouth, just the way I did with a horse. "Let's go."

He looked at me again, that growl back.

"Sorry."

He opened his wings and took flight, the ground far below us in a split second.

I leaned forward over the horn and kept my head behind his neck, away from the wind that hit me like a thick wall. He climbed and climbed, and I held on with all my strength so I wouldn't topple back and splatter against the ground.

He finally leveled out, so high in the sky that the details of the island were difficult to make out. He glided next to his brother Pyre, just beneath the clouds, and they looked at each other as they soared.

Ivory smiled at me and shouted, "Isn't this amazing?"

I'd captured the duke's daughter from the castle and assumed I'd have to coerce her into cooperation. But it led to an adventure I couldn't have anticipated, and now we flew together side by side, on the only two free dragons left in the world. "Yeah...it is."

THE OCEAN WAS a static mass beneath us, an endless sea of gray. It was cold up in the clouds, but not nearly as cold as it would be down below, the waves splashing over the hull and soaking our clothes. A trip that would last several days passed in the blink of an eye, and we spotted land up ahead.

"That was quick."

I would have been quicker if my wings had been stronger.

It was dusk when we arrived, when the land officially appeared directly beneath us.

"Should we stop?" Ivory shouted from the back of her dragon.

I wasn't landing our dragons anywhere they could be vulnerable—and they would be vulnerable anywhere outside of HeartHolme. "No. We'll be covered by the night."

"But how will we see where we're going?"

"I'll figure it out."

We continued to soar through the sky, the wind so strong it made my eyes smart if I didn't crouch behind the drag-on's neck. The world below was dark, not a single torch visible from this height. The world was dark, just as eerie from the skies as it was from the ground. "Turn slightly right."

Storm corrected his course and headed farther south.

I knew we'd reached HeartHolme when I saw it.

Ivory saw it too, based on what she said next. "Huntley!"

The bonfires on the outskirts of the clearing were lit, illuminating the massive army that stormed the gates of Heart-Holme. Ten thousand strong, at least. There were so many that I couldn't believe they were Necrosis.

But they must be.

They used their bodies to make a physical ladder at the gates, and dozens were crawling over the edge and infiltrating the city.

HeartHolme had fallen.

"Fuck," Ivory said. "We couldn't have arrived a moment later."

I didn't come here to fight.

"You aren't going to fight. You're going to burn." If Necrosis breached the gates, that meant my mother must be dead. That meant Commander Dawson had fallen. That meant... Ian probably hadn't survived the night. "Burn them all."

Ivory stared at me as she never had before, her eyes full of genuine sadness, as if the same thoughts had crossed her mind as they did mine. "Come on, Pyre. Light 'em up." She went first, diving down toward the gate.

Pyre opened his mouth in the middle of the dive, and the stream of volcanic fire emerged, twenty feet long, the flames red and orange. It lit up the night, paused the battle for just a moment as everyone stared.

The flames hit the stone gate, catching the ladder of Necrosis on fire, and they collapsed to the ground, their corpses set ablaze.

"That's my girl." I patted Storm's flank. "Drop me off at the wall."

I refuse to land.

"You see the mountain above the gate?"

Storm continued to fly, his wings spread wide. *Yes.*

"Drop me off there. I'll climb the rest of the way."

Why?

"I need to help my people behind the wall. Continue to circle and burn Necrosis down below."

Necrosis. He said the word, tested it in his mind.

"They don't have weapons against dragons, so stay in the sky and they can't hurt you. Burn as many as you can."

Storm dropped down to the rocky outcropping and landed on the slanted surface. It was a heavy thud, and then he slid an inch or two, the rock slippery. *Hurry.*

I climbed down and slid along the smooth surface a few feet before I regained my footing.

Good luck.

"You too."

He opened his wings and took flight again, his dark mass disappearing overhead instantly.

The fire from Pyre's snout lit up the darkness in the field once more, taking out hundreds of Necrosis in a single line.

They would retreat. Wouldn't have a choice.

I navigated down the mountains, slipped in some spots, and somehow made it to the top of the wall without sliding down and breaking my skull. The torches illuminated the chaos, Necrosis that had vaulted over the wall and killed the Runes, leaving their mangled bodies in piles everywhere.

My mother wasn't among them. Nor my brother.

My feet hit the wall, and I pulled out my ax, ready to slice through skin, muscle, and bone. I came up to one from the rear and sliced his head clean from his shoulders, his forearms marked black with hunger. I took out the remaining ones that had just scaled the wall, and I turned my attention to the battle below.

The cannons had been turned to the inner wall, as if they intended to blow it apart to save the rest of HeartHolme, but the soldiers hadn't survived long enough to accomplish that. I made it down the stairs—and that was when I saw my brother.

His eyes were on the sky, seeing Pyre release another ball of fire. Necrosis was everywhere, ten to one, and that brief glance to the sky nearly cost him his life. Necrosis rushed in and struck their sword down on his shoulder. His armor protected him, but it dented and made him grimace.

I sprinted down the stairs and threw myself into the fray. My ax swung and came down right on the invader's skull, nearly cleaving it in two. I kicked him back and swung my ax again, hitting another Necrosis nearby. It all happened so fast. I couldn't even see my brother's reaction. I killed a couple more, and when I didn't have any more coming right at me, I turned to look at him.

His sword was deep in his enemy on the ground, and with his eyes on me and his breathing heavy, he yanked it out. The disbelief was on his face, the words impossible to find. His eyes were wide, utterly shocked.

"Let's kill the rest of these motherfuckers and call it a night."

"NECROSIS RETREATS!" Commander Dawson stood on the top of the wall, his chest plate broken nearly in two from the sword he'd taken to the chest. His helmet had cracked at some point because he wasn't wearing it, and a streak of blood stretched down his forehead.

Most of Necrosis had been taken down, and only a few stragglers remained behind. They didn't make it past our final line of defense and had been unable to invade the city where our citizens were hunkered down in their homes.

Ian took out the last one, stabbing his sword down the back of his neck and into his spine.

He crumpled to the ground.

Then it was silent. There were no shouts of victory. No applause. Morale was so low it was as if we'd lost.

Ian was out of breath as he looked at me, and as he tried to put his sword back in his scabbard, he missed. Too tired to care, he just threw the sword on the ground. "Fuck it..."

"Son."

I turned when I heard her voice, a voice that had been in my life since the first time I opened my eyes. There was a lot of resentment, a lot of danger, but at the end of the day, she was still my mother.

One vambrace was missing and she had a nasty cut on her arm, and her clothes were torn as if Necrosis had grabbed hold of her and tried to rip her in two. One eye was so swollen it was completely shut. She'd taken one of the worst beatings I'd seen—and that made me want to chase after Necrosis and finish what they started.

She got to me as quickly as she could and latched on to me. "My boy, you saved HeartHolme." Her arms circled me for a hug, and she squeezed me so tight. "I've never been so proud."

My arms reciprocated, and my heart held on to those words. "HeartHolme wouldn't be here to save if it weren't for you and Ian." I pulled away and examined her arm. "Your arm is broken."

She pulled it from my grasp. "Didn't even notice." That affectionate look was in her eyes like she didn't feel an ounce of pain. Her love for me was triumphant over any kind of suffering. She shifted her gaze past me to Ian next.

I stepped back and let them have their moment.

My brother looked at her with a slight shield in his eyes, buffering himself for whatever disappointment she would unleash.

She was a foot shorter than him, but she put her hand on his shoulder like she had the height. "Are you hurt?"

He shook his head.

She brought him in for a hug and squeezed him tight. "You did great today."

He held on to her, and after a long stretch of silence, he spoke. "You did too, Your Highness."

She pulled away and looked him in the eye. "HeartHolme stands because my two sons defended her."

"Your daughter, as well," Ian added.

Her affection dropped, and she turned away, back to her role as queen. "Take the injured to the infirmary. Open the gates and burn Necrosis on the field. The battle has ended, but the night has only begun."

Everyone got to work because there were no breaks under Queen Rolfe.

Ian walked up to me, the fatigue noticeable in his body by the way he dropped his shoulders, the way he'd left his sword on the ground. Blue eyes shifted back and forth as they looked into mine, as if he didn't quite recognize me. "So, you did it."

"My wife, actually."

"Necrosis would have overrun HeartHolme if you hadn't gotten here when you did."

I gave a nod.

"Looks like your wife is a hero."

"Don't tell her that." I gave a slight smile. "It'll go straight to her head."

The smile didn't enter his lips, but it appeared in his eyes. "Mother will have to like her now."

"She better," I said. "How's Elora?"

"She stayed in the city, so she's safe."

"Good." I felt goddamn lucky that everyone I loved had survived the night.

"You know, she was worried that once the dragons could fly, Ivory would take them straight to Delacroix."

"I'm aware of Elora's paranoia. Looks like she'll have to shut her goddamn mouth now."

He cracked a smile.

That was when I pulled him for a bear hug, a hard embrace that we hardly ever shared.

He reciprocated immediately, as if he knew it was coming. "Thanks for having my back."

"I always have your back, little brother. And your front."

36

IVORY

The remaining forces of Necrosis retreated into the darkness, disappearing from the light of the bonfires. When I saw Storm swoop down beside us, I realized that Huntley was gone.

Pyre answered my unspoken question. *He's behind the wall.*

Probably fighting the Necrosis that invaded the city. "My home would be gone if it weren't for you guys."

Pyre glided toward the field below, tilting his wings so he could make a gentle landing. *I wouldn't have wings if it weren't for you.* Once he was on the ground, he folded his wings. *My wings are tired. I need to rest.*

"You both deserve it. I'm sure they'll have something good for you guys to eat."

Do they have cow? It's been a long time since I had cow.

I chuckled. "I'm sure we can arrange something." I slid to the ground and looked at the scattered bodies of Necrosis. Some of them had died at the beginning of the battle by arrows, but the rest of them were charred by the dragons. I grabbed one and dragged it to the center of the field.

What are you doing?

"Making a pile so we can burn the bodies."

Pyre and Storm did the same, grabbing a handful of corpses in their big jaws and claws and tossing them onto the pile.

"Why don't you eat them?"

Pyre dropped another pile on top. *They smell.*

"Because they're dead?"

No.

We gathered all the bodies into a pile in the center of the field. It was an impressive mound, but only a fraction of what had marched on the gate. Far more got away than perished, and something told me we would face Necrosis once again.

The gates to HeartHolme opened, and wagons guided by horses rolled onto the field.

Horse sounds pretty good.

"You aren't eating a horse."

Pretty much the same as a cow.

"No." I gave his wing a gentle slap. "Horses are special to us."

The wagons stopped far away, like the dragons were too terrifying to approach.

"Okay, let's back up. I think they're scared of you."

Scared of us? Why?

I turned to look at Pyre and gave him an incredulous look. "Pyre, you're a dragon that just defeated the most formidable enemy in these lands. You two are the single most powerful beings here right now."

Pyre stared at me like he just didn't get it.

I gave a sigh. "You'll get your confidence back. Come on, let's move away." We backed farther away from the pile so the men could throw the corpses on top. They added Necrosis to our existing pile and made a new one for the Runes who had sacrificed their lives so HeartHolme could prevail. The pile of Necrosis didn't bother me, but the big pile of Runes pulled at my heartstrings.

When the last corpse was thrown on top, the wagons pulled away.

"Baby?"

I pulled my eyes away from the pile of Runes and shifted them to Huntley. He was exactly as I'd last seen him, not a mark on him. The blade of his ax stuck out from behind his back slightly, and his armor didn't have a scratch. His intense gaze was on me, the same look he'd worn when he'd taken me behind the rocks.

"You alright?"

I gave a nod, rendered speechless by that look.

From behind him came Queen Rolfe, Commander Dawson, and his brother Ian.

My eyes shifted to my mother-in-law.

She wasn't her same regal self. Her clothes were ripped in many places, and half of her face was bloody from the battle. One of her forearms was secured in taut gauze tied to a wooden plank. She looked at me with the same stoic expression that Huntley wore at times. She should be on her knees, thanking me for what I'd done for her city, but the gratitude never came. Instead, I received a long, hard stare.

And then a nod.

Huntley looked at Pyre. "Go ahead."

Pyre sucked the air into his lungs before he released it as fire, torching the pile of dead Runes. The blaze turned into an inferno, and the flames leaped up high into the sky. The flames were so hot that they burned the flesh before it could start to smell.

Storm engulfed the other pile in flames.

Even from the distance we stood, the flames were hot on my skin, as if they were right against my face. The crackles and pops of the fire weren't subtle and soothing like they were in the fireplace. They were loud and explosive, violent. We all stood there and watched the flames burn the bodies to ash.

Huntley left his family and crossed between the two pyres toward me. The heat must have been unbearable that close, but it didn't seem to bother him in the least, not when his look was hotter than both bonfires.

He came to me, his large body blocking out the flames behind him the closer he drew. I already knew what would happen once he reached me, but I was just stunned that he would do it. Though, when it came to Huntley, nothing surprised me anymore.

He wrapped his arm around the small of my back and gave me a deliberate tug against him, his other hand sliding into my hair and pulling it from my face as he kissed me. It wasn't quick. It wasn't appropriate for an audience. But as if his own mother wasn't watching, he kissed me like nothing in the world was going to stop him from having me.

THE DRAGONS WERE FED and then escorted to the empty cavern in the mountainside. It was bigger than the one they had at the island, so there was plenty of room for both of them, away from the rest of society.

Neither one of them seemed to mind the accommodations, not after everything they'd been through, and they were both tired, so a long night of sleep with full bellies was all they cared about at the moment.

The rest of us went to the castle at the top of the cliff.

What I wanted most were a shower and some sleep, but everyone else had been fighting for their lives all night, so the last thing I would ever do was complain. We made it to her study near the back window, the place I'd seen her when I'd been inside the castle before.

Commander Dawson was still at the gates, cleaning up the destruction the battle had caused. Uninjured soldiers helped, putting HeartHolme back together as soon as possible, as if nothing had happened in the first place.

It was just us, Ian, and Queen Rolfe.

She sat on her throne, her hair a mess after being stuffed underneath her helmet, the feathers crumpled in different places. Her armor had been removed, showing the full damage to her clothing underneath. She looked like a beggar on the street, holding out a cup for a few coins. "I'm a woman of many words, but now, I have none." Her eyes dropped for just a moment, weary. "Without the dragons, HeartHolme would have been claimed by Necrosis. Every man, woman, and child would have perished—their souls as well. I set you on this journey in the hope you would succeed, but never the expectation."

It was finally a version of her I liked, a version that wasn't hard like iron, but vulnerable and deep.

507 THE BROKEN QUEEN

"We lost many people tonight. Many perished before they could witness the fire in the sky. It's not a victory I can celebrate, not when I didn't protect every single soldier who pledged their life to HeartHolme." Her eyes dropped again.

"It was an army of ten thousand," Ian said. "Maybe twenty. Our inability to prevail had nothing to do with you as a leader and everything to do with the numbers."

Queen Rolfe looked at him, her eyes still hollow. "A ruler doesn't make excuses."

"Not an excuse," Ian said. "It's a fact."

She turned her gaze to Huntley. "While we won this battle, it still feels like a loss. HeartHolme will need time to recover before we march on Delacroix, and I'm sure you need to recuperate from your arduous journey." Her voice was still full of solemnity, her heart burdened by the dead. "Time is of the essence more than ever, now that we know Necrosis wishes to wipe us from the face of the earth. I will take command of the dragons and take back all the Kingdoms."

Everything had been going well...until we hit that little snag. "No one takes command of the dragons. They're here of their own free will, as allies and friends. They're not servants. They don't take orders from anyone."

Huntley angled his head to look at me.

Queen Rolfe turned ice-cold once again. "Your mission was to bring the dragons here for my use."

"No. Our mission was to gain them as allies—which I have done. They're not to be used. They're not horses."

Her stare continued, so focused it seemed as if she would never blink.

Huntley broke the tension. "The dragons have been subjected to torture and cruelty. Their wings were clipped like turkeys. The only reason they're here is because they trust Ivory. Ivory will be their keeper. She will ask for their cooperation and permission throughout this process."

The tension left my chest when he came to my rescue.

She studied him but gave no argument. "You can speak with them?"

Huntley nodded. "They only speak with those they trust, so I don't expect they'll speak with you or anyone else here."

"Do they speak with you, son?"

"Only Storm."

She gave a slight nod. "With the help of the dragons, we don't need an entire army to take Delacroix. We'll take one with us and leave the other behind."

"They won't be separated." I didn't even have to ask.

Her eyes shifted back to me. "One must guard HeartHolme in my absence. You've seen the power of Necrosis yourself."

"Be that as it may, they're brothers," I said. "They won't separate."

She turned back to her son, as if asking for confirmation.

He gave a nod. "We'll have to travel under darkness and make sure no one sees the dragons. That way, Necrosis will assume they're still at HeartHolme. As long as they think the dragons are here, they won't attack."

With her elbow propped on the armrest, she brushed her fingers across her chin. Her nails were painted black, the same color as the armor she discarded. "I will consider our course of action as I return HeartHolme to its former glory. For now, you're dismissed."

She didn't thank me for what I'd done, and I felt stupid for being disappointed. There was nothing I could do to gain her acceptance. If securing the dragons for the war and saving HeartHolme didn't get more than a nod, then nothing would change our circumstances. She would always hate me—and the feeling was mutual.

Ian turned to leave, and I did the same.

"Mother."

I stilled when I heard Huntley's address.

"Ivory saved me from the Teeth, and she wasn't even my wife at the time. On the island, the outcasts captured me and dragged me back to their camp. If she hadn't commanded one of the dragons and come to my rescue, you wouldn't even have been able to bury your son. She did what nobody else could and healed those dragons, and then she convinced them to come all the way here to help us. You owe her more than your coldness. You owe her more than your indirect gratitude. You owe her more than a fucking nod. You will thank my wife for what she's done for all of us—and you will embrace her as a daughter because she's the woman I love."

My heart tightened so hard I couldn't feel any part of my body. My lungs tightened too, so there was no breath in or out. It was surreal, so surreal I wasn't even sure if what I thought happened actually happened. I turned back around, seeing Huntley face off with his mother like I wasn't in the room.

Queen Rolfe held his gaze, the hardness gone, a different look having replaced it.

Huntley stood his ground and waited.

I didn't even care if she thanked me. All I cared about was the confession he'd just shared with his family—and with me.

Queen Rolfe gripped the arms to her throne as she rose to her feet. One step. Two steps. Her eyes remained on Huntley. Then she slowly turned her head and finally looked at me, like it took all her strength to cooperate. With her eyes on mine, she finally conceded. "Thank you for everything you've done for HeartHolme. You're officially a Rune. And you're officially a Rolfe."

OUR HOME FELT EXACTLY the same.

It was as if we'd never left.

He made a fire right away and used the heat to draw a bath in the tub. Neither one of us spoke as we went about our routines. I hung up my weapons next to his against the wall, shed all the filthy clothes I'd worn for days and tossed them in the hamper, and then the two of us both took a hot bath to wash away the weeks of grime that had oiled our hair and coated our skin.

I didn't address what he said, and he didn't act like he said it either.

The shock hadn't worn off for me yet. He just didn't seem like a man capable of those kinds of feelings, let alone saying them out loud. Our marriage started off as a political convenience, and I wasn't sure when it became genuine. It felt like it'd always been genuine.

Once we were dry, we returned to the bedroom. I hadn't slept for days, and while I was exhausted, I wasn't sure if I could sleep. Not after everything that had happened. Not after what he'd just said. Not when the sunlight came through the window because the sun had risen at some point.

"If you've got a problem, give it to me straight."

I had just closed the curtain when his deep voice shattered me. I flinched on the spot, the aggression enough to make my bones tighten. I turned back around, the room much darker now that the sun had been shut out.

In just his underwear, he stood there, his muscular arms at his sides, his jaw clean because he'd shaved off his beard. His eyes were intense, as if we were enemies rather than lovers. "I don't have a problem."

"You haven't said a word to me."

"You haven't said a word to me either."

His eyes narrowed even more.

"I...I didn't think you felt that way."

He cocked his head slightly as if in disbelief.

"I was just surprised...is all."

"Surprised?" His tone became clipped, hostile. He came toward me.

Instinctively, I backed up, as if we really were enemies.

He flattened his hand to my stomach and pushed me up against the wall. He lowered his head, so we were eye level, his open palm taking up my entire torso. "A man shouldn't have to tell a woman how he feels. It should be obvious in everything he fucking does. And I've made it's pretty fucking obvious." His eyes shifted back and forth as he looked into mine, and he pressed his hand a little harder into my stomach as if I might try to get away. "I don't talk about raising daughters like sons with any whore I've had in my bed. I don't challenge my mother for a woman who means nothing to me. I've never called another lover 'baby,' and I never will. Don't act surprised. Don't act like you had no idea that I would slit my own throat before I'd let anything ever happen to you." He dropped his hand and finally let me go, finished making his point.

"Why are you so angry right now?"

"Why? Because I told my whole fucking family that I love you, and you didn't say a goddamn thing. That's why."

"I was just shocked—"

"Get the fuck over it." He turned away this time and faced the bed, showing me his muscular back.

"You know I love you." The words came out, my mind no longer in charge of my heart. "I know I've made it pretty obvious too..."

He stilled for a while before he slowly turned back to me. "Then grow some balls and say it—"

"I love you." My eyes started to fill with tears, and I didn't even know why. Everything hurt. Like my heart was a dam that was opening for the first time, everything came flooding out. The release was powerful, so powerful it actually hurt. "I've loved you for a long time..."

His eyes were focused once again, looking at me with that intense expression that was so fierce it was sharper than a sword straight out of the forge. His arms hung by his sides as he came closer to me, as he backed me up against the wall again.

My heart was beating so fast it was going to give out. There wasn't enough blood to feed it. Enough air in my lungs.

He scooped me into his arms and lifted me up, my back against the wall. Instead of kissing me, he held me there, his eyes on my lips as if he was waiting for the right moment to feast on my body and soul.

His eyes lifted to mine, and he finally kissed me, a soft embrace that was delicate and gentle, but packed with passion. His eyes were on mine as he gave me purposeful kisses, his fingers kneading my bare ass as he held me without complaint.

My arms circled his neck, and I got swept up right away, lost in his kiss, lost in the most powerful chemistry I'd ever felt.

Without breaking the moment, he carried me to the bed and rolled me onto my back, his hips staying between my thighs. His hand yanked at my underwear and pulled them over my ass and down my legs, and then he pushed his down to his knees.

He positioned himself between my legs, my head on the pillow in the center of the bed, and he inched himself deep inside me as his eyes remained locked to mine. Farther and farther, he went until there was nowhere else for him to go.

My ankles locked around his waist, and I moaned as I felt every inch of my husband.

"Baby." He started to rock, taking it slow, his eyes on mine the entire time. "I love you."

I moaned when I heard him say it again, listened to the depth of his feelings in just those three little words. "I love you too." My arms scooped underneath his arms and held on to his back as he made love to me. "I love you so much..."

37

HUNTLEY

The morning light struck the cobblestone pavers, giving a brilliance that reflected back onto the buildings. Heart-Holme was as glorious as it'd always been, the vile Necrosis getting nowhere near it. No innocent citizen had been lost in the battle. We'd done our job and kept our people safe.

Ian walked beside me. "Woman you love, huh?" There was a smile in his voice, a teasing taunt.

I ignored him.

"I'd started to wonder."

"Now you don't have to wonder anymore."

"I like her, for what it's worth."

I turned to look at him.

"Not that my approval matters to you."

"It does."

"Elora has been concerned about Ivory's loyalty. Said she would take the dragons to Delacroix and stab you in the back. I told her she was being paranoid, but you know how she is."

"Yes."

"But I suspect she feels differently now."

"Let's not forget how stubborn she is." We reached the door to her forge, and once I tried the knob, it opened. Weapons were sprawled across the counter, and barrels of arrows were scattered everywhere. It was a mess, not neat and tidy like it normally was. The forge was cold and quiet, like it'd been off all night. "Elora?" We stepped farther into the room, and that was when I spotted her on the couch clear on the other side. A blanket was pulled over her shoulder, and a stain of drool was just underneath her resting head.

Ian shook his head. "Disgusting."

I raised my voice. "Elora."

She gave a jump this time, jolting upright and pulling her dagger out of her belt. She blinked a few times before she realized it was us. The dagger was returned to the scabbard before she dragged her fingers across her face. "Shit...it was a long night." She pushed herself off the couch and went right toward me, her chest hitting mine as she wrapped her arms around me.

I caught her and squeezed her back.

She stepped back after a moment. "I went to your house yesterday, but there was no answer."

Ian gave a grin.

I sidestepped the statement altogether. "I'm glad you're alright."

"I'm alright?" Her hand planted on her chest. "You're the one I was worried about. I'm so glad you're back. I'm so glad this fucking nightmare is over." She ran her fingers through her hair. "When we realized the size of their army...I didn't think we were going to hold HeartHolme. Queen Rolfe always has a trick up her sleeve, but unless she had ten thousand soldiers tucked in that sleeve, I knew we had no chance. But of course...Huntley saves the day."

"My wife," I said. "My wife saved the day." I turned to Ian and placed my hand on his shoulder. "And my brother. My mother. And my sister. We all worked together to protect our people."

For the first time, Elora didn't fire off any shots at Ivory.

"Where is she anyway?" Ian asked.

"Still asleep." I'd made a fire and prepared a small breakfast before I left. It would make her a little less pissed when she realized I'd gone without saying goodbye.

Elora crossed her arms over her chest. "How do you know when you get to Delacroix, she won't—"

"Enough." I sliced through her suspicion with my sharp words. "I won't listen to this bullshit anymore."

"I'm trying to protect you—"

"I don't need your protection. I'm a grown-ass man who can make my own decisions. And I know that I can trust her as much as either of you. A knife could have been in my back many times, but she's the one who stopped the blade."

"Does my opinion mean nothing to you?"

"I could ask you the same thing."

Her eyes narrowed.

"Get over it, Elora."

"You don't have the approval of your family. You should be ashamed of that."

"Do I look like the kind of man that needs approval from anyone?" My eyes shifted back and forth between hers. "If I were, I wouldn't have a woman like her, a woman who doesn't give a fuck what anyone thinks of her either." I stepped closer to her. "Let me make this perfectly clear. She's my wife, and she's staying my wife. We'll take Delacroix and the Kingdoms together. You can be stubborn like Mother and exclude yourself from our relationship, or you can pull your head out of your ass and see her for what she really is. She brought those dragons here and saved us all, and if you still don't approve of her, you never will. So no, I don't care about the opinion of someone who's inca-pable of making a decision rationally rather than judgmentally." I stepped away, not feeling the least bit remorseful for the callous way I'd just spoken to my little sister, the woman who was still a girl in my eyes. I'd taken her under my wing and protected her from the world ever since she was born, but I wouldn't put up with this anymore.

I walked through the shop and brushed off the rage in my soul. It was infuriating to watch my family judge Ivory because of the blood in her veins rather than the love in her heart. My opinion was as good as gold in any other capacity, but when it came to Ivory, I was a lunatic.

"Huntley."

I kept my back to her. I wasn't in the mood for an argument.

"Maybe you're right..."

I stilled because I couldn't believe the words I'd just heard her speak.

"I'm just like Queen Rolfe. I can't see past my own hatred."

I turned back around, seeing her soften like a flower petal in the rain.

"I'm willing to give her a chance. But until she delivers what she's promised, I can't trust her. Not fully."

I walked back to her, my shoulders a little less stiff. "Hope for the best but expect the worst. That's what my father always used to say."

Ian nodded like he remembered.

Her eyes stayed on me. "Are we okay, then?"

"We'll always be okay, Elora."

A soft smile moved on to her lips. "Does that mean...you can introduce me to the dragons?"

"They're pretty terrifying."

"Psh. So am I."

I smiled, knowing our relationship was back to what it used to be. "Alright, then."

Elora turned to Ian. "Have you been close to them?"

He shook his head. "Just seen them in the sky."

"How big are they?" she asked.

"Fucking big," Ian said. "A single one is nearly as big as the castle."

Her eyes widened. "Whoa..."

They talked a bit about the dragons, the stream of fire they released, the way they could ignite an entire pile of bodies and char the flesh before it could even burn. Ian turned the conversation back to business. "I told Huntley about the sword, but I didn't tell him about the man who broke in to your shop."

"Someone broke in to your shop?" I immediately asked.

"He's the one who left the Ice." She extended her hand to Ian and snapped her fingers. "By the way, give it back."

Ian sighed before he removed the scabbard from his belt and handed it over.

Elora pulled the blade from the scabbard and presented it to me. She tilted it back and forth slightly, showing the way the crystals caught the light. "He only gave me enough to make two, so I let Ian borrow mine for the battle."

"Who has the other?" I asked.

"Mother," Ian answered.

"Do you notice a difference?" I looked at my brother.

He nodded. "Necrosis usually takes four to five good hits. With the blade, only one."

If every soldier had an Ice blade, that could make a huge difference. Our biggest disadvantage was their strength. Regular guys couldn't match it even with their armor and weapons. "Elora, do you know where to find more?"

"No," she answered. "The guy didn't say."

"And who is this person?" My eyebrows furrowed.

"No idea." She put the blade back into the scabbard. "Didn't tell me his name."

"Is he a Rune?"

She shrugged. "I think...but I'm not sure."

"What did he look like?"

"Uh, tall, broad-shouldered, blue eyes, handsome, quiet..."

"Handsome?" Ian asked incredulously.

"What?" she snapped. "You asked what he looked like."

"Are you sleeping with him?" Ian snapped.

"If I were sleeping with him, wouldn't I know his name?" she snapped back.

A slight grin moved on to his lips. "Not with you—"

She kicked him hard in the shin. "Motherfucker…"

He groaned as he leaned down, but he still laughed through it.

I didn't find the exchange the least bit funny. "Elora, you need to tell me everything you know about this guy."

She turned on me. "And I just did. You literally know everything I know now."

"What did he want?" I asked. "He just helped you for no reason?"

"He said he would want something in return if we prevailed."

"So, you didn't tell me everything," I said coldly.

Her eyes narrowed. "Okay. Well, *now* you know everything."

"If he was a Rune living in HeartHolme, there would be no need for deception." He wouldn't know that Necrosis was coming before we did, and he wouldn't have the very element that was most effective against killing them either. "He has to be Teeth or a Plunderer. And he has access to HeartHolme."

"Did he look like Teeth?" Ian asked.

"I mean, he didn't push out his teeth at me," Elora said. "Think I would have mentioned that..."

"Plunderer?" Ian asked.

"They look just like us, so how am I supposed to know the difference?" she asked with a shrug. "I think all that matters is that he wanted us to defeat Necrosis, which means he's their enemy and our ally. We'll know more about him when he tells us what he wants."

"We need to get more Ice," I said. "That could make a huge difference in the next battle. Instead of hiding behind our walls, we could send our men into the field."

"He said that was all there was," she said. "It's so rare that people don't even know it exists."

"I refuse to accept that answer," I said. "There's more—and he's going to help us find it."

"Wait..." Ian rubbed the back of his neck as he kept his eyes on the floor. "Could he be Necrosis?"

The thought hadn't occurred to me, and once he suggested it, a rock dropped into my stomach. My eyes went back to my sister. "Elora?"

"I mean, he didn't *look* like Necrosis. He wasn't covered with black spots or anything..."

"They only wear those marks when they're weak," I said. "Their features tend to be more prominent. Did you notice that?"

"He did have sharp features, but so do the two of you." Her eyes switched back and forth between us. "So that doesn't mean anything."

"Guess not," Ian said.

"Elora, when he approaches you again, you need to get everything out of him this time," I said. "Ian, you should stick close by while I'm gone."

"Gone?" Ian asked. "I'm coming with you."

"Mother and I will leave to take Delacroix," I said. "That means you'll be in charge of HeartHolme while we're gone."

"Commander Dawson can take the position," Ian argued. "Now that the battle has been won, I need to return to the outpost anyway."

"Those are the queen's orders, Ian." Ian showed great leadership in the battle against Necrosis, and he was the right person to oversee HeartHolme in the queen's absence. He lacked confidence in himself, born from years of disapproval from our mother. "You're the best person for the job."

Ian didn't argue anymore, but he looked disappointed.

"We'll be leaving soon," I said. "So, I need you to do something for me, Elora."

"Sure," she said. "Anything you need."

"I need you to make armor."

She looked me up and down even though I wasn't wearing any. "You already have my best design. I haven't made any improvements since."

"It's not for me."

Her eyes narrowed, probably thinking of Ivory.

"It's for the dragons."

WHEN I WALKED in the door, she was sitting at the kitchen table eating the leftover bacon and toast that was still sitting in the pan. In one of my shirts that fit her like a blanket, she had one leg propped up her chair while the other rested on the floor. "You know I don't like waking up to you being gone."

"That's why I made you breakfast." I approached the table then leaned down and kissed her.

She stilled at the affection before she gave me a kiss back.

"What?"

"What?" she said back.

I pulled out the chair and sat down. "You hesitated."

"We've just never done that before. You know, kiss good-bye, kiss when we see each other..."

With my arm over the back of the chair, I stared at her.

"Not that I don't like it..."

"You have a funny way of showing it."

"It's just weird, you know? To think of where we started... and where we are now."

"I never think about where we started. Doesn't matter anymore." She had no resemblance to the man who'd taken everything from me. She didn't remind me of everything I lost. My mother and sister were still in that place, but I hadn't been there for a long time. "When you're finished, I need you to help me with something."

"What is it?"

"Elora is going to make armor for the dragons. Need to get them fitted."

She was about to take another bite of her toast when she hesitated. "She can do that?"

"Elora can do anything."

"You think the dragons need it?"

"I think if they're the last free dragons, we need to do whatever we can to protect them."

"No argument there." She abandoned her food and got to her feet. "Let me get dressed and we'll go—"

I yanked her onto my lap then pulled her into my chest.

Her arms were around my neck, her fingers in the back of my hair. Her lips landed on mine with the softness of a rose petal, and her fingers fisted my strands instinctively. She could feel my hardness underneath her, because she rolled her hips slightly, playing with it. "I guess there's no rush, right?"

PYRE AND STORM emerged once we approached the cavern. Their scales immediately shone in the sunlight, dark green and cobalt blue. They both dipped their heads to examine us, and Pyre rubbed his hard cheek against Ivory in greeting.

Storm was cold like me—and preferred to stare. *They've fed us well.*

"Those were my orders."

But we wish to fly.

"You can fly at night."

I want to fly in the daylight.

"Soon."

Ivory laughed at something Pyre said, and I didn't think dragons could smile, but he smiled at her.

"We're going to outfit you with armor," I said. "Do you have any objections?"

Armor?

Pyre turned to me.

"My sister is a blacksmith. The best blacksmith I've ever seen. She's made the armor and weapons for our army that have protected us all our battles. She'll protect you as well."

Has she made dragon armor before?

"No. But I assure you, she can do it."

Storm looked at Pyre. Pyre looked at Storm. A silent conversation ensued.

I waited for a response, but nothing was forthcoming. "What are your concerns?"

Storm turned back to me. *That we won't be able to fly.*

"Then don't wear it."

We will try.

When I turned around, I saw Queen Rolfe approaching with Ian and Elora. Commander Dawson was there, escorting her as her private guard. She was back to her regal attire, her dark hair smoothed out and braided with feathers. Her eyes were on the two beasts behind me as if I wasn't even there.

She came to a halt a way back, her eyes wide as she examined the two dragons before us. Her arms were rigid by her sides, and her eyes combed over their scales. She'd never seen a dragon like the rest of us, and it took her just as long to believe her sight.

Ian was stone-faced with his hands behind his back.

Elora looked like a child eager to rush ahead.

When Mother regained her composure, she stepped forward. "I'm Queen Rolfe of HeartHolme, and I'm very happy you two are here. When my home was faced with doom, you came to the rescue with fire and teeth—and I'm forever grateful for your intervention. If there's ever anything I can do for you, please don't hesitate to ask."

Another cow.

I gave a Storm a cold look.

She said I could ask for anything.

"Not now, alright?" I whispered.

Is it customary for humans to make meaningless offers?

I turned forward and ignored him.

Queen Rolfe continued. "Our next plan is to take Delacroix, the kingdom that once belonged to my late husband and me. My eldest son tells me you've pledged your loyalty until we prevail over these lands. That debt will not be forgotten." She took a step, her hands behind her back. "To prepare, Elora will build your custom armor and saddles for riders. Once that's complete, we will move forward. I will make sure you're comfortable in the meantime."

Elora came closer, her measuring string wrapped around her shoulder. "Is it okay if I approach?"

No.

I turned back to Storm.

Ivory spoke next. "They'd like me to do it...if that's okay."

Elora couldn't hide her disappointment, probably because she wanted the honor of touching a dragon. "Uh, sure. I'll tell you what to measure, and you give me your readings." She placed the measuring string in Ivory's hands. "This is the biggest I could find...so I hope it works."

"I'll figure it out." Ivory took it and walked to Pyre, who immediately lowered himself to the ground so she could reach the areas of his body.

I turned to look at my mother and sister and watched them watch Ivory.

I could definitely see it then—see them look at her differently.

38

IVORY

We sat across from each other in his favorite pub, a few blocks away from his gated home. The ale was good and the food was hot, and since I'd never been a picky eater, a hot roast beef sandwich with a pile of gravy on top was just fine.

He'd returned to the bar a while ago, and while he got service from the barmaid right away, he'd also gotten the attention of someone else. A blonde with ringlets in her hair, her body language relaxed at the counter, her eyes possessing a flirtatious smile.

Did that bitch not see me?

He spoke to her as he waited for the barmaid to refill his glass.

I'd lost my shit once before and stabbed him out of jealousy, but I wouldn't humiliate myself again. I kept my eyes on my food and then drank more of my ale, but he was taking so long I would need a refill by the time he came back.

He finally got his ale and headed back to me. His muscled frame fell into the chair across from me, and he took a deep drink before he picked up his fork and stabbed it into a hot piece of meat slathered in gravy.

My eyes glanced back at her.

She was still staring at him.

I gave her a wave.

She swiveled her ass on the barstool and faced forward again.

What I thought, bitch.

His eyes were down on his food. "Going to stab me again?"

I ignored the question. "Who is she?"

"Jenny."

"That's not what I asked."

He took another bite then cracked a small smile.

"Are you going to tell me?"

"Baby, what does it matter?"

"It matters because she's under the impression you're still available."

"Not true."

"That's not what I saw."

"Well, I told her I was married, so now she knows."

"So, she *was* hitting on you?"

"Baby, come on." He took another drink. "Look at me."

"Wow...you're such an asshole."

This was all just a big joke to him, and he smiled in amusement. "I used to be her client. Told her I was married, and then she asked if Ian might be interested."

"Can you really be her client when she clearly wants to fuck you for free?"

He kept his eyes down on his food and took another bite.

I never got an answer to that.

"You're the most jealous woman I've ever been with."

"Because I'm your wife who doesn't appreciate other women hitting on you? When I'm ten fucking feet away?"

He chewed his food, the amusement in his eyes.

"This isn't funny."

"Look, when we're done here, I'll fuck you so hard that you'll forget about the whore at the bar, alright?"

I rolled my eyes. "Fuck you."

"You want me to fuck you right here? Because I will."

I ignored him.

He dropped his fork and got to his feet.

"Alright, sit the fuck down…"

He got back into his chair and resumed eating.

We ate our lunch in silence, and Ian walked in a moment later. He said hello to a few people before he made his way over to our table. His civilian attire still denoted his status, wearing a crisp black shirt with matching trousers. His eyes glanced back and forth between us, as if he could detect the hostility. "Is this a bad time or…?"

"No." Huntley finished his food and pushed his empty plate aside. "My wife is just pissed off at me right now."

"What'd you do?"

"*I* didn't do anything," he said. "A whore tried to book me for the night."

Just hearing that pissed me off all over again.

Ian gave a slight nod.

"Told her I was married. Then she asked if you'd be interested."

Ian perked up at that. "Yeah?"

"She's the blonde at the bar."

Ian scratched his jaw before he gave a discreet glance over his shoulder. "Is she any good?"

"Are you fucking kidding me?" I dogged my husband hard, because if he answered that, he really would get stabbed again.

That subtle smirk was on his lips, and it was infuriating. "Baby, you're the best I've ever had. Don't act like you don't know that."

That made me feel a little better, but I was still simmering beneath the surface.

Ian glanced at her again before he faced us once more. "Elora is almost done with the armor. I imagine you'll leave in a few days."

I dreaded leaving HeartHolme. Not because we'd have to travel the entire way on foot to protect the location of the dragons, but because I'd have to look my father in the eye before I betrayed him. I would strip him of his throne, and Huntley would imprison him for the rest of his life.

None of that would have been possible if it weren't for me.

Maybe he deserved it. That didn't mean I wanted to be involved with his punishment.

"I don't know how long we'll be gone," Huntley said. "You'll need to keep an eye on Elora."

Ian gave a slight sigh. "I always keep an eye on her."

"No offense to either of you, but she seems like someone who doesn't need to be watched." Elora had the mouth of a soldier and the stare of a falcon. She could build weapons and dragon armor. Just as capable as a man, if you asked me.

Huntley stared at me. "She's our sister. We'll always keep an eye on her."

———

HUNTLEY MADE good on his word and made me forget all about that blond bitch at the bar. He kissed me everywhere. Made me tug the sheets off the mattress. Made me writhe as if it was our first time rather than our hundredth. When the fun was over, he fell asleep right away, one arm behind his head, the sheets pulled to his waist.

Sometimes I just stared at him, admired his hard body with chiseled lines, the dark hair on his chest, the prominent V at his hips. Even when he was at rest, his body was flexed like he was in war.

This was a man.

And everyone before were boys.

I pulled on one of his long-sleeved shirts and moved to the dying fire. I added a couple logs without waking him then sat in the high-back armchair that faced the fire. With one knee to my chest, I watched the flames dance. They were wild and unbridled, unlike the fire that Pyre and Storm produced, which was purposeful and straight like an arrow.

I knew our time here was limited, and I wondered when we'd return after we reached Delacroix. In order to take the

Kingdoms, we'd have to remain in those lands, so this home would be abandoned.

I'd miss it.

Two dragons would fly high over Delacroix, casting shadows the size of clouds on the ground, blocking out the sun entirely in some instances. Citizens would scream in fright, assume their doom had arrived. Commander Burke would notify my father of the siege, but he would have no idea I would be the one leading the charge.

Pyre would land on the ground—and my father would see that I was the rider.

The guilt was like bile in my throat. It made my stomach roil the way it did when it was desperate with hunger. Acid had replaced the blood in my veins. As if I had been corrupted, I felt the tentacles of darkness wrap around me and pull me under.

Even if my father were guilty of all these travesties...it still sucked.

Huntley dropped into the chair beside me in his underwear. His big fingers slid across his face and caught the sleep in one of his eyes. It was still too early for bed, and neither one of us had had dinner yet. He watched the fire for a while before he turned to look at me. The firelight highlighted one of his cheeks. His bent arm supported his chin, his fingers lightly touching the coarse stubble.

I knew it was written all over my face.

"I'm sorry."

He knew. He knew so well. He was the other side of my coin. The blood to my heart. The beat to my drum. "The look on his face...I don't want to see it."

"You don't have to."

"Yes, I do." This was all my doing—and I wasn't a coward. "I want to confront him anyway. Sometimes I wonder...I wonder..." I couldn't bring myself to say it, let alone think it.

He continued to stare. "What is it, baby?"

"I wonder if he had anything to do with my mother's death." Even if he was as evil as Huntley proclaimed, I just couldn't believe he would do such a thing. "They were fighting a lot before she passed. And then she just got sick... and the priests couldn't figure out what was wrong with her."

"Why would her death benefit him?"

"I don't know...maybe he wanted his bed to be full of whores instead of her." He'd tried to keep it from me, but I knew the truth. I knew when he wasn't on official business, he was drinking and fucking like a teenage boy. I expected that behavior from Ryker, but not a grown man who should be a role model to his children. "I wonder about our past, where we come from, who else he left behind...if he ever loved me." I kept my eyes on the fire and could feel his stare. "He's always preferred Ryker over me. Never really spent any time with me. The only time he ever took an interest in me was when he taught me how to fight...and plotted to marry me off. But both of those things were to benefit himself, not me."

His stare continued.

"Not only do I dread seeing the look on his face when he's seen what I've done. But I also dread facing those questions...and getting the answers I don't want."

"Look at me."

The gentle command in his voice made my eyes water because I already knew what he was going to say.

"Come on."

I finally tore my eyes away from the flames and met his hard stare.

"Whether he loves you or not, it doesn't matter. Because I love you now, and I will love you forever." His gaze was sharp like a blade, powerful like the magic of Adeodatus. "No matter your age, you're the woman I want in my bed. I don't want a woman I bought. I want the woman I earned. I will be a damn good father to the children you give me, and I will love my daughters more than my sons simply because they'll look like you. I'm your family—and that's never going to change."

Two tears spilled over and streaked down my cheeks. "I know..."

AFTER LEAVING the tropical paradise of the island, the cold weather was harsh. Whenever the sun was out, the dragons left their cavern and basked in the sun, just the way pets found that perfect spot on the living room floor.

I sat in front of Pyre on the ground, the sun hitting my back while it hit him right in the face. His eyes were closed as he enjoyed it.

You seem sad.

"I am a bit sad... It's complicated."

I can try to understand.

"Well...Delacroix is where I'm from. I grew up there with my brother. I thought the kingdom had been in our family for generations, but then Huntley told me that wasn't true. It actually belonged to his family...until my father barbarically claimed it for himself. He did some other terrible things, things I won't repeat."

That's hard to believe since you're so kind.

"Thanks."

Does that mean you're going to kill him?

"No. Huntley promised me he wouldn't. But we're going to remove him from power. He'll probably be a prisoner for the rest of his life."

And you feel bad because he's your father.

"Like I said, it's complicated. He's going to see me show up with two dragons and married to his enemy. That's a lot to take in. I know I shouldn't feel bad, but I can't help it."

Family is complicated.

"Yes."

Storm and I are fellow hatchlings, but we don't always get along.

"This is more than not getting along. My father raped and murdered people..."

I'm sorry.

"Thanks."

You can make your own hatchlings with your husband.

"He said the same thing."

I'm sure they will be beautiful.

"Yeah...I think so too."

Ivory, something is happening.

I looked up to see three carriages leave the path and hit the grass as they approached us. Six enormous horses led the carriages, so the cargo in the rear must be heavy. They came to a standstill feet away, and then Elora hopped down from one of the carriages.

"Your armor must be ready." I got to my feet and dusted off my breeches.

I hope it's not too heavy.

"We'll see."

The men began to pull out the pieces, working together to bring the enormous plates across the grass toward the dragons. They looked heavy, but they couldn't be that unwieldy if the men could actually move them.

Elora set down the first piece. "I know they prefer you when it comes to proximity, but I really should be the one to do this. I just want to make sure everything is on right and secured before they test it out."

I turned to Pyre. "Is that okay?"

I suppose.

I gave her the go-ahead.

Elora didn't make small talk with me and barely looked at me, but she didn't seem hostile either, so that was a win.

It took a long time for Elora to fit each piece, even with the help of the men. She attached the breastplate, the metal rings that covered different parts of the neck while allowing for movement, attached the braces to the arms and legs, and then carefully installed the armor that went over the top of the wing. "This isn't tough armor like everything else, but it's so light that you should be able to fly. I can't attach it to the underpart of your wing. Otherwise, you won't be able to get off the ground." She worked to put everything together, and by the time she was done, Pyre looked like a whole different dragon.

The armor was black and matte, having no shine whatsoever. There were hints of red in the joints of the plates, made of a softer material that allowed for movement. The bolt and pins in the armor were pronounced and thick, and that added to the aesthetic.

Pyre moved his wings a bit and tried to take a look at himself. *How do I look?*

"Uh, badass."

Really? Me?

"Yes, you. I wish you could see yourself."

Storm came next, and once all the armor was attached, Pyre could get a good look. *Wow. That is badass.*

"See? Now you think you can fly?"

We shall see. Pyre opened his wings and gave a hard flap as he pushed himself off the earth.

"Be careful."

He got off the ground and continued to flap, but he lost his height a couple times, as if he didn't know how to flap his wings with the new weight. But he kept trying, and soon, he got the hang of it. He soared through the sky, a behemoth of teeth, fire, and wings.

Storm took off and joined him, and then they started to play fight in the sky.

Everyone was mesmerized.

"Elora, you nailed it."

With her arms crossed over her chest and her head tilted back, she watched. "Yeah...I think I did."

"On your first try, too."

"What can I say?" She brushed off her shoulder and gave me a smile. "I'm that good."

Did she just smile at me?

She looked up at the sky again, the pride in her eyes. "I've made a lot of great things...but nothing as special as this."

WE WERE LED to the grand table near the sea of windows.

Queen Rolfe was already there at the head of the table, in her black dress with sleeves, a chain necklace across her front that attached her cape to her garment. With feathers woven in her hair and dark makeup around her eyes, she looked wild and authoritative at the same time.

Commander Dawson was to her left. Ian was on the other side of him, dressed in a similar fashion.

I knew the seat to the queen's right was reserved for her right-hand man, Huntley.

Huntley took that seat, so I sat in the chair beside him, unsure if I was even allowed the join the table.

With her hands together on the table, Queen Rolfe held her silence as she considered her opening words. "The dragons are ready for the siege, and I think we are as well. I suggest we depart at sunrise. With the dragons at our disposal, we don't need an army, not when we're catching them by surprise. Two dozen soldiers should be plenty to secure the castle. There will be no resistance from the civilians, not when we're the rightful rulers, and not when we have two dragons that can burn their town to splinters."

My heart was beating so fast, picturing the attack on the place I once considered home.

"The soldiers and I will take the tunnel to the top, and you'll meet us in the woods. At sunrise, we'll take Delacroix. That way, they can see the full glory of the dragons that serve us."

"They don't serve us," I said. "They're our allies." I'd already said that once, and I'd better not have to say it again.

Huntley turned to me. "Her Highness means that in a different way than you're interpreting. Everyone here serves Queen Rolfe. Not literally, but by loyalty and of free will."

"Just want to make it very clear that the dragons will not be enslaved by any master ever again, and if that's your intention, then I'll no longer be your ally." The words left my mouth with the sharpness of Huntley's ax, and my eyes had no hint of regret.

Queen Rolfe stared at me with stony silence. "It is not my intention."

"Then we won't have any problems."

Queen Rolfe turned to Ian. "I appoint you as Heart-Holme's keeper. You fought bravely against Necrosis, and I have full confidence that you will protect our people in my absence."

Ian stared at the table before he finally gave a subtle nod.

Huntley watched his brother.

"Your task is to investigate the whereabouts of Ice and harvest as much as you can. Elora will need it to outfit our army with as many weapons as she can. I believe we won't hear from Necrosis for a while, but I have no doubt they'll return eventually, even if they think the dragons are here."

Ian gave another nod. "Yes, Your Highness."

"And you're to detain the mysterious man Elora spoke with. I want to know everything about him—and who holds his allegiance."

Ian nodded again.

"We'll send our missives by crow—and hope they can make it to the top of the cliffs."

"I'm sure our falcons will be able to do it," Commander Dawson said. "Communication will be imperative at this time, especially if the Teeth and Plunderers realize that the queen is absent from HeartHolme."

"What of the outpost?" Ian asked. "We can't leave it abandoned. It'll be overrun, and we won't be able to reclaim it."

"Send Geralt," the queen said. "He'll be in command of it now." She looked around the table. "If there are no other concerns, we'll prepare for our journey in the morning."

Huntley turned to his mother. "Elora did an incredible job outfitting the dragons. I hope you express your awe as well as your gratitude. She didn't take up a sword in battle, but she's won our wars."

Queen Rolfe stared at him for a long time, and her stony stare was even more intense than his. "You're dismissed."

We all left the table, and I was happy to be out of there.

"Huntley, stay."

Commander Dawson and Ian walked out, and I took up the rear.

"You too, Ivory."

I stilled in front of the door, and instead of walking through it, I closed it.

Queen Rolfe addressed Huntley. "Speak to me like that again in front of an audience, and I will strip you of all your titles. Do you understand me?" She scolded him without raising her voice, without even appearing angry.

Huntley remained quiet.

"If you want to comment on my parenting abilities, you will do so in private."

"It's the first time I've heard you acknowledge that she's your daughter in over a decade."

The tension was so thick it felt like a cloud of smoke was in the room. I didn't want to be there, didn't want to feel her hostility and wrath.

Queen Rolfe stared him down. "If Klaus had raped your wife while in captivity, and she gave birth to a boy who had his eyes and his teeth, would you love it like your own?" As if she had a knife between his ribs, she twisted it and dug even deeper.

Huntley remained still, but his breathing changed, and that gave away his cards.

Her eyes shifted back and forth between his. "So, don't you dare judge me, Huntley. Because we both know you would kill that child the second it emerged from her womb. Stab it right in its little beating heart."

He couldn't hold her gaze any longer.

I'd never seen Huntley break contact first.

"My husband is still alive because he lives in you. Every time I look at your face, I see the man I pledged my life to. His soul is gone from my reach, so my soul withers a little more every day. If I didn't have sons who bore his resemblance and spirit, I would have taken my own life long ago. That is the greatest testament to my love for you two—the fact that I'm still here. I know we don't agree on everything, and I know I'm harsh sometimes, but you've never once doubted my affection. I can't pretend to feel that way toward Elora. I won't insult her by pretending that my love for her is comparable to my love for you. Perhaps that makes me a monster, but I really don't care."

Huntley still didn't look at her.

"I'm grateful that you and your brother can see your similarities more than your differences, that you can give her the love I never could. I understand she's a victim as much as I am and doesn't deserve my absence, but I also don't deserve to be burdened by this issue for the rest of my life."

Huntley stared at the floor for a while, his stony expression identical to the stone keep.

She waited, as if she knew that wasn't the end of it.

"You're right," he whispered. "I wouldn't be able to do what I'm asking you to do."

Despite her clothing and her confidence, she didn't look like the queen anymore. She was just a mother.

"But you're the most inspiring person I've ever known...and you're a hell of a lot stronger than me." He raised his head and looked her in the eye. "I think you could...if you tried." With that, he stepped away, ending the conversation by turning his back on her.

She watched him walk away, her eyes not sharp with authority, but soft with vulnerability. She stared at him as he looked out the window, studied him like she saw him in a brand-new light. Then her eyes flicked to me.

Every muscle in my body tightened once I was the recipient of that stare.

She didn't ask me to approach, but I walked over her to her anyway, following a command that was never given.

Her expression was different now, not soft and vulnerable like it was for her son. But it wasn't callous either. "I never properly thanked you for what you've done for Heart-Holme and all the people I've vowed to protect. I would have fought until my dying breath like we had a chance, but deep in my heart, I knew we never did. Because of your unique abilities, you were able not only to heal the dragons, but to convince them to help us in this fight, and you've managed to earn my son's heart...a man who's always been heartless. You've earned my respect—and it's time that I give it."

Rendered speechless, I didn't know what to say.

"All I've ever wanted for Huntley is a woman who can hold her own, a woman who does more than birth his children. A woman who will take up a sword and defend her family just the way he would. And that's exactly what you are."

Honestly, that was the nicest thing anyone had ever said to me, and it meant a lot more coming from somebody like her.

"I hope you can find it in your heart to accept my apology, but if you can't, I understand."

All the animosity I felt toward her disappeared instantly. I'd always hated her as a person but admired her as a queen. But now, I admired her as both. It took a lot to admit shortcomings, especially for someone who never had to admit anything at all. "Of course I do."

Her eyes narrowed slightly, showing the same look of surprise that Huntley showed on occasion.

"My husband is the man of my dreams because of you."

Her eyes narrowed a little more, this time with a contraction of emotion.

"I admire you as both a mother and a queen—and I'm honored to serve you."

Her chest rose with the deep breath she took, and all her rigid majesty disappeared. She looked at me the way she looked at her sons, with a twinge of vulnerability, with a dash of emotion. "Thank you, Ivory."

I backed away and looked at Huntley by the window.

He was leaning against it, arms across his chest, a slight smile on his lips. He pushed off the wall with his hips and approached his mother with his arms by his sides.

Queen Rolfe didn't look at him, as if it was too much for her.

He continued to stare down at her, his eyes affectionate the way they were for me sometimes. "What did I tell you?" His arm circled her shoulders, and he drew her in closer. "Knew you'd like her."

The smile spread to her lips.

"Thank you." He kissed her on the hairline before he released her. "Love you."

Her eyes softened altogether as she gazed at her son, giving him a look of love that my mother used to give me. "Love you too, my boy."

I opened the door to the servants on the other side. They carried two trays of dinner, just as I asked them to do every night for the foreseeable future. I didn't let them into my bedroom to set up at the dining table anymore. Just took the food and shut them out. I balanced both trays and carried them to the dining table.

Effie was in one of my long-sleeved shirts, her hair slightly damp from the shower she'd just taken. "They must know you have someone living in here."

"I'm sure they do." I set everything down and opened a bottle of wine.

"Won't that information make it back to your father?"

I poured the two glasses then recorked the wine. "Don't care if it does."

"He would just be fine with it?"

"I don't care who sleeps in his bed, and he doesn't care who sleeps in mine." I took a seat and dropped the linen in my lap.

She moved to the chair across from me. "Must be nice to be a man..."

"It is."

We ate together just as we did with all our other meals. She'd been staying with me for weeks. The Blade Scions had left after they cleared our operations, but I didn't take her back to the house where she would spend all her time alone. When she was with me, she was safe and fed, and she gave me good sex every night.

With her head tilted down to her food, she spoke. "We both know I can't stay here forever."

I didn't want to think about it.

"I have to find my family. I have to go outside. Right now, I'm a rat living in the cracks in the floor."

"A very cute rat."

She gave a little smile.

"I know I'll have to travel to the Capital soon. I'll take you with me then."

"And what will I do there?"

"I'll buy you a house."

"That didn't answer my question."

I pushed my food around with my fork. "We'll find your family. Then they can move in with you. You can start new lives."

"The Capital is really far away..."

"We'll make it work." I wished she could stay in Delacroix, but other people in the town would recognize her, and that would compromise the ongoing lottery. There were other villages closer by, but they didn't have the same infrastructure to keep her safe. Also, I didn't have much of a reason to visit those other places, so it would be even harder to see her.

A knock sounded on the door.

Effie flinched, as if she wasn't sure if she should dart into the washroom.

I dropped my fork and got to my feet, then I nodded toward the bathroom.

Effie disappeared.

I opened the door and came face-to-face with Commander Burke. "Something you need, Commander?"

"Your father has requested your presence." His eyes purposely shifted past me to the table with two dinner plates, as if to make a point. Then he walked down the hall-way, his boots loud against the thick rug and the hardwood.

My father hardly asked for my attendance in the evening, so whatever it was, it was probably important. I threw on my attire before I took the stairs to the next landing. He was at the grand dining table, his dinner laid out before him. In his hands was a roll, which he ripped in half before stuffing one piece into his mouth.

I took the seat on his right, the plate already prepared with food for me.

He chewed the enormous piece of bread as he stared at me, the food hardly able to fit inside his mouth.

"Enjoying that roll, huh?"

Annoyance entered his gaze as he forced the food down his throat. "Word has reached my ears that you have a long-term guest staying with you."

I didn't dodge the accusation or sugarcoat the truth. "You've never been concerned with my personal life before."

"Only when a guest becomes a resident—and it sounds like that's what she is."

"Don't you have whores who live here—"

"We agreed that you would wed Lady Elizabeth at the Capital. Did we not?"

No, we didn't agree on anything. "Oh shit, is that tomorrow?"

My father glared, not the least bit amused by my smartass comment. "Ryker. What did I tell you about getting serious with a woman who fucks men for a living?"

"She does it for free, so your concern is unfounded."

"Ryker." He slammed his closed fist on the hard table. "I'm sending you to the Capital next week to woo Elizabeth, and you'd better be unencumbered when that happens. With Ivory gone, that's our only path to the throne."

"King Rutherford has three sons. I'm not going to marry someone to be fourth in line."

"You'll be first in line—eventually." He grabbed his ale and took a drink.

I heard the warning in his voice, crisp and sharp. "What are you implying? You're going to kill all three of them?"

"*I* won't be doing anything." He said nothing more and left it at that.

He'd mentioned something like this before, but I didn't think he was serious. I spent my summers in the Capital growing up, spent time with Maddox, Jaime, and Peter in the gardens, sailing their little sailboat in the harbor, skipping rocks on the ocean. They were rambunctious and cocky at times, but they'd never done anything that deserved this treason. "Delacroix is more than enough for me. I'm happy to inherit your title when your time comes."

He picked up his chicken leg and took a few bites before he slowly turned his head and regarded me, his eyes as sharp as a spear. "Well, it's not enough for me. The Kingdoms will be ours before my time comes."

I hadn't touched my food, not when my stomach was full of bile, not when Ivory's words rang with truth. "When you came to the top of the cliffs, why didn't you take the throne in the first place?"

He finished the rest of the leg, eating everything down to the bone. Juice dripped from his lips, and he didn't bother to wipe his mouth even though the linen was right on the table. "Because Rutherford was in charge—and I had to bide my time. Now that you're of age, it's time."

"I think we should wait until Ivory returns. She can marry Maddox. No one has to die." It was all a ploy to stall, to spare myself from marrying a woman I didn't even know. Ivory was already married, but that fact didn't matter right now.

"Who knows when she'll return."

"You could send men to find her, just the way you did with me."

"Remember how that worked out? All of them are dead— because of you."

I felt like shit about that, but I also felt worse that he was willing to send an army after me but not his daughter.

"You're going to the Capital next week. Break it off with the girl."

I stared at my full plate, unsure what to do. There was no way I was ending things with Effie. But I didn't know how to get out of this either. I could just be a dick to Elizabeth so she wouldn't accept my marriage proposal. That was the only solution I could think of. "Father...there's something I've been meaning to discuss with you."

He grabbed his next piece of meat and ate with his hands.

"I understand the lottery serves a greater purpose to us all. But that solution is temporary, and over the course of time, it's costly. Lottery winners are selected every two weeks, so over the course of decades, that's a lot of people that are leaving Delacroix."

"If you're worried about population control, we've got too many people as it is."

"I'm more concerned about the morality of the situation."

He stopped eating and gave me his direct stare.

"Necrosis is an enemy always sitting just on the horizon. They haven't provoked us yet, but they could defeat everyone at the bottom of the cliffs at some point, and then we'll be next—"

"Your imagination is running wild right now."

"It's not my imagination. It's a possibility. And if that happens, we won't be able to fight them."

"We'll be long dead and gone if that ever happens."

"But what about my children? And their children?" The man I'd admired most of my life looked totally different to me now. He was truly selfish. Was truly indifferent to the plights of other people. A ruler should care more about his citizens than himself.

"I live in the moment, Ryker. Not the past. Not the future."

Roughly translated, I don't give a shit about anybody but my wine and my whores. "I think it's something we should be concerned about. I think if we unite all our forces, there's a chance we can defeat Necrosis—"

"Where is all this hogwash coming from?" He pivoted in the chair and stared at me head on. "You're fucking a girl who wins the lottery, and now your world view is upside down. Is that the woman staying in your quarters?"

Shit.

"Because if it is, I'll push her throat down on my blade."

"It's not." I blurted out the answer with confidence and held his gaze like my life depended on it. "Knowing someone who won the lottery did make me question everything. I wasn't able to save her, but the impression she left on me was eternal. I'm just suggesting an alternate course of action, because what we're doing right now is buying us time, not fixing the problem."

He seemed to believe me because he faced forward again. "No."

I knew my father would be unresponsive to the suggestion, but I didn't anticipate his coldness. I didn't suspect it would unveil his true character, the character that had always been there but I'd never noticed. Or didn't want to notice. "Father—"

"When we were stuck down there and the Rolfes ruled the Kingdoms, do you think they gave a damn about us?"

His gaze was so sharp it scratched my eyeballs.

"They let us suffer. Let all of us suffer. So you're damn right I'll do the same. I'm not going to risk my life and everything I've worked so hard for to march on an enemy that can't even touch me. They can all be damned for all I care."

***

I PULLED my shirt off and tossed it aside. My boots were kicked off next, my breeches afterward. Walking through my bedchamber, I ripped everything off as I went along, not even noticing Effie at the dining table.

"What happened?"

My glass of wine was still where I'd left it, so I downed the rest of it before I took a seat. "Just a bunch of bullshit."

Her eyes softened with pity. She looked even more beautiful when she did that, empathetic. "I'm sorry."

"He wants me to go to the Capital next week. That's when I'll get you settled into your new place."

"Why does he want you there?"

I almost didn't look at her when I answered. "Wants me to woo Lady Elizabeth."

The light was immediately snuffed out of her eyes. "Oh…"

"Don't worry. I'll be a dick so she won't want me."

"You don't have to do that—"

"I don't want to marry her."

"Well, it's not like you can marry me."

My eyes took her in, thinking of my sister who married the enemy. If she could choose the worst possible person, I should be able to choose whomever I wanted. "I've been dragging my feet for a while, knowing what he would say. But I finally did it, and…it was worse than I ever expected it would be."

"Really?" she whispered. "What did he say?"

"First, he basically admitted he wants to stage a coup against King Rutherford. He'd kill all his sons, leaving no heirs, and then kill him next." My eyes dropped to my empty wineglass. "Then I'd become king, through my marriage to Elizabeth. The whole thing is just barbaric."

Effie was silent, her expression doing all the talking.

"Said he didn't give a damn about anyone at the bottom of the cliffs. Didn't care about the lottery. Didn't care about protecting future generations. But he did say something else…"

"What?"

"That when the Rolfes ruled the Kingdoms, they did the same thing."

"Yeah."

"So, he doesn't owe anyone anything."

"Huntley isn't like that—if that's what you're thinking."

I slouched in the chair as I stared at her.

"He and Ivory are determined to do the right thing—for everyone. So, if you have any doubt about helping them, it needs to be assuaged now. If you stand by your father's side, nothing will ever change. But if you stand with Ivory, this world could be better. For all of us."

I WAS UP AT SUNRISE.

The fire was dead in the fireplace, and Effie's naked body was wrapped around mine. Her hair was matted in different ways, from the way I'd fisted it last night, from the way she'd lain on the same side all night so she could hold me close. I placed a kiss to her shoulder before I slipped out of bed and got dressed for the day.

The castle was quiet, the guards ready for the morning shift to replace them at their posts. Breakfast wafted from the kitchens, and just by the smell alone, I knew honey-smoked ham was on the menu. I made it downstairs, passed the guards at the front, and stepped into the daybreak.

It was a cool morning, a cloudless sky. I looked down at the city below then glanced up at the sunrise. It was just below the clouds beneath the edge of the cliffs, but the color of the sky was slowly changing, from pinks and oranges to blues and purples.

And then I saw it.

It started in my periphery, coming from the north, a dark spot against a soft sky. I turned to get a better look at it, to make out the expansive wings that held enough weight to keep the creature afloat. "What the...?" I stepped closer and squinted.

There were two.

Two fucking dragons.

Headed right toward us.

40

HUNTLEY

"Storm, make a perimeter of fire around Delacroix." We'd waited for Queen Rolfe outside the tunnel in the woods, and once we had our meager army, we'd marched on the city and arrived at sunrise like we planned.

Ivory grabbed my wrist. "We agreed to leave Delacroix unharmed."

I twisted out of her grasp. "I told him to make a perimeter, not burn the city or its inhabitants. We must display our power if we want this to end peacefully. Our dragons are armored and can burn this place to ash if he doesn't surrender."

Ivory searched my gaze before she gave a nod.

Storm jumped into the sky. *I burn.* He opened his mouth and shot out a stream of fire, burning the fields around the exterior of the city, preventing anyone from entering or departing. The green was lush and green, but it sparked like desiccated firewood.

I watched him go, watched his powerful wings carry his mass as well as his armor.

Faron would be scared shitless once he saw it.

"Let me handle this."

My eyes narrowed on her face. "I don't think that's a good idea."

"He's my father—"

"And that's exactly why you shouldn't." We stood together in the field, Pyre by our side for protection. The screams came a moment later, everyone in the city panicking as they saw the cobalt dragon armed to the teeth surround them in fire. "I will handle this." I turned away before she could argue with me.

Queen Rolfe stared at the castle, glorious in her tailored armor, her eyes fixated on the structure she'd once called home. "A part of me is happy to see this place again. But another part of me wants to burn it to the ground—out of spite." She continued to stare, her eyes on a window at the top. "I've thought about this day for a long time. Every moment since the last day I stood on these lands."

"I know, Mother."

She finally pulled her gaze away and inhaled a slow breath. "I can taste his blood on my tongue."

I'd kept my promise a secret to her so far. If I'd told her a long time ago, we may not have reached this moment. "When Ivory agreed to help me, she gave me one condition."

She stiffened.

"We may punish her father however we wish. But we must spare his life."

She'd never looked at me like that before—like she wanted to kill me. "And you agreed?"

"It was the only way."

Her head moved forward again, as if she was ashamed of me.

"We'll still take back our home. We'll still get our revenge. It's just not exactly how we pictured it."

She visibly shook, she was so angry.

"It's better to accept the compromise than forfeit the victory altogether."

"How dare she defend him?"

"She doesn't. Whatsoever."

"Then how can she plead for his life—"

"It doesn't matter. Those were her terms. We must honor them."

Her hands went to her hips, and she dropped her stare to the grass beneath us. "I need a moment."

"Of course, Your Highness." I stepped away and returned to Ivory.

She stared at my face, her eyes shifting back and forth.

"I just told her."

"She didn't know?"

I stared.

"What if she does it anyway—"

"She won't."

"But what if—"

"We made an agreement. We will hold that agreement."

Storm landed on the other side of us, the ring of fire secured around us. We were just outside the gates, the soldiers visible up the hill as they organized into their ranks as if they would march on us.

I'd already called their bluff.

The gates opened, and men approached.

"Huntley."

I turned back to my mother.

Her arms were back to her sides, her spine perfectly straight. "Take the throne in my name. I would do it myself —but I'll kill him."

I nodded then faced the men who marched toward us. "Get behind me, baby."

"I'm not a coward—"

"Now."

She didn't test me and shielded herself behind me.

I recognized Faron as he drew closer. His green eyes. His dark hair that was now peppered with gray. His shoulders used to be broader, and he used to be thinner. Age had weakened his muscles and extended his stomach. A ruler should be strong, always ready for combat, not lazy with a belly full of booze. When he was just feet away, I saw his most defining feature.

The scars on his left cheek.

They were still there, just faded.

Motherfucker probably had no idea who I was—but he was about to find out.

Ryker was on his right, in his full armor with two short swords at his hip. His eyes immediately narrowed on my face because he remembered me from last time. His eyes shifted left and right, looking for his sister.

I was surprised Faron had the balls to leave his castle and face me like a man.

Perhaps he was Ivory's father after all.

He stared me down.

I did the same time to him.

Nothing was said. The fire crackled around us, and it was hot enough to reach my skin through my armor.

The memory of that night was scarred in my mind, and now that vivid memory looked different, because I replaced his old face with the new one. With the wrinkles and fat. I pictured him on top of my mother, his round belly shaking with the thrusts.

I'd thought I could keep my promise, but now I wasn't so sure.

It was the hardest thing I'd ever done. "Surrender. Not only will your men and city be spared, but your life as well. Resist, and we will burn your castle to the ground and build a new one on top of it. We will burn your armies until they're fiery corpses. We will burn your crops, so your subjects starve. We will leave this place inhabitable."

His eyes shifted to Pyre and studied him for a long time. "Dragons are supposed to be myths. Supposed to be legends told by firelight. And yet, you have two. How?"

His entitlement only angered me, but I didn't show it. "Because I'm the true King of the Kingdoms."

He straightened at my words.

"I've been forsaken for twenty years. But no longer. Surrender."

It didn't seem like he knew who I was, not even with that blatant hint.

"You don't remember me, do you?"

His eyes narrowed.

"I was a boy then. Weak. Powerless. Defenseless. Tied to a chair and forced to watch my mother be subjugated to cruelty that still haunts my nightmares."

His eyes flicked to my mother—like he knew.

"Look at her again and see what happens."

His eyes turned back to me.

"Now I'm a man. A man who's killed Necrosis. A man who's felled yetis. A man who's survived blizzards and storms, who's survived a fall from the top of the cliffs to the ice-cold tundra below. A man who was raised by a queen who has bigger balls than you ever will. In my father's name, I take back what is mine. Now drop your sword and bend the knee."

Faron held my gaze but didn't move an inch.

"Bend. The. Fucking. Knee."

"You said you would spare my life. Why?"

My jaw clenched and my teeth ground together, because all I wanted to do was give a flick of my sword and slice his head from his shoulders. I wanted to stick his head on a pike in the market for all the citizens to see. I wanted to throw the rest of his body over the cliff—where it belonged. "Because my wife asked me not to."

Raw confusion took over his face.

Ivory stepped out from behind me and revealed herself.

His eyes shifted to her face, and at first, there was just pain. Pain at the betrayal. Pain at the secrecy. Pure and raw devastation.

That gave me a bit of satisfaction.

But then that pain transformed into rage. Blinding rage that stretched out his wrinkles, that furrowed his eyebrows, that made an ugly man that much uglier. "Ivory—"

"It's true... You really did that." The tears were in her voice but absent from her face. It wasn't a question, just a painful realization. Elora's existence was enough evidence, but hearing me describe it again without his objection was the final nail in the coffin. "How could you?"

"How could I?" he asked incredulously. "You're the one who betrayed your own family. Your father. Your brother. You gave the enemy the keys to our kingdoms. You married the man who will strip away everything I worked so hard for—"

"Worked so hard for?" she snapped. "Murder and rape. That constitutes hard work?"

"He's a pretty man who's tricked you into bed and fooled your heart, but he's no better than me. While we suffered down below and begged for asylum, they rejoiced up here and abandoned us to our misery. We made it to the top of the cliffs in peace, and you know what they did?"

Ivory stood beside me, breathing hard.

"They forced us back down. Threatened to kill us if we didn't return. Your husband can pretend he's better than me, but he and his whore mother—"

My sword was out of my scabbard. "Just give me a reason."

Her hand went to my wrist and steadied it.

He watched me for a while before he turned his gaze on Ivory. "They aren't better than us, despite what they say. They're lies, Ivory. And you're too stupid to see that."

"Maybe you're right," she said. "Maybe all of that is true. It doesn't justify what you did to her. Nothing ever justifies holding a woman down and forcing her against her will, and I'm absolutely ashamed to call you my father."

His look of rage continued, reserved for Ivory.

"We're going to change this world. We're going to unite the Kingdoms and take down Necrosis once and for all. There will be no lottery. People won't be confined to the bottom of the cliffs against their will. Our world will be a free place—for everyone."

"That's the stupidest thing I've ever heard."

Ivory stilled, as if her father had crossed the gap between them and slapped her in the face.

"Did you really stab me in the back for *this*?" he asked, unable to contain his attitude. "For a plan that has no chance of success? I gave you a life of luxury and royalty, and this is how you repay me? Judge my sins all you want—but we're family. And you don't do that to family. You don't do that to your father. To your brother. You're ashamed of me? I'm ashamed of you. I'm ashamed that my daughter is too fucking stupid to know how the world really works."

For the first time in her life, Ivory was rendered speechless.

I stepped forward with my sword at my side. "Bend the knee."

His eyes flicked back to me, vicious.

"Bend the knee. Or die."

His face contorted into an angry look of malice. He couldn't contain it, couldn't prevent himself from rupturing. He withdrew his sword and swiped to cut me across the throat.

I blocked the hit, pushed his sword down, and then punched him so hard in the face he fell back. "Bend." I stood over him and kicked him hard in the back. "The." I grabbed him by the shoulder and forced him up, on his knees. "Knee."

41

IVORY

Once my father officially surrendered, his army did as well.

The ring of fire around the city burned out, the screams of the citizens abated, and it looked like a normal day once we were at the castle. Storm perched on top of the castle and admired the view of the city below, and Pyre lay on the grass of the castle grounds, enjoying the sunshine as it heated the metal of his armor.

There was no resistance from any of the soldiers or the guards, and that showed me how faint their loyalty had been. I suspected it wasn't because of their lack of morals, but their lack of belief in their ruler.

I stood in front of the castle and looked at the city that used to be my home. It was exactly the same, but it felt different now. Felt like a foreign place I'd never been.

Huntley handled the conquest as if he'd rehearsed it in his head a hundred times. As if this was another city that he'd brought to its knees. Queen Rolfe took a step back, and that told me how deep-seated her hatred was for my father. This day should have been joyous for her, but the past was still too traumatic, twenty years later.

My father was taken to the dungeons, and the few men that refused to surrender were slain. The takeover was fairly bloodless, went far better than I thought it would, but I hadn't expected it to hurt so much.

Ryker appeared in front of me, but I didn't even see him approach.

"I know you hate me right now... I'm sorry."

"I don't."

I let his face come into crisper focus, let his handsome features become clear.

"You did the right thing."

"I did?" I whispered.

He nodded. "Everything you told me about him, I didn't really believe it before, but when I spoke to him...I saw it."

"Yeah..."

"And I really saw it today."

I gave a nod.

"It's hard to fight your enemies, but it's even harder to fight your family. You're brave, Ivory."

"Brave?" I whispered. "I don't feel brave. I feel like shit."

"Don't. The cycle will never end unless we break it. And if we succeed, this world will finally be different. It's worth a try."

"You've really come around."

He gave a shrug. "The Rolfes abandoned everyone just the way Father did. That means anyone in this seat of power will do the same. If we've found someone who will change that, then we've got to support him."

"Yes."

"And you didn't kill him—so your loyalty remains intact."

"Despite everything he's done...I could never do that."

"I know," he said. "Me neither." His hand went to my shoulder, and he gave it a squeeze before he pulled me into his chest. "It's nice that we're together again."

I clamped down on him and held on tight, even though his armor was hard and uncomfortable. "I missed you."

He pulled away and gave me a smile. "Whoa, let's not get carried away."

My wall of sadness was shattered, just for a moment. "How's Effie?"

"Up until two dragons headed straight for the city, she was doing well. Been staying with me in my bedchamber."

I waggled my eyebrows. "Has she now?"

He rolled his eyes.

"Told you."

"Guess she can't stay mad at me forever...not when I'm this sexy."

"Okay, we're done here."

***

HUNTLEY HAD his men stationed throughout the castle, and he employed the new guards under his wing. He was busy running the place and getting everything in order, so I went down to the basement to visit my father.

If I told Huntley what I was doing, I knew he would talk me out of it, but I still had more to say to my father, things I didn't say on the battlefield, things I didn't want to say in front of an audience and two dragons.

I made my way down the stairs and found him in his cell.

It was more luxurious than a regular prisoner's cell. It had a full bed, a shelf with books, an armchair, and a fireplace with a stack of wood. Other than the iron bars of the cell and the brick that lined the walls, it was practically a royal bedchamber.

He sat in the armchair in front of the fireplace, one arm on his knee, his eyes on no spot in particular.

The love between parent and child was unconditional, so even though he deserved this sentence, it still hurt to see him that way, to watch him rot in a cell for the rest of his life. It hurt to know that my own father was the source of incredible pain to the man I loved. It made me feel like shit, and then I felt even shittier for having any feelings toward my father at all.

His eyes flicked to me, stone-cold.

I stayed a few feet back from the bars, not that I expected him to reach for me.

"What will you do with Ryker?"

"Nothing. He's free to do as he wishes."

A glimmer of relief moved into his gaze, and that made it hurt a little more. "Good."

I'd come all the way down here, but now I didn't have the words.

"I know you're the only reason they haven't killed me." His eyes shifted back to the fire. "While I appreciate that, death is preferable to a cage. You should know that."

"I do know that. But this imprisonment doesn't need to be forever."

After a pause, he looked at me again.

"After you serve some time, I think an apology would go a long way."

He leaned back in the chair, releasing a quiet sigh. "Sweetheart, apologies mean nothing between enemies. Apologies are meant for those you love because they're the only ones who will forgive you."

"And Huntley is family—because he's my husband."

With one hand on his knee, he stared. "I should have sent men after you. I knew you would return, but I didn't expect it would be in this condition. Did he force you? I imagine he did—to make me suffer."

"No, he's not that kind of man. Our marriage started off as an alliance, but now I love him with all my heart."

He looked away.

"I can convince him to release you. You just need to serve some time, apologize and mean it, and pledge yourself to our cause. You know King Rutherford, so I know you have great insight into how we can either convince him to join us or remove him from power."

"If you hate me, you would hate him a million times worse. If you try to take away his crown, he'll grip it tighter and tighter, just like a snake around its kill. Don't waste your time. It'll just make you look weak."

"Well...that's helpful. And I'm sure you can be helpful in other ways."

He stared at the fire.

"This is your chance for redemption, Father."

He wouldn't look at me.

"I want to hate you, but a part of me believes you aren't that man anymore. I want to believe that you fell in love with Mom and had us...and that's the moment you changed. That you aren't the same man who did those terrible things. Tell me that's true."

He kept his gaze averted.

"Please..." I needed to believe that to sleep at night, to release this burden from my heart.

"I loved your mother, when I thought I would never love anyone. She gave me a beautiful daughter and a proud son. Yes, those events changed me, softened me. So did the luxury, the wine, and the power. I'm not the same man who conquered Delacroix, but I'm not the man you want me to be either." He looked at me again. "A clan of yetis destroyed our home. Killed my brother. My mother too. The Teeth took our weakness as an opportunity and invaded. So, we climbed to the top of the cliffs."

"You *climbed*?"

"With ropes and spikes," he said. "We made it to the top, and I begged for asylum. Queen Rolfe has no memory of this, because I spoke to her husband, the king. I told him of the harsh winters. Told him about the Teeth that feasted on our blood. Told him that our afterlives were at risk with Necrosis. He barely looked at me before he took away our equipment and sent us back down there."

My heart tightened.

"I'm not sorry that I returned with a vengeance. I'm not sorry that I killed King Rolfe, not when he couldn't care less about the death of my family. I'm not sorry that I did exactly what he would have done if our positions were reversed. I will do anything to survive—and I won't apologize for it. Your husband can pretend to be the hero all he wants, but that's only half the story. My actions were a *reaction*—not a provocation."

No one was right. No one was wrong. I could see that now.

"I took it too far with his mother. I admit that. And I took it out on her sons when I kicked them over the side of the cliff. But he damned my family—so I damned his. Maybe I should have been the better man and exiled them into the woods instead. But my anger got the best of me."

My eyes dropped to the floor.

"I think your plan is foolish. You'll never gain unanimous cooperation from all the Kingdoms, let alone all the barbarians down below, even if it's against a common enemy. You'll get yourself killed, along with everyone else you love. And even if by some small chance you actually succeeded, Necrosis is too strong. I've fought them before—and you have no idea what that's like."

I hesitated, because when he put it like that, I felt hopeless. "I know it's going to be hard, and it would be easier just to not bother, but this world is never going to change unless we end Necrosis. I want a better world for my children.

Worrying about your children's well-being is hard enough, but worrying about their afterlives too...that's unbearable."

His eyes shifted back to the fire.

"Apologize...and join us."

He stayed quiet for a while. "Even if I did, it wouldn't make a difference."

"It would make a difference, because I know my husband, and he would do anything for me."

The silence stretched for a long time, his eyes focused on the fire that blanketed his cell with warm light. He rubbed his hand down his coarse beard before he gave a sigh. "I'll consider it."

"Thank you." My father was more stubborn than I was, so any reflection at all was huge. "Can I get you anything? I'm sure I can grab something from the kitchen, along with a bottle of wine."

"Sure." He looked at me again, his eyes tired. "But instead of wine, make it scotch."

42

HUNTLEY

The last time I'd walked through this castle, I was Mastodon, a Blade Scion who only showed my eyes through my helmet. The mask was enough to disguise my fury because no one seemed to notice my need for bloodshed.

But the castle was mine now—and it still didn't feel like home.

Nothing had changed. The rugs were the same. The paintings on the walls were too. It even smelled the same, as if I'd just returned home after a very long trip. I eyed the chandelier hanging from the ceiling, knowing one of the crystals was missing because we'd been playing in the house and chipped one of them. Our parents never discovered the transgression.

A guard passed me.

"Where's Queen Rolfe?"

"I haven't seen her, sir." He continued on his way.

Once we'd infiltrated the castle, my men threw Faron in his cell, and I hadn't seen her since. The takeover was a smooth transition because most of the guards had no interest in resisting. They returned to their posts as if they served the same master. Maybe it was the dragons outside that made everyone obedient. This conquest definitely wouldn't have been possible without them.

I searched the castle but didn't call her by name. The study where my father used to occupy his time was empty. The royal bedchambers were empty too. I checked the kitchens, the grand dining room, everywhere.

She was nowhere to be found.

Where would she go?

Once I began to worry, I checked every door I came across. "Mother?" I did a quick scan then moved to the next door and then the next. I descended the stairs, moving toward the basement underneath the castle.

That was when I realized where she was.

In the dungeon.

Slitting his throat.

I took the stairs two at a time and reached the basement. All the lights were on, but it was still dark without the windows letting in the light. I was just about to turn right and head toward the dungeons when I heard it.

A woman crying.

I stilled as I listened, not recognizing it.

I turned the other way and followed the sound, moved down the hallways until I came to a large room with portraits stacked against the walls, crates on the floor, dusty paperwork on the counters.

On her knees in the middle of the floor, she held a portrait in her hands.

A portrait of my father.

Her sobs were so strong that her body shook. Tears streaked down her face like rivers and splashed into her lap, leaving stains so large I could see them from where I stood by the door. Her cries had the same ferocity of a child, of a little girl screaming because she was scared, screaming because her world had come down around her.

Other pictures were on the floor around her—portraits of us.

She brought her forehead down on the edge of the frame and continued her sobs, let her tears hit the canvas and streak down. It didn't seem like she had any idea I was there. If she did, she would swallow her emotions and pretend she was perfectly fine, hide all her pain from me.

I hadn't really understood the depth of her suffering —until now.

I couldn't bear the sight any longer, so I left the room, evaded the sound of her cries, but no amount of distance could ever silence their memory. The moment would haunt me as long as I lived, the strongest person I'd ever known defeated by her grief.

The memories washed over me.

He held her down by the back of the neck and forced himself inside her, and not once did she cry, not once did she drop her strength. She gave him no satisfaction, and she maintained her strength to make it easier on me.

But now I saw what it had done to her.

Had truly done.

All these years later.

The stairs were beside me, but I kept my eyes down the hallway, the hallway that led to the cells. My sword felt heavy on my hip. My heart was too strained to pump. A flush of heat ran through me, heat that burned with white-hot fire. My jaw clenched so hard that my lips started to quiver, screams of blood lust wanting to escape my lungs.

I moved past the stairs and deep into the hallway. The glow of the fire became brighter and brighter as I approached. Soon, the shadows were visible, his silhouette cast across the wall. He sat in the armchair, his eyes down on the fireplace.

He didn't look at me, as if he expected me, or expected someone.

I unlocked the door and swung it open.

That was when he regarded me, and one look at me told him my purpose. He didn't rise to his feet to face me like a man. He just sat there, his shoulders defeated. "I knew you would come."

I unsheathed my sword.

"I won't beg for my life." He remained seated and turned back to the fire. "So get it over with."

I grabbed him by the neck and slammed his head back, forcing his gaze on me. "I was too young to defend my father. Too weak to save my mother. Too small to defend my kingdom. But I'm a man now—and you're the one who's small."

His eyes didn't flinch. They were defeated, knowing his life was forfeit.

"Fuck. You." I squeezed his throat and forced him to gasp for air—and then I stabbed my sword right into his throat and through the back of his head, pinning him in place just as he had to my father on his throne.

He died instantly, his eyes still open, blood dripping from his mouth into his lap.

"Ahhhhhhhh!" Metal clanked against the stone floor. A bottle shattered. The screams continued to pierce the silence. "Noooo!"

Even her voice wasn't enough to destroy my satisfaction, my blood lust, my all-consuming need to avenge my father.

"You promised me!" Her voice was choked with sobs, so soon, her words became incoherent. "You...promised... You... God."

I finally turned around and faced her, faced the consequences of my actions. "He deserved it."

She was on the floor, her back against the wall, rocked with the same sobs my mother had just cried.

I stepped out of the cage, stepped over the broken glass from a shattered bottle. The metal tray was on the floor, bits of food scattered in other places from when she'd thrown it. The longer I watched her suffer, the more it hurt. "You know he deserved it—"

"He tried to come to Delacroix after his family was killed by a yeti attack...and your father exiled him." Her hands left her face, her eyes red, her skin blotchy. "Your father exiled him. He left him to die down there." She climbed to her feet, swaying side to side because she was too weak to stand.

"Doesn't justify what he did—"

"He was going to apologize—"

"Don't want his fucking apology!"

"He was going to help us with King Rutherford—"

"I don't need his goddamn help. He killed my father, raped my mother, and destroyed my family! My father has been avenged, and I know he's proud of me this very moment. My mother got the closure she deserved. She can move on with her life now, knowing she never has to see that motherfucker again. I have no regrets."

More sobs exploded from her mouth. "You promised me..."

I blew out a drawn-out breath.

"You promised me...you fucking promised me."

"And I meant that—"

"That was the one thing I asked. Now his blood is on my hands because I helped you get here. You made me kill my own father."

"No—"

"Fuck you."

"Baby—"

She slapped me hard across the face. So hard it emphasized her strength. "Don't you dare." She turned away and headed to the hallway.

I went after her. "Ivory—"

"We're done." She turned back around and faced me, rivers of tears running down her cheeks. "We're so fucking done."

Everything hit me at once. All the euphoria I'd felt just moments ago was obliterated. The satisfaction was gone.

The pride. The closure. Now my heart broke in two when I saw the pain I caused, the damage, the devastation. I'd just destroyed the one thing that mattered most to me.

My wife.

She walked away—and this time, I didn't go after her.

I heard her cries all the way down the hallway, all the way up the stairs, and even long after she was gone.

IVORY WAS BETRAYED by Huntley and wants out. Will Queen Rolfe grant her an end to their marriage? Find out in **The Three Kings.**

Printed in Great Britain
by Amazon

37570702R00341